ACER
No Prisoners MC Book 3

by Lilly Atlas

Lilly Atlas Books

ISBN: 1-946068-09-8
ISBN-13: 978-1-946068-09-5

For the two coolest bikers I know. Known to us as Nonna and Opa.

After one unforgettable night with a dangerous outlaw, Fia knows she must limit contact with the kind of man who could never fit in her wealthy circle. Unfortunately, she can't keep their brief but passionate encounter far from her thoughts. When she seeks him out for reasons unrelated to their chemistry, the worst happens, and Fia is attacked by a madman. With her life turned upside down, she finds help from the one person she can't get out of her mind.

Betrayed by someone he should have been able to trust above all, Acer spends the next two decades of his life avoiding entanglements that have any chance of ending with a knife in his back. The MC life provides a safe way to have personal connections and loyalty due to its simple rule: betray the club and punishment will be severe. Still, he keeps a large part of himself locked away inside, hidden even from his MC brothers. When the woman who's been messing with his head for months reappears in his life needing sanctuary, Acer jumps to her aid. He's committed to helping her reclaim her life but determined to keep her at arm's length in the process.

As Acer and Fia fight their growing feelings, his club is in danger from a new and different kind of enemy. Will his refusal to put his full trust in anyone, including the woman he's falling for, end up destroying more than betrayal ever could?

ACER
No Prisoners MC Book 3

Prologue

Adam straightened his Armani tie, leaned back in his chair, and flicked his gaze to the clock above the judge's bench. Ten minutes earlier, the overweight bailiff had announced the judge had reached a verdict, and it would be delivered in fifteen minutes.

He wasn't worried.

There were very few things in life he had to worry about. Wealth and a prominent family paved the way to an easy existence. Apparently, his attorney agreed if the self-assured smile he wore was any indication. He sat on Adam's right grinning like he didn't have a care in the world. In the rows behind them, Adam's father, mother, and grandmother sat, also confident in the trial's outcome.

"Jesus, Acer, how can you sit there looking so calm and collected?" Adam's dark-haired friend Derek spoke to his left. Derek, whose leg bounced like it was attached to a live wire, and whose crinkled thrift store suit had never met a tailor. Behind him, Derek's mother sat, fidgeting just as much, if not more, than her son.

Derek was his best friend, his brother. Adam recalled the day they met, just over five years ago, like it was yesterday. At thirteen, he'd been independent beyond his years. Having no siblings, a father who cared about nothing beyond making money, and a mother who lived her life squandering that money, left Adam with little to no parental supervision. Most afternoons he headed to a less affluent part of town and hung out at a neighborhood diner, eating loaded fries and nachos.

He'd loved that diner. It wasn't fancy, wasn't expensive, but it was honest, delicious, and full of friendly people who didn't put on pretentious airs. Derek's mom worked the afternoon shift as a waitress while Derek bussed tables. Acer observed him for months, envying the easy and close relationship his friend had with his mother.

One day, he overheard a conversation between Derek and his mom about their broken computer. Derek needed it to complete his homework, but she couldn't afford a new one or even repairs on the one they had. Adam jumped in and offered to help fix it. He walked the two miles home with them and had their old Acer computer up and running in no time. Their friendship cemented, Derek called him *Acer* from that day forward.

He'd take a bullet for the guy, but it wouldn't have killed him to shave his scruff for their day in court. "You should have let me buy you a decent suit, Der."

His friend's deep blue eyes narrowed while his lips pressed into a thin line of displeasure. "Seriously? That's what you're thinking about? You do realize, in five minutes we might end up with a prison sentence for felony aggravated assault? And you're sitting there like your waiting to find out if you...fuck, I don't know. Something unimportant."

Adam chuckled. "Derek, calm down. We've talked about

this a hundred times." He flicked a look at their attorney, ruffling through his briefcase, his salt and pepper hair in an immaculate style, then lowered his voice to a whisper and leaned closer. "My dad and Judge Morrison have played golf together once a week for the past twenty years. It's in the bag. We're getting off scot-free. Won't even have to do five minutes of community service. Chill out."

Derek snorted, his hyperactive leg picking up speed. "Must be nice to have so much money."

Adam frowned. Money and status had been a constant burr on the ass of their five-year friendship. Derek's family was dirt poor. His mom busted her butt at three shit jobs to feed him and his sister while his dad drank the day away in their crappy trailer on the literal wrong side of the tracks. Their life situations couldn't have been further away on the spectrum. Yet, somehow, they clicked.

Adam admired the freedom Derek's lack of money afforded. He'd never told his friend that; Derek would think he'd lost his mind, but it was true. Derek wasn't expected to take over a family business he detested. Derek wasn't expected to flirt and court senator's daughters while leaving their virtue intact. Derek didn't have to hide his love of motorcycles because it wasn't proper or posh enough for his circle. Derek didn't have to live in a world as phony as a bad wig.

"Look, man, answer me one question. You regret what we did? Same thing happened tomorrow, would you do anything different?"

Derek shot daggers at Adam with his glare. "Hell no! Acer, you saw what he was doing to her, what he was about to do to her."

"Well then, there you go. Bottom line, we stopped that piece of shit from raping your sister. My dad's connection to the judge will keep any blemishes off our records, and you'll be free to start Marine boot camp next month."

Derek ran a hand through his shaggy brown hair. "I hope you're right. Now that we're eighteen, we'll be in a shitload of trouble if this doesn't work out like you say."

Adam leaned back in his chair once again. Derek needed to have a little faith.

Hell, even if he ended up with prison time, he wouldn't change a damn thing about that day.

Two months ago, almost to the day, Adam had attended his senior prom at the outrageously expensive and exclusive private school his parents shelled out for. Derek's family couldn't have afforded one day of the tuition, let alone a whole year, so he went to the public school in town. Since he hung around Adam nearly every day after school, a fair number of Adam's classmates knew Derek, and his fifteen-year-old sister, Penny.

Brandon Epley, a hotshot jock from the football team, invited Derek's sophomore sister to be his date. Derek flipped his shit at first. He'd been protecting his sister from their drunk of a father's violent outbursts for years and was forever in big brother overdrive. But, for a girl with no money and an underprivileged upbringing, an invite from a popular kid at a wealthy school was a dream come true.

Penny had pouted and batted her baby blues at her big bro until he relented and promised not to mess with her date. There wasn't much Derek wouldn't endure to see her smile.

Unfortunately for Penny, her dream date turned into a dark nightmare. Adam and Derek discovered her and her companion in a bedroom at an after party. Penny was struggling beneath one-hundred-eighty pounds of bastard. Her screams disappeared into the pulsing beat of techno music pounding through the party house. Adam opened the door, mistaking it for the bathroom, only to encounter an appalling scene. Brandon's pants were around his ankles and her simple dress was shoved past her waist.

Without a second's hesitation, Adam ripped the man off Penny and shouted for Derek, who waited in the hallway. Together, they beat the ever-loving shit out of Brandon while Penny righted her dress and sobbed on the bed. Once the jock was a bloody mess on the floor, Derek gathered her up and carried his hysterical sister home.

Since that night, Penny had been a timid, frightened shadow of the happy high-schooler she'd once been, and it broke Adam's heart. He wasn't blood, but with no siblings of his own, Derek and Penny were all but family.

Not for one second, did he regret his actions that day. Hell, he wished he'd had five more minutes with the guy. His sense of justice may not coincide with that of the law, but so what?

So they'd broken Brandon's nose, jaw, and one of his eye sockets. So they'd busted a few of his ribs. So he'd needed some plastic surgery on his smug face. What they'd prevented him from doing to Penny was far more severe.

The guy's affluent parents didn't share Adam's vigilante thirst for retribution, or maybe they did. They pressed formal assault charges and before long, Adam and Derek found themselves cuffed awaiting interrogation in the downtown Dallas police station. Even a night in jail hadn't changed Adam's satisfaction with the conclusion of that night.

It was their word against Brandon's, and since the asshole hadn't actually penetrated Penny, there was no physical evidence of sexual assault. On the flip side, there was plenty of evidence of Adam and Derek's attack against him. Partygoers were too drunk and too busy trying to score to pay attention to anyone other than themselves and their potential conquests, and no one had even noticed Penny disappear upstairs with Brandon.

So, here they were, awaiting the verdict on their felony assault charges. The fucked up legal system prosecuting the guys who stopped a bastard from raping a girl. No, Adam didn't feel one bit of remorse for his actions. The guy needed to be taught a lesson, and he and Derek had done just that.

He glanced across the courtroom at the bastard himself, sitting with his parents, a pitiful, wounded-animal look on his face. Adam had to give the guy props; he sure knew how to play the game. His crooked nose and fading bruises gave Adam a small sense of satisfaction. Sure, he'd have it fixed by a plastic surgeon to the stars, but for now, the visual reminder of the ass beating was a welcome sight.

He rolled his shoulders and looked toward the judge's bench as the bailiff emerged through a wooden door to the right of the bench.

Nothing to worry about.

"All rise for the honorable Judge Morrison."

Adam pushed up from his chair.

Derek stood next to him, a trembling mass of nerves, the leg still bouncing.

Discreetly, Adam gave him a gentle tap on the side of his thigh. The fidgeting ceased and Derek nodded, gathering his strength.

"You may be seated. I've reached a verdict in the case of The People vs. Wellington and Roberts."

Advised by their lawyer and Adam's father, he and Derek waived their right to a trial by jury, opting instead for a bench trial. Why bother with a jury when the judge was in your pocket?

"In the case of The People vs. Wellington and Roberts, I find the defendant, Adam Wellington, not guilty of felony aggravated assault."

The look of relief on his Derek's face was almost comical. His own mouth turned up in a victorious grin. Okay, maybe he *had* been a little apprehensive, not that he'd ever admit that to Derek. Ten more seconds and he'd announce Derek's innocence. Then they could leave this shit in the past.

"I find the defendant, Derek Roberts, guilty of felony aggravated assault."

Derek blinked.

Adam whipped his head around, staring at the judge. He must have heard incorrectly. The words, *five years* and *prison*, melded into the background against the sound of blood rushing in his ears. Adam couldn't think; he could barely draw a breath. Behind him, Derek's mom broke down in harsh sobs. Next to him, Derek stood with a dumfounded expression of shock on his face.

Somewhere in the recesses of his mind, he could hear the prosecutor congratulating the Epleys. He couldn't risk turning around. One look at Brandon's self-satisfied face and he wouldn't be able to restrain himself.

Judge Morrison's expression was a blank mask, no indication of the reason he had screwed Adam and his father over.

Dread overtook Adam, and he turned around, meeting his father's cold stare. A tiny, almost imperceptible smirk lifted one corner of the man's mouth, and Adam knew. This was his father's plan all along.

Two police officers crossed the courtroom and secured Derek's hands behind his back. Adam stood by in stunned and helpless silence as though viewing a horror movie in slow motion. His limbs weighed a hundred pounds and his tongue filled his mouth, cutting off the ability to speak.

Derek was gone in seconds, dragged out of the courtroom

by the grim-faced officers. His mother's soul-wrenching sobs cut like a knife into Adam's heart.

He'd done this. He'd promised his friend they'd be exonerated. That his family would take care of him. And here Adam stood, free as a bird, while Derek, who trusted him, was being hauled off to jail. His life was over. No Marine Corps, no time with his family, no future.

He turned his attention away from the door Derek had disappeared through, in time to see Derek's mom being ushered out of the courtroom by her sister. Her deep sorrow would haunt Adam for years to come, if not forever.

"I'm sorry, Adam." His attorney patted him on the shoulder.

Adam didn't bother to turn around. The scumbag didn't sound sorry at all. Hell, he was probably in on the scheme from its inception.

In the blink of an eye, the courtroom emptied and Adam found himself alone, staring at nothing.

A throat cleared behind him and he whirled around. His father, no, Reginald—he'd never call the man father again—lingered just three feet away, his eyes alight with triumph. Adam curled his fists against the urge to wrap his hands around the man's throat.

"Why?" he asked, his voice raw with grief.

"Because he's beneath you, he's beneath us." Reginald punctuated his point by pointing toward the door Derek left through each time he said the word *he*. "I've always told you that. For the past five years, I let him distract you from your responsibilities, from your family obligations. You're not a child anymore, Adam. Time for silly games with trailer-trash is over. You will assume your position in the family company as I've planned your whole life."

From the doorway of the courtroom, Adam's

grandmother gasped. She gaped at her son with eyes full of disbelief and horror. Adam loved her and her rebel-spirit above anyone else in his screwed-up family. She bought him his first motorcycle and allowed him to keep it hidden at her house. She stuck a condom in the back pocket of his jeans on more than one Friday night. She encouraged Adam to pursue a degree in computer science rather than join the family empire. Reginald had no idea Adam accepted an admission to Harvard for computer science.

He wouldn't be joining the family company for anything in the world.

"Fuck you and your hotels. Do you have any idea what you've done here today?" Venom dripped from Adam's words.

Reginald just smiled. "I'll give you a few days to get over your tantrum, but I expect to see you in the office on Monday. School's out. Time for your real education." He turned and left the room, walking past his mother as though she wasn't there.

Impenetrable steel doors slammed down around Adam's heart, locking his emotions so tight, he was surprised his grandmother couldn't hear them as they landed. Never again would anyone have the power to betray him as his father just had. Never again would another human being possess his full trust. Adam Wellington was dead. From this day forward, he wouldn't answer to that name again.

He'd be Acer from now on. And Acer had no father.

Chapter One

Fia stepped into the ballroom and smoothed an unsteady palm down the front of her deep purple dress. She pasted what was probably an overly syrupy smile on her face and nodded at the pompous son of a California State Senator who raised a hand in greeting as she approached. It wouldn't serve her well to wear her anger on the outside, so she put years of practice and grooming to good use and played the rich, friendly, tolerant-of-jerks socialite.

The senator's son abandoned his conversation with a politician whose name she couldn't recall and strode toward her, a smug, women-love-me-for-my-money-and-looks smile on his face. Fia resisted the urge to roll her eyes. Gordon had been pursuing her for a while now, and she had less than zero interest in the man who thought he was God's special gift to females everywhere.

He gripped her hand in a limp hold and drew it to his lips, kissing her knuckles in an old-world gesture. "Good evening, Serafina. I must say, you look lovely tonight."

She winced. Strike one. She hated her full name. It was

too pretentious, too formal, too…celestial. "Hello, Gordon. You're looking very handsome yourself, and please, I much prefer to be called Fia."

He wrinkled his perfect nose. "I don't know why you insist on people calling you by that foolish nickname. Serafina is a lovely name, and you should be proud to have it." Still holding her hand, he drew her out on the dance floor.

It took every ounce of restraint she possessed to avoid ripping her hand from his feeble hold. Arrogant jerk didn't even have the decency to ask if she'd like to dance with him. No, he just assumed any woman would be honored to have the privilege of being lead around the floor by his greatness.

Sure, his five-hundred-dollar haircut had each platinum strand coiffed in a perfect arrangement, and his manicured nails were impeccable, but the soft hands they adorned did nothing for her as a woman. A man needed a few calluses. Nothing felt better against her skin than the subtle scrape of a man's rough hands. Gordon's metaphorically turned up nose and literal lack of work ethic didn't exactly get her motor revving either. Some things a thousand-watt smile and striking deep green eyes just couldn't overcome.

She hated these events. If rich people actually donated as much money to the charities as they spent on the balls and banquets, the unfortunate would be much more fortunate. But, tonight's charade was for a cause she supported wholeheartedly, so she was here. And with no desire to embarrass herself or her family, she'd behave. Even if that meant enduring a dance with a man who viewed himself as an angel sent to earth for the sake of the fairer sex. Fia preferred her angels with a bit of a crooked halo. Her own was just a bit off kilter.

Today had been a long day full of frustrations and failures. What she really wanted was peace, quiet, and a warm bath overflowing with bubbles. Oh, and wine, lots of wine. But she wanted to show her support for the cause, so her wishes would all have to wait a few more hours.

Once a year, at a different one of his prestigious hotels, Reginald Wellington held a large gala to raise money for state penitentiaries in whichever state the event was held. Money raised was used to provide counseling services to inmates in that state's prison system.

When Fia was in college, she had a friend who ran into some trouble with the law and spent a year in jail. After her release, she remained on a straight path and was now a successful defense attorney, but her time in prison had taken a large psychological toll, and Fia had watched her friend struggle with a consuming depression for years.

This event meant something to her, and with her own career in jeopardy, it gave her something to focus on besides her drama. She had some significant life-decisions to make, and no clue which direction she should take.

With a sigh, she left her head and allowed Gordon to draw her into his embrace if only to avoid an uncomfortable scene. Conscious of keeping a bit of distance between their bodies, she swayed with him to the music.

Too bad he couldn't take a hint.

He leaned down and brushed his nose along the curve of her neck. "You smell lovely, Serafina."

She recoiled from his unwanted touch. Did the man know any complimentary words besides lovely? "Fia," she ground out between clenched teeth.

As though she were a child who said something cute, he chuckled against her ear, and she pulled her head farther back, narrowing her eyes at him. He really was handsome, in a straight-off-of-a-magazine-cologne-advertisement way. He was tall and wore a designer suit well. Unfortunately, she'd

12

seen him at the country club, and what lie under the suit could only be described as soft. He was a man who spent his time indoors, behind a desk.

Not her type.

"Okay, fine, *Fia*."

"Thank you."

While they danced a familiar waltz all society girls learned by age ten, Gordon rambled on about his ambitions to assume his father's seat in the senate, and she tuned him out, instead letting her gaze drift around the room. After scanning past several acquaintances, her focus landed on a man standing in the corner with a scowl on his face as he listened to an older gentleman speak.

She couldn't quite put her finger on what it was about the man that captured her attention. At first glance, he looked similar to many of the other males in the room, expensive tuxedo, expertly styled dark blonde hair, flawless facial features. Then he shifted his gaze and his eyes locked with hers. The energy flowing from him was almost palpable, like that of a caged tiger seconds away from attempting escape. She shivered. If all that power was unleashed, the effects could be devastating.

Gordon twirled them and Fia lost sight of the intriguing eye candy.

As they turned, Gordon let out a surprising and unrefined curse. "Shit, there he is." He shook his head. "And I wagered this would be the year he finally quit turning up here and upsetting his family."

Fia drew back and looked up at him. "Who are you talking about?"

He spun her a second time so they both faced the very man she'd been studying, only he wasn't in the same spot he'd been in seconds before. The back of his head drew farther away as he trailed after the man he'd been speaking with.

"See the blonde guy, the one walking out of the room?"

"Yes, I see him, who is he?"

"That's Adam Wellington."

Her jaw dropped and Gordon chuckled. She knew the name well, at least the rumors surrounding it. Her father and Adam's had been friends for the past ten years. Reginald Wellington owned this and many luxury hotels around the world.

Adam was a bit of an urban society legend. She never laid eyes on the man, but she'd always been curious as to whether the tales were accurate. Story was, he'd dropped out of society to join a gang after a friend of his went to prison for assault.

While it was enthralling, Fia wasn't stupid enough to believe the story was that simple. It took guts to leave the fold. The idea of throwing all this aside, all these fluffy parties and endless senseless conversations, for a life without rules was appealing. Not that she'd ever be daring enough to achieve such a thing herself, but her curiosity about the man who did was definitely piqued.

"He comes to this one charity event every year. No one knows why." Gordon went on, his tone almost mocking. "Some say he's planning something. Biding his time until he can get back at everyone he blames for his low status in life now."

Fia rolled her eyes. "That's the stupidest thing I've ever heard."

The man in question turned, meeting her gaze as though he heard her from fifty feet away. Like a deer caught in blinding headlights, she froze under his attention. Why was it this particular event he attended each year? What was his connection to this charity? Had he been in prison? His eyes smoldered with a mixture of anger, frustration and...could that be desire?

As though his attention had been physical instead of visual, her nipples tightened in the confines of her bra. Damn, he gave off some powerful sexual energy.

A ripple of nervous energy ran its way up her spine and her stomach fluttered. She tore her gaze away and stepped back from Gordon as the song ended. "Thank you for the dance, Gordon. Please excuse me, I'm going to get some air."

"Would you like me to join you, Serafina?" His tone suggested she'd be getting more than air if he escorted her.

Strike three, you're out Gordy. She tried not to show her revulsion.

Much as he'd done moments ago, she hovered close to his ear. "No, Gordon, I'd like a moment alone. And if I have to tell you to call me Fia again, I'll be doing so while you're doubled over with my knee against your balls," she whispered.

She turned and walked away from a slack-jawed Gordon, heading in the opposite direction of the mysterious Adam Wellington.

Whoops. So much for acting like a lady.

Chapter Two

Acer laughed out loud, a full, this-is-truly-hilarious kind of laugh. "Let me get this straight. You want me to be a coyote? For you?" The fact that the man thought Acer would do anything for him, for any amount of money, was comical in and of itself, but this took the cake.

Across the round oak table in a luxury suite two floors above the gala, Reginald frowned at him, not a strand of silver hair out of place despite his growing displeasure. Though his lips turned down, the expression above his mouth didn't transform one bit, too much Botox to allow for a raised eyebrow. "I don't know what you find so amusing, son."

Acer leaned forward and rested his forearms on the table. His voice lowered to a lethal tone. "I'm no longer your son. You lost the right to call me that twenty years ago, when you fucked over my real family. What I find amusing, Reggie, is that you think I'd put myself, and my club, on the line to help you do anything."

Reginald's eyes narrowed, but he rallied and shrugged, twisting a gaudy jeweled ring around the ring finger of his right hand. As far back as Acer could remember, his father did that when his frustration rose.

"This isn't about helping me or our personal family issues, it's strictly business."

Acer held in his laugh this time. "You want to use my club to smuggle Mexicans across the border so you can exploit them for cheap labor. You have any idea how crazy ICE is down in Arizona? Any idea the shit-storm of Feds I'd be bringing to my club? You're as crazy as you are evil."

If his MC brothers could see him now, dressed in a tux, without his cut, surrounded by the rich and elite, he'd be tormented for life. They rubbed his face in his posh upbringing at least ten times a day. But, he'd made a promise to his grandmother on her deathbed. Derek's incarceration weighed on her almost as much as it did Acer. That was the reason she set up this charity, and the reason Acer agreed to attend it each year, even after she passed. To honor his lost friend.

He held his father's gaze. "And you and I both know how fucking evil you are."

His father abandoned the unaffected act and rose, slapping his open palm against the heavy table. The clank of the metal ring against the wooden surface reverberated through the room as the two men stared each other down. "Don't act like you're above the law. You and your precious club are nothing but a band of common criminals. Don't act like I'd be sullying a pristine reputation."

Acer stood as well. With a three-inch height advantage over his father, the older man had to tip his head to maintain the stare. It gave Acer a secret thrill to be glaring down at the man for once. "Never claimed to be a choir boy. But I'm not going to put my family at risk to help you. That's the bottom line. We done here?"

"Your family?" Reginald scoffed. "You made the mistake

of putting scum above your real family once before. You learned a hard lesson. Maybe you need a refresher, *Adam*."

The reference to Derek pierced Acer's skin like a deep splinter, as did the emphasis on his given name. He should be grateful Reggie didn't call him Acer. No one referred to him as Adam in his everyday life—they valued their noses too much— but hearing the nickname Derek had coined leave Reginald's lips may have sent Acer into a frenzy. "There's a lot more to family than some genes."

"You're a fool to pass up this kind of money." A bit of desperation worked its way past the anger in Reginald's tone.

Acer had more money than he could spend in three lifetimes, and the No Prisoners had what they needed to be comfortable. "I'm here for one reason and one reason only, because I made a promise to your mother, my grandmother, on her deathbed. The least I owe her is to keep my word. I owe you nothing and there isn't a damn thing I need from you, old man. Especially not your filthy money. This bullshit is over."

Reginald moved from the table and stood in Acer's path, blocking the exit. His eyes narrowed and his voice lowered to a lethal level. "I can make things uncomfortable for your club, Adam. My connections are far reaching."

Acer laughed again, a cold mirthless sound. "Knock yourself out. I'm not a trusting eighteen-year-old boy you can screw over anymore. I bet my *connections* would trump yours any day." He stalked around the table and strode toward the door, unwilling to listen to his father's pathetic threats. As he plowed past, he bumped the old man with his shoulder.

"This is happening, Adam, and in Arizona. I offered you first rights, remember that. And remember, no matter how much leather you wear or how many tattoos you get,

Wellington blood will always flow through your veins."

Hand on the door handle, Acer paused. "Keep your business the fuck off my turf and I don't give a shit what you do." He flung the door open and lengthened his step as he made his way to the elevator and down one flight to the gala.

His first move upon entering the ballroom was to hit the bar. The collar of the tux was too tight around his neck and pent up energy that had no release fired his nerve endings.

He needed a stiff drink.

And a hard fuck.

In the many years he'd attended this event, he'd never picked up a woman. Pampered society princesses didn't pique his interest, and while a one-night stand was just that, he couldn't stomach the thought of sleeping with someone who represented everything he despised.

A pair of whiskey-colored eyes flashed in his mind. The eyes belonged to one hell of a sexy woman who caught his attention a few times tonight. He'd been captivated by the feisty sparkle in her eye and the lack of sparkle on her dress and around her neck.

The majority of the women in attendance dripped with flashy diamonds and colorful jewels dangling from heavy chains. Status symbols screaming, *look how much money I have*. This woman had small teardrop diamonds hanging from each ear and an equally humble solitaire diamond on a delicate chain around her neck. Yet he didn't get the impression the tasteful accessory choice was due to lack of coin.

She was understated and classy, though her body was anything but understated. That eggplant gown fit her like a second skin, molded to her mouthwatering curves. The dress had only one strap, leaving a single creamy shoulder bare; temptation for every man in the room.

Christ, now he was semi-hard with no relief in sight.

Both pissed off and aroused, not a good combination.

He held up a finger to signal the bartender and seconds later, his chosen drink appeared. The man was good, paid attention to his clientele. Acer tossed back the twenty-one-year-old Glenlivet and sighed. One thing he hadn't shaken from his fancy upbringing was the love of good scotch.

The walls of the ballroom seemed to shrink in on him and his tie grew tighter around his neck. He needed air before he lost his shit and started a fight with some unsuspecting self-centered asshole he recognized from his former life.

Acer hastened his stride and made his way toward a set of French doors leading to a large balcony. It wasn't far enough away from the crowd, but it would have to do for now. In two hours, this farce would be over and he could catch a good night sleep before he rode back to Arizona.

He loosened the knot at the base of his throat with one hand as he pushed the double doors open with the other. Ahh, peace, quiet, and solitude.

Almost.

A woman stood with her hands wrapped around the railing of the balcony, staring out into the night, looking lost and a bit pissed off if the angry sigh she emitted was any indication. One look at the eggplant colored fabric and the blood heated in Acer's veins. It was as though he'd conjured up the woman he'd been lusting after only moments before.

She was so deep in thought, she didn't notice him breach her sanctuary. Enjoying the second of being undetected, Acer swept his gaze up and down her sexy figure. She was bent slightly forward, which only served to draw his attention to her ass, and damn it was a nice ass. She wasn't a stick figure like most of the ladies here. Her body was just a bit rounded, that ass perfect for gripping as he pounded into her.

He cleared his throat. "You look like you are enjoying your evening almost as much as I am."

The woman jumped and gasped as she spun around, a hand pressed to her chest. Whiskey eyes met his gaze. She obviously belonged here, expensive dress, fancy hair, but something about her led him to believe she was like him. Here out of obligation and sick of wealthy snobs. Maybe it was the spark of sass that lit her eyes. He didn't see that feisty glow in any of the too-sophisticated and cultured women here. Learning just how feisty she was would be fun, especially if it extended to the bedroom.

And damned if he wasn't sporting a full-blown erection now.

~ ~ ~ ~

Fia's heart galloped so fast and so loud she was half convinced Adam Wellington could hear it. "Holy crap, you scared me." Scared was an understatement. She'd been so lost in her own world, she almost screamed when his voice rang out. She chuckled. "Though I suppose it was my own fault. I was a million miles away. You're—" She caught herself before she said something stupid like *you're the one everyone talks about, the one they all call a criminal.*

The dark blond god with the regal face walked toward her, his gait confident without crossing into arrogance. He held out a hand and gave her a panty-melting smile. "Acer," he said. "Black sheep of high society."

Even as her mouth turned down in confusion, she extended her hand. "Acer? I thought your name was Adam."

He engulfed her hand in his much larger one, slowly, letting his fingers glide along her palm in what could be described as nothing other than sensual. A zing of awareness shot from her hand straight to her core. The man was lethal.

He smiled again.

Yep, melted panties.

"I see you've heard of me. My name is Adam, but the only people who call me that are the pricks in that ballroom. Since you don't look like a prick, I went with my preferred name."

She laughed. He was a refreshing change to the stuffy businessmen and political hopefuls with whom she usually socialized. "I have heard of you. Terrance Caldwell, oilman extraordinaire, is my father. He and your father are friends. My given name is Serafina, but don't call me that if you expect me to answer. I'll reserve judgment on whether or not you're a prick, but nonetheless, call me Fia."

He gave her another one of those break-out-the-condom smiles and released her hand. She immediately missed the feel of his skin against hers.

Not good.

It hadn't been *too* long since she'd been with a man, but long enough that her body perked up and wanted to beg for his touch.

Acer reached with his now free hand and tucked her hair behind her ears. Forward, considering they'd just met, but the move didn't feel presumptuous, it felt oddly...intimate. She swallowed and tried not to stare at him like she was in heat.

"I like your hair, Fia. It's short and sassy, like you seem to be."

She smiled at him. "Thank you." She kept her hair on the shorter side, an A-line bob a smidge longer than her chin. He described exactly what she loved about the style. It was chic and sassy, and the fact that she didn't have long hair like everyone else she knew, drove her family nuts. Bonus.

"So, Fia." He chuckled at the play on words and she rolled her eyes. "What has you running from the party to the safety

22

of the fiftieth-floor balcony? Boyfriend troubles?"

She snorted. "Not hardly. Shitty day. Work troubles, actually."

"What is it that you do?"

She studied him for a moment. Too frequently, if she told the truth she was met with scorn and judgment, as though her chosen profession was below her station in life. But Acer's life choices certainly weren't understood or accepted by the upper echelon, at least not according to the whispered buzz. Perhaps something they had in common. "You haven't heard yet? Huh, I'm surprised. Usually, my parents warn every man within a three-mile radius. I'm the porn queen of Los Angeles."

Chapter Three

Acer choked on his saliva and tried to draw in a breath as Fia released a throaty laugh. The sound was intoxicating and negated any anti-erection effect the choking spell may have had on his dick.

"That was kinda fun," she said with a grin once he'd regained control of his airway. "I don't know you, but I get the feeling not much takes you by surprise. I'm happy to be the one to break the mold."

Nothing surprised him. Not anymore. That was for sure. He trusted no one and rarely gave anyone else control over his life, so no, surprises weren't commonplace. But he had to admit, her statement shocked the breath right out of him.

Sexy, witty, and bold. A lust-inspiring combination.

"Okay, you had your fun," he said. "Now, I'll take an explanation because, babe, I've had…encounters with a few women who work in the adult entertainment business and I can assure you, you aren't one."

She laughed again and his dick twitched. How would she sound if she were moaning instead? Preferably while his cock plunged deep inside her.

"I think I'll take that as a compliment. I'm a designer,

lingerie designer. I do mostly custom pieces." She held out her hands and shrugged. "Akin to porn in my family's eyes."

Jesus, did that mean there was something dirty and sinful underneath that dress? Or maybe something frilly and virginal. Either way, he was on board. "Custom lingerie, really? There a big market for that?"

"You wouldn't believe how much rich women will pay, and how far they will travel for custom lingerie made from the finest material." She lifted her stubborn chin and stared straight at him, the spark in her eyes daring him to belittle her profession.

He got the impression she was used to having to defend her career choice. Not surprising given her presence at this event. Most women here were arm candy, trophy wives, or hopeful singles shopping for one of those roles. Businesswomen weren't the norm. Especially not businesswomen who specialized in sexy.

"At ease, there, soldier," he said. "You won't find any judgment here. I happen to think lingerie is one of the best inventions out there."

Her stance relaxed and she sent him a grateful smile.

He leaned against the balcony wall. "So, what's the problem? You need someone to give you some advice on which designs work? I'm more than happy to fill that role. In fact, we could head on up to my room and you could give me a private showing of your collection right now."

Fia laughed, as he'd intended, but not before a flare of interest lit her eyes. For just one second before she laughed at his blatant and poorly executed pick-up line, her prideful expression turned hungry.

Damn, if she kept that up she might not make it out of this hotel tonight.

"As generous and selfless as your offer is," she said with a wink. "That's not the problem. I'd rather not get into my troubles right now. I just met you; no need to bore you to tears just yet."

"Come on, spill it." He stepped closer and ran a hand down her arm, from her shoulder to her hand. Halfway to her wrist, she shivered and goose bumps rose beneath his palm. He linked their fingers and gave her hand a little squeeze.

Her eyes widened and she tensed slightly but didn't pull away.

"I need something to distract me from how much I hate everything about being here. You won't bore me. I'm sure you've heard hundreds of stories about me, and I can promise you that no more than ninety percent of them are true." He played with her fingers as he spoke, enjoying the feel of her smooth skin under his coarser fingertips. Would his rough hands bother her? He may be rich, and he may be well educated, but he wasn't soft. His chosen life as a member of a one-percenter motorcycle club saw to that. Women of her caliber often found that unpleasant. Another reason he stayed far away from rich girls.

She must have recognized the contrast to the men in her social circle because her focus darted to their hands then back up to his face. The gown she wore covered every inch of her chest, not even a peek of cleavage showed, but when her breathing sped up and with it, the rise and fall of her breasts, she might as well have been naked.

He gave her hand a gentle squeeze and the momentary spell was broken.

"Okay, but now you lost the right to complain if you lose interest," she said.

He nodded. She was such a welcome reprieve from the rest of the evening. Her sassy personality was as sexy as her gorgeous body. He bet she'd get along really well with Lila and Emily, two of his brothers' women.

What? Where the fuck did that thought come from? This woman would never be within ten miles of anyone from his club. Her existence and his might as well be oceans apart. One night per year spent back in her fancy world was disturbing enough. Bringing her into his might push him over the edge.

She licked her lips and he nearly swallowed his tongue. Dam that mouth was enticing. "I lease a storefront on Rodeo Drive," she said.

Her statement knocked him out of his thoughts. The woman wasn't kidding. She had some high-end clientele.

"I stock a handful of retail pieces, but the majority of my work is custom like I said. So, women with more money than they know what to do with come from all over to commission pieces. I take precise measurements, and meet with them to formulate designs based on their specific desires." She sighed and shook her head, frustration returning to her face. "Or at least I used to. My landlord sold the building out from under me, and my lease doesn't carry over to the new owners, so I'm out on my ass."

He frowned. "That can't be—"

She held up a hand, stopping the inquisition before it began. "I don't know all the details, but my lawyer assures me it's all legal."

"Maybe the new owners will let you stay through the completion of your lease."

She shook her head. "The new owners are my parents. They've gone from verbally attacking what I do to actually sabotaging it. The pattern will just continue now. Anywhere I set up shop, they'll find a way to buy the building and boot me out, they as much as told me so."

She pulled her hand from his grasp and jammed them both on her hips. "They don't even live in LA. My whole family still lives in Texas, where I grew up." A spark of frustration lit her amber eyes. "Apparently, my indecent business is just too embarrassing for them. Since I often sell to women in their social circle, even so many states away, they see it as low-class. They'd rather me hang off some politician's arm with a fake smile than run a successful business. My parents and I have always gotten along well enough, but now... I'm just not sure where we stand." She pressed her lips together and shrugged, her chest rising and falling in time with her shoulders. "So there you have it. Sorry you asked?"

"Jesus." He turned away from her and stared out at the city, her story hitting too close to home. The memory of being stabbed in the back by his father too near the surface, especially tonight when the old man was trying to drag him back into a world he loathed.

"I'm not sure Jesus is too fond of what I sell either," she said in a deadpan tone.

Acer turned back. She looked at him with a half smirk on her face. He threw his head back and let out a hearty laugh. With one line, she yanked him from his dark thoughts. Not an easy feat. "So, you're an entrepreneur, the sexiest woman at this benefit, and apparently, a comedian. Anything else I need to know about you?"

There it was. That surge of heat. Her face flushed to a pale pink and her eyes darkened. The visible rise and fall of her throat as she swallowed drew his gaze like a heat-seeking missile. At some point tonight, his lips would be on that neck, of that he was sure.

She tilted her head as a small grin played across her tempting mouth. "And you are smooth with the words, huh?"

"You should just do it all online." The idea popped in his head and was out of his mouth before he had time to question the wisdom of messing in someone else's business affairs.

Her mouth opened, closed, then dropped open again. "What?"

"Your business. Forget the storefront and just sell online."

After just a second, she caught up with the directional shift in the conversation and shook her head. "Eighty percent of my revenue comes from custom designs. I need to meet with clients, take accurate measurements, show them samples, then do a fitting to make any small adjustments before the piece is finished. I can't do that on the computer."

"Look, I'm not trying to tell you how to run your business, but, you can. Well, most of it anyway. Just use Skype. The women can go to any tailor they choose and Skype you in. You can display samples and supervise to make sure their tailor is measuring the way you want. Then at the end, you can go to them for a fitting. Do it in their homes, or have them come to yours if you'd rather. I bet your customers would love how personal it is. I promise I'm not just butting in. This is right in my wheelhouse. I run all our business affairs and know my way around a computer." That was putting it mildly, and he'd never tell her what his *business affairs* actually were, but it was close enough.

She opened her mouth, but he cut her off before she could argue. "The ones who travel are willing to pay to come to you, right? If you don't want them coming to your house, I'm sure they'd be willing to pay you to fly to them for a fitting. In fact, they'd probably prefer it."

He needed to shut his mouth or before he knew it, Fia would be calling him with computer questions at all hours. Sure, he wanted to sleep with her, but that's it. When this event was over, and he walked out the hotel doors tomorrow morning, there would be nothing tying him to this world for one entire year.

Not even a sassy woman with whiskey-colored eyes and a hypnotic laugh.

~ ~ ~ ~

Fia blinked at him, which was only slightly less embarrassing than gaping with her mouth hanging in the breeze.

The man was a genius. He was also get-horizontal hot, confident, mysterious, and there was a slightly…dangerous air about him. But for now, he was a genius.

Could it really be that simple? Well, no, of course it wouldn't be *that* simple, but the idea was solid, and with a little fertilizing, it could grow into something real, and possibly quite profitable.

He raised one eyebrow at her. "Nothing to say, Fia?"

"It's actually a really great idea. I need to give it some serious time and thought." She laughed. "But you very well may have just saved my business. I suppose I owe you one, now."

Acer's entire demeanor changed in an instant. For one second, his gaze dropped to her chest, then back up to her face and his eyes smoldered with undisguised desire. He went from intelligent business advisor to hungry male animal in the blink of an eye.

He stepped close to her, so close she had to tip her head back to see his face. The heat radiating from his body wafted across her skin, raising her temperature until she felt almost feverish. Two seconds of his nearness affected her ten times more than an entire dance in Gordon's arms.

"In that case, I'm going to need to request a private consultation," he said. "You happen to have any samples you could show me?"

That was an invitation if she ever heard one.

She clenched her fists to keep from reaching up and yanking his mouth down to hers. "Just one set." One set that was currently on her body.

He must have caught her meaning because he smiled a predatory grin. "Perfect, that's exactly what I'm in the market for."

"My consultation fee is pretty hefty."

One eyebrow arched. "I thought we already established that you owe me."

"True." Beneath the underwear they spoke of, her nipples beaded, abraded by the lace. Fia clenched her teeth, unwilling to release the needy sound that threatened to escape.

"You know what? I believe in supporting the small business owner. I'll make you an offer." He bent his head down to her ear. "How's five orgasms before the sun comes up? That sound reasonable?" As he whispered, his lips brushed her ear.

Hell, yeah, that sounded reasonable. It sounded fantastic. "Um." Words were hard to conjure. "I think...um...I think I can work within your budget."

He chuckled against her ear. "Room sixty-seven twenty-four, ten minutes, smartass."

He nipped her neck, not a bite really, just a grazing of his teeth along the tender skin and goosebumps rose all over her body. She couldn't quell the visible shudder that traveled through her muscles. "You smell fucking delicious, Fia."

You smell lovely, Serafina. Gordon's words from just twenty minute ago floated through her mind. No contest. She'd take fucking delicious over lovely any day. Fucking delicious meant he just might want to eat her up. Her empty pussy clenched and moisture drenched her panties at the thought of his mouth between her legs.

Acer pulled back and winked at her like he knew the direction of her thoughts, then turned and strode back into the banquet hall his gait confident once again, as though he hadn't just been whispering filthy promises in her ear.

Fia blew out a shaky breath and remained where she was. The past fifteen minutes had been a whirlwind and she needed to gather herself. If she tried to strut across the balcony as Acer just had, her trembling legs would likely crumple beneath her, leaving her in an aroused heap on the floor.

She liked sex. She had sex. Not enough to make her promiscuous, but enough that she knew what she wanted in a partner. Unfortunately, no man had ever quite fit the bill of exactly what she was looking for. Acer, however, was nothing like the sedate bankers and upper-class men she typically went out with.

Was she really going to do this? One-night stands weren't her thing, and she had no doubt that's all this would be. All it could be. If the rumors were to be believed, he lived a dangerous life on the wrong side of the law.

Instead of turning her off, that fact only ignited every bad boy fantasy she'd ever had.

Yes, she was going to do this. She was a big girl, she made her own decisions, and tonight she was going to have a little fun.

Or, if the expression on Acer's face was any indication, a lot of fun.

The man's hands were callused after all.

Chapter Four

Fia's stomach fluttered with a mix of anticipation and nerves as she rapped her knuckles in a soft knock on the large, black oak door with the brass six-seven-two-four.

He didn't make her wait long. Acer opened the door before her fist was back at her side.

Her jittery stomach kicked up a notch at the site of him. He'd shed his shoes, jacket, and tie, and the top two buttons of his crisp white shirt were open, revealing a small expanse of skin she couldn't wait to taste.

He was mouthwatering.

And for tonight, he was hers.

"Hey," she said in more a whisper than a greeting.

He smiled at her as though he could read her thoughts. "Come in. Would you care for a drink?"

In the hand not holding the door open, he had a glass tumbler with a shot or two worth of liquor. Maybe a drink would settle her a bit. He was so calm, confident, and she didn't want to appear a nervous amateur.

"Sure. Whatever you're having." She stepped into the suite and glanced around, taking in the opulence of the heavy drapes and mahogany furniture. It wasn't her style; she preferred a more modern look, but someone liked it because the suite went for nearly a grand a night and it was a coveted room in this high-class hotel.

Acer shut the door behind her and moved to the bar, pouring her a drink. "I can tell by the look on your face that you're about as into the décor as I am."

She snickered and spun around, watching him as he prepared her drink, his laidback manner helping to put her at ease. Something, though, maybe the laser stare he pierced her with across the ballroom, led her to believe the man under the tux could be intense and formidable. "Yeah, it's not really my thing. No offense to your father."

Acer grunted as he walked toward her. He'd polished off his own drink but held hers out. She took it from him and brought it to her hips. After draining half the glass in one healthy gulp, she held it at her waist. Now what?

Acer reached out, wrapped his free hand around her upper arm, and pulled her flush against him.

Fia couldn't suppress a startled yelp as she gripped his hips in an attempt to steady herself. He reached back and set what was left of her drink down on the bar, hard. The sound of sloshing liquid registered in some small part of her brain, as he wrapped a strong arm around her waist.

Before she could process the press of his firm body all along her torso, his mouth descended and took hers in a kiss that consumed. Whiskey, good whiskey, and a hint of cigar smoke mixed with his natural spicy flavor and overwhelmed her senses.

The man could kiss.

The command in his actions intrigued her. In her head, she'd answered the door, they chatted, flirted, then one exploratory kiss would lead to another until they were ripping each other's clothes off to get to skin. She hadn't quite expected him to pounce on her like this. She'd longed to find a man who took control in the bedroom, complete control. So much of her life was spent under the control of her overbearing parents that she tended to take the dominant role in the bedroom.

She met too many men who reminded her of her father. She couldn't trust them enough to give up her control. She wanted a strong man who she could count on to give her what she needed without her having to take the reins and get it for herself. Was Acer that man?

Was that why she had such a powerful reaction to him from the moment she first laid eyes on him during her boring dance with Gordon? Or was it her dance with boring Gordon?

After who knew how long, he broke away and stared down at her. Her chest heaved with the effort to catch her breath and heat radiated from her face. If she'd been wet out on the balcony, she was soaked now. This was the first time she'd had such a powerful and immediate physical reaction to a man, and she couldn't wait to see what came of it.

"Unbutton my shirt." His voice was deeper than it had been on the balcony.

"What?" Her mind still spun from his kiss.

"Take off my shirt."

There it was again, the commanding control, this time in his voice instead of his actions. A shiver of excitement raced up Fia's spine. This night might be more than she'd bargained for. But exactly what she needed.

~ ~ ~ ~

Acer stared at the little vixen who had his dick so hard it could drive a stake through the ground.

She tasted as sweet as he expected, but it was her sassy side that drew him the most. He'd enjoyed verbally sparring with her out on the balcony almost as much as he enjoyed her mouth under his. She was intelligent, quick-witted, and, despite who her family was, she was the antithesis of the spoiled rich girls this charity event overflowed with.

"Yes, sir," she said of his request to unbutton his shirt. The comment was full of snark instead of obedience.

As different as she was from the women here, she was also night and day from the women who hung around the club. Those women were only interested in two things—the size of his dick and the size of his wallet. Fia respected his opinion and his advice on her business. She was independent, intelligent, feisty, and seemed to be an ally as far as frustrations with their socioeconomic peer group.

Not that it mattered.

They played in two different camps and after tonight, the chances of running into her again were in the negative percentile.

Her small hands reached up and started with the top button. One by one, she popped them open, her gaze riveted to her task. At one point, her tongue peeked out and licked along her bottom lip. Acer groaned, imagining that tongue flicking across his dick.

Her lips twitched in a small smile. The minx enjoyed torturing him.

Instead of opening the panels of the shirt when she ran out of buttons, she placed both of her palms flat against his stomach and slowly slid them up to his chest.

His cock twitched in his pants and his stomach muscles clenched beneath the caress. The same smile she'd had seconds ago reappeared on her lips and as she continued her journey upwards. She rose on her toes as she reached his shoulders, and pushed the fabric back and off his shoulders.

Her eyes widened as his skin was revealed.

36

Acer tensed. Women unfamiliar with the MC scene typically had two reactions to club members, fear and distrust or a morbid curiosity of the tattooed bikers.

He had quite a few tattoos across his arms, sides and a full back piece that had taken upwards of twenty hours to complete. Across the right side of his chest, the Chinese characters for the word *brothers* were tattooed along with his and Derek's birthdates. Despite how chill she seemed, Fia was a society princess. Would she recoil at the amount of ink he wore?

"Your nipple is pierced," she said.

"It is."

She stared at the barbell through his right nipple like she was figuring out the answer to a riddle. "Does it make it sensitive?" She ran the smooth pad of a finger from one end of the metal to the other, raking her glossy nail over his nipple as she traversed it.

His entire body jolted as though he'd been shocked.

She chuckled. "I guess so. It's sexy." She ran her hands over his body from shoulders to navel and he ground his back teeth together to keep from grabbing her. She circled him and, when she reached his back, released a surprised gasp. The entire expanse was covered in with the No Prisoners' logo, prison bars pulled open at the center with a skull bursting through. The words *take no* were inked in an arc across his shoulder blades and *prisoners* rounded out the bottom.

"Well?" He couldn't keep the bite out of his voice.

"Well, what?" Fia stepped back in front him and frowned.

"Say what you're gonna say."

Her scowl deepened, then her eyes widened and she smirked. "Ohh, I get it. This is a test. What happens if I fail? You gonna put a stop to this right now? I think that big bulge in your pants says otherwise."

Her voice held some bite of her own, and he didn't blame her. Christ, he'd invited her up here with the promise of hot sex and now he acted like an emo teenager. What did it matter what she thought of him or his ink? She was just another lay. She didn't need to respect him and he didn't need to respect her. Hell, they didn't even need to like each other. But he did like her, and for some fucked up reason, he did want her to like him.

"Okay. I'll say what I was gonna say." Her tone mocked him. She placed her hand on his abdomen again and walked around his body, trailing her fingers as she moved. "I'm not an artist in the conventional sense, but I'm a designer. I sketch, work with colors, shapes, lighting for photo shoots. So, I think that gives me the right to call myself an artist."

As she spoke, she traced the soft tip of one finger across the letters on his upper back. Acer couldn't prevent his eyes from dropping closed. Her touch was intoxicating, gentle, yet arousing.

"I think your tattoos are gorgeous, stunning. As an artist, I can appreciate the talent it takes to draw these intricate designs, work with the colors and shading. And that's with pencil and paper. To do it with a needle on someone's skin? That kind of talent is beyond me."

Her hand left his back and in the next moment, she was in front of him again. "I also think it's hot as hell. Sue me. I like ink on men." She shrugged. "I like the way it outlines your muscles and moves with you as they flex. And this—" She gave the barbell a little tug. "I already told you I thought it was sexy. Kind of a naughty secret. I'm the only one here tonight who gets to see the real you beneath the tux. To everyone in the ballroom you look like a polished businessman, but I get to reap the benefits of this bad boy undern—"

That was enough. He grabbed her ass with both hands and lifted her, spinning around and walking until her back met the nearest wall. Her eyes flew wide open and she gasped, clutching his biceps like he was a buoy that would save her from drowning. The stretchy material of her dress rode up her thighs and bunched at her hips, allowing her the freedom to lock her legs around his waist. "I'm going to fuck you so hard, you might not be able to leave this hotel for a week."

Her pointed heels dug into his back and her soft body molded against his. She slid her hands into his hair and grasped the strands between strong fingers. "Guess I passed, huh?" she asked before she yanked his mouth down to hers.

Christ, she was going to give as good as she got. Acer faltered for one second. The small part of him that had worried over her reaction to his ink also wondered how she'd respond to his alpha bedroom tactics. Needless worry. She was fire in his arms.

He pressed his erection to her core as his tongue tangled with hers. She moaned into his mouth and he increased the pressure of his pelvis against hers. She ground her mound against his hard-on and he nearly shot off into his pants.

He was going to give this woman a night she'd never forget. Then in the morning, he'd be on his way back to Arizona, doing his best to forget her.

Chapter Five

Fia took a deep breath and wiped her sweaty palms down the front of her black leather leggings. In the six months since she spent the night with Acer, she'd fantasized about this moment far too many times. Imagined what she'd say if she encountered him again.

She'd planned a script in her head, word for word. A rehearsed speech was safer than winging it. If she didn't have something prepared, she was likely to blurt out how she couldn't stop replaying every moment, every touch, and every orgasm from that night. He'd delivered on his promise of five orgasms by morning and threw in an extra one for good measure.

Simply stated, Acer had ruined her for other men. She hadn't had a flicker of interest in anyone since him. If she wasn't careful, she'd admit that too, and ask him if she'd imagined the emotional connection she remembered, or if he'd felt it too.

For the past few months, she'd thrown herself into her work, focusing on converting her business to an online format. She still had a few kinks to work out, but so far, Acer's idea had been wildly successful. Her retail sales were up sixty percent. Women from all over the world were discovering her website and ordering her designs. The custom side of her business had slowed a bit, but that was intentional as she used her time to focus on increasing her retail sales.

She had yet to travel out of LA for any custom orders, but worked with a local clientele for now. She wanted to be confident with her new system before traveling all over the country. A few of her loyal customers came to her and she worked with them right out of her home, an experience they all loved since it was private and comfortable. A home office was something to consider moving forward. Without a doubt, she owed her increased success to Acer.

Never did she envision she'd seek him out, though. And certainly, not to give him news of a potential threat to his club. Okay, sure, she could have called with the concerning information, but she'd jumped on the first excuse to see him in person.

Her stomach flip-flopped and rolled. Three days ago, she'd walked into her favorite lunch spot only to see the back of Reginald Wellington's head sitting at a booth. She'd met the man on numerous occasions, and would have greeted him under normal circumstances, but now that she'd slept with Acer, it somehow felt like a betrayal. She didn't even know the details of Acer's family problems, but that had no bearing on how she felt.

Of course, the hostess seated her at the booth directly behind the man, but she'd remained quiet and out of sight behind the high back of the booth.

While she couldn't see him, she could clearly hear his side of a phone conversation, and the dialogue was unsettling, to say the least. Unable to fully grasp the context, she did pick up on the fact that Reginald had some ill-intended plans for

Acer and his motorcycle club.

Who knew how Acer would react to the information? She didn't know him well enough—didn't really know him at all —to gauge his reaction. For all she knew, she could be setting off a shit-storm of epic proportions. But for the same elusive reason she avoided speaking to Reginald, she felt compelled to share the information with Acer.

So here she was, parked outside a no-frills gym surrounded by motorcycles, nervous as a virgin on her wedding night. She pressed a hand to her stomach as though she could calm the raging waters inside. "Suck it up, girl." The weak pep talk did nothing to soothe the racehorse galloping in her chest. "On three, you coward," she muttered. "One, two—"

Before she hit three, she wrenched the car door open and made her way across the parking lot. When she reached the entrance to the gym, she hurried inside before she could talk herself out of this madness.

The heady aroma of sweaty male surrounded her like a thick blanket. She blinked as her eyes adjusted to the bright lighting in the gym after being out in the dim shades of twilight. All around her, tattooed and muscled men dressed in leather and chains shouted, cheered, and yelled profanities at a raised boxing ring in the center of the room. No one paid her any attention, so she slipped between and around many large bodies, farther into the gym and tried to get a better look at the main event.

Two men circled each other like caged animals battling to claim the dominant role. One man had his back to her, and he dipped left, dodging a quick as lightning strike. The fist flew past him, missing his face by centimeters.

Impressive.

The same man bounced on the balls of his feet and the duo spun around so she was no longer staring at his back.

Oh. My. God.

Fia's jaw dropped and the breath stilled in her chest. Acer.

A split second later, Acer rammed his fist into his opponent's stomach in a move that would have taken Fia out for the next week. His opponent doubled over in pain, but she barely paid him any attention. All she saw was Acer. He was shirtless. His upper body gleamed with sweat and his muscles bunched with exertion as he fought. Muscles that had pressed her down into the mattress, and against the wall, and had wrapped around her as he took her from behind.

She'd explored every inch of that body, more than once, and had committed it all to memory, but the reality of it right in front of her was just as powerful as it had been all those months ago.

A throbbing began between her legs and she shifted. Her body was pissed that it hadn't seen any action beyond her own hand and vibrator over the last six months. Damn that man and his effect on her. The purpose of this visit was to deliver unsettling news, not drool over her real-life fantasy.

~ ~ ~ ~

Acer's opponent rose from his hunched position, shook out his arms, and rallied. Nice recovery. Acer hadn't held back too much on that particular punch. He blocked a jab and landed a left hook to the side of his opponent's head. This was too easy; the kid was inexperienced and far too predictable, coming at him with the same combination repeatedly. He could have ended it in the first round, but the crowd preferred a little show.

Acer dodged another jab and nearly fell over as a flash of glossy, honey-colored hair shining amid all the black leather crossed right into his field of vision. He knew that hair, and he knew that gorgeous face.

Fia.

Holy. Shit.

What the fuck was she doing here?

Pain bloomed in his jaw and radiated through his head as his neck snapped back with the force of a blow he hadn't seen coming. His adversary grinned like a cocky fool.

The bell dinged. Round two over.

Acer jogged to his corner and spat a small amount of blood into a bucket. Mouthguard was a damn joke. Still hurt like a motherfucker to get hit in the mouth, though it had to be better than having a tooth go through his lip.

Maybe she'd been a hallucination, his mind playing tricks. Bringing his fantasy to life. He blinked and scanned to the right. Nope, that was definitely Fia, in the flesh.

"What the fuck was that bullshit?" Jester bellowed as Acer sank to a stool and grabbed his water bottle. "You completely lost focus at the end. You could have taken this loser without him landing one punch but you were MIA for a second. What gives?"

Acer shook his head but didn't answer, his attention riveted to Fia.

"Oh, Jesus." Jester groaned as he followed Acer's stare. "Seriously? You gonna throw this match cuz you see some hot piece of ass?"

He ignored Jester's continued ranting and focused on Fia. She should not be here. Christ, she looked like every biker's fantasy come to life, standing there in the tightest leather pants he'd ever seen. On top, she wore a pale pink, flowy tank top that shimmered in the light. Black heeled ankle boots made her legs appear miles long. If only she'd turn around, he could see exactly what those painted on pants and boots did for her sexy ass.

He lifted his gaze to her face and found her staring right back at him. Her eyes widened slightly when they met his, and she licked her lips. The sight rocketed his mind back to that night six months ago and the way those lips wrapped around his cock with a tighter, wetter suction than he'd ever experienced.

That mouth of hers was dangerous.

Despite the aching in his jaw and the six-foot-five angry man hollering about what an idiot he was, Acer's cock stirred. Anyone ever won a mixed martial arts match with a boner? He didn't plan to be the first to find out. He tried writing complicated lines of computer code in his head; anything to avoid humiliation.

A biker he didn't recognize, but who looked far more like he belonged here than Fia did, approached her. She smiled at him and Acer's blood curdled. The assholes here would eat her alive, and smiling at them would only encourage the feeding frenzy.

The man slung an arm around her shoulders and said something that made her throw back her head and laugh, exposing the smooth column of her throat. More than once, she'd shivered beneath him when he nipped her there.

Enough was enough. This match was over. No more fucking around. The bell dinged and the middle aged, balding ref moved to the center of the ring and held up his right hand.

Acer hopped up, assuming a fighting stance with his fists at chin level. Across the ring, his opponent did the same. In his periphery, Acer noticed a second soon to be dead man approaching Fia. Gone were the shining eyes and bright smile from seconds ago, and in its place, was a bit of discomfort.

The ref dropped his hand and backed to the edge of the ring. Acer charged, meeting his opponent on his side of the ring. The newbie scrambled and threw a sloppy punch Acer sidestepped with ease. He dropped his shoulder and powered an uppercut to the guy's gut, followed immediately by a straight jab, and a nearly lethal left hook to the side of the head.

Acer wasn't the best striker—not like his club's VP, who was named for it—he did his best work on the ground. But something about seeing Fia get hit on by men who wouldn't hesitate to fuck her over enraged him.

The young fighter crashed to the ground and laid still, the steady rise and fall of his chest dispelling fears of a serious injury. Noise in the room ceased except for the sound of the referee counting. "Eight...nine...ten. Knockout."

Thunderous cheering and boot stomping erupted before the words were out of the ref's mouth. Behind him, Jester's shrill whistle cut through the celebratory ruckus. "Damn straight. That's what I'm talking about, brother. Wait... where the fuck you goin'?"

Acer tossed his grappling gloves and mouthguard into a corner of the ring, and slipped between the ropes, passing Dr. Lila Parker as she climbed up to assess the other fighter. She was his VP's wife and served as a medic of sorts for the monthly Friday Night Fights.

"Damn, Acer, where did that come from?" she asked as he passed.

He nodded but didn't answer her, his focus like a laser on Fia and her admirers.

"Acer?" Lila called to his retreating back.

He lifted a hand in acknowledgment. Hopefully she wouldn't tell her ol' man he blew her off. There'd be an ass chewing later for sure.

He shoved his way through the crowd, shaking off the back slaps and praise until he reached Fia. Her back was to him now, and he wrapped a hand around her upper arm, drawing her away from her fan club.

"Hey, man, what the fuck you think you're doin'? I'm talking to the lady."

"Acer!" Fia's face lit up at the sight of him. That delighted smile hit him harder than any punch his challenger could have thrown.

"The lady's mine." Acer growled down at the punk who dared to touch her. His head was shaved except for one short, but wide strip down the middle, like a tire track. One of his front teeth was missing and he smelled like a marijuana dispensary. Christ, had he really just claimed the woman out loud? He had less than no rights to her, nor did he want them, but she inspired some kind of unwelcome Neanderthal possessive instinct.

Fia's eyes widened, but she wisely kept her mouth shut.

"Maybe she don't wanna be yours. Maybe we should take this outside and see who the lady wants to go with." Tire Track took a menacing step forward.

Beside him, Fia laughed. "Did you see what he just did to that guy in the ring? He destroyed him in five seconds. Move along, buddy." She waved her delicate hand with its pale pink nail polish in a shooing motion.

Acer gritted his teeth and held back his laughter. He loved her sass, but she needed to learn when to keep a lid on it. Around here, it wouldn't fly. He gave her upper arm a light warning squeeze. What was it about this woman that made him want to slay her dragons then fuck her for hours?

She was fearless, he'd give her that. Smart-mouthing this white trash was ballsy but reckless.

Tire Track's expression darkened and he took a step toward Fia. Wrong move. Luckily, the man wasn't quite as stupid as he looked. He stopped dead in his tracks when Acer speared him with a look that told him he'd cut his nuts off if he came within another foot of Fia.

Tire Track shrugged, then held his hands up. "Okay man, plenty of pussy in the sea." He turned and ambled off.

"Acer, holy crap that was insane. You were amaz—"

The second Fia's new friend was out of earshot, he spun her around to face him. It took all his strength to focus on getting rid of her and not the feel of her silky skin beneath his hand. Her entire body had been just as soft and supple.

"What the fuck are you doing here, Fia?" He lowered his voice and ignored the spectators milling around them.

Her smile flipped upside down. "I know you're surprised to see me, but I need to talk to you about something."

And he needed to get her out of here. He wasn't free to leave yet, and couldn't babysit her for the rest of the night. Striker had a match later and Acer was coaching since Jester had to split early. He hated to be a dick to her, but it was the fastest way to get her to leave. "You looking for another fuck, babe? Been thinking about me for the last six months?"

She jerked her arm away from him. "Don't be an asshole, Acer. It wasn't good enough that I'd hop on a plane to come looking for it. There's plenty of men in California who are up to the task."

Even though he didn't believe a word of it, her comments hit below the belt.

He crowded her until she walked backward, her spine hitting the wall after a few steps. He didn't stop until their bodies were plastered together, his hard-on pressing into her stomach. It wasn't private, but at least they weren't in the center of a throng of bikers anymore.

She gasped and tried to glance around his body. "Acer," she said, pushing against his chest. "What the hell are you doing?"

Her hands on his naked chest only served to make him

harder. "Checking something." He crashed his mouth to hers with no mercy.

Fia moaned into his mouth and melted against him without an ounce of resistance. Her arms closed around his upper body, holding him flush against her.

Christ, she was just as sweet as he remembered. Six months of trying to figure out how she'd gotten under his skin, and how to excise her were fruitless. Every memory and unwelcome emotion came rushing back.

He tore his mouth away and whispered in her ear. "I call bullshit, baby. You damn well know how good it was. Now, get the fuck out of here. This is not the place for you." He took a step back. Her loose shirt clung to his sweat-glazed torso and slowly peeled off his body as he pulled away. Christ, even that fired his blood. The need to fuck her right here against the wall intensified by the second.

She shook her head, her eyes dazed, a red flush on her face. "No, wait," She grabbed him by the waistband of his boxing shorts.

He raised an eyebrow. "Really, babe? Right here? It's not exactly private, but I'm game if you are." Thankfully, no one paid them any attention as they drank their beer and geared up for the next match.

The spark was back in her eyes. "If you'd stop trying to scare me away for just one minute and listen to me, I'll tell you why I'm here, which is not for a quick fuck in the middle of a crowded gym."

He loved her spunk. He also appreciated that she was intelligent and saw through him. Shouldn't have underestimated her. With a sigh, he ran a hand through his damp hair. "Why are you here, Fia?"

"I need to talk to you about something, but this is not the place."

His eyes dropped to her flat stomach and she laughed. "I'm not pregnant, Acer, though I will remember the two seconds of horror on your face for the rest of my life." She laughed again. "Good stuff. Hey, where's your nipple ring?"

He rolled his eyes. "I wear a spacer when I'm fighting. Too risky otherwise. Get to the point, babe."

"Huh?" She seemed to have lost her train of thought somewhere between his nipple ring and his pecs. "Oh right. It's about your father, and concerns your club."

She had his full attention now. "Fuck, you serious?"

She nodded and released his shorts.

"What do you know? Did he send you with a message or something?" Flashes of how Jester met his woman ran through Acer's mind. She was sent by an enemy of the club to siphon information in exchange for saving her brother's life. In the end, it all worked out, but not before putting Emily's life in danger and dragging Jester through hell. Acer's trust was limited to his brothers only, and even with them, he was cautious.

"What? Of course not. I overheard a phone conversation your father was having. If he knew..." She shook her head. "Let's just say I was very discrete."

This wasn't good. His father could be ruthless, and her knowledge of his more nefarious business practices could be hazardous to her health.

Acer scratched at the scruff on his chin. "You're right, this is not the place. I'm stuck here for a few more hours, but I can meet you at your hotel? Where're you staying?"

"Well, your family doesn't seem to have any hotels here, so..." She winked.

Acer laughed. "Yeah, our town isn't quite grand enough for a Wellington monstrosity."

"I'm at a motel two towns over, Sunset Inn, room twenty-three."

He nodded. "I'll be there by midnight. You need a ride back?"

She shook her head, the tips of her hair brushing back and forth over her bare shoulders. He'd liked it six months ago, but it was longer now and he had the urge to wrap it around his fist, tilt her head back, and devour her talented mouth.

"I have a rental," she said.

He gave into partial temptation and pressed his torso against her once again. "Go straight there and don't leave. It's not the best area." He captured her bottom lip between his teeth and gave a light tug before pulling back. "Say, 'yes, Acer'."

"Yes, Acer," she parroted with enough attitude in her voice that he smirked.

"Smartass." He dropped a quick kiss on her upturned mouth then turned and gave her a gentle nudge toward the door. "Go, see you at midnight."

She turned around, mischief sparkling in her whiskey eyes. "Going. And nice win, hot stuff. Never knew two men fighting could be so sexy. Think I may have found a new sport to watch." She winked and turned again, walking toward the exit with a sexy sway to her hips.

Acer shook his head and kept his gaze on her until she disappeared. That smart mouth of hers was going to get her in trouble. He had a few ideas for how to keep it occupied so she couldn't sass him so much.

Unwilling to watch the other men as they ogled the sensual twitch of her ass while she walked, he spun back toward the ring. Shit, how much time had he spent talking to Fia? With a turn of his head, he scanned the room. Jester stood in the ring staring down at him with a shit-eating grin on his face.

Fantastic.

He'd given the jokester enough fuel to torment him for a long time.

Fuck it.

The woman who'd plagued his erotic dreams for the past six months was here, and there was no way he was letting her leave without a repeat of the best night of sex he'd ever had. After that, he was done. He knew better than to get involved with anyone. Tonight, he'd purge her from his system and resume his normal life, unencumbered by constant thoughts of Fia.

Chapter Six

Man, the desert was eerily dark. Even with the high beams blaring from her rented BMW, Fia missed the glow of streetlamps along the highway. Countless miles of unlit road loomed ahead. She flicked her gaze to the rear-view mirror. Nothing but endless blackness behind her too. She shuddered. This certainly wasn't somewhere she'd want to run out of—

She gasped and darted her attention to the gas gauge. She expelled a harsh breath. Okay, half-full tank. Thank God. She attributed the momentary freak out to the horror-moviesque setting. Woman alone, driving through the pitch-black shroud of the desert night… Okay, so her imagination was running away with her, but it was scary as shit out here.

With a shake of her head, she turned up the radio. Maybe the music would drown out her overactive imagination. After settling on her favorite Sirius country station, she returned her eyes to the road. Something darted in front of her car, and she screamed.

"Shit!" She jammed her foot on the brake, pressing it to the floor of the car. Her body flew forward only to be jolted back against the seat by the stiffening seatbelt. The breaks squealed, easily heard over the loud twang of the music, and the smell of burning rubber filled the car.

"Oh my God." She placed her shaking hands on her head and breathed to calm her pounding heart. "Get it together, girl," she muttered, spreading her fingers to peek through the windshield. Just ten feet in front of her a mangy coyote with beady yellow eyes stared at her as though annoyed that she dared to interrupt his evening.

After a sharp tap on the horn, the coyote fled. "Fia, you're such a chicken." With unsteady hands, she resumed driving. This damn motel couldn't materialize fast enough.

Finally, about a half mile ahead, faint light of the tiny town that housed her motel glowed against the dark backdrop. With a sigh of relief, she rolled her shoulders and added more pressure to the gas pedal.

Three minutes later, she threw her car in park and dug through her purse. "Come on, room key," she muttered. The goal was to spend as little time outside the exterior door to her room as possible. Finding the key card took twice as long as it should have since her hands were not fully back under her control. Damn coyote.

Key in hand, she stepped out of the car and did a quick scan of her surroundings. Aside from three other parked cars, the lot was dead silent and nearly as dark as if her eyes were closed. Dim light from the Sunset Motel sign, missing the *u* and *o*, was the only illumination, and it was far from adequate.

Fia shivered and dashed toward the hotel door. She slid the keycard into the slot and frowned at the red light blinking back at her like an evil eye. After a second attempt, she groaned. "Come on, you can't be serious," she muttered, trying and failing for the third time. "Damnit."

"Trouble, miss?"

Fia shrieked and her hand flew to her chest. In the span of one second, her heart rate shot from almost back to normal to dangerously rapid. She stared at the source of her fright. The skinny man with long, scraggly hair, who'd checked her into the hotel, stood just a few feet away. "Holy crap, you scared me to death, Mr.—I'm sorry, I don't recall your name."

"Just call me Mike," he said.

He'd unnerved her when she met him, his mud-colored eyes lingering too long on her chest, and his smarmy grin betraying his inappropriate thoughts. Now, she felt a cautious relief that he'd stumbled upon her.

"Mike, my key card doesn't seem to be working. Should I take it to the office to get another one?" She longed for a luxury hotel with fifty floors, where all the entrances to the rooms were *inside* the building and lit by bright, cheery hallway lights. Why did Acer have to live in a tiny town with no lodging options?

Mike shook his head. Greasy strands of hair fell in front of his eyes as he advanced on her. "Let me give it a try first."

"I've tried it three times already. I'm pretty sure it's just broken."

He winked a brown eye. "Sometimes it just takes a man's touch."

Seriously? She wanted to roll her eyes but refrained. He offered help and all that mattered was getting in that room as fast as possible. Acer would be by in about two hours and she needed the time to mentally prepare both for giving him potentially disturbing news and for being alone in a room with him and a bed.

Mike stepped close, too close, and wrapped his hand around her wrist. He pulled the keycard from her grasp, but didn't release her.

She tried to wiggle away, but his grip was solid. His hand on her arm caused her to shiver, and not in a good, excited way. More due to unease and a bit of fear. It was okay; she had a knee and knew how to ram his balls if he went any further.

He slid the card in the slot. Same result as her, the flashing red eye. "Huh, looks like you're right. It's not working." He chuckled.

She swallowed and twisted her wrist yet again. "Would you please let go of me, Mike?"

He turned to her and her stomach soured at the lewd, gleaming excitement that shone in his eyes. "I don't think so."

In a move that was so sudden she couldn't have done a thing to prevent it, he wrenched her arm behind her back and shoved her face-first against the wall. Her cheek scraped against the rough stucco surface of the building, still warm from the desert's heated day. She winced and bit back a cry of pain.

Fight, fight, fight, her mind screamed at her, but he had her immobilized and outmatched by his surprising strength. "Mike, what the hell are you doing? Get the fuck off of me."

He rustled around behind her, and she struggled in vain. The wall abraded her face, but she ignored it, the stinging preferable to whatever he had planned.

Without warning, he grabbed a fistful of her hair and yanked her head back, clamping a cloth over her mouth. She increased her efforts to escape and thrashed against him, trying to kick him or scream or do anything to attract attention and help. It was all a wasted effort. The angle of her neck made it difficult to breathe or fight back with any effectiveness.

A pungent odor singed her nostrils and in seconds, an

intense tingling spread throughout her limbs. Darkness ringed the edges of her vision and shrunk inward. Her muffled screams were ineffective, only serving to inhale more of whatever noxious chemical he forced over her mouth.

Panic like she'd never known flared.

"Nighty, night," Mike whispered in her ear.

Just before her vision went black, thoughts of Acer filled her mind. What would happen when he came looking for her? Would he find her alive? Would Mike hurt him?

~ ~ ~ ~

At five minutes to midnight, freshly showered and sporting a tender bruise along his jaw, Acer pounded on the door for the third time. Flakes of peeling paint drifted to the ground with the power of his fist. "Fia, open up," he shouted.

Where the fuck was she?

He stomped toward the office and yanked the glass door open. A high-pitched jangle of bells made him wince. The shrill sound was a harsh contrast to the quiet night. Behind the desk, a girl, probably eighteen or nineteen, with spiky purple hair and a hoop through her lower lip sat, her thumbs flying over the screen of a cell phone.

"Need a room?" she asked without diverting her attention from the device.

"No." His tone was severe, a no-nonsense bark.

She jumped and the phone fell from her fingers, landing on the desk with a clatter. Her blue eyes widened to the point of comical as she took in his No Prisoners' cut.

Being feared definitely came with its advantages.

"I need some information. I'm looking for the woman staying in room twenty-three. You see her tonight?"

"Uhh...well...I'm not supposed to give you any information about the guests." Her voice quivered and she sounded like she feared he was going to pounce on her any second.

He relaxed his stance and gifted her his most charming smile. "Listen, it's really important." He dug his wallet out of his pocket and pulled out five bills. He made a show of placing each bill on the counter, holding back his laughter when he reached one hundred dollars and she licked her lips. "Promise I won't tell a soul you gave me any info."

Money worked in almost any situation, and this was no exception. The girl scooped up the bills as though they might run away if she wasn't fast enough. "I haven't seen her. Let me check the computer." She hunted and pecked across the keyboard, then leaned back to wait while the ancient machine churned. "Hmm, looks like she checked out this evening, about two and a half hours ago. That was right before my shift started, so I wasn't the one to check her out. Sorry. Uhh, can I still keep the money?"

"Sure, kid," he said.

Goddamnit, where the hell had Fia gone?

He stepped back out into the cool evening air and glanced around. Well, he could follow the road out of town, see if he could track her down. The question was, whether or not he should bother. She'd obviously chickened out, turned tail, and run. Hopefully not straight to his father.

She seemed legit, and based on the troubles she had with her own family six months ago, he didn't think she'd be working for his father, but he never took anyone at face value anymore.

After he had returned from the charity gala in LA, he'd filled his club president in on his father's request for assistance shuttling illegals across the border. Shiv was as against the ideas as Acer was. He'd mentioned the threats his old man dealt as well, but Shiv wasn't concerned. His father could cause some headaches for the club, but nothing they couldn't handle.

Acer scratched his chin and mounted his bike. He checked his phone one last time. Nothing from Fia. She hadn't answered or returned any of his six calls.

He could go to her home. Finding the address would take all of five seconds, just as finding her phone number had. If he showed up where she lived, she'd have no choice but to deal with him. Did he want to go that route? He'd think on it for a few days then make a decision, one that didn't involve his cock and its yearning to be back inside her.

Fia messed with his head, and in his life, that was dangerous. Acer didn't care how happy his brothers were with their women. They just didn't know yet how devastating the fallout was when the person you trusted most in the world stabbed you straight in the back.

Chapter Seven

Fia awoke with a harsh jolt. There was no dreamy ease into wakefulness, or comfortable snuggle into her feather pillow as she blocked out the world for a few more minutes. Her muscles contracted in a painful spasm, her eyes flew open, and heat as hot as a brick oven engulfed every inch of her skin.

Before her mind had a chance to register fear, her heart raced and her mouth dried up as though stuffed with yards of cotton. Sweat poured off her face and landed on her chest, rolling in itchy rivers to her stomach.

In an automatic movement, she lifted a hand to wipe the offending perspiration away. Her forearm brushed across a naked breast, and then the fear came in an avalanche of horror and panic.

Jesus Christ, what the fuck happened to her clothing?

She looked down at her unclothed body, streaked with dirt and sweat. Tears filled her eyes as memories assaulted her. Memories of Mike holding that pungent cloth over her face until she passed out. Memories of...what? The last thing she recalled was darkness encroaching on her vision. The rest was a vast chasm of blankness, until she woke up seconds ago.

She glanced at her nudity again as the tears spilled down her face. Why the hell had Mike taken off her clothes? What did he plan to do with her? What had he already done to her?

She drew her knees up to her chest and wrapped her arms around them, burying her face against her legs. The sobs began as small choked sounds and increased until they racked her. For what seemed like endless minutes, her body heaved with the furious force of her crying.

Eventually, she ran out of steam and went from full body spasms to small hitches in her breathing. Tears slowed to a trickle.

Think, Fia. Move. Be smart.

Now that the despair had quieted, her mind allowed some of the anger in. It was right. There would be plenty of time for tears later, if she survived this.

Crying would do nothing to help her situation. She lifted her head and forced herself to her feet. Pain lanced her right ankle and she peered down. "Oh my God." She whimpered but held back a second round of tears. Around her red, raw ankle, a metal cuff with a thick chain kept her bound to the floor.

Her legs trembled. "You're fine," she told herself. "Just shaky legs." She looked around the room. It was empty except for one small folding chair about ten or so feet in front of her, next to the door frame. The door appeared to be missing, wood trim splintered as though someone wrenched it from its hinges in a violent outburst. On the wall behind her, a boarded-up window was too far out of reach. She stood on a dusty cheap wood floor in the back corner of the room, opposite the door.

How long would it be before Mike came in? Was he even

here? Maybe he'd just left her to die. Her stomach cramped and her left knee buckled. She leaned her damp back against the wall and tried to lower her bottom to the ground in a controlled fashion. Her legs shook with such force, she slid much faster than intended, landing with a rough thump.

She grunted and ignored the sharp pain in her tailbone. With trembling hands, she gripped the metal chain and tugged as hard as possible. No give. She was well and truly trapped in a room with no weapons and no chance for escape.

Soul deep helplessness swamped her and she began to cry again. A heavy trudge of footsteps sounded in the hall, growing louder with each stomp. Her head snapped up and her stomach clenched as the breath stilled in her lungs. She sat still as a corpse as though not moving could somehow make her invisible.

Within seconds, Mike filled the doorway. "You're awake." His gleeful voice made every hair on her body rise to attention, as though preparing for battle. "Took me forever to drag ya in here last night. You were dead weight. Thought I mighta killed you." He chuckled. "Looks like I didn't. Now we can play." A sinister smile that she'd only ever seen on psychopaths in the movies formed on his face.

Fia quaked with such violence, had anyone else been present, they would have thought she was having a seizure. She tried to speak, but the muscles in her jaw trembled as hard as the rest of them, clanking her teeth up and down and rendering her mouth useless.

Mike held a smoldering cigarette in one hand and the other moved to the fly of his jeans. Fia's attention was immediately drawn to the bulge behind the zipper. She gagged and her stomach heaved with enough force to expel her internal organs, but nothing came up. It had to be over fifteen hours since she'd eaten, and the searing heat of the room had probably pulled every ounce of water out through her skin.

He lowered the zipper as he advanced on her with slow steps.

Each click of the opening zipper was like a countdown to her doom, edging close to zero at an alarming rate. "N-no," she managed to whisper. "Please, no." The words were rough and her dry throat ached with the effort to speak. She scrambled as far into the corner as possible. The thought of his hands on her, of what lay behind that zipper was worse than her darkest nightmares.

Mike laughed and continued forward. When he was within striking distance, Fia's fight-or-flight instinct kicked up in full force. Fleeing was impossible, so she went with her only option. She hit, kicked, tried to bite and head butt, anything to prevent what she feared was about to happen. Mike ignored the blows that connected and jammed the glowing end of his cigarette into her side.

Fiery pain bit into her and stunned her into immobility. She cried out and flopped against the wall, the searing burn seeming to originate from every cell in her body.

"That's better," he said with another evil smile.

Fia didn't know why he abducted her. Didn't know if he'd ever let her go. Didn't know if she had the power to fight him. The one thing she was sure of, though, was that her nightmare had just begun.

~ ~ ~ ~

Acer growled at his phone for what had to be the fiftieth time in the past twenty-four hours. If Fia was pissed at him for his treatment of her at the gym, the message was well received. This cold shoulder act was enough to drive him nuts.

He'd give her one more day, then he was flying to

California and busting down the door of her Beverly Hills apartment. No way would he tolerate his woman hiding from him like this.

His woman? Where the fuck had that insane thought come from? She was in no way, shape, or form, his anything but pain in the ass. For all he knew, this was some plan concocted by his asshole of a father to mess with his head.

In his gut, he knew that wasn't true, but his head ruled the show and had decided twenty years ago, that the word trust didn't belong in his vocabulary. That was the reason Fia wasn't his, and would never be his.

It was times like this, even so many years later, when he missed Derek the most. His friend would have knocked him upside the head and told him to quit whining. But speaking to Derek wasn't a possibility, today or any day.

His phone rang and he slammed it against his ear without checking the number. "Fia?"

"Uh, no, but I'm definitely going to have some questions about that later. You sure sound anxious to talk to this broad." Jester laughed.

"What the fuck do you want?"

"Yikes, brother. Cranky much?"

"Answer the damn question, Jester." Acer gripped the phone until his palm ached.

"Church, thirty minutes. You know that guy we lent money to for helping us out with info on that last gun shipment?"

Acer grunted.

"Well, he missed his very strict payback deadline. Shiv's fit to be tied. See you in thirty. Can't wait to chat." Jester laughed then disconnected the call.

Fuck. This was an annoyance he did not want to deal with. He rose from his couch. Well, maybe it would distract him for a few minutes from the mind-fuck that was Fia. He grabbed his keys and strode out his door.

One week. Seven days. Then he was flying to fucking California.

Chapter Eight

Fia could no longer narrow the aches and pains down to specific parts of her body. Everything hurt. She was a giant throbbing ball of pain.

That wasn't entirely true.

The pain between her legs was the worst, though to be honest, the physical discomfort was probably amplified by the psychological trauma that accompanied the violation. The searing pain on the right side of her ribs, where Mike had ground out no less than seven cigarette butts against her sensitive skin, rivaled a close second. After that, she was just one mass of discomfort.

A strange thing happened after days of constant terror. She became slightly detached, like her physical body and her fears were two separate beings in the room. Her physical self remained naked, chained by the ankle to a large metal ring bolted to the floor, unable to escape.

But her thoughts? They floated somewhere above her, a mix of anxiety, disbelief, and hopelessness. That was until Mike returned. When he returned, terror wrapped its long fingers around her throat and threatened to choke her.

The sound of his keys turning the deadbolt set her off

each and every time, with this being no exception. She'd figured out at some point that she was in a house. Maybe more like a shack. It was certainly small. She could hear almost every move Mike made when he was there, even if he wasn't in the unfurnished room with her.

Her breathing sped and her heart pounded as she prepared for battle. Inside the house had to be close to a hundred degrees, and sweat poured off her, but she ignored it. That discomfort was the very least of her worries.

She had no weapon, agonizingly little strength, and even less energy, but she'd fight him until her dying breath. No matter how long he kept her prisoner or what he did to her, she'd fight him every single time. There was always a chance, slim as it may be, that she could inflict some damage and get the upper hand.

She'd been trying for three days to get out of the chain that bound her to the floor and was no closer than she'd been when she arrived. That meant she'd have to kill him. She couldn't incapacitate him and run. She'd have to kill him… somehow, and take the phone he always kept in his back pocket. Only then would she stand a chance.

She was okay with that. She was ready to take his life. He deserved it for what he did to her, and who knew how many other women. Maybe at some point in the future guilt would come, but for now, she had no reservations.

A loud banging noise from somewhere in the house caused her to jolt. She drew her knees up and wrapped her arms around them in a weak attempt to shield her body from his impending lust-filled gaze. Not that it mattered. Mike had already seen everything she had to offer. That, and worse. Still, the instinct to preserve even an ounce of dignity was strong.

Seconds later, he burst in, a crazed and frantic look in his eyes. He stopped dead in his tracks, almost as if he'd forgotten she was there.

She kept quiet, pressing hard to the wall. Putting as much distance as possible between them was always the goal. There had been a few lucky times when he came in the room, mumbled some frustrated, incoherent words, then left without so much as a glance in her direction. Other times, she wasn't so fortunate. Which way it would go was always an unknown, so her first act was to remain quiet and pray to be ignored.

"You don't have time to deal with her," he mumbled. "They're going to be here any minute."

Fia held her breath. He gripped a hammer in one hand, and a faded backpack in the other. This was the first time he'd had any object in his hand besides a cigarette. If she invoked his wrath and he came at her with the hammer, there was a good chance she wouldn't survive. Aside from muttering her name, he paid her no attention as he walked to the far corner of the empty room.

With a curse, he dropped to his knees, lifted his right arm, and sent the hammer crashing through the wood floor.

Fia jumped and slapped a hand over her mouth, holding in a hysterical shriek. Would he turn that hammer on her next? She slid a finger into her mouth and bit down, the acute pain keeping her from completely freaking out and making a sound that would draw his attention. He appeared in his own world and needed to stay there.

After a few seconds of bashing the hammer into the floor like a madman, he reached into the hole through the splintered wood and pulled out a thick wad of cash. Into the backpack it went, followed by another, and another still.

Holy shit. That was a lot of cash. Where the hell had it come from? What the hell was he planning? The room spun, but she didn't dare breathe and refused to blink.

Mike zipped the bag and stood, making a beeline for the door.

Just when she thought she was safe, he stopped and pivoted back. His gaze landed on her, an almost loving expression on his face.

She shifted her focus to the wooden floor. *Keep silent. Leave*, her mind screamed. *Just leave. Please, please walk out that door.*

"I may not be back for days. They're coming for me." With that cryptic statement, he turned and ran out of the room. The slam of the front door reached her seconds later.

Fia sucked in a gulp of hot air as relief and terror coursed through her in equal measures. Her body trembled and her thoughts raced.

He was gone.

Maybe for days.

Thank you, God.

But how the hell would she get out of here? He hadn't fed her since she arrived, and she'd only had one bottle of water. Already, she was so weak and dehydrated, position changes made her dizzy. How much longer could her body hold out?

"It will damn well hold out until you get out of this fucking chain, Fia," she ordered herself. With nothing else to do and no immediate fear of Mike's return, she could focus all her attention on getting free. If only he'd left the damn hammer.

She gripped the thick metal ring around her ankle and gasped as white-hot pain shot from her foot to her knee. The ankle was raw and bloody from her repeated attempts to work the metal shackle off her foot. She was no doctor, but the skin beneath and around the cuff didn't look healthy. The flesh was an angry shade of red, and her entire calf was swollen from knee to toes. Infection had to be setting in. It was difficult to tell if she was feverish because the room was so blasted hot, but a time or two she'd shivered with unexpected chills. A fever may have been the culprit.

The idea of removing the cuff from her throbbing leg abandoned, she moved on to the metal plate bolted to the floor.

Rising to her feet on quaking legs, Fia took a deep breath and willed the room to stop spinning. She straddled the metal plate and pulled on the chain with all her might. There was about a centimeter of wiggle. It was a start.

Her right leg buckled and she sat on the ground, hard. The rough landing jarred her battered body. With both hands, she grasped the iron ring that attached to the metal plate and worked it back and forth. Maybe, if she tugged at it long enough, she'd loosen the bolts enough to remove it from the floorboard. She'd work at this twenty-four hours a day if she had to.

No fucking way would she die in this hellhole.

~ ~ ~ ~

"Don't look much like the fucker's home. How much you say he owes the club again?" Jester tied his shoulder-length dark hair back at the base of his neck as he spoke.

"Forty thou," Acer replied, not bothering to look at Jester, his attention fixed on the house twenty feet away.

Acer, Jester, and Striker sat on their bikes in the street outside a house on the outskirts of Crystal Rock. They had a debt to collect, a large one.

Shiv was pissed, and if the money wasn't recovered tonight, then he wanted the man to have a firm understanding of what happened if you fucked with the No Prisoners.

"Why the fuck did we give him all that money? We a fuckin' charity now?" Jester asked.

"We only let him borrow thirty. Other ten is a missed payment penalty. Next payment is due tomorrow and a little birdie told us he's not good for it. Shiv's orders. Take it up with him," Acer replied.

Striker grunted. "It was a thank you. You know how he warned us the cops were sniffing around that last gun shipment." He shrugged "Guy told us he needed thirty large and asked for ten in exchange for the info. Shiv offered the whole thing as a loan in hopes of earning future info. He knows now it was a dumb move." He sighed and ran a hand over his face. "Christ, eleven on a Monday night. You boys know what I could be doing now instead of this shit?"

Acer thought from the start lending this asshole money was an irresponsible move, but he didn't make the decisions. He followed orders. "You got more power than all of us, VP. You want to be home fucking your ol' lady, you coulda made that happen. Looks like you want to be in the trenches with us after all. Married life getting stale already?"

Striker flipped him off.

"You in a funk again, Acer? You've been in a shit mood for the past three days, ever since I caught you devouring that pretty little thing at the fight." Jester blew into his closed hand. Now that the sun had set, the temperature was dropping at a rapid rate.

Christ. Fucking Jester and his big mouth.

"What? Why am I just hearing about this now?" Striker turned and gave Acer a toothy grin. "You know, come to think of it, you've been in a piss poor mood for months now, ever since you got back from LA." Jester tapped a thick finger against his lips as though deep in thought. "Hmm, this dame at the gym was classy, Lila classy. She from LA? She have anything to do with your six-month long PMS?"

Acer hopped off his bike and charged toward Jester, the

man's giant size be damned. Striker stopped him with a none-too-gentle slap to the chest.

"No time for this, kids. Save it for the playground tomorrow." Striker's phone buzzed and he peered down at it. "Guys are in position around back. Plan is to go in hard, drag him out. If he can't pay up, he gets an ass beating he won't forget."

"And if he ain't here?" Jester asked. "Because it doesn't look like anyone's home."

"Toss the place, maybe we can find some of what we're owed."

Jester snorted. "Not likely."

"Shut up and move." Acer barked.

Jester grinned and turned to Striker. "See what I mean, VP? Cranky, cranky."

Striker laughed. "Just go, Jester. Take that clown-sized foot out of your mouth and boot in the door, will ya?" He drew out his weapon and Acer followed suit, flicking off the safety.

"Yes, sir," Jester said as he snapped a salute. He lifted what had to be a size fourteen foot and planted it next to the doorknob. Without even so much as a grunt of effort, Jester kicked and the door swung wide open. Silence greeted the group. "Well, that was anticlimactic."

"Isn't that Emily's line?" Acer asked with a laugh.

"Oh, so you're a comedian now?" Jester flipped him off. "First, you're a moody asshole, now you're a funnyman. Hard to keep up. And I'll have you know, Emily comes at least—"

In a poor attempt at disguising a laugh, Striker coughed. "Get in the fucking house."

The house remained soundless as a tomb. Looked like Jester's assessment was right, the prick wasn't home. People tended to make some noise when a group of angry bikers bashed in their door in the middle of the night. Unless he was hiding.

Acer scratched the back of his neck. An itch had formed the second Jester booted in the door. Something didn't feel right about this entire situation. Were they walking into an ambush? Didn't seem likely. The place was tiny; not much space for people to hide and attack. Still, the itch grew more aggravating with each passing second.

Senses on full alert, Acer stepped into the house. Heat blasted him from every angle. "Christ, it's hot in here."

Jester tromped straight back, down a hallway leading to what Acer assumed was a bedroom or two. Acer located a light switch next to the door and flipped it up. Light from a ceiling fan flooded the room.

Aside from a recliner, tiny television, and small folding table, the living room was bare. The table lay on its side on the floor, with a cup of whatever this loser had been drinking spilled next to it. A half-eaten hamburger lay across the room, probably flew there when the table upended.

"Looks like he may have torn through here in a hurry." Striker said from behind Acer. His VP stood in the doorway, surveying the room with a frown.

"Would have been too easy if he were here waiting with cash in hand," Acer said.

Striker grunted. "I'm getting too old to chase down assholes for money."

"Send prospects next time." Acer kept his focus on the dark hallway Jester disappeared down. The unease scratching at his nape hadn't subsided when they entered the quiet house. If he was being honest with himself, the edgy feeling began three days ago, when Fia up and disappeared. He frowned. He had to quit thinking about her. She didn't disappear; she ditched him.

"I would have sent prospects this time, but Shiv wanted it done by us. I think he realized he fucked up lending this guy cash." Striker grunted and waved a hand around. "Let's do a quick and dirty search, then head out."

A high-pitched yelp followed by a weak sounding, "Don't come any closer," drifted down the hallway. What the hell? Acer's itchy neck turned into a screaming gut. Something wasn't right here. He knew it deep in his bones. He looked at Striker who had his pistol aimed at the hall, finger on the trigger.

Jester emerged from the hallway, his lips pressed together in a grim line of displeasure. The bleak look in his eyes alerted Acer to the fact that shit was about to hit the fan. "We got a problem, boys, a huge fuckin' problem. There's a girl back there."

"So what?" Striker asked. "Tell her to keep her mouth shut, growl at her a bit so she gets the picture, and send her on her way."

Jester shook his head and curled his fists at his sides. "I don't think she's here willingly. She's naked, dirty as my bike after a sand storm, and chained to the fuckin' floor. I tried to help her, but she freaked out when I took one step toward her. I think my size scared her. Acer, maybe you'll have better luck, and, Striker, I think you need to call Lila."

"Shit." Striker drew out his phone and stepped back out into the night.

Acer's blood ran cold. Memories of Penny from years ago —scared, trembling, and trying so hard to keep her dignity— assaulted him. Anger warmed his veins and he started to sprint down the hallway.

Jester's meaty palm on his shoulder halted his progression. "It's bad, brother. You go charging in there with that murderous expression, you'll scare the shit out of her."

Acer blew out a breath and rolled his shoulders. "I'm cool."

"You sure?"

"Yeah, I won't go in all crazy."

"Okay." Jester moved to the side and let Acer pass. He had to turn sideways to fit past Jester's huge form in the hall.

As he approached the dim room Jester had emerged from, he heard soft but accelerated breathing. Blood pounded through his veins and his gut churned. Nothing angered him more than mistreatment of a helpless woman.

He stepped into the doorway and turned his head toward a shadowy corner in the far left of the room, where a frightened gasp came from. Jester was right, someone was huddled in the corner, but aside from the fact that it was a small person, so probably a woman, the room was too dark to discern anything else. He pulled out his phone and activated the flashlight, filling the room with a surprising amount of light.

"A-Acer?" The low sound was so full of anguish and despair that the walls around Acer's heart vibrated.

Two terrified, pain-filled, and very familiar eyes stared up at him from the face of the battered woman huddled in the corner on the dusty floor. Fia. He took two steps closer and came to a staggering stop as though he'd been slammed in the stomach by a two-by-four. The room spun. He fought to find air. This could not be happening. He closed his eyes and counted to five before opening them again. No, it was real, not a figment of his tortured imagination.

Fia was the abused woman.

She was naked, as Jester said, and a metal cuff around her ankle held her chained to a ring on the floor. She was covered with dirt and bruises and her shoulder-length hair hung in stringy strands around her face.

Nausea swamped him at the sight of those bruises. Deep purple marks marred her thighs, her chest, her face. Thoughts of what she must have endured made him physically ill. Her hands were also raw as though she put up a hell of a fight, and Acer felt a tiny surge of pride.

For months, his dreams were plagued with memories of the way those whiskey-colored eyes glazed with pleasure when she came. Those same eyes, now broken and petrified, would forever haunt his nightmares.

Chapter Nine

"Fia?" he croaked, unable to make his voice work properly. His throat had dried up and constricted. He felt like he was choking.

"A-are you really h-here?"

Her whispered question knocked him out of his stunned state. He tore off his cut, letting it fall to the floor. Without a second thought, he yanked his sweatshirt over his head, leaving him in a white T-shirt. He rushed toward her, coming to a stop when she shrank even farther into the corner. "Fia, I'm really here. I won't hurt you."

At the sound of her name, she met his gaze, but confusion filled her eyes, as though she hadn't heard him. The last thing he wanted to do was scare her, but she seemed to be in shock and he needed her alert.

"Fia," he said again, putting a bit of snap in his voice.

She jumped, but her gaze cleared and she looked right at him.

"Baby, I promise I won't touch you, but I need to get closer to see what I'm dealing with, okay?"

She nodded and her body visibly relaxed just a fraction. She sat with her legs drawn up and arms across her chest, a weak shield for her nudity. She was small and vulnerable, and the thought of finding out exactly what she had endured made him want to murder someone. No, not someone. Mike, the bastard whose life now had a very imminent expiration date.

"Fia, I have a sweatshirt for you. Can I help you put it on? It will be hot in here, but it's chilly outside and you'll feel better covered up."

She nodded. "O-okay."

Acer crouched next to her and slipped the sweatshirt over her head. His hand brushed her shoulder as he drew the soft material down her body and she flinched in a violent jerk. She let out a small pain-filled groan and his hard heart cracked a little. "Sorry, baby."

He'd slipped the fabric down her back and over her bent knees, covering every inch of her exposed body. "There you go, hon. No one can see anything anymore. Let's get you out of here."

"Thank you," she whispered. With a trembling hand, she pointed toward her foot. "I can't get out."

Acer looked down at her right leg. Holy fuck. He clenched his teeth so hard, a trip to the dentist just might be in his near future. He willed himself to remain calm, not let the flame of anger burn bright enough that Fia could see. She didn't need to see him lose his shit. It would do her no good.

The leg was swollen so big, there wasn't any space between her skin and the cuff. The abused skin around the metal was red, raw, and oozing a yellowish discharge. Hopefully, the infection was localized. If it had traveled too far up the leg, there was a chance she could lose it. How could anyone abuse such a thing of beauty? How could a man destroy something that was built for pleasure, not pain?

"Look at me, Fia."

She slowly lifted her head until eyes full of despair met his gaze.

"I don't care if I have to rip this place apart one nail at a time. I am getting you the fuck out of here, and there is no way in fucking hell that bastard will get anywhere near you again. Okay?"

Her eyes filled with tears. "Okay."

"I'm going to go get something to bust you out of here." He started to rise to his feet.

"No!" Fia gripped his hand with startling strength. "P-please don't leave. You can't leave. I can't——"

"Shh, baby, it's okay." He gave her hand a gentle squeeze. "I won't leave. I promise. I'm just going to poke my head out the door and call for my friend. I won't leave your sight."

She nodded and released the vice grip.

Acer popped up and stuck his head out into the hall. Jester hovered by the front door, talking to someone outside, probably Striker.

"Jester, I need a crowbar. I think one of the guys had one in case we needed it to bust in here."

"Is she okay?" Jester asked.

Fia's eyes were closed and she shivered in the corner, despite the sweltering heat of the room and the added warmth of the sweatshirt.

"I don't think so. Did Striker reach Lila?"

Jester nodded. "He did. Be right back with that crowbar." He jogged outside.

Acer closed his eyes and rested his forehead against the doorframe for a second. No, she wasn't fucking okay. She'd been raped. He knew it in his gut. There was only one time in his life Acer had cried, a horrible day six months after Derek was incarcerated, and he recognized the choking feeling that accompanied tears the first time. He squeezed the doorframe until his knuckles ached, the physical discomfort detracting from the emotional turmoil.

With every fiber of his being, Acer wished Mike was there. He'd take that crowbar to the bastard's head and wouldn't stop until he was one hundred percent certain he'd never be a threat to Fia again.

Acer straightened and walked slowly back toward Fia. He sunk down next to her so he wouldn't frighten her by looming above.

"What day is it?" She shifted and did a terrible job of masking the pain.

"Monday. Monday night." He couldn't take much more of this. Seeing her this way was a true test of his self-control and ability endure torture.

"Three days. He might come back," she whispered, her voice weak and hitched.

"Not while we're here," he responded. "He knows we're after him. He's not stupid enough to go where we are. Though I wish he was." He couldn't keep the hardness out of his voice.

Fia's eyes widened, but not with further fear, with surprise. "Thank you for helping me."

"Baby, I'd walk through hell to get you out of here if I had to." He meant it. There was no mountain he wouldn't climb to see her safe and out of this hellhole.

A soft knock had both of their heads whipping around. Even though he wasn't touching her, he felt Fia tense. Her body was so rigid, it was obvious from two feet away.

Jester waited with his hand out, holding a crowbar.

"Thanks, brother." Acer stood and reached for the bar. Sweat rolled down his face. Christ, he needed out of this oven.

He turned back to Fia and made sure to keep his voice low

and gentle. "Honey, this is Jester. He's a very close friend of mine, and I promise he will not hurt you or touch you in any way. You got me?"

Fia nodded, her wary attention completely focused on Jester.

"Brought her a bottle of water too." Jester tossed it and Acer caught it one handed.

"Thanks brother." He opened the cap and handed it to Fia. "Whoa, easy there, babe. Drink slowly."

Fia nodded and stopped trying to guzzle the entire bottle in two seconds. She cast a wary glance at Jester. "Thank you. That's so good."

"I'm going to bust this metal ring out of the floor with a crowbar, okay, hon? We'll figure out how to get the cuff off your ankle later on. Then we'll take you to get checked out by a doctor."

At the mention of a doctor, Fia tensed again. The urge to run out of this house and search for Mike so he could tear the man apart was almost too hard to ignore, but Acer forced himself to focus on Fia instead. He'd have all the time in the world to track the man later.

"The doctor's a woman, babe. A close friend. I promise she'll be gentle and discreet. She's used to dealing with... delicate situations."

Fia nodded. "I trust you, Acer."

She was a fool to give anyone her trust, but this wasn't the time for that conversation.

Acer wedged the flat end of the crowbar under a corner of the metal plate that held Fia trapped. It wasn't difficult; the plate was loose. Fia must have been working on it for days. Had she been in here much longer, she might have been able to pry it out. Pride at the way she fought to free herself flared. She could have easily given up, but she was a fighter through and through.

He slammed his foot down on the bar and the metal plate popped right out. He whirled around when a soft chuckle sounded behind him.

"Sure, it's easy when you have a giant crowbar." Her voice was weak, but now that she was free, it was growing stronger, and a tiny grin curved her pretty mouth.

He blinked at her. Christ, she was nothing short of amazing. Covered in bruises, sweat, and dirt, and obviously in pain, she was still able to bust his balls. So damned admirable. It was no wonder she'd turned his world upside down these past six months. He chuckled. "Smartass."

It would take her a long time to heal, both physically and mentally, there was no question, but in that moment, with the small glimpse of the sassy Fia he was so drawn to, Acer had no doubt she would survive this ordeal.

Whether or not he would recover from the horrifying sight of her injured and chained to the floor like a dog was another question entirely. And the last question—what would he do about the burning need for revenge—well that was a question he had a firm answer to. Mike was a dead man walking.

~ ~ ~ ~

If it wasn't for the reality of a physical agony and burning humiliation, Fia would have thought she was dreaming. Or maybe that she'd been held by a psychopath long enough she went crazy herself. But the agony and the heat in the house were too real to be conjured up by her mind.

"Fia?"

She jumped. Geez, was she doomed to be so skittish now?

She glanced up at Acer's handsome face. He looked rattled and a bit unsure of himself. This was the first time she'd seen him looking anything other than strong and confident.

"Can I pick you up? Would you rather try to walk on your own?"

The thought of anyone, even Acer, touching her made her want to throw up. And that made her angry. For months, she'd craved his touch and now…

"I can do it myself." Her voice sounded like someone had taken sandpaper to her vocal cords.

He frowned and a brief flash of hurt crossed his face, but he recovered in an instant.

Fia braced one hand against the wall and forced her legs to uncurl. As she rose to her feet, the cuff around her ankle shifted and the heavy metal rubbed her mistreated skin. She gasped. The area under the shackle burned with a raw intensity and a trickle of blood rolled down her foot, leaving an itchy path in its wake.

The waves of Acer's fury were palpable. At his sides, his fists were clenched so tight veins popped out. She appreciated his restraint when he obviously wanted to snatch her up and run from the house.

She struggled to her full height and the room flipped upside down. "Woah." She sucked in a breath and reached for the wall with both hands, needing a stable surface to ground her. Her legs shook so hard, her knees banged together. "Ouch."

"Fia, please. You're two seconds away from falling over. I swear on my life, hell I swear on my bike, I won't hurt you."

Acer's sweatshirt fell well past her ass, down her mid-thighs, but, with a lack of undergarments, she still felt exposed and vulnerable. She sagged against the wall and a ghost of a smile twitched her lips. "So you value your bike more than your life?"

"Fia…"

The anguish in his voice was her undoing. She sighed. "I can't walk. I'm too weak and dizzy."

Before she finished her statement, Acer was at her side. One arm slid around her shoulders and the other slipped behind her knees. He lifted her in a hold so gentle, tears stung her eyes. Somehow, he managed to drape the metal chain over his shoulder so it hung in as painless a position as possible.

"Thank you." She rested her head against his chest. Despite the intense temperature of the house, the warmth of his body comforted her. After days of harsh treatment, his tender touch was almost more than she could handle. She owed him so much more than she could ever repay. If he hadn't been here tonight... She forced the sickening thought out of her mind.

"When is the last time you had anything to eat or drink?"

Fia shook her head against the firm muscles of his chest. She'd loved the way it had felt pressed against her as he rocked into her, so strong and sexy. Would she ever find anything sexy again? Was she doomed to live out the rest of her life fearing and detesting a man's touch? What a depressing thought. "I...um...I haven't eaten since I've been here. I had a little water today. No, wait—I think it was yesterday." She shrugged. "I'm sorry, everything's a blur in my head."

"Fucking animal," Acer ground out. He walked with her into the hallway and out into the dark night. Cold air washed over her and she shivered in his arms. "Do you want me to see if someone has a blanket?"

The genuine concern in his voice warmed her. He probably wouldn't agree with her, but he was a damn good man. She was now well acquainted with the difference between good and bad men. "No. It's chilly, but it was so hot in there that it feels really good."

Acer grunted. "Fucker had all the doors and windows closed. Makes it like a pressure cooker."

"Lila is on her way here. She'll drive you guys to the hospital." The unfamiliar voice startled her so bad she visibly flinched in Acer's arms.

"Shhh, it's okay, baby. Fia, this is Striker, he's our VP. Lila is his wife, and she's the physician I mentioned."

Fia stared at the handsome man with disheveled dark hair and chocolate dark eyes who'd spoken. He stood about ten feet away and nodded at her, but didn't make a move to get closer. His face was tight, angry, almost as angry looking as Acer's.

Striker spoke again. "She's going to take you in the employee entrance of the hospital. It's much more discrete, and she can get you in and out without being seen by too many people."

"Thank you," Fia said. She did not want word of this getting out. Her family was well known enough that it had the potential to be splashed across national headlines.

A small sedan pulled up in front of the house and a petite, beautiful woman emerged. Striker met her at the curb and gave her a quick kiss before taking her hand and leading her up to where Acer stood with Fia.

Fia watched the effortless way with which the couple interacted and touched. She'd been like that once, but that easiness was wiped out in just three days. She didn't feel comfortable in her own skin anymore, let alone with other people. She tolerated Acer's touch in this moment because the alternative was falling flat on her face.

"Fia, is it? I'm Lila, his wife," she said with a smile as she tilted her head in Striker's direction. "We're going to get you to the hospital so I can examine you and provide whatever treatment you might need."

"Thank you," Fia said. She must have said it fifty times in the last ten minutes. It was about all she had the energy to say; her reserves were draining fast. It wouldn't be long before she fell asleep whether she wanted to or not.

The smile fled Lila's face and she turned all business. "Acer, you are sweating like a pig. Why don't you hand Fia off to Striker and he can load her in the car while you take a second to wipe off."

"No!" Panic clawed at her at the thought of another man holding her. As soon as the word left her mouth, embarrassment flooded her. "Sorry," she whispered.

Acer gave her a slight squeeze. "Thanks, Stitch, but as long as Fia doesn't mind the smell, we're good. I'll ride with her in the back of your car. I left my phone and cut on the floor in there. Can someone grab it?"

"Got it." Jester's voice came from behind him.

Lila nodded. "Okay, let's roll."

"Close your eyes, babe. It will take us twenty minutes or so to get to the hospital. I won't let you go until I'm sure you are awake and aware of what's happening. Okay?"

Fia nodded and took a moment to study Acer's face as he spoke to one of his MC brothers. Something would have happened with him three nights ago if they'd been able to meet up at her motel. Whether it would have just been another night of mind-blowing sex, she couldn't say for sure. But she didn't think so. The deep connection they seemed to share would have only been ignored for so long. No, she had a feeling something significant may have started between them that night.

Sadness lay on her as heavy as a lead blanket. Mike stole that chance from her. He stole a lot from her, but that might have been the greatest offense. Because now? Now she was damaged, emotionally and physically. And what man wanted a woman with so much baggage? Especially if there was a chance that woman had lost all ability to be intimate with a man. Not a confident, sexual man like Acer, that was for sure.

Despite her churning thoughts, her muscles finally relaxed into Acer's hold. His comforting words gave her body the permission it needed to shut down for the first time in three days. She trusted he'd keep his word, keep her safe. Her heavy eyelids dropped closed and fatigue overwhelmed her. Plenty of time later to despair over missed opportunities.

Chapter Ten

Cool air blew from a vent in the ceiling and wafted down onto Fia's mess of a body. It was wonderful to no longer be pouring sweat and sucking in hot, stale air. She felt a bit strange—disconnected and floaty. Lila had given her some pain medication and promised it wasn't too strong. The prospect of being out of control terrified her, but the pain had subsided to a dull ache, and she had to admit the floaty feeling wasn't unwelcome.

She'd take it. She'd pretty much take anything to be free.

The door pushed open at a slow pace and her body lurched. This new and oversensitive startle reflex was going to take some getting used to. Though she supposed she should cut herself at least a little slack since she'd only been free for two and a half hours.

Lila poked her head into the room. "Hey, sweetie, okay if I come in? I knocked but I don't think you heard me."

"Sorry, I was lost in thought." She chuckled. "Or maybe that was the Vicodin. Please, come in."

Lila stepped into the room. She'd changed from the jeans and T-shirt she'd had on when Fia first met her, and now wore a pair of green hospital scrubs. "How are you feeling?"

Fia sighed. Good question. She took inventory of her aches and pains. "Not too bad, physically. Whatever you gave me really helped with the discomfort."

Lila sent her a sympathetic smile. "I know it's not the same thing at all, but I was attacked and kidnapped about a year ago. I was luckier than you, but I know a little something about fear and trauma. So, if you need to talk, please consider me."

Nothing but kindness and sincerity radiated from Lila's gaze. From the moment she was rescued, every person Acer introduced her to had been above and beyond kind. Here she was, supposedly in the presence of dangerous motorcycle gang-bangers, and they couldn't have been nicer. Couldn't have treated her any better than they did. She tried to think of who, in her real life, would have had such compassion and taken such good care of her, and she came up blank. It was a sad commentary on her group of uppity friends.

"Thank you. My brain feels a little numb now, but I'm sure it's all going to come crashing down around me at some point."

Lila nodded. "Yeah, it probably will."

"Is, um, did Acer stick around?" Lord, she sounded like a middle-schooler with a crush on the cool kid.

Lila laughed, a genuine full out laugh. "Is Acer still here? Honey, if I don't let that man in here in the next thirty seconds, Striker might have to knock him out cold to keep him away. No man acts as anxious to see a woman as he is if she's a stranger. You know him, don't you?"

She knew him all right. Every sexy inch of him. Fia nodded.

"Well, it's obviously your story to tell, and I'll let him in here in a minute. I just wanted a private moment to go over a few medical details with you." She turned to the computer on wheels next to Fia's bed, typed in a password, and opened the electronic medical record.

Fia picked up the bed control unit and raised the head of the bed. "Lay it on me."

Lila slipped into professional mode. "The rape kit came back positive. We collected enough DNA to send to the police if you'd like us to."

Fia forced her face to remain neutral as she listened to Lila. Of course, the damn rape kit was positive. She was raped. She took a deep breath. Lila was just doing her job.

A soft hand wrapped around hers and squeezed. "I've given this speech more times than I should have to, but it never gets any easier. I'm so sorry this happened to you, Fia."

"Thanks," she managed to squeak out. What else was there to say? Everyone would be sorry it happened to her, and while she probably would have said the same thing to others, it didn't help anything. Everyone's sorrow wouldn't diminish her pain or fear. It wouldn't get rid of this new flare of anxiety she experienced every time a man came near her. She sighed. Again, not Lila's fault. She just said what one says in these types of situations.

"I sent the swabs off to the lab with a rush request, but at this time of night, the best we can hope for is results in a few hours. I recommend you get tested again in a few weeks because some diseases can take longer to show up."

Her stomach turned over. She hadn't even thought about diseases. As if this situation wasn't shitty enough, she now had to worry that Mike had left her with a horrific parting gift. Anger bubbled under the flat mask she forced her face to show. Rage was a hundred times preferable to the numbing fear and despondency she'd been battling for days. Rage she could work with.

"You have an IUD, so pregnancy isn't an issue," Lila

continued.

Thank God.

"As for the rest, you're severely dehydrated, which I'm sure comes as no surprise, so I'm going to keep you until tomorrow afternoon so I can give you a few more bags of fluids. The wound on your ankle was showing signs of a pretty significant infection, as were the burns on your torso. I cleaned and bandaged each of those wounds as well as started you on a broad-spectrum antibiotic that will basically knock out any type of skin infection. The MRI showed the bone is clear of infection, which is very good news. Other than that, it's bruises and scrapes, which I'm sure are painful, but not life-threatening."

The barrage of clinical details was just too much information to fully process. Half of her mind wasn't fully convinced she was out of that house and safe. The other half was trying to process what to do now that she was free. There simply weren't enough narcotic-soaked brain cells left to digest the mountain of medical data.

Lila plowed on, seeming unaware of the fact that half the information was falling right back out of Fia's ears. "I strongly recommend counseling, Fia. These kinds of things are difficult to move past without help."

Right, counseling. Because talking about it would be a piece of cake. Geeze, she sounded like an ungrateful bitch. Lila was amazing, and of course, she was right. How did someone get on with their life without some assistance after this kind of trauma? "Thank you for being so amazing about this, Lila, and for getting me in here without being seen. You don't know me and didn't have to go so far out of your way for me."

"It wasn't a problem at all, sweetie. You obviously mean something to Acer, so I'll do anything I can to help because he means something to me. Now, I need to let him in before he self-destructs." She winked.

Fia's heart rate kicked up and she smoothed a hand over her hair. It was a pointless gesture. He'd seen her when there was no lower to go, but she wanted to somehow erase the mental image of her in that house from his mind. A boxy hospital gown and ratty hair weren't the way to do that.

If it was even possible for him to forget.

Lila returned with Acer and Striker in tow. Dark circles rimmed Acer's eyes. He looked like he needed to sleep for a decade. He shouldered Striker out of his way and stood next to the bed. He lifted a hand as though to touch her, but dropped it back down to his side. Sadness swamped her. Just a week ago, she would have begged for that touch. Now, she was relieved he knew enough not to crowd her. Depressing.

"Hey, baby," he whispered, his eyes bleak and stormy.

"Hi."

"Hey, Fia," Striker addressed her.

He stood at the foot of the bed with an arm around his wife's shoulders. There they were again, the happy couple, relaxed and completely at ease with each other. Was there even a smidge of a chance for that in her future? "Hello, Striker."

"Look," Striker ran his free hand through his dark hair, mussing it further. "I hate to have to do this now, but I have to bring it up and I don't know if I'll see you again." He sighed and flicked a glance toward his wife. "I need you to leave our involvement out of this, with the cops I mean."

Beside him, Lila gasped and slapped his chest. "Striker! Now is not the time for this discussion. Geez, if I'd known you were going to talk about this, I would have made you wait in the hall." She scowled and Fia couldn't help but smile at her mamma bear proactive attitude toward her patient.

Striker gave Lila a look that would have had most people quivering in their shoes. Not his wife, though. She gave him her own obstinate look right back.

He relented first with a roll of his eyes. "Babe, there is no other time. Her parents will be here in a few hours."

Her parents? Though she wasn't looking at Acer, his stare was so strong she practically felt it. Someone called her parents? Of course they had. What did she expect? She couldn't stay here, and they were her emergency contacts. It was the logical thing to do. Sure, they had some major issues revolving around her career, but they were family. Maybe this ordeal would help mend their differences.

"Please." She motioned for him to continue. "Just say what it is you have to say. I can handle it. Do you not want me to go to the police?" She wasn't sure she wanted to. Could she handle the interrogation, investigation, and maybe even a trial?

"No, I'm not saying that. I just need you to leave any mention of the No Prisoners out of it. You'll need to come up with a believable story of how you escaped, a story that does not involve anyone in this room."

"She gets it, Striker, that's enough. It's time for you to go." Acer's dismissal was spoken in a gravelly tone.

Striker narrowed his eyes and appeared about two seconds away from punching Acer. The last thing Fia wanted was for him to get in trouble on her behalf.

"Come on, Striker, let's give them a few minutes." Lila tugged her husband's hand and he relented, following her out of the room.

Fia had to admire the way she handled her man. She did owe him a little peace of mind though. "Striker?"

From the doorway, he turned around.

"After all you've done for me, I would never put your club

in jeopardy. You have nothing to worry about."

"Thank you. I hope you feel better soon." He slipped through the door and she was alone with Acer.

He dragged the hard vinyl chair from the corner of the room next to the bed. He dropped into it and they stared at each other for long seconds. Fia wanted to say something, but she was at a loss for where to begin. Really, they didn't even know each other, and now they were connected by a bond of horror.

Finally, Acer broke the silence. "Can I hold your hand?"

Her heart squeezed in her chest and she nodded. Such a simple gesture, but that he knew enough to ask made tears spring to her eyes.

With a gentle touch, so opposite the hard expression on his face, he picked up her hand and pressed a kiss to her fingertips. Then he placed it palm down on the bed and rested his forehead against her knuckles. "I'm so sorry, Fia," he said, the words slightly muffled by the sheets.

Her throat thickened and she tried to swallow, but the muscles wouldn't obey. His voice was so full of despair she felt an instinctive need to comfort him. It couldn't be often, if ever, that he let his guard down like this. "Acer," she whispered. "None of this is your fault."

He barked out a harsh laugh and raised his head. "Everything about this is my fault. When I saw you in the gym on Friday—" He shook his head. "God, you looked amazing, Fia. Like a fucking dream. Then those assholes were chatting you up, flirting, eyeing you like they had some right to you. I saw red. All I could think about was getting you out of there before one of them crossed the line. And, now—"

"Acer, stop." She lifted her hand to his cheek. Day old stubble made it rough against her palm. "Just stop. I won't listen to you do this to yourself, so if that's why you're here, you can go. You and I both know who is responsible for this, and isn't you. So, either we move off this topic or you leave."

He smiled at her. "I'm glad to see your snarky attitude is still perfectly intact."

Fia chuckled. This was what she needed. A moment of normalcy. "Don't think anything in this world could knock that out of me."

Chapter Eleven

Acer wanted details. He needed them like he needed his next breath. Needed to know exactly what the motherfucker had done to his Fia. The need to know ate at him until it felt like an actual wound. "Tell me," he said.

She watched him with wide eyes for a moment and his stomach bottomed out. She might not tell him a word. She didn't owe him anything. She wasn't his. He needed to keep that at the forefront of his mind. "Please. I need to know."

With a heavy sigh, she tugged the bottom of the blanket high enough it exposed her bandaged leg. "Well, this is infected." She grimaced as she lifted the sore limb.

"Shit, babe." Acer covered her back up. "Keep it still."

"I'm infected, dehydrated, and bruised as crap. But I'm alive and out of there, thanks to you." Her eyes shone with a gratitude he didn't deserve.

"Fia, don't start thinking I'm a hero. That's the last fucking thing I am."

She pointed a finger at the door. "Uh uh, we already had this conversation. Either can it with the guilt, or take your ass out of here."

He brought her hand to his lips again. "I have one more

question."

"Please don't ask it." As though she read his mind, she turned her pleading eyes on him. "You already know the answer. You found me naked. You know the answer. I'm not ready to say it out loud yet. Please talk about something else."

He dropped his head and stared at the stark white sheets. Having a knife stabbed into his gut would be less painful than hearing Fia had been raped, and though she couldn't say the words, she'd confirmed what he'd held out a tiny hope hadn't happened. His head swam with a maddening swirl of emotions. He had a strong feeling that something had been taken from him, something precious and rare. But he wasn't the one violated and Fia wasn't his, so the feeling had no basis in reality. That reminder didn't make the sentiment go away. "Lila called your parents. It wasn't me. I wasn't sure if that's what you'd want, but she obviously didn't ask my opinion."

She chuckled. "I figured it wasn't you." With a sigh, she shrugged. "Look, we have our troubles, but they're still my parents. I'm sure they'll help me through all this. It was the right thing for her to do." She gave him a half smile.

Was it the right thing to do? She had a few serious issues with her parents, but family banded together in times of crisis. Didn't they? He almost snorted out loud. His sure didn't. *Ask her to stay.* He shook his head at the ridiculous voice in his head. She couldn't stay with him, probably wouldn't stay with him. He ran her out of the gym and into the arms of a madman. He was the last person who should see her through this trauma. "Can I ask you something?"

"Sure."

"This probably isn't the time for this...but...anyway, why did you come to the gym? You said there was something you had to tell me." He still held her hand, needing that connection.

Fia's eyes widened and her jaw dropped open. She sat straight up in bed with a wince. "Oh my God. I'd forgotten all about that. Shit!"

"Honey, lay back and relax. I wouldn't have asked if I knew you'd get all worked up." He wanted to crawl into the bed next to her and hold her until his mind was satisfied that she was actually safe. But he didn't. He had no rights to her, and after what she'd just been through, the thought of a man in her bed was probably repulsive.

"I'm fine, Acer. And it's very important. I overheard a phone conversation your father had. I was in a booth behind him at a restaurant. I don't think he knew anyone was there or he wouldn't have spoken so candidly."

Acer froze. His father's threats had been in the back of his mind the past few months, but with no further communication, he assumed the old man was all talk and bluster. Now, unease crept up his spine. She wouldn't have traveled to a different state to tell him something that wasn't significant.

"What did you hear?"

"I didn't quite understand it all, but he spoke to someone about a project starting in Arizona, near the border. He talked about packages coming from Mexico and being delivered to the site of his new hotel, which I think is on the outskirts of Vegas."

"Yeah, from what I hear, he's trying to pull traffic off the strip. He say anything else?" Packages his ass. Those *packages* were illegal workers shuttled across the border only to be exploited by his prick of a father.

Fia smoothed a wrinkle in the blanket that covered her hospital gown. "Yes." She met his gaze and her eyes were somber. "He said he offered you a chance to get in on the deal months ago, and you declined. Then he lowered his voice and I could barely make out what he said, but it was something about your club. I'm sorry it's not more, and now that I say it out loud I realize I may have overreacted, but at the time I felt like you needed to know."

Acer blew out a breath and leaned back in the chair. His mind whirled with possibilities. He'd kept one eye on the border traffic for the first two months after speaking with Reginald, but found nothing. Time to do a little investigating. He'd have to take this to Shiv as well. Damn his old man and his greed.

"You know what he was talking about, don't you?" She worried her lower lip between her teeth.

Acer took her hand again, interlacing their fingers this time. Her hand was warm and small. Like she was. "Yeah, baby. I know exactly what he's talking about."

"And you're not going to tell me, are you?"

He smiled at the spark of annoyance in her voice. "No. You're already too involved. And now that your parents are coming, people will find out you were here. It's too risky."

She nodded. "Just be careful."

Guilt hit him full force. Here he was thinking about his own problems when Fia had just barely been pulled out of hell. "I'm such an asshole. We shouldn't be talking about any of this now. You need to rest."

"Oh, no. Not you, too. Everyone is going to be telling me I need to rest and heal and all that crap. From you, I need normal. Promise me."

"Babe—"

She shook her head. "Not from you, Acer. Please. It's different with you."

This was the perfect opportunity for him to remind her

they weren't anything to each other, and that's the way it needed to stay. She belonged in Beverly Hills, not the off-the-grid town of Crystal Rock. He opened his mouth to tell her just that. "I promise." The words slipped out before he had a chance to stop them.

"Good. Now I'm tired and I need to rest." She shot him a sassy smirk. "So go talk to Striker, I know you're dying to."

Acer laughed at the way she used the words she'd just admonished him for, he couldn't help it. She was hilarious, and sweet, and sexy even in a hospital gown. He should be shot for having those thoughts about her right now, but he couldn't help it. Everything about her called to him.

"All right, baby. I do need to talk to Striker, but I'm going to sit with you a bit more."

She opened her mouth, no doubt to tell him she was just going to sleep, but he cut her off. "Sleep. I'll just sit here while you drift off."

She smiled. "I'd like that."

Her eyes fluttered closed and within seconds, the even rise and fall of her chest alerted him to her slumber. The muscles in her face relaxed, making her look younger than her thirty years. She was small, helpless and delicate, dwarfed by the large hospital gown. Purple circles ringed her eyes and her face and arms bore the bruises of a brutal assault. The marks didn't detract from her beauty, but they roused a protective instinct he hadn't felt since Penny. Only it was different this time, with an adult intensity he hadn't experienced twenty years ago.

He did need to speak with Striker, but all he wanted to do was watch over her while she slept. That fact alone was enough to uproot him from the chair.

The moment he stepped from the room, he was bombarded with a flood of unfamiliar emotions he'd been holding at bay for hours. He rested his back against the wall outside Fia's room, needing a moment to clear his head.

He didn't do emotions, feelings. Two decades ago, he locked down his heart and closed off the ability to feel anything besides anger.

Sure, he loved his club brothers, would die for them. But even they didn't have all of him. No one knew about Derek and Penny, no one knew where he disappeared to one weekend each year when he went to the prison charity fundraiser. The club's harsh policy on loyalty was one of the main draws. The rules were simple: betray the club and you pay, severely. It was the closest he could get to a guarantee of trustworthiness. And even then, it wasn't a true guarantee. Members had betrayed the club in the past. But retribution was swift and harsh, and that gave him a sense of security and comfort. Fucked up as it may be.

Allowing people too far into his personal shit gave them power over him, gave them control. Acer was never powerless, nor without control.

But now, standing outside the room of a woman who'd been beaten, raped, and terrorized, a woman he knew intimately and who'd pierced his armor in an unsettling way, Acer struggled to keep the walls around his heart from shattering.

The guilt was hardest to ignore.

She didn't blame him now, but she would. At some point, when the trauma wasn't so acute, she'd realize that if he hadn't rushed her from the gym, none of this would have happened. And then what would he do when Fia no longer looked at him with admiration and wonder, but a darkened anger?

Acer took a breath and pushed off from the wall. He needed to find Striker. Problems for his club were the number one priority. Fia would be fine. She was strong, and she had her family in her corner. She wasn't his to heal, wasn't his to worry over, and he didn't want the position anyway.

He strode down the hall in search of Striker, ignoring the voice in his head whispering, *liar*.

Chapter Twelve

A subtle sense of déjà vu scratched at the back of Fia's neck as she wiped her sweaty palms down the front of her baggy jeans. She wasn't outside the gym, and she wasn't technically here for Acer, but she was outside the No Prisoners clubhouse and just as nervous as the first time she'd come to this town.

That wasn't true.

The stress was greater this time around. She was here for a reason, but as with her first trip, she could have called. Something had to be done to snap her back to reality, back to her life. For two weeks, she'd hidden. She was tired of hiding at her parent's home, tired of being afraid, and tired of her family. Acer offered to send a club brother to look out for her until Mike was caught, but her father refused in dramatic affront. He hired a security firm, but it didn't do anything to allay her fears. Instead, the large men hovering around only increased her nerves.

Enough was enough. It was time to face her fears head on, and, never one to do things in half measures, she decided to go straight to the source of her fears, Crystal Rock, Arizona. She'd slipped out in the middle of the night and drove the trip from Texas to Arizona, the thought of a crowded airport enough to make her physically ill.

What had the therapist called it, flooding? Immersing herself in the phobias until the fear subsided.

Easier said than done.

She opened her car door and forced her body out into the hot desert sun. After two steps toward the door, the world spun, her vision blurred, and her chest constricted.

Shit, not a panic attack, not now.

Fia turned around and took the two steps back to her car. She bent forward and placed her palms down on the hood of the car, ignoring the heat that seared her skin.

In, out, in, out, she chanted in her head over and over in an attempt to regulate her gasping breaths. Within a minute, her heart rate began to slow and the pressure in her chest subsided, allowing her breathing to calm as well. At least she was finally gaining some measure of control over the paralyzing anxiety.

She straightened and tried again, this time on weak and shaky limbs. The panic attacks always left her drained. "Suck it up, girl," she murmured to herself.

As she approached the door, the feelings of fear and unease started to abate. There was a good chance Acer was behind those walls, and the thought of being near him steadied her, made her feel safe.

It was a stupid thought. They were nothing to each other but a one-night stand plus a one-night horror show, but at this point, she'd take anything that made the fear diminish.

"Well, hey there, gorgeous. You going inside?" A very tall, thin, almost gangly man stood about fifteen feet away, holding the door to the clubhouse open for her.

"Oh…yes…I…um…" She had to get it together. There was simply no other option. Well, there was, she could live in her parent's house forever, sleeping in her teenage bedroom and hiding from reality while she slowly went out of her mind.

She cleared her throat and tilted her head back to get a full view of his face. "I'm sorry. Yes, I'm on my way in."

He winked. "No worries, I have a tendency to make women speechless."

Fia laughed, and it felt great. Humor had been lost on her in the past weeks.

"You looking for someone in particular, doll?"

She looked up at the slender giant. "Actually, yes, I'm looking for Striker."

The man's mouth pulled down and he stepped in her path, effectively blocking the entrance. "You know he's got an ol' lady right? They're fuckin' tight, so if you're here to shit on that, I'm gonna have to tell you to turn around."

She gasped. "What? No! I'm not here to…shit on anything. It's business, strictly business. I know Lila."

His face hadn't kicked back up into a smile, but he nodded and moved aside. She passed through the entrance, careful to stick close to the right side of the doorframe so as not to brush against him. Last thing she needed was another panic attack.

"Yo, VP. Classy lady here to see you. Says it's business," he called into the room. "He's at the bar, darlin'." He pointed at a large mahogany bar generously stocked with bottles.

Her face heated as the five or so large bikers in the room all turned and stared at her. "Thank you…um…"

"Gumby."

She smiled. It fit. "Thank you, Gumby."

"No problem, doll. You looking for a little entertainment after your meeting, I'll be right across the lot, in the garage." He winked again and left.

It was such a normal thing, a handsome man making teasing, flirty comments, but it no longer felt normal to her. She'd tensed at his words and had to work to keep from running away.

"Fia?"

She turned toward the bar and met Striker's gaze. "Striker."

"Hey, come have a seat."

"Thanks." She walked to the bar and sat on the empty stool beside him.

He leaned in like he was going to kiss her cheek, but must have sensed her distress, because he halted at the last minute and patted her shoulder. "Want a drink?"

So what if it was two on a Saturday afternoon? She obviously needed something to help her relax. "Sure, I'll have a beer, thanks."

Two seconds later, a half-full tumbler of amber liquid was plunked down in front of her. She looked at Striker, whose ice-blue eyes were alight with mischief. He really was attractive. Lila was a lucky woman. His dark brown hair was once again disheveled, and a few days' growth of beard dotted his jaw line, giving him an edge that on him was very attractive.

"Thought bourbon might be more effective. You look like you could use it."

The man was observant.

"Thanks." She took a sip and almost moaned as warmth coated the back of her throat and traveled down to her stomach. "That's good stuff."

"Damn straight. I don't give the good shit to just anyone either." He smiled and tapped the bar. An identical glass appeared before him. "Beat it, Prospect," he ordered the very young looking man who delivered the drinks. "So, Fia, I assume you're not just here to drink my booze."

She shook her head and took a healthy gulp of her drink. Once the young man he called Prospect was out of earshot, she spoke. "I'm not. First off, I wanted to thank you, and your wife. You guys were——"

He placed his hand over one of hers on the bar and she forced herself to keep still when every instinct screamed at her to yank her hand away.

Face the fear. Flood it.

He wasn't going to throw her down on the bar and attack her. The intelligent side of her knew that, but the damn fear made rational thoughts evaporate. She used her free hand to take another drink, get her mind off the feel of him touching her.

"Not necessary, hon. For real." He released her hand and straightened on the stool. "I don't want to hear it. You're Acer's. Enough said."

His comment made her inhale a sharp breath, unfortunately with a mouth full of bourbon. She coughed and sputtered, the hot burn of embarrassment heating her face.

"Shit! Sorry, hon." He moved in like he was going to whack her on the back, but she waved him off.

"It's fine," she said around a wet cough. "You just startled me. I'm not Acer's anything. Nothing at all. We haven't even spoken since I was here last."

He stared at her, as though he could see into her brain. "We'll see."

She shook her head. There was nothing to see.

"The man's working through his own issues, hon. Anyway, back to why you're here."

What did he mean by that? Acer's own issues? Thoughts for another time. She took a deep breath. "I never went to the cops. Not here, nor once I got to California."

If the situation hadn't been so serious, she would have laughed at the comical expression of surprise that crossed his face.

"Why the fuck not? Because of what I said? Shit, Fia. I just told you to leave us out of it. Lila's gonna have my ass." He ran a hand through his hair, mussing it even further.

She reached out and placed a hand on his forearm. "No. That's not why. Well, maybe that's a tiny piece, but I just couldn't go. I don't really expect you to understand, but the thought of it—" She shrugged. "The thought of all the interviews, and the time, and the reliving of it all. I just couldn't. And Lila knows. She called me because the cops never requested the rape kit. I'm assuming she didn't say anything to you because I'm technically a patient and she wanted to protect my privacy."

Striker nodded as though he did understand. She liked the man. He was intense, but not a brute, and not one to bullshit. "Okay then, what's the problem?"

"My family is the problem. They are pushing me to go to the cops, hard. Truthfully, I think they want the story to hit the news. Any publicity is good publicity, right?" She rolled her eyes.

"Christ, sounds like your parents are some serious assholes."

She half smiled at him. "They have their moments. Thing is, I've refused so many times, they are threatening to take things into their own hands. My dad's mentioned on more than one occasion that he's going to go to the media. I don't think he's bluffing. I wanted to warn you guys, and make sure you knew I had no part in it."

Another second under Striker's piercing stare and she'd start to squirm. "Thank you, honey," Striker said. "It's a problem, but nothing we can't handle. I appreciate you coming to me with this."

"Least I could do." Unsure of what to do with herself now that she'd delivered the message, she swirled her finger in the condensation that collected on the bar around the base of her glass.

"You know you could have just called, right? Both Acer and Lila gave you their numbers."

She nodded.

"You hanging in, honey?" Striker asked.

"I'm fine." The automatic answer was out of her mouth without a second of thought, having repeated it so many times over the past two weeks.

When Striker didn't reply, she sighed and dragged a drop of water across the smooth surface of the bar with her fingertip. "I'm pretty shitty. And I just needed...out. I should never have gone with them in the first place, but I was hurt and scared, and like a little kid, I hoped my parents could fix it. Pathetic, huh?"

He gave her a small smile. She was grateful he didn't try to crowd her space but remained a safe foot and a half away on his barstool. "Not pathetic at all, hon. You got a place to stay?"

"No, this trip was a bit of an impulse."

"Stay with us, for as long as you need. Lila will be thrilled."

"No, I can't. You—"

"It's not open for discussion." His mouth smiled and his eyes were easy, but his tone brokered no argument. The man was obviously used to having his orders obeyed.

She should go, but she could stay. Was it a horrible idea? Couldn't be worse than the notion of going back to her parent's home in Texas. She wasn't thriving at their house, she was hiding. And the pressure to go to the police and media would soon be unbearable.

If she stayed here, there was a chance she could breathe again. Get over some of the paralyzing fear that was now a constant in her life.

She should stay.

"Well, maybe just a few days. Thank you. I'd love to see Lila." And Acer, but closed her mouth before those words escaped. Decision made, Fia took a deep breath. It came easier, perhaps easier than it had in the past two weeks. Maybe there was hope for her yet.

Chapter Thirteen

Acer bent his left ear toward his shoulder and winced at the crack that resounded through the room. The noise was unpleasant, but some of the tension that had built in his neck released with the stretch. He glanced at the clock on his laptop.

Damnit, two-twenty-seven. He'd been holed up in Striker's room at the clubhouse for nearly five hours, and not a fuckin' thing to show for it.

The door flew open and Jester burst in without knocking. No surprise there. His brother's giant body and even more outstanding personality went where it wanted when it wanted.

"What the hell you been doing in here for so long, nerd? You got a chick stashed somewhere?" He made a dramatic display of looking around the room, knowing full well that Acer had been working all day.

"Just me." Acer closed his laptop and swung his feet off the bed, landing his boots on the floor with a thud.

With a snort, Jester crossed his arms over his chest and leaned against the doorframe. "Figures. You know, now that I think about it, I ain't seen you with a woman in a while."

He had no idea.

"Anything you want to tell me?" Jester loved nothing more than ribbing everyone he knew. He wouldn't stop until Acer shut him up.

"Yeah, actually there is. I'm gay."

Jester's eyes widened and his arms dropped to his sides. "Oh, shit, well…um…that's…you know…"

Acer burst out laughing.

"Fuck you!" Jester scowled. "You're such an asshole."

"Nothing less than you deserve, brother."

Jester grunted and pointed to the closed laptop. "How's that coming?"

Acer blew out a breath. He leaned forward and propped his forearms on his thighs. "It's not. I can't find shit. My gut is screaming at me that I'm missing something, but I've looked at weeks of satellite imagery. Lots of traffic across the border, but that's typical, and nothing to suggest anyone is trying to fuck with us in any way. It's making me twitchy."

Jester moved into the room and sat next to Acer on the edge of the bed. "Maybe she was wrong. She could have misheard." He paused then spoke in a lower tone. "Maybe your old man sent her here with the message."

Acer turned his head and gave Jester his best hate glare. "No fuckin' way would she do that."

Jester raised an eyebrow. "You gotta consider it as a possibility, brother."

"Yeah, you would know." The moment the words were out of his mouth, Acer wanted to kick himself. Sure, Emily was initially sent by their enemies, but she acted against her will and did her damnedest to protect the club. Jester's mouth thinned in an expression of extreme displeasure, but thankfully, he didn't try to knock Acer's lights out. Getting hit by Jester was never an experience anyone wanted.

Acer dropped his head into his hands. "Sorry, Jest, that was a shit thing to say. I told you this was making me twitchy."

And why the hell didn't he consider the possibility that Fia was sent by his father? Because he felt some kind of strange connection to her? Because even though he'd only fucked her in about one one-hundredth of the ways he wanted to fuck her, she was still the best he'd had? Because he felt responsible for the trauma she'd endured? Because he still dreamed about her almost every night? Only now, his dreams started out an erotic pleasure and ended in a nightmare of horrifying memories that had him waking in a cold sweat.

He never took anyone at face value, and none of those reasons were enough to do so now.

"Yeah...about that." Jester clucked his tongue.

Acer sat straight up and looked Jester in the eye. "Ahh, so that's what this is really about. You drew the short straw."

Jester snorted and ran a hand across his chin. "Something like that. Look, you've been off for months, but the past two weeks you've been a miserable prick. The way I see it, it's gotta be the chick."

"Leave it, Jester." He was not about to discuss his complicated connection and confounding feelings for Fia.

"At the risk of sounding like a pussy, you feel something for this one?"

"Christ, you are turning into a pussy." He flicked his wrist and imitated the crack of a whip with his mouth. "This what happens when you board the monogamy train? Just another reason to stay far away."

Jester laughed and shrugged like he didn't care one bit if Acer thought he was losing his edge. "Maybe, but all the sex sure is nice. That woman can't keep her hands off me. I'll tell ya, if I were a lesser man, I might have a hard time keeping up with her needs. Good thing I'm such a virile stud." He thumped a fist against his chest, a smug smile on his face.

Acer rolled his eyes. "Just stop talking. You're starting to use words that are too big for you." He stood. "Let's go, I need a drink." He started toward the door but was halted by Jester's hand on his shoulder.

"Seriously, brother, you gotta snap out of it. Shiv's asking questions. He's gonna leave you out of shit if you can't stay focused on the game."

Acer nodded. "I appreciated the warning." Jester was right. His head had been fucked up for the past two weeks, the past seven months really. "Thanks, I'll pull my head out of my ass."

"Works for me." Jester clapped his hands once then rubbed them back and forth. "To the bar!"

Acer followed him downstairs. When he neared the bottom, he heard the sound of Fia's laughter. It was a laugh he'd recognize anywhere. One that haunted his dreams. Maybe he was losing his mind. Hallucinating after spending such an inordinate amount of time obsessing about her. He scanned the room and stopped dead in his tracks.

Fia sat at the bar, drinking with Striker. Or at least it was some version of Fia. Not the Fia he knew. Not the confident, sexy, vivacious Fia he'd touched, tasted, and fucked all night long. This was a haunted Fia, with flat, shuttered eyes, unstyled hair, and baggy clothes that might as well have been a metal chastity belt.

Heaviness settled on the left side of his chest. It wasn't that Fia no longer looked pretty; she'd be beautiful no matter what she wore. No, the deep sadness came from knowing she wore these clothes as a shield of armor to keep men's interest at bay. She was a shadow of her normal self, and that made his stomach ache.

"Oh goody. This day is about to get a lot more interesting," Jester said.

He drank in the sight of her. Letting her leave with her parents had been a mistake. They hadn't done right by her. One more error added to his scorecard.

Well, fuck that. She was on his turf now, for whatever reason. This time, he'd keep her here, with him. He couldn't do a worse job of helping her than her negligent family had. And he'd use his last breath to get the old Fia back if he had to.

~ ~ ~ ~

Tiny hairs rose on the back of Fia's neck and she swiveled around, making eye contact with a stunned Acer. The invisible connection she felt to him, even after everything she'd been through, was overwhelming.

He looked mouthwatering in dark jeans that hugged his waist and were obviously of higher quality than most of the men here. On top, he wore a plain, light gray T-shirt and the same black leather vest he'd worn when she last saw him. In fact, each man here had the same No Prisoners vest, though each bore different patches.

As usual, his hair was impeccable and he radiated a vibe of refinement. Fia wasn't sure why the combination of polished sophistication and down and dirty biker was so appealing to her, but it was. Or maybe it was just the man himself.

As though drawn by a magnetic force, Acer veered straight for her, ignoring the big man beside him who spoke. She recognized him from the night they'd rescued her. His size terrified her at first. Now she had to admit he looked like an oversized teddy bear. Probably not something she should mention to him though.

Acer stopped right in front of her and lifted her right hand, the same hand he'd held in the hospital. He brought it to his mouth and pressed a kiss to her palm before cradling her hand in his larger one. The tender gesture brought tears to her eyes, but she refused to let them fall. Crying in a room full of bad-ass bikers would take mortification to a whole new level.

There was no fear, no tension, only relief at being near him. It was like the permission she'd given him to hold her hand in the hospital two weeks ago still counted and they both knew it.

"Hey, gorgeous," he whispered.

Beside her, Striker cleared his throat. Fia's entire body heated in embarrassment as she realized every man in the room was focused on their show. She tried to pull her hand back, but Acer held it captive in a firm but affectionate hold.

"Hello, Acer." Her focus jumped around the room, taking in the men who observed them. The massive one who had been on the stairs with Acer had an arrogant smirk on his face. Gosh, what was his name? She must have been introduced to him but had little chance of remembering a quick introduction from that devastating night.

"Ignore them," Acer said. "What are you doing here?"

Striker jumped in. "Her parents are threatening to go to the media. They know we were involved and want to splash it all across headlines."

"Shit." Acer scrubbed his free hand over his face. "I never should have let you leave with them. I'm sorry, Fi."

She squeezed his hand. He needed to stop accepting blame for things that weren't his fault. "What else could you have done?"

"I could have had you stay here, with me. Which is what I'm doing now. Hope you didn't pay for a hotel, you're coming with me."

Seriously? He wanted her with him. She wasn't sure if she should be elated or terrified. "Acer, I already told Striker I'd stay with him and Lila."

"Well, untell them." He glared and Striker and Fia couldn't help but chuckle at the pissed off expression on his face. She longed to take him up on his offer. In the three minutes he'd been standing there, she felt safer than she had in the past two weeks at her parents' house. The situation was just so complicated. She wasn't the woman she'd been when they first met, couldn't function as that woman had any longer.

"Please." Acer's whispered plea and the sincerity shining in his eyes made the decision for her.

"I'm sorry, Striker," she said in an overly sweet voice. "Thank you for your kind offer of hospitality, but it appears I'm requested elsewhere."

Striker smiled and patted her on the shoulder, ignoring the real and true growl that came from Acer when he touched her. What the hell was wrong with him? He was acting like a possessive ape. She ignored the small thrill that sound evoked.

"Well, normally I'd put up a fight, just to bust his balls," he said jerking his thumb at Acer. "But you lit up like a damn Christmas tree when he came in the room. If he can put that look back on your pretty face, who am I to stand in the way?"

It really didn't matter what look Acer put on her face. Nothing would come of it. She was damaged, the thought of being intimate with a man made her want to bury her head in the sand. This was just a chance for something different. A chance to get away from her real life and figure out who she was supposed to be moving forward. It had nothing to do with Acer.

Keep telling yourself that, Fia.

Chapter Fourteen

Fia stepped out of her car into the sweltering heat for the second time that day. She scanned the area with a smile on her face. Acer lived in the small downtown area of Crystal Rock, in an apartment above a coffee shop. From the outside, it didn't look like much, but knowing what she did of him, the interior would be a pleasant surprise.

He swung a long leg over his bike and pulled off his helmet before he strode to her. "I'll take your bag," he said of the one small suitcase she'd thrown some clothes in five minutes before she jumped in her car.

"Thanks." There wasn't any point in arguing that she could carry it herself.

"You can keep your car parked back here as long as you want, there are always extra spots and no one will bother it."

"Thanks," she said again.

He chuckled. "You know any other words?"

Warmth spread across her face. "Sorry, I guess I'm a little unsure of myself here."

He stroked a finger down her cheek but kept out of her personal space. The tenderness and warmth of the simple touch was more intimacy than she'd allowed anyone in the past two weeks. Friends and family squeezed her hand, patted her shoulder, but that was all she tolerated. Anything further and panic wound around her like a boa constrictor. "It's just me, Fia. You have nothing to prove to me. I don't have any expectations."

She did though. She had to prove that Mike hadn't destroyed her soul. Prove it to Acer. Prove it to herself most of all. "It's not that. It's just, well, we really don't even know each other, and I'm barging in your life like I have some right to be here." She sighed and toed a jagged rock with her sandal. "Mostly, it's just being back here, in Arizona, where...you know." With a swift kick, she sent the rock bumping across the paved lot. "It just has me a little on edge."

His features darkened, but his touch remained light as he placed a hand on her back and guided her to the outdoor steps. "Go on up. We'll talk inside."

She preceded him up the stairs and waited until he joined her on the landing. With him blocking her view, he punched five numbers into a keypad below the doorknob and twisted it open. "This keypad unlocks the door. I'll program a unique code for you so you can come and go as you please. Don't share it with anyone."

He wouldn't be sharing his personal code with her. Interesting. She may trust him, but apparently, that trust wasn't returned. It shouldn't bother her; she was the one who pointed out how they knew nothing about each other. Two intense experiences, a night of brain-melting sex and a dramatic rescue from a kidnapping, gave a false sense of closeness. In actuality, they were all but strangers. Still, here she was putting her full trust in him. Some measure of reciprocity would have been appreciated.

"You gonna bake out there all day, hon?" Acer's voice cut

through her musings and she jumped. The hair-trigger startle reflex hadn't diminished over the past weeks.

"Sorry, babe, didn't mean to scare you." He reached out as though to grab her arm and pull her in the apartment, but he dropped his hand at the last second, a look of uncertainty on his face.

She waved it off and stepped into the foyer of his apartment, grateful for the rush of cool air. "It wasn't you. I was lost in thought. Besides, anything and everything makes me jump out of my skin these days."

He studied her as though he wanted to say something, but instead, moved around her and punched another code into a keypad next to the door. "I'll program a code for you to the alarm as well."

She nodded. "Some pretty high tech security you got here."

"Yeah, well, I have some pretty expensive computer equipment. And let's just say I don't want the information on it getting into the wrong hands."

Yikes. It was easy to forget who he really was when he spoke so well, looked so good, and attended high-class galas, or at least one high-class gala. But she'd be wise to remember that under the shiny exterior was a man with tight control over every aspect of his life. A life she knew little about beyond rumors and hearsay, but if her Google search was accurate, included at least some level illegal activity.

"There are multiple security cameras around the exterior of the building including right here outside the door. They are all accessible through my phone, and I'll set yours up too. Anyone comes to the door, you'll know exactly who it is before you answer it. You can talk to them through the intercom, using your phone, as well. You're safe here, Fia, and I want you to feel comfortable."

She exhaled about ten pounds of pent up tension. "Thank you." Sweeter words had never been spoken. What an ignorant fool she'd been in the past to blindly believe she was safe. When she recalled the number of times she'd neglected to lock her apartment door at night, she wanted to travel back in time and scream at the naivety of those actions.

He nodded. "I'll give you the grand tour later, Come on into the kitchen for now. I want to get this conversation over with before we do anything else."

Oookay. She trailed behind him down a short hallway. About a third of the way down, Acer hung a left and she followed into a small but luxurious kitchen. The cabinets were dark, almost black with a sandy stone counter top. A stainless-steel oven was built into a wall and matched the refrigerator on the opposite wall. In the far corner, a round table with four chairs boasted a cozy eating nook.

She whistled. "This is nice, Acer."

He shrugged and shot her a grin. "I guess a little bit of that silver spoon is still stuck in my mouth."

"You can take the boy out of the money…" she said in a singsong voice.

He laughed and pulled out a chair. "Have a seat. Want a beer or a glass of wine?"

"Oh, wine would be perfect."

A few moments later two glasses and a bottle of merlot were plunked down on the table. Acer held his out to her and she touched her glass to his. It was good stuff, and if the label on the bottle was any indication, expensive stuff.

Being with Acer like this, in his personal space, was nice, almost domestic, and maybe if she drank enough wine, she could forget the real reason she was here. She studied him openly as they sipped in silence until she could no longer hold back a burst of laughter.

He lifted his eyes to meet hers. "What's so funny?"

"You are." She winked at him. "You're a fascinating contradiction. Leather and miles of tattoos, expensive wine, fancy education, motorcycle club, charity galas."

One eyebrow shot up at the mention of his education.

She raised her glass to him. "I can google with the best of them. I know you graduated from Harvard with a computer science degree."

He looked away and hot shame heated her from the inside out. Geez, she must seem so ungrateful. Here she was, making him uncomfortable when he'd been nothing but amazing to her. "Acer, I'm sor—"

He shook his head. "Don't sweat it, babe. I want you to tell me why you haven't gone to the police."

Guess he preferred to talk about her hot-button issues rather than his own. She swirled the wine and stared at the legs that trailed down the inside of the glass. Once upon a time, this man wanted her, as a woman. They'd shared the most intense sexual experiences of her life. The idea of allowing him to see how ugly her life had become was grossly unappealing.

She almost laughed out loud. He'd seen her at what could only be described as the very worst moment of her life. A simple conversation should be a cakewalk in comparison.

But it wasn't. Some small part of Fia-the-woman, who hadn't been completely demolished by Mike, didn't want Acer to remember her as the damsel he rescued. Didn't want him to remember that Mike had violated her in the worst way possible, reducing her to a mess of nerves and constant anxiety with a newfound fear of men.

"Fia?" The sincerity in his gentle tone convinced her to open up.

"I'm a mess," she whispered, staring at the table. The

humiliation of that admission burned in her gut. "Most days I feel like I'm climbing a muddy hill in a down pour. I dig my foot into the muck, grab a chunk of soft earth with my hands, and haul myself up with every last ounce of strength I have, only to slip ten feet farther down the hill. I'm getting nowhere."

Warmth engulfed her hand as Acer slid palm over knuckles. She lifted her gaze until she encountered his concentrated focus. There was anger in his narrowed eyes and tense shoulders, guilt and remorse too. Selfish as it was, she didn't have the capacity to try to decipher his emotions. Not right now.

"I have these panic attacks, I freak out if I'm touched, I wake up screaming at night. It's bad." She shook her head. "The thought of seeing him again, of prolonging the amount of time I have to think about it and relive it with a trial…"

"Look, I'm not exactly a fan of the cops or the legal system." He rubbed a hand over his face. "But, don't you want him punished?"

"Of course, I want him punished. I just don't want to have to be the one to do it. Looks like under all my tough talk and attitude, I'm quite the coward." Tears filled her eyes and she was helpless to stop them from falling.

"Jesus, Fia. Is that what you think of yourself? That you're a coward?" He brought her hand to his lips and nipped at the knuckles.

Seven months, ago his teeth grazing her skin would have had her wet and climbing on the table ready for all he could give her. Now, she was just glad she didn't shiver in revulsion.

"You seem okay when I touch you." He dropped his forehead to their joined hands. "Christ, baby, I should have kept you here with me. I'd never for one second have allowed you to think those toxic thoughts. It was a mistake to go with your parents."

Her heart squeezed at the deep self-loathing in his voice. For the first time since she was abducted, she became aware of the fact that the ordeal she went through may have had a profound impact on him as well. Was it misplaced guilt, or was it possible he cared for her on a deeper level?

She sifted her free hand through his hair. A small bit of stress evaporated as she shifted her focus to the comfort of someone else for a moment.

~ ~ ~ ~

The raw urge to ride to Texas and pound her parents into the ground was almost too strong to ignore. Fia wasn't weak, she wasn't a coward, she was traumatized. Had her family done their job and supported her, she'd have been able to face the idea of a trial, Acer was certain of that.

Part of him—the part that beat the shit out of Brandon Epley for daring to lay a hand on his friend's sister—was glad Fia hadn't gone to the police. He wanted a shot at the asshole, and if Mike was buried in the system, Acer might never get his chance to make him pay.

Fia deserved to know he would take care of Mike for her. That she'd get justice, at least his brand of justice, without ever having to be within a mile of the man who caused her such pain. "There hasn't been any sign of him since we found you."

She inhaled a sharp breath. "How do you know?"

Acer shrugged. "I've got eyes on his house, his bank account, credit cards. He hasn't shown up for work. There was one hit on his ATM card in New Mexico a week ago. I sent a few prospects to investigate, but he was in the wind by the time they got there. Wherever he is, he's staying off the grid."

Her eyes widened and her mouth opened as though to speak but she snapped it shut again. She looked away for a beat then turned back to him. "So you've been searching for him?"

Acer nodded. "As much as I can, but I don't think he's in the state."

She remained quiet for a tense moment. "Will you turn him in to the police if you find him?" she finally asked.

"No."

"What will you do?" Her volume dropped to a notch above a whisper.

"Handle it." He watched her closely for any signs of distress, disgust, or shock at his declaration. Sure, he didn't voice the actual words, but she was an intelligent woman. She knew what he meant.

Fia took a large gulp of wine and ran a hand through her limp hair. "So…" she began. With a heavy sigh, she took a visual tour of his kitchen until her gaze landed back on him with nothing else to delay her question. "So, if I wasn't here, if we weren't having this conversation, you'd track him until you found him and…handle it."

It was said as a statement rather than a question, but he answered her anyway. "No. That's my plan regardless of this conversation. Regardless of whether you go to the cops or not, whether he's incarcerated or not. Prison would make it difficult, but there are plenty of ways to reach a man inside. I have some friends in low places." He couldn't soften the deadly tone.

A flicker of relief crossed Fia's face, as though she preferred his method. She clearly wanted Mike gone, dead, never having the opportunity to hurt her or anyone else. But she was too good a person to come right out and ask him to kill Mike.

"I think—" She swallowed and his eyes were drawn to the delicate rise and fall of her throat. He remembered the sensation of her pulse, fluttering under his lips.

Christ, this wasn't the time for those thoughts. He should be castrated for those thoughts.

"I feel like I'm supposed to object, to ask you not to take matters into your own hands. But all I can think about is how much I want him gone. How I need to be completely certain he'll never be able to hurt me or anyone else again."

"What happens to him won't be on you, Fia. You aren't making this choice; you aren't asking this of me. In fact, I'm not sure I'd agree if you asked me to back off. Your conscience can be clear, hon. You with me?"

She nodded. "And your conscience?"

He gave her hand a squeeze. "You may not want to admit it to yourself, but you know who I am, what I am. You've heard enough stories. I won't lose one wink of sleep."

"Will you tell me—"

Hell no. He shook his head. "No details. I won't put you at risk that way, and details won't help you recover."

She shook her head and held her hand up as though to ward off his statement. "Oh, no, no. I don't think I want the specifics. Will you just tell me when it's over? I'm not sure I'll ever feel safe until I know." Her voice shook like she was straining to keep herself together. Mike's death couldn't come soon enough.

"That I can do."

She took another sip of her wine. "Thank you," she whispered.

They stared at each other across the table, a sizzle of energy snapping and buzzing between them. She may be suppressing it, afraid of it, trying to deny it, but it was there and she had to feel it too. The chemistry between them was off the charts.

This would be the perfect moment to take her back to his big bed and spend the next twenty-four hours making her forget every second of the past month. But she wasn't there yet, not even close.

She'd get there. Acer would make sure of it, and not just because he wanted to fuck her more than he wanted his next breath. But because she deserved to have that moment when her eyes glazed over and nothing registered but intense pleasure. She deserved to kick the trauma so far into the past it would never reappear in her mind. And she deserved to live again.

Alarm bells sounded in his head, warning him that he was treading on emotional thin ice. He silenced the blare. This wasn't about emotions. Had nothing to do with emotions.

This was just paying a debt. He had thrown her into this mess; he'd guide her out.

A loud pounding caused Fia to jolt so hard she knocked her wine glass over with a clatter. "Shit! Sorry, Acer. I'm so damned jumpy. At least it didn't break."

He swatted her hands out of the way and righted the glass. "And at least you guzzled your drink so there was nothing left to spill," he tossed over his shoulder as he made his way to the door, his eyes on his phone.

Fia's laugh followed him down the hallway. "That too."

"Acer, open up. It's Lila! I know you have Fia in there and we want to see her."

He groaned and turned to Fia.

"We?" she asked.

"You'll see," he said. He deactivated the alarm and pulled the door open, moving quickly to the side to avoid the three women who practically fell into the apartment.

"Geez, Acer. Took you long enough." Emily said with a

roll of her pale blue eyes. She brushed her long ink-black hair out of her face and dropped a quick kiss on his cheek.

"Fia, meet the No Prisoners' pep squad," he said of Striker and Hook's wives as well as Jester's live-in girlfriend. He viewed all three women as an extension of his MC family. Each had been through tough times of their own and, with the help of their men, come through shiny and new. He prayed the same would happen for Fia. Even though he wasn't her man.

"Fia!" Lila moved her tiny body into the hall and the two women embraced in a tight hug. Fia didn't seem at all phased by the physical contact with another woman. Then again, it wasn't a woman who'd chained her up, beaten her, and raped her.

"What are you ladies doing out without your ol' men?" He closed the door behind the group.

It was Marcie's turn to roll her bright green eyes. "Stuff it, Acer. We're supposed to tell you that there's a meeting with Shiv in half hour. You go and we'll keep your lady entertained." She was so bubbly she practically bounced as she walked, her long blonde ponytail swishing back and forth.

Acer turned and sent a questioning look Fia's way. Her eyes were wide and she shifted from side to side in a nervous gesture, but a ghost of a smile tilted her lips.

"Don't worry about me. I'll be fine. Go do your thing."

He really didn't want to leave her so soon, but what choice did he have? At least the ladies were here so she wouldn't have to be alone in his apartment five minutes after arriving. He nodded. "Okay, I shouldn't be long. I'm going to set the alarm so don't try to leave until I get back, any of you." He shot them each a stern look. "Make sure the girls take good care of you, Fi."

"Seriously, Acer, how much trouble do you think we are?" It was Emily who asked the question.

Of the three women, he was closest to Emily. Surprising, considering how she and Jester met. Emily was sent by an enemy of the club to extract information from a No Prisoner. Acer leaned in to press a chaste kiss against her cheek. "Lots of fuckin' trouble."

All four women laughed and he covered his ears. "Thank fuck for this meeting or I just might die."

"Get out!" Lila shoved him toward the door.

He sent a wink over his shoulder to a wide-eyed Fia and set the alarm before securing the door behind him.

For the first time in as long as he could remember, he had no interest in meeting with his club brothers. Shiv was concerned about his focus, but concentrating would be an extra challenge tonight with half his mind back at the apartment with Fia. While he knew staying with her twenty-four-seven wasn't realistic, leaving her felt like shit.

This meeting better be damn quick.

Chapter Fifteen

"So," Fia said to the three women who stared at her like she was a sparkly diamond they couldn't wait to inspect. If one of them whipped out a loupe, she just might bolt, alarm or no alarm. "I'd ask you to sit or offer you something to drink, but Acer hasn't even given me a tour yet, so you probably know where things are better than I do."

The blonde with emerald green eyes and a long blonde ponytail smiled and held out a hand. "I'm Marcie, and this here," she pointed next to her at the woman with raven hair and unique light blue eyes, "is Emily. She's the only one who's been here before. But, girl, we have no problem making ourselves at home. That's the price Acer pays for leaving us alone in his apartment with his expensive booze." She headed down the hallway as though she owned the place.

Wow, the woman was a ball of energy.

Lila linked her arm through Fia's and gently tugged her down the hall after Marcie.

"Hey, you think Acer will care if we crack open another bottle of wine? This stuff looks pricey." Marcie called from the kitchen.

"I don't kn—" Fia wrung her hands at her waist.

Behind her, Emily laughed. She seemed the most mellow of the gang. "Are you kidding me? I have a feeling Acer will let Fia do whatever the hell she wants."

"Well, I'm not—" She rubbed her forehead where a dull ache was forming.

"Yeah, he won't care at all, Marce. Open it up!" Lila let go of Fia when they reached the kitchen.

Apparently, she wasn't going to be able to get a word in around these three. And why were they so certain she had Acer wrapped around her finger?

Marcie made herself at home, opening cabinets until she discovered where Acer kept the wine glasses. "Bingo! Three glasses coming up since I see you already have one, Fia."

The table in the eat-in space was small and round but had enough chairs for the women. Each took a seat while Marcie played hostess and poured the wine.

Fia took a small sip. It was even better than the last bottle, but she hadn't eaten in a while and didn't want to get drunk. Having dulled reflexes and not being in full control of her faculties was out of the question these days.

Lila swallowed a sip of the cabernet, closed her eyes, and smiled. "Mmm, Acer is my new favorite person."

"Amen," Emily said.

Lila turned her attention to Fia. "Okay, honey. I'm not one to bullshit, so I'm going to get the hard stuff out of the way right now. That way you can enjoy your wine without wondering when it's going to come up. We're all so sorry for what happened to you. Each one of us," she said looking around the table, "has had some variety of trauma in our lives. We won't push, but any one of us is more than willing to listen if you need an ear or a shoulder to cry on."

Fia's eyes flooded and she willed away the tears. She would

not become the weepy woman who cried every five minutes. "Thank you," she whispered. "None of you know me at all, yet you're all so kind. In my world, that kind of sincerity is rare." They'd shown her more compassion and caring in five minutes than anyone from her parent's Texas circle had. It was both a heartwarming feeling and sad commentary on her life.

Lila snorted. "Don't I know it."

Huh, she'd have to ask Acer about that later.

"Look, you may not be Acer's girlfriend, or whatever," Emily broke in. "But you are the only person we've ever met who has a non-club related connection to him. Everyone teases him about his past and makes lots of assumptions, but we don't actually know much. And we've never been introduced to anyone from his past. That makes you part of our inner circle, our family. No matter what you guys end up being to each other."

They'd be nothing to each other. She could just imagine it. *Hey, Acer, I can't stand to be touched and it may be years before I can have sex, if ever. Wanna go steady?* The idea was laughable, but the heartfelt sentiment behind Emily's words chased away a bit of her loneliness.

"Thank you, guys. I'm excited to get to know all of you."

"So, Fia, what is it that you do?" Marcie asked before she tipped back her glass and polished off the wine. "Good thing you drove, Em." She reached for the bottle and refilled her glass.

Emily flushed bright red and turned to Fia. "Yeah, tell us what you do?"

"I'm a fashion designer, but I strictly do lingerie, mostly custom pieces."

Three sets of wide eyes and three broad grins stared back at her. "Uh, what?"

Marcie broke the silence. "Oh my God, it's fate."

What on earth was she talking about?

"So." Lila's eyes sparked as she spoke. "A lot of MCs make their ol' ladies—"

"Their what?" Seriously? Old ladies?

The women laughed. "It's just the term for a woman in a serious relationship with a club member," Emily explained.

"Ah, interesting." She wasn't sure how she'd feel being called an old anything, but it seemed to roll off these women's backs.

Lila chuckled and sipped her wine. "Anyway, they make them wear a leather vest, similar to the member's cut, with a patch that says 'property of' whoever it is they are with. It's archaic, and thank God, the No Prisoners don't have that little tradition. That being said, there's just enough caveman in each of our guys that we know they would love it if we wore one, at least in private if you get my drift."

Emily chimed in, more animated than she'd been until now. "For months, we've been saying that it would be so much fun to design No Prisoners lingerie that said *Property of Jester*, in my case, across the backside. Holy shit, my man would go crazy if he saw that."

"And it would have to be leather, of course. With *Take No* and *Prisoners* on the bra cups. Good, huh?"

Fia burst out laughing. She knew just enough about these men to know the girls were right. They'd go insane. "I'm in, so in. If you girls are serious, I can get measurements from you now and show you some different design options. I've cut back on much of my work since…" She cleared her throat. "Anyway, I'd love something to keep me busy while I'm here, so I don't go stir-crazy, or worse, Acer-crazy."

"I can't believe this is happening, I'm so excited!" Marcie practically bounced in her chair.

"Oh, we're serious." Lila's grin was wide and excited, like Marcie's.

The women's enthusiasm was contagious, and Fia found herself eager to focus her attention on a work project. She hadn't touched anything business related in the past two weeks. It felt good to have something productive to focus her energy on.

Only Emily looked slightly uncertain. The reaction was surprising given her friend's elation. Fia was just about to tell her there was no pressure when she chimed in. "Okay, I'm game too." But she didn't look quite as pumped as the other two.

"I'll be right back." Fia dashed to the front door where her suitcase still sat and pulled out her laptop, sketchbook, and a binder of sample materials. She'd thrown them on top of her clothes as a last-minute thought; work had to begin again sometime.

When she returned, the wine glasses were topped off and the ladies were ready to begin.

After much laughter and friendly arguing over design ideas, Fia glanced up at the clock. She blinked her heavy eyelids in case she'd read the numbers wrong. Had two and a half hours really flown by that fast? Her first thought was that she'd spent an entire two and a half hours without thinking of Mike once. Progress.

The second thought was what the hell was keeping Acer?

Chapter Sixteen

Acer coasted to a halt and dropped his feet to the ground, raising his middle finger to the camera over the traffic light. Every damn time he rode through town, this blasted light snagged him, like it had some kind of sensor and turned red when it saw him coming.

A few times, he'd been tempted to hack into the department of transportation's server and have a little fun, but there was a good chance he'd cause an accident or two so he never gave into the urge.

He wanted this meeting over as fast as possible. Fia didn't know where anything was in his place. Hell, he hadn't even shown her where she could sleep.

In his guest room.

Not his bed.

Thanks to Mike. Mike, who raped her and stole her confidence and comfort with men. Mike, who Acer had all but admitted to Fia he planned to kill. Her reaction to that admission caught him off guard. The trauma was still so acute. In another few months, she'd be disgusted by the thought of him taking another person's life.

A loud rumble caught his attention and he turned his head

left, in time to catch the blur of a motorcycle blow past him on the cross street, going at least seventy through downtown Crystal Rock's thirty mile-per-hour roads.

What the fuck?

It was hard to tell due to the speed of the bike, but he'd swear the rider wore a No Prisoners' cut. It didn't make any sense, though. The clubhouse was in the opposite direction and Acer was running late, so whoever this was should have been there already.

The light blipped green and he started to turn left toward the clubhouse.

"Fuck," he spat out as he looped around and sped right instead, following the path of the unknown biker. For two weeks, his gut had been unsettled. Something stunk like a week-old diaper, and this just may be his first solid lead. He couldn't ignore his unease any longer.

He gave the bike more gas and the needle climbed well over seventy. About a mile down the road, he glimpsed the tail end of a bike as it again made a right turn and disappeared out of sight.

The road the mystery biker took was long, winding, and led thirty miles out into the desert, ending just one mile shy of the border in the middle of nothingness. The churn in Acer's gut increased until it was a gnawing pain. This entire situation was fucked, and he had a sick feeling he knew what he'd encounter.

He eased off the throttle a hair, dropping his speed to about eighty, not wanting to alert his target who was about a mile and a half ahead.

Fifteen minutes later, as he approached the highway, he slowed to a near crawl. Up ahead about a mile, right where the highway dead-ended, three bikers were parked on the side of the road. He was too far to make out the patches on their cuts but knew deep in his gut what it would read.

It became clear as crystal. He needed to get back to alert the club. Now that he had a specific area to focus on, he could revisit the satellite imagery and confirm his suspicions.

Hatred for his father burned like acid, scarring the walls around his heart. This was why Fia shouldn't be so free with her trust, and this was why he'd hold back with her, no matter how much he wanted to keep her close. No one would hesitate to stab you in the back if it served their purposes, blood and family be damned. At least with his club, the members knew the severe price of betrayal. Fear of the fatal consequences was enough to keep most in line.

His engine roared as he cruised to the clubhouse at top speed. Shiv would be pissed he missed the meeting, but he'd be more pissed when he discovered why.

Twenty minutes later, Acer slowed to a stop in the lot outside the clubhouse. His jaw ached and gray dotted the edges of his vision, the anger in him rivaling that of twenty years ago.

He stomped through the gravel lot, into the clubhouse and straight back to the chapel. Before he wrenched the door open, he blew out a breath. Letting down the club was a sin none of them wanted to commit. And while he knew his brothers wouldn't hold his father's actions against him, in his own mind, he was responsible.

Twenty-five sets of eyes trained on him the moment he stepped in the room. Striker stood, his mouth set in a grim line, but Shiv, his club president, was the first to speak. "Where the fuck you been? You got something more important to do than be here for church? Huh, Acer? Like playing house with your lady friend, maybe?"

Acer didn't bother to take his seat at the table. Angering Shiv further wouldn't be wise. He shook his head. "I ran into some trouble on the way here."

A low murmur sounded around the room.

"Shut the fuck up," Shiv barked. "Grimm Brothers?"

Jester grunted. "Can't be. They're too busy killing themselves fighting over Snake's abandoned throne. No one's seen or heard from him since he was discharged from the hospital."

Acer shook his head again. "Not Grimms. Saw a biker on my way here, heading out into the desert, toward the border. Guy had a No Prisoners' cut. Followed him until he stopped and met with two others. Both had cuts as well, but I was too far to see the patches."

Shiv slapped his palm against the table to quiet the uproar that ensued. "You think it's a chapter from another state? Lucky is coming from Vegas, but not for a few days."

"Definitely wasn't Lucky, guy was too heavy."

"So who the hell do you think it was?" Striker asked.

Acer ran a hand across his jaw. He hadn't bothered to shave that morning since his only plan for the day had been to work on his computer at the clubhouse. Now, after being out in the heat for an hour, the stubble itched like a wool sweater. "I think it's Reginald Wellington."

"You think your old man was on a bike in Crystal Rock?" Gumby's eyes widened.

"Gumby, shut the fuck up and let him finish." Hook shook his head.

"I obviously haven't had a chance to investigate it yet, but my theory is that he's got guys wearing our cuts, or something very similar, smuggling illegals across the border like he planned all along. They get busted and the Feds start sniffing around us."

"Jesus, you rich pricks have some fucked up families." Jester's comment evoked a round of snickers.

Tip of the iceberg.

Shiv jabbed the smoldering end of a cigar into an ashtray, then leaned back in his chair, linking his fingers behind his head. He pierced Acer with a penetrating glare. Shiv could keep his cool in the tensest of situations, but Acer wasn't so stupid as to believe his president wasn't simmering on the inside. A man didn't get to be MC president by losing his cool in every situation, but he sure as hell didn't rise to the top by being soft either.

"Here's what we're gonna do, boys. Acer, I want you to do some computer voodoo and figure this shit out. If you're right, we gotta cut this off at the balls. I don't give a shit what your old man does at the border, but I won't tolerate any blowback on my club. Hook, I'm putting you in charge of getting any weapons off the premises. Store them at the warehouse for now, until we come up with a better idea. ICE paying us a visit is one thing. They call their buddies at ATF we need to make sure they don't find shit. Get the prospects hauling it today. We good?"

The men grunted their approval.

"All right. Get the fuck out of here. Acer, hang back for a second."

He waited until the room cleared out, then took a seat at the large rectangular table, opposite Shiv.

"Heard about your girl coming into town." He lit another cigar and exhaled a cloud of white smoke.

Acer didn't bother to correct him. If people thought she was his, they'd be more inclined to leave her alone.

"Appreciate the heads up about her family wanting her shit broadcast in the media. You good to handle it?"

"I got it." He'd be placing a friendly call to her father tonight.

Shiv nodded. "Let me know if you need anything from

me. As for her, bring her around anytime."

Acer tensed. He loved his brothers, but most of them were dogs when it came to women. They'd hit on anything with tits and were aggressive about it. "I'm not sure she's—"

Shiv waved the hand holding the thick cigar. "I know what happened to her. I warned the boys she's yours, off limits. She did us a solid with the heads up. She's welcome here."

"Thanks." The club was the closest thing to family, brothers, that he'd allow himself. And while a part of him was always cautious and distrustful, he was confident he had their loyalty as they had his.

He lifted his chin at Shiv and rose from the table. When he was halfway to the door, Shiv called out. "Hey, Acer?"

He turned around.

"Good to have you back, brother."

When Acer stepped back outside, the glowing sun rested lower in the horizon, taking with it some of the scorching heat. Jester, Striker, and Hook huddled around their bikes laughing at something Jester was saying.

"You good?" Striker asked as he approached the group.

"I'm good." That was enough. These men knew him well enough to know he'd never vomit his feelings over his family drama. Hell, he had no feelings on the matter. His father was a faithless asshole whose only loyalty was to the green in his wallet. That's all there was to it.

"We're gonna head back with you, pick up the girls since it's getting late. You mind if I leave Em's car at your place until tomorrow?"

"Nah, brother. Leave it as long as you want." He climbed on his bike, careful not to let the little spark of anticipation show at the thought of returning to his apartment, where Fia was waiting for him.

Chapter Seventeen

Acer opened his door to the sound of feminine laughter. Not flirty, giggly laughter, but hysterical, loud hilarity.

"Aww shit," Hook muttered behind him.

"What?" He waved the guys into his apartment and secured the door.

Striker groaned and pinched the skin between his eyebrows. "Any chance you thought to lock up your liquor before you left?"

Jester laughed. "Obviously not, because that is the sound of some very drunk ladies having one hell of a time. What are the chances they're naked and swatting each other with Acer's swanky goose down pillows? Feathers flying all around, then one of them might accidentally—oof! Ouch, that hurt, dipshit!" He rubbed his ribs where Hook's elbow had jabbed. "Was it something I said?"

His brothers all laughed then collectively rolled their eyes when a high-pitched squeal came from Acer's guest room.

"I'd say the chances of a pillow fight are slim and none. The more likely question is what are the chances we'll have to tie them to our backs to keep them from losing them halfway home," Striker said with a grin.

Acer wasn't quite sure what all the grumbling was about, but then, he didn't have an ol' lady to manage.

The group made their way down the hall. Acer was relieved Fia seemed to have found her way around the apartment. Although, he had a feeling the other ladies were the adventurous ones.

He reached the guest bedroom before the other men and came to a dead stop at the sight before him. Fia sat cross-legged on the bed, next to Emily. The other two were sprawled on the floor, leaning against the wall with three, presumably empty wine bottles scattered around.

Shit, that was a two-hundred-dollar bottle of wine.

He returned his attention to Fia, and in that moment, she could have robbed him blind and he wouldn't have given a shit. She'd piled half of her hair in a messy bun on top of her head, giving her a casual and relaxed look, and she'd changed into a sunny yellow tank top. It was still too loose on her, but at least it wasn't the obvious man repellant she'd had on earlier.

What captivated him, though, was the wide, happy, and almost carefree grin on her face. Her eyes sparkled with mirth and she resembled the Fia he recalled from seven months ago. The Fia he hadn't been able to keep his hands and lips off. Hell, if hanging out with the ol' ladies and drinking his expensive wine put that look on her face, she could have at it.

"At least my woman looks sober enough to stay upright." Jester shoved Acer aside and barged his way into the small room, his enormous bulk monopolizing the space.

~ ~ ~ ~

Jester surged into the room and Fia tensed. He was so large, the space in the bedroom seemed to shrink before her eyes. Someone that size would be impossible to protect herself against. He had easily three times the muscle mass of Mike, and Mike had been able to overpower her so easily. Jester could—

Fingers of panic began to squeeze the air out of her lungs. God, no. Not now. They would think she was a basket case.

Jester approached Emily, captured her face between his mitt-sized hands, bent his head down, and kissed her for all she was worth. Right before their lips met, Jester's mouth moved, a breath away from Emily's. Fia only caught him say, "I love you," because she sat an inch away from Emily. No one else in the room noticed.

Fia's breath came easier, but something clenched deep inside her. Would she ever have that? That closeness? That physical comfort with a man? Hell, would any man even want that knowing what she'd been through?

Heat flooded her cheeks and she shifted her gaze, embarrassed to be gawking at them with such blatant interest. Acer rested against the doorframe, his toned arms crossed over his firm chest, his concentration on her. A knowing, sexy smile tilted up his tempting mouth and his eyes darkened. Was that desire? Was it possible he still felt an attraction toward her?

The spell was broken when Hook cleared his throat. "If you'd move your big ass out of the way and let someone else in the room, I'd show you how it's really done."

Marcie laughed from the floor. "I'll come to you, baby," she said. She grabbed the top of a modern, gray nightstand next to the bed and hauled herself up. "Woah." Her back hit the wall and she giggled.

"Jesus, a little sloppy there, Marce?" Hook shook his head.

She giggled again. Hook hip-checked Jester out of the way and moved into the space. He slid his arm around his wife's waist and guided her out of the room, again ramming

Jester's body with his.

"Okay, okay, I can take a hint." Jester broke off the kiss, slid his hands under Emily's backside, and lifted her straight off the bed. She yelped and wrapped her legs around his waist. "Later guys." He followed Hook and Marcie out of the room, his arms full of happy female.

Striker was next to collect his lady and before she knew it, Fia was alone in the room with Acer.

Her insides twisted as apprehension settled in her chest. "I hope it's not a problem that I set up camp in here."

He moved into the room never shifting his attention off her. She couldn't meet his eyes, his intense gaze too powerful. "No problem at all, hon."

Fia nodded and smoothed a hand over the soft, royal blue comforter on the queen-sized platform bed. He had great taste. The bed was low to the ground with a large tufted gray fabric headboard. A contemporary gray dresser with a wide mirror was opposite the bed. It fit him. Clean, modern, masculine, expensive, but not fussy.

She peered up at him. "Did everything go okay?"

"It went fine." His answer was reflexive, but she would have sworn she saw a flicker of anger in his eyes.

She really had no right to question him about it, so she didn't. "Are you hungry?"

He ran a hand over his flat stomach. "Actually, now that you mention it, I'm starved. You want to order something in?"

"Oh well, um, we were hungry and couldn't get something delivered since you set the alarm, so we...um...well, we raided your kitchen. I made some stir-fry with what I could find. I hope that's okay. There's quite a bit left over if you want some." She averted her gaze again. If he wasn't attracted to her before, this nervous rambling would reel him in like a hungry fish for sure.

She hated this person she'd become. This woman who lacked confidence and whose spine was as pliable as a wet twig. Old Fia would have told him she made him dinner and if he didn't like it, he could eat a sugar packet.

He stood in front of her now, far enough away that she didn't feel crowded, but close enough that he was able to reach out a hand and gently tip her chin up. "Babe, for as long as you're here, it's your place too. Got it? You don't have to ask me for shit. Use what you want, eat what you want." He glanced at the wine bottles on the floor with a grimace. "Drink what you want."

Some of the tension left her muscles, and she chuckled. "Yeah, sorry about that. There was no stopping them."

He snorted. "They are a force. Come on." He gripped her hand and gave a light tug. She followed him back to the kitchen.

"Sit," she said. "I'll get it for you. I may have a little more myself."

She busied herself nuking the leftover stir-fry and preparing plates, aware of Acer's heavy gaze on her the entire time.

He moved his arms from the table so she had space to place his plate. "You been on a bike before?" he asked.

With a smile, she sat across from him. "Actually, yes. A few times."

Acer's mouth flattened and he stopped the fork halfway to his mouth. "When? And who's the asshole who had you on the back of his bike?"

Fia laughed. That sounded distinctly like jealousy. "It was in college. Geez, almost ten years ago, now. I had a friend with a motorcycle. I used to ride with him sometimes. No big deal. But I loved it. So, if you're offering, I'm definitely game."

He grunted but didn't say anything else and she assumed it was man speak for *I'm not sure I like it, but you can ride on the back of my bike anytime.* She grinned as a bit of excitement stirred. Riding on the back of a motorcycle again would be a lot of fun.

They ate the rest of their meal in silence, but it wasn't uncomfortable. It was intimate, almost…domestic. Was this what the other couples were doing right now? Were they sitting down to a home-cooked meal before they retired to their bedrooms to spend the rest of the evening making love?

She hoped so; someone ought to get some tonight. God knows it wasn't going to be her. It might never be her again.

~ ~ ~ ~

Acer depressed send on his phone and lifted the device to his ear. Fia had retired to bed about an hour earlier and he waited until he was confident she was asleep before placing a call to her father. He'd spent that hour doing a little digging on Terrance Caldwell and his oil empire. The ease with which he found some dirt to use as leverage was laughable. People had no idea how, with just a few keystrokes, their skeletons came tumbling out of the closet.

After the third ring, a thick Texas drawl, laden with sleep came through the phone. "Who the hell is this? You have any idea what time it is?"

"It's ten here in Arizona, so I guess that puts you at about midnight, Terry."

Caldwell grumbled, no doubt at the informal use of his name. "Who the hell is this?"

"Well, Ter, it's Adam Wellington." Dead silence left a wide void between the men. "Thought that might get your attention."

"Goddamnit. I knew that little tart would run right to

you."

Acer tsked. "Terry, is that any way to speak of your only daughter?" He hardened his voice. "Especially knowing the trauma she's suffered."

Caldwell's sneer could be heard through the phone. "Yeah, because of you and your gang of miscreants. What's it gonna take to get you to send her back to Texas? You want money?"

Like a jagged knife, Caldwell's words stabbed straight into the heart of Acer's guilt. "No. I do not need your money. And what is Fia, thirty? I can't exactly *send* a grown woman anywhere like she's a child. Even if I could, your house would be the last place I'd allow her to go. She tried that already. Your idea of helping your daughter recover is to drag her through media hell to get some publicity for your struggling oil corporation."

Caldwell's intake of breath had Acer smiling. "That's right. I know all about your financial troubles. I know about your girlfriend too. Cute girl, but come on, Ter, she's gotta be what, ten years younger than your own daughter?" He clucked his tongue. "I wonder what Mrs. Caldwell would have to say about your infidelities?"

"Alicia? How did you—"

"Shut the fuck up." Acer's voice was thick with menace. "We both know your corporation is failing. We also know Mrs. Caldwell's parents were nice enough to die early, leaving her the fortune. Without her, your kingdom would crumble. Bet Alicia wouldn't be too eager to suck your wrinkled dick then, huh? Back the fuck off Fia or the media will get a story they'll find much more interesting than the kidnapping and rape of your daughter. Do you understand me?"

"I don't know who you think you are to threaten me." His

words were bold, but panic was evident in the way his shrill, wheezy pitch.

"I'll ask you one more time. If you don't answer correctly, this picture I have from a security camera of young Alicia with her hand down your pants outside a very well-known Dallas hotel goes straight to every media outlet I can think of. Do you understand me?"

Silence ticked by for one, two, three beats of Acers heart.

"My finger is hovering over *send*."

"I understand."

The defeated attitude was music to Acer's ears. He disconnected the phone without bothering to respond and dropped it next to him on the bed.

Christ, had it really been less than twelve hours since Fia walked back into his life. She had a long way to go to recover from her trauma, but she'd get there. Acer would make sure of it. He'd do whatever the hell he had to, to help the old Fia return to life. Then, he'd set her free. Because as much as he enjoyed their little family-like dinner this evening, he knew all too well it would never work out in the long run.

She'd betray him, or he'd betray her. It's just how it was. People couldn't be trusted.

Both their families were the perfect example.

Chapter Eighteen

Fia glanced up from the small sketchpad she had doodled on and chuckled. Acer and Hook had shoved tables aside and danced in a circle around the middle of the clubhouse sparring and taking shots at each other.

Acer was different today—lighthearted and almost playful. It was a side of him she'd never seen before. Sure, she didn't know him all that well, but she'd been living with him for two days and was coming to learn his moods.

A club brother from their Vegas chapter was due into town any minute. Apparently, he and Acer were tight and she attributed his good spirits to manly excitement over his buddy's visit.

A shrill whistle had her turning her attention to the entrance. Marcie and Emily stood with their arms linked at the elbows. Marcie's free hand was in her mouth and she whistled again. "Get him, baby," she called to Hook.

Hook diverted his focus long enough to blow Marcie a kiss. In the two seconds of inattention, Acer's gloved fist connected with Hook's jaw.

Hooks head snapped back and Marcie winced. "Oops, sorry, honey."

"No worries, babe. He hits like a chick."

The reverberation of motorcycle pipes filled the room, drowning out any comeback Acer may have fired. Striker and Jester came through the door and the mock boxing match broke up. Both Marcie and Emily sought out their men, winding their arms around each other like they couldn't bear to be apart. Lila had a shift at the hospital and would join them for a barbecue at the clubhouse later.

"Sounds like Lucky's here." Acer sidled up next to Fia and grabbed her hand. "Come meet him." He pulled her off the barstool and followed the rest of the gang out to the parking lot.

A man backed his bike into a spot next to Acer's and killed the engine. He pulled off his helmet and shook out his dark, shaggy hair before waving at the group.

"Uhh, holy crap! Is that—?" Emily's mouth dropped open.

"Colin Ferrall?" Fia finished for her.

Emily laughed. "Why didn't you guys tell me Colin Ferrall was a member of the MC?"

The men groaned as one unit.

Striker coughed, disguising a laugh. "And now you know why he's called Lucky."

Fia frowned and looked at Acer. "Because he's Irish?"

Striker laughed again and answered for Acer. "Not exactly." He winked at her. "It's because when it comes to the ladies, he's the luckiest damn son of a bitch I've ever met. Not one of us stood a chance at scoring whenever we were out with Lucky."

"He speaks the truth. Not to mention he's a former Marine sniper. Don't know what it is, but something about that fact makes the ladies line up for a shot at him." Acer chuckled and slung an arm across her shoulders. It was such an innocent gesture, one befitting a friend, but her muscles seized. His arm might as well have weighed five-hundred pounds, it felt so heavy across her back. "Oh, shit, sorry," he whispered as he started to move his arm.

"No!" She grasped his hand, securing him in place. "I'm okay. Leave it there. You just startled me." She had to start somewhere. Baby steps.

"You sure, babe? You're so tense I might snap you in half."

"I'm okay." She put some force behind the words this time.

"All right." He squeezed her shoulder and let the subject drop.

Colin Farrell's doppelganger approached, one dark eyebrow arched and the same side of his dark goatee raised in a smirk. "You guys talking about my sexual prowess yet again?"

Striker snorted, grasped Lucky's hand, and leaned in for a back-slapping man-hug. "You wish, my friend. Good to have you here."

"Thanks, brother."

"Damn, girl, you get more gorgeous each time I see you. Got any sugar for your Uncle Lucky?" He held his arms out and accepted a hug and a peck from a giggling Marcie. "And you must be Emily." He lingered a bit with Emily's hug, until Jester's growl made her laugh out loud. With a wink for Fia, Lucky released Emily to her grumbling man.

"And who might this be, Acer?" He stepped in front of Fia, so close she could count his eyelashes. "Another gorgeous ol' lady for your chapter? Damn, they grow 'em pretty around here. Although, Acer, I gotta say this one looks a bit uncomfortable with you. He not keeping you satisfied, darlin'? You know, Ace, if they're standing like a marble statue next to you, you must be doing something wrong. You can come to Uncle Lucky too, darlin'. I'll get you to loosen up for sure."

Silence descended on the parking lot like a thick, dense fog, distorting reality. Old Fia would have had a snappy comeback and a wicked insult to hurl right back at Lucky, faster than a boomerang. New Fia's legs trembled like a newborn foal at his intrusion in her personal space.

Acer's brother. He was Acer's MC brother. He wasn't Mike, and Acer would never let him hurt her.

Lucky reached out and tried to lift Acer's left arm from around her shoulders. In the next instant, quicker than she could blink, Lucky was laid out on the ground, blood pouring from his nose.

Fia gasped and stared at Acer like he had two heads. Guilt and embarrassment heated her face until she was sure it glowed like a burning ember. What the hell? He'd just sucker punched his good friend. For her. All because she was two shakes away from a full-on freak out.

Jesus. Her mess was hemorrhaging into his life, becoming his mess.

"Fuck, Acer! What the hell, man?" Lucky's thoughts mimicked her own.

"Don't you fucking touch her." Poison dripped from his tone, and if she hadn't known better, she would have said he looked like a jealous man.

Lucky sat up and raised his hands in surrender, blood dripping onto his clothes. "Dude, did we just meet? You do know how I joke around, right?"

"Okay, normally I'd let you two pound each other until you were both as ugly as Hook here—" Jester started.

"Fuck you," Hook said.

Jester flipped Hook the bird. "But Fia looks like she might cry, so I'm breaking this shit up. Baby, why don't you and Fia go to our house for a while. Let the boys work out their shit. Acer can come get her in a bit."

"Sure," Emily said. "That okay with you, Fia?"

She looked at Acer, but he wouldn't meet her eyes. She'd ridden in on his bike, so she had no other transportation, nowhere else to go. She laid a hand on Acer's arm but he still refused to look at her, almost like he was embarrassed by his impulsive behavior. Fine then, he could just come pick her up at Emily's whether he wanted to or not. "Sure, let's go."

As she walked away, she glimpsed Lila striding from her car toward the melee.

"Oh, come on! I've been at the hospital for fifteen hours. Now I come here and need to play doctor to you two morons?" She threw her hands in the air. "Not doing it. I'll lend Lucky a tampon he can shove up his nose, but that's all. I'm off duty." She stepped directly over Lucky's supine form and strode straight for the clubhouse.

Despite her swirling emotions, Fia chuckled.

This was one crazy family.

~ ~ ~ ~

Acer wasn't quite sure when his brain decided knocking Lucky on his ass would be a good idea. Maybe it hadn't. The action seemed more like a reflex than a conscious choice anyway. A man intimidated Fia and Acer's knee jerk reaction was to end it, violently. Not to mention the thought of a man touching her didn't sit well with him for reasons that had nothing to do with her anxiety, but that was something he didn't have time to think about.

The way he saw it, Lucky was damned lucky he didn't take out his hatred for Mike on him and keep at him until he was a limp mess.

Fia walked away from him, Emily's arm around her, her shoulders slumped in dejection. He'd fucked up by not acknowledging her. Hell, it wasn't her fault that he had an animal instinct to kill anyone that made her feel threatened.

Maybe it was for the best. Better for her to realize now that she shouldn't put her trust in anyone.

With a sigh, he rolled his shoulders and extended a hand to Lucky—not the hand that throbbed from his buddy's granite jaw.

Lucky stared at the offered palm for a moment, like it might be a trap, but he relented and allowed Acer to pull him to his feet.

"Aww, look at you two making nicey-nicey now." Jester grinned and rubbed a hand across his stomach. "All this fighting has made me hungry. Think I'll follow the women to my house and see if I can't get them to make me a feast."

Acer snorted. "Good luck."

Lila returned from the clubhouse, a roll of paper towels in one hand and two long necks in the other. "Here." She shoved the paper towels in Lucky's hands and passed the beers off to Acer. With a frustrated sigh, she pointed to a picnic table near the entrance. "Sit, drink, sort out your nonsense. Nice to see you Lucky. Don't tilt your head back, lean it forward and pinch your nose with the paper towels for twenty minutes."

"Thanks, mom." Lucky smirked.

Striker swore under his breath and Lila shot a death glare at both Lucky and Acer. Acer felt about five inches tall, having been the cause of all this drama. Striker kissed his wife, then everyone left Acer alone with Lucky.

They sat next to each other at the wooden picnic table. Acer rested the frosty beer across his throbbing knuckles. The annoying pain was less than he deserved, going off on a brother like he did.

"Okay, I'll risk another fist to the face by talking first. I obviously stepped in a serious shit pile that I'm completely in the dark about. Wanna fill me in on why you went postal on my face the minute I looked at your woman?" He held out a bottle opener attached to his key chain.

"Thanks." Acer popped the top on his icy bottle and took a long drink. The cool liquid lowered the heat of his temper. "She's not my girl. She's just—" How was he supposed to describe Fia to Lucky when he didn't know what the hell she was to him? "She was raped. Recently. She's just staying with me while she figures some shit out."

"Jesus." Lucky held a wad of paper towels against his nose, his voice nasal. "She the girl you guys helped out a few weeks ago?"

Acer nodded and took another drink. "Yes. She just needs a place to crash while she tries to get past this shit. I know her, from…from even before all that. Blew her off at the last fight and she got snatched on her way to her hotel. I owe her."

Lucky snorted then coughed. "Ow, fuck. Bad idea. So here I came with my inappropriate jokes, and I got too close and freaked her out, huh?"

"Something like that."

"Shit, sorry, brother. I'd have clocked me too." He pulled the towels away from his nose and faced Acer.

"Still bleeding."

"Jesus, brother. I'd say you hit like a girl, but my fucking face hurts like a mofo." He tossed the bloodied towels on the bench next to him and grabbed fresh ones. "I'll apologize to…"

"Fia."

"Fia, tomorrow."

Acer shook his head. "Not necessary. She won't hold a grudge. In fact, she'll probably tear me a new one for hitting you." He'd gladly take it to see some fire in her eyes.

"Sounds feisty."

"She was."

"She'll get it back. You're like a dog with a bone until you get what you want, so she'll be okay." Lucky slapped Acer on the back.

If only it was that simple. Lucky hadn't seen Fia chained to the floor, bruised and terrified. People don't always come back from that kind of trauma. Yet the glimpses he'd seen of the Fia he once knew gave him hope.

He polished off his beer. "Anyway, enough about my shit. You were all sorts of shady on the phone. What's with the visit?"

Lucky's eyes clouded over and it had nothing to do with the purple shiner blooming around his orbit. With one last gentle swipe under his nose, he ditched the towels. "It's not a visit. At least I'm hoping it's not. I'd like to patch over."

Christ. Now he knew how Lucky felt, blindsided by a powerful blow. "You shittin' me? We've been trying to get you here for years and you always said you'd only leave Vegas in a body bag. Wait, you in trouble?"

Lucky hesitated just a second too long. "Nah, nothing like that. Just need a change."

It was tempting to call him on his bullshit. Moving your whole life and patching over to a different chapter was more than *just a change*. He'd give Lucky a pass for now, but at some point, he'd press the issue. For now, he'd do a little behind the scenes digging.

If Lucky came bearing trouble, the club needed to know.

Nothing like being an untrusting bastard.

Chapter Nineteen

"This is going to be perfect, Fia. We looked into having this made by an online mass producer, but wanted something that wasn't cheap or cheesy." Lila flipped through the pages of Fia's sketchbook a week later with a smile on her face. "I really love how you were able to make each one unique."

Fia nodded. "I've ordered the materials I need, which should be delivered in the next few days. After that, I'll just need a few weeks to complete all the work. Think Acer's gonna mind my sewing machine in his apartment?"

Lila waved her hand in a dismissive motion. "Please girl, I keep telling you that man would count the grains of sand in the desert if it made you smile."

Fia rolled her eyes. Lila had told her that a number of times, and it may be partly true, but not for the reasons Lila wanted to believe. No, her new friend had woven some romantic story in her head, when in reality, Acer had a misplaced sense of guilt over the night she was abducted. As soon as she was back to her old self, he'd be absolved of his guilt and their lives would continue on without each other.

She reminded herself of that daily, in hopes of quelling the disappointment that came each time she thought of leaving. So far, no luck.

"How are things going at the apartment?" Lila's face showed nothing but genuine concern.

Fia sighed. "Okay. I've been working on a few designs for clients, trying to get back into the swing of things."

Lila opened her mouth then closed it again.

"What?" Fia asked.

"Okay, can I ask you a question that's none of my business?" She shrugged and flashed Emily a sheepish grin.

"Well, I guess so because now you have me curious." She knew what the words would be before the left Lila's mouth.

"Anything happening between you and Acer. You know… *happening*, happening?"

Even though she anticipated the question, hearing the words and having to talk about this was difficult. Fia closed the sketchbook and gave Lila her full attention. "No. I'm not there yet. Sometimes I wonder if I'll ever be there. The only man I feel remotely comfortable around is Acer, but I'm so worried that I'll freak out. I think I may be more scared of my own reaction than of actually doing anything physical." She smacked her lips. "Wow, bet you didn't expect me to spew all that on you."

Lila laughed. "I'm an emergency room doctor, hon, I've had much worse on me. What I went through was a minor violation compared to what you endured, but I was touched against my will by a man. It took me a little while to get comfortable in my own skin. I'm not trying to tell you how to feel at all, or how long it should take you to heal, but I will say that Striker helped me through it all. Acer would do the same for you if you wanted him to. I know without a single doubt that that man will never hurt you, rush you, or push you into anything you aren't comfortable with." She squeezed Fia's hand. "I didn't know you before, but I see you starting to come out of your shell. You're healing, Fia. And I'm confident you'll get all aspects of your life back, including your sexuality."

Fia's eyes flooded. "Thank you so much, Lila," she whispered. "You don't know how much I needed to hear that. I get so caught up in my head, I forget that I have made progress and I am moving forward."

"You sure are, hon. Well, I hate to drop all that on you and run, but I'm covering half a shift today for a colleague whose kiddo has a dance recital." Lila hopped off her barstool and gave Fia a quick kiss on the cheek. "You okay here? The boys should be back in an hour or so."

"I'm good, thanks. I'm working on some designs for a client who is getting married in a few months. Plenty to keep me busy." She returned the peck to Lila's cheek. "And you work too hard."

Lila rolled her eyes. "Ha, you sound like my husband."

Fia laughed. "If I wanted to sound like your husband it'd be more like, 'babe, you fuckin' work too fuckin' hard. Fuck!'"

Lila burst out laughing as she gathered her purse. "Well, well, Miss Fia. Seems like you're getting to know us pretty well." She wiggled her fingers in a wave and walked toward the door.

Huh, she *was* getting to know this group well, and she really enjoyed them. They were loud, fun, outrageous, sometimes vulgar, and closer than most family. It would be hard to leave.

But she would be leaving.

Her life was in California.

She bent her head back down to her sketchbook. No point in dwelling on it. It's just the way things were.

"Excuse me. Hey, I'm talking to you."

Fia jumped and spun around on the barstool. "Oh, shit, sorry, I was in the zone."

She blinked and stared up at a Barbie doll come to life. Actually, two of them. She blinked again. Had she been staring at the sketchbook so long she was now seeing double?

"Hey, Cha Cha, Babs! Long time no see. Get you girls a drink?" The young prospect behind the bar was going to need a towel to wipe the drool if his tongue lolled out any farther.

Cha Cha? Babs? Were these girls poodles? No, they were at least five-foot-ten, platinum blonde, beautiful women with huge knockers, tiny waists and golden—if not slightly orange—spray tans.

"Aww, ain't you sweet, Prospect. We'll be having lots of drinks in a bit. We're looking for Acer." Blondie Number One's eyes lit up and she licked her lips like Acer was an ice cream cone she couldn't wait to devour.

"He's not here right now, and, uhh...well...this is Acer's..." The prospect coughed, clearly not having a clue what Fia actually was to Acer, but he pointed to her nonetheless. "Yeah, I'll be right back, gotta hit the can."

The chicken scurried off toward the bathroom. Blondie Two's face morphed into disbelief as she looked at Fia and laughed. "Good one. We'll hang out until he gets back. The three of us always have so much *fun* together. Know what I mean?" She snapped her gum and tossed her nearly white hair over her shoulder with a wink of a heavily made up eye, before strutting toward a group of club members on the other side of the room.

Saliva curdled in Fia's mouth as she watched the twitch of two tight asses under shorts that were probably a toddler size. If either woman bent over she'd get a clear view of a hoo-ha, and probably a nipple as their matching tube tops didn't appear too substantial either.

She glanced down at her own outfit. She'd worn shorts today as well, the first time since…well, the first time in a while. They practically reached her knees. This morning she'd considered it a small victory. Now her face burned with humiliation and her clothes felt more like a burlap sack than an outfit she was proud of.

Were these the kind of girls Acer went for? Of course they were. They were hot, willing, adventurous, and probably didn't have a panic attack when a man got too close.

The rancid taste in her mouth was nauseating and the air in the room grew too stale to breathe. She shoved her sketchbook in her bag and jumped down from the barstool. She needed to get away before she lost her shit in front of Acer's family and two members of the Malibu Barbie ménage.

Seconds before the door closed behind her, the prospect's angry outburst flew through the air. "Where the fuck did Fia go? Acer warned me she was not to leave under any circumstances. Fuck! I'm a dead man."

The sense of relief that hit her when she stepped outside was staggering. "Oh, crap," she murmured. She rode in on the back of Acer's bike. No matter. A walk would do her good. It was broad daylight, no reason to be nervous taking a walk alone.

She glanced at the overcast sky. Even Mother Nature wanted her to get some exercise. The cloud cover kept the temperature in the high eighties. Mild for the desert as she was coming to learn.

With sure steps that looked more confident than she felt, Fia made a left out of the clubhouse and started her journey. Her thoughts raced and she worked to keep from feeling sorry for herself. Just a little over three weeks had passed since the MC found her and rescued her from an endless nightmare. She needed to cut herself some slack. She seemed to be the only one who expected her to be back to who she was before Mike.

Mike. There still hadn't been any sight of him. Did he really leave the desert? Was he hiding somewhere close? Fia lifted her head and scanned her environment suddenly very aware she was alone and vulnerable.

This had been a bad idea.

She wasn't ready for this.

A familiar yet unwelcome tightening in her chest alerted her to the oncoming panic attack. She could not lose control out here. Anything could happen to her if her senses weren't on full alert.

Her heart rate kicked up to a sprint and the edges of her vision blurred. A deep breath was near impossible. She needed to brace against something, to support herself so she could ride it out.

On trembling legs, she stumbled off the sidewalk and into what appeared to be a park. A handful of people milled around, some looking at her with curious expressions.

Fia leaned her back against a tree and bent forward, her hands propped on her knees. The position helped draw in a steady breath. She shook out her hands, hoping to calm the pins and needles shooting from her wrists to her fingertips.

In, out, in, out.

Willing to try any trick she could think of, Fia conjured up an image of ocean waves gently rolling onto the beach and pulling back out to sea.

It didn't work.

She jerked and spasmed with the force of her choppy breaths. Her vision tunneled and her heart felt as though it would burst from her chest. She was seconds away from passing out, alone in a park where God knows who could drag her off to—

Her stomach heaved and she gagged.

If she could just draw in some air…

~ ~ ~ ~

Lucky cruised to a stop at a red light and glanced around. Coming to Crystal Rock had been the right decision. Already, he felt more at peace than he had in months. He'd only thought of Kori twice—make that three times—since arriving.

Next week, the brothers would vote and if all went his way, he'd patch over to this chapter and leave Vegas in the past. Even though he was only a few hours away, it was far enough to ease some of the pain in his soul.

The light turned green and he squeezed the clutch. What the hell?

He eased his bike to the side of the road and dropped the kickstand, pulling out his phone at the same time.

Acer answered on the second ring. "What's up brother? Not finding enough to keep you entertained in our shit town?"

Lucky ignored Acer's teasing. "Hey, man, where are you?"

The playful note left Acer's voice. "On my way back to the clubhouse, about ten minutes out. Why? You got trouble?"

"I'm across the street from that park about a mile from the clubhouse, looking at your girl. I don't know what she's doing here, but it don't look good, brother. I think she's about to flip her shit."

"Fuck!"

Lucky flinched and held the phone away from his ear.

"Why the fuck isn't she at the clubhouse?"

"Don't know, brother. Something must have happened. Want me to try and talk to her?"

"No. Yes. Shit, I don't know. Just don't scare her. I'll be there in ten minutes." Acer disconnected the call.

"Right," Lucky said to dead air. He was damn good with the ladies, but ladies in the throes of an emotional crisis were an entirely different manner.

He jogged across the street and approached Fia, slowly, so as not to startle her. The sounds of her gasping breaths and sobs tore at his heart. No wonder Acer's head was all fucked up over this gal. He didn't even know her and he wanted to scoop her up and fight her demons. "Fia?"

Her body jolted and she lifted her head, her eyes wide and full of terror. Tears streamed down her face and her breathing was too fast and ragged.

"L-luc-ky?" she managed to get out between pants.

"Yeah, baby. I'm just gonna stand here with you, okay? You concentrate on taking deep breaths and I'll make sure nobody bothers you."

"T-thank y-you." The words were high pitched and raspy.

"Shh, don't try to talk, just breathe."

Lucky mean-mugged a few bystanders who gawked at Fia like she was an attraction they purchased a ticket to see. No one stuck around long when they took in his cut and realized who glowered at them. After a few moments, the hitches in her breathing grew less frequent and she was able to rise to a full stand.

She covered her face with her hands. "God, Lucky, I'm so embarrassed."

"Shh," he said again. "Let's sit on that bench right there. Acer is on his way." He pointed to a dark green bench about fifteen feet away.

Fia's legs wobbled and he wanted to wrap an arm around her for support but some instinct told him to maintain his distance.

She plopped down on one end of the bench and he took the other, conscious to leave a few feet of space between them.

"You want to talk about it?" Part of him hoped she'd say no. He had enough of his own troubles without taking on anyone else's.

Chapter Twenty

Did she want to talk about it? About how she fled the clubhouse because she was jealous of the boobsie twins and their wild threesomes with Acer? About how thoughts of Mike caused a full-blown panic attack—the worst one yet—in the middle of a public park?

No, she didn't want to talk about it. She didn't want to think about it. She didn't want it to ever have happened.

"I've been told I'm a good listener."

She couldn't help but smile at the arrogant grin on Lucky's face. He was so full of himself, it crossed the line from irksome to amusing.

"Also been told I'm handsome as hell, smart, good in bed, a damn fine cook, hung like a horse, and amazing with power tools." He held up his hands and shrugged as if to say, "what are ya gonna do?"

Fia laughed. "Anyone ever told you how cocky you are?"

He winked. "I thought I covered that with hung like a horse."

She rolled her eyes. "Okay, Mr. Ed, I'll talk. If it will get you to stop telling me how wonderful you are, I'll talk."

"Manipulative. I'm manipulative too."

She snorted and looked over the park. Maybe it would be cathartic to talk about it. There were times she wanted to open up to Acer, but he already felt guilty and pitied her. The thought of making it worse was unappealing. Lucky didn't give a shit about her, not really. So maybe it would help to get it out.

"I was, uh, at the clubhouse this afternoon and these two women came by. They were…well they were stunning." She kept her eyes trained straight ahead.

Lucky draped his arm across the back of the bench and faced her. "All right, I like how this story is starting out."

She faced him and rolled her eyes. "I'm sure you do. Anyway, they asked for Acer, insinuated that they'd all…you know." She rolled her hand in a flourish.

"Ahh, yes, ménage-a-biker." He bobbed his eyebrows up and down.

Lucky was a scream and she appreciated his levity more than she could express. It put her at ease, made him easy to talk to.

"I looked at them, and I looked at me——" she gestured to her clothing, "——the me now, that is, post-assault. I just felt so inadequate. Here they are offering kinky sex on a platter, and I…well, I…"

She what? How to even put it into words?

"You're not sure you're ever gonna be able to fuck again." That's how.

"Jesus, Lucky." Her face flamed.

"Well that's it, ain't it? Don't need to sugar coat it for me, babe. It's only been, what? Three weeks? You gotta ease off yourself."

She pulled at a thread on her frumpy shorts. "I know, I know. I just saw them and needed to get the hell away for a bit. So I went for a walk, my mind wandered to…bad memories, and, well, you saw the result."

"I'm gonna say something now, before Acer gets here, because if he heard me say it, he'd kick my ass so bad I wouldn't be able to ride for a month." He leaned back on the bench and rubbed a hand over his defined chest.

She kept her gaze on him. What on earth could he possibly have to say?

"When you're ready, and you will be ready, I have no doubt. When you're ready, if you need someone? You come find me."

What? "Um, Lucky—"

He leaned forward and squeezed her shoulder. "I'm dead serious, babe. I'm putting the offer on the table, just in case you were thinking that no one would want to fuck you after what you went through. So that's one less thing you have to worry about, okay?"

"I, uh." She nodded, at a loss for words. She had to admit, in a weird way, his offer lifted at least one of her worries.

"Here comes Acer." Lucky stood. "I'm gonna talk to him for a sec then I'll send him right over. We won't be out of eyesight."

He started to leave, but she grabbed his hand and he turned back. "Thanks, Lucky." His unique blend of arrogant humor came just at the right time.

He squeezed her hand and winked. "Told you I was good, baby."

Fia smiled and watched him amble across the park until he met Acer. Even from fifty feet away she could see the fearsome frown on Acer's sensual mouth.

~ ~ ~ ~

Acer's eyes narrow, his fists clenched and he broke into a jog when he witnessed Fia take Lucky's hand and smile up at him as though he was her savior. He itched to ram his fist into his friend's face, again. Another black eye to complete the set.

Lucky strode toward him and met him about halfway between his bike and Fia.

"Get the fuck out of my way," Acer snapped, coming to a stop inches from Lucky's smug grin. They were the same height and stood nose to nose. Acer snarled. Lucky's smirk shone like a giant bull's-eye.

"You need to reign in your shit, brother. Six feet of pissed off biker is the last thing she needs right now."

"And you're an expert on her needs?" Jesus, where had that childish remark come from? Lucky was dead on. A seething man would only freak her out. He didn't want to admit it, but he wanted to be the one to comfort Fia, and the fact that Lucky got to her first—got to her at all— stung like a swarm of angry bees.

"Oh man, you are so far gone over this woman." Lucky laughed.

Acer lunged for him.

He held up his hands in a gesture of surrender. "I'm done, I'm done." The smirk left his face. "It's fun to bust your balls, but your girl was in a bad way when I found her. Turns out two stacked blonde skanks came 'round the clubhouse asking her where you were and tossing out hints about your sex games."

What the fuck?

"She started to compare herself to them. She's worried she'll never be able to fuck again. Then she got an up close and personal view of what type of playthings you like."

Fia talked to Lucky about sex? That knowledge settled in his gut like ground glass. Frustration and a bit of jealousy rumbled in his chest.

Lucky laughed. "Come on, you can't be surprised she feels

that way. Anyway, she split and went for a walk, started thinking about the asshole who hurt her and she freaked the fuck right out."

"So what'd you tell her?" Acer ran a hand down his face.

"Told her to cut herself some slack, then told her I'd be more than happy to fuck her. She just has to say the word." The smirk was back.

Acer lifted his gaze to the sky. "Swear to God, if you weren't my brother—"

Lucky laughed. "You got it from here? Now that I've done my good deed for the day, I'm feeling the need to reward myself with a lap dance or ten. I'm meeting some of the guys at Black's."

"Have fun," Acer said, but his focus was on Fia. He took a breath and calmed the beast raging inside him. From the moment he took Lucky's call, until he could see for himself she was unharmed, a restless energy had been zinging through his blood.

She gave him a small, sad smile as he sat next to her on the bench. Unlike Lucky, he didn't give her space. He sat close, plastering his side against hers. She wasn't caged in and had plenty of room to move if she felt uncomfortable, but he needed to feel her, at least a little.

"I'm so sorry I interrupted whatever you were doing. And I'm sorry if I embarrassed you or the club. And please don't be mad at the prospect who wasn't supposed to let me leave. I snuck away when he was in the bathroom."

He frowned. Leave it to Fia to worry about someone else. "Don't worry about him, I'll deal with him, later."

"Is he in trouble?" She fingered the hem on her shorts.

"Yes." He damn sure was in trouble.

"Any chance you could cut him some slack?" She gave him a sweet smile.

"No, babe. It was his job to look after you. That meant not letting you leave. It also meant making sure you weren't disrespected or embarrassed. I'm not gonna kick his ass, but I'm not going to let it slide either."

She sighed. "Lucky told you, huh?"

He nodded even though her gaze was on two children throwing a ball on the other side of the park and she couldn't see it. "It was more than a year ago."

"What?" She turned her head.

"Those girls." He dragged a hand through his hair, yanking hard on the strands. "It was once, more than a year ago. It was the anniversary of something I'd rather forget, and I got so shitfaced I'd have slept with a rattler if it slithered into my bed. I barely remember it, and will not be buying another ticket for that ride."

"Shit, Acer, you do not owe me any kind of explanation about your sex life. We aren't, I mean I can't even..." She held out her hands and shrugged.

He gripped her shoulders and turned her so her upper body faced him. It was the boldest move he'd made in terms of touching her, and he didn't miss the tension in her posture, but he ignored it. What he had to say was too important. "Fia, you are fucking amazing. You're stronger than any women I've met. You're sweet, sassy, brave, and so damned sexy I've been hard more often than not since you moved in. I respect the hell out of you, baby. We've been intimate, you're currently living in my apartment, and no matter how often we tell ourselves it would never work, there is some kind of connection between us. So, yeah, you deserve an explanation."

Silence followed his monolog and he risked a glance at her.

She stared at him, slack-jawed and eyes glossy with unshed tears.

"One more thing." Christ, if he continued with this emotional diarrhea his dick would shrivel up and fall off.

Fia took a deep breath. The curve of her breasts rose and fell, drawing his gaze. His cock twitched in his pants and he shifted to accommodate it. Maybe he wasn't in any imminent danger of losing his man card.

"What is it?" Her voice was soft, as if she was in awe.

He grasped her chin between his thumb and forefinger, lifting until they made eye contact. "When you get there, and I promise you'll get there, when you're ready to fuck? No way in hell do you go to Lucky or any other man."

Her eyes widened and a split second of uncertainty flashed. Acer leaned in until his mouth was against her ear on the side of her body closest to the bench's backrest. She still wasn't boxed in and could hop up if his nearness overwhelmed her, but it was definitely an invasion of her personal space.

She stopped breathing, her body rigid, but she didn't pull away.

"It's been seven months for me, baby. I'll die before I let another man have what's mine. I'll wait as long as you need to be ready, but I will not sit back while you seek out another man." His lips brushed against the sensitive skin of her ear as he spoke and a subtle shiver coursed through her.

She was closer than she thought. Closer to Old Fia.

He drew back, curious at her reaction, and if the issue of his celibacy weren't so grim, he'd have burst out laughing at the caricature of shock on her face.

He linked his fingers with hers and tugged her to her feet. "Come on, babe, let's go home."

It wasn't her home. California was her home.

The disappointment that hit each time he thought of her leaving was growing harder to ignore.

Chapter Twenty-One

Fia thanked God Acer's headboard was made of strong, solid wood. She gripped it so tight, it might have snapped in two were it composed of weaker material. With a low moan, she peered down at Acer as he licked through her saturated folds. The sexy sight of her legs straddled around his face amped up her desire.

This was exactly what she needed, what she'd craved for so long. Acer's hands were full of her ass, and he squeezed tight, bringing her more firmly against his mouth where he proceeded to drive her straight to insanity.

"Good, baby?"

"Yes, yes, so freakin' good." She panted as she rocked her pelvis against his mouth. Acer wrapped his lips around her clit and sucked. She gasped and threw back her head as she flew toward an explosive release. Almost there, just one more

—

What the hell?

The incredible sensations disappeared as Acer's mouth left her body and he squirmed out from between her legs. "No! What are you doing? I was so close!"

Acer curled his strong body around her back. "I know," he

whispered in her ear. "I want you to come with my cock inside you. I want to feel you squeezing me like you can't get enough."

"Ohh," she moaned as he pushed his full length inside her. He started a heavy rhythm that had her climbing again in no time.

"Yes, Acer," she cried as she pushed back to meet his thrusts. She was teetering on the edge. If only he'd touch her clit, one quick glance of his fingers would do it.

Fia's heart pounded and she stared into the dark and quiet room. Acer's eight hundred thread count Egyptian cotton sheets were tangled around her legs, and her hand, not his, was buried between her thighs and she was lying in his guest bedroom. Alone.

Damn, that dream had seemed so real. Her body hummed with unfulfilled need. The source of the dream was no mystery. Knowledge that Acer still wanted her, that he refused to let her sleep with another man, had been running through her mind all evening. She was the last woman he'd slept with, for crying out loud. That knowledge freed something in her.

She could go in there now. In just a few minutes, he'd have her screaming out his name with the much-needed release. Unless of course she freaked out and had a panic attack the second he touched her.

It just might be a risk worth taking.

On the other hand, she could just take care of the problem herself. She hadn't masturbated since…everything, but before that? Between the time she'd slept with Acer in LA and the day she went to the boxing gym? She might as well have taken out stock in the vibrator company, she'd used the damned thing so many times. All with fantasies of Acer as her chosen pornography.

Well, it was nice to know she could still feel desire. If only she could keep herself from having an anxiety attack whenever a man got close to her.

Fia kicked her legs, loosening the mummy wrap of the sheets. She sat up and scrubbed a hand over her face. The clock next to the bed read almost two in the morning. Acer would most likely be asleep. She'd just go out into the kitchen, make herself a cup of chamomile tea, and relax.

Lila's words rumbled around in her head, reminding her she had made progress, she was strong, and she was healing. "What you need to do is go in there and have sex with Acer," she muttered. "Stop hiding and just do it." Her stomach rolled over with nerves. Was she really ready for this?

She shoved off the bed and wrenched the door open, tiptoeing toward the bathroom. She'd seen condoms in there a few days before. After rummaging through the cabinets and finding a foil packet, she stared at herself in the mirror. "You can do this. It's Acer. You've already slept with him," she told the woman in the mirror, who looked a bit green around the edges.

She was getting so sick of that woman. It was time for that woman to take a hike and for Old Fia to come back to life. She closed her eyes, counted to five, then opened them again. The same woman stared at her, but this time, Fia realized something different. The woman in the mirror looked exactly like Old Fia. The eyes were the same, the smile was the same, the hair was the same. New Fia hadn't completely taken over. If Old Fia was still there in her looks, she had to be alive inside her as well. With a surge of confidence, Fia started down the hallway, only to come to a frozen halt outside Acer's closed door.

Open it, Old Fia whispered in her mind. She reached for the doorknob only to have New Fia screaming, *Run!*

She couldn't do this. She wasn't ready. For crying out loud, she was a thirty-year-old woman, standing in the hallway at one in the morning, nerves strung tight as guitar strings. Was it hot in here? She fanned herself and rolled her eyes. Looked like it was going to need to be ice water instead of hot tea. Then she could return to her lonely bed where erotic dreams and unfulfilled desires would torture her.

Damn anxiety.

Old Fia's disappointment sitting on her chest like an elephant, she took two steps toward the kitchen. She clenched her fists, the crinkle of the condom wrapper loud as a cannon's roar.

Screw it.

Without indulging in another thought, she spun around, gripped the doorknob, and slowly twisted so as not to startle Acer. When she met resistance, she pushed the door and took one giant step into the room.

Okay. She made it. She was in. Nothing in this room reminded her of being in Mike's house and that was extremely important.

Now what?

A soft snore drew her attention to Acer's large bed. She loved that bed. It was four-poster modern platform bed. A striking piece that drew the eye. The contradictions of style a perfect representation of the man himself. Old world polished, merged with modern edgy.

Acer lay on his back, one arm thrown above his head and the other resting on the ripples of his bare stomach. Fia leaned against one of the posts and watched the steady rise and fall of his chest for a moment. The predictable movements soothed her raw nerves.

Damn, he was handsome. She allowed her eyes to take a visual tour of his body, starting at his face, moving to his chest where she paused to remember how he'd bucked each time she flicked that nipple piercing, then trailing her gaze down, down, down, until—

Acer was completely nude.

Hello! The sheet, having slipped down his body, now pooled across his lower thighs. Fia tiptoed closer for a peek. His legs were out straight, about shoulder width apart, and his soft cock rested against his thigh.

Her stomach clenched at the sight of his naked body. That body had given her so much pleasure at one point, and if his shouted responses had been any indication, she'd pleasured him as well. Could she do that now? Thoughts of taking him inside her once again conjured up equal amounts desire and apprehension.

Well, maybe a little more apprehension, if she was being honest. Okay, a helluva lot more apprehension. That didn't mean she couldn't overcome it.

It was now or never. A part of her knew that if she didn't go through with this now, it would be ages before she gathered the courage to try again.

With trembling hands—trembling more with desire or nerves, she couldn't say—she shimmied out of her panties. She placed the condom on the bed next to Acer's hip and drew the sheet away from his legs.

Would it be crazy to wake him up after she was already astride him? She covered her mouth to hold back a spurt of laughter. Wasn't it every man's fantasy to wake up with a naked and eager woman straddling them?

So, she was willing, but not exactly eager, and there was no way in hell she'd be getting any more naked than she already was. The cigarette-singed skin on her ribs had mostly scarred over, but seeing another man's initial branded on a woman had to kill a boner faster than a bucket of ice. The cami was staying on, no matter what happened.

Ignoring the instinct to flee, she braced a knee on the bed and swung the other leg up and over a still sleeping Acer. His thighs were rock solid between her own. She slowly lowered her hips until Acer's muscles grew rigid like steel beneath her.

Shit! He was awake. Fia's stomach rolled. She couldn't do this. She wasn't ready.

Chapter Twenty-Two

Acer woke with a start. His heart pounded and his hand reflexively grabbed for the nightstand next to the bed where he kept his nine-millimeter pistol. He had a few weapons stashed around the apartment but liked the smallest and lightest next to his bed for quick access and easy maneuverability.

Before he had a chance to wrap his hand around the piece, the fog cleared and he realized what had woken him. "Christ, Fia! I could have shot you. What are you doing in here?"

His eyes adjusted and his cock hardened in the same instant. Fia straddled his thighs wearing nothing but a skimpy, tight-as-hell, light purple tank top, her bare ass hovering just an inch above his thighs.

Her hair was loose, a rumpled mess around her shoulders, like she'd just woken up as well. Her eyes were wide and her chest rose and fell in a rapid dance as though she'd been running.

She looked sexy, she looked terrified, she looked... determined.

He held statue still, waiting for her to answer his question, afraid to scare her.

She pressed her lips together and held up a condom. Where the hell had she gotten that?

"I-I want to have sex."

Her words entered through his ears and shot straight to his dick. Christ, he wanted that too, but... "Babe——"

She ignored him and pointed to his erect dick, which thickened further just from being the momentary center of her attention. "It seems like you're up for sex as well."

Fuck yeah, he wanted sex. But like this?

"Fia, you don't have to——" He tried to reason with her, but his brain was still half asleep and two steps behind.

"You game?" she asked.

The firm set of her jaw let him know she wasn't kidding, but the minute waver in her voice betrayed her true trepidation.

She wasn't actually here for sex, or at least not pleasurable sex, she was here to excise a demon. Part of him wanted to refuse. When he fucked her again, he wanted it to be hot, wild, and needy, not...therapeutic. But he'd promised himself he'd do anything in his power to help her overcome the trauma and get back to being herself. And if this was what she needed, he'd do it. God forbid he turned her down and she sought it elsewhere.

"I'm in."

"Good." She rushed on, her eyes trained on his pierced nipple. "I have it all figured out. I will do all the work. But I need you to not touch me. I don't think I'm ready for that." She looked up at his face and he saw the uncertainty in her gaze. "Okay?"

Acer gripped a side of his pillow in each hand. "My hands won't leave the pillow."

"Thank you."

This situation was so tense it was almost comical. Apparently, though, his cock didn't seem to care. It was rock hard and would take any opportunity to be inside Fia. He stared at the ceiling as he listened to her rip open the condom wrapper.

Never had he been in this submissive position before. He liked control, and even if a woman was on top, he was in control. Promising Fia his hands would remain on the pillow added an entirely new level to this encounter. He didn't think there was any other woman in the world he'd let have this much control over his body.

"Jesus Christ," he cried out as her small hand circled his length, rolling the latex on.

She stilled. "Oh God, did I hurt you?"

He laughed. "No, babe, I just wasn't expecting it and I almost cut our night very, very short."

Her blush was adorable. "Oh. You good now?"

No. "Yeah."

While he clenched the pillow, she finished rolling the condom on, then rose on her knees, positioning herself directly over the head of his straining cock. With a deep breath, she began to lower herself onto him. She winced when the tip prodded her entrance.

For Acer, the pleasure was so intense he saw stars, but it didn't detract from what was happening here. She wasn't ready. Not by a long shot. She was stressed, and dry, and treating this like it was an unpleasant chore she needed to power through. He'd seen her aroused, passionate, begging for more of his touch. This was unacceptable.

"Fia, stop," he ordered her.

"No, Acer, it's okay."

"Babe, it's not okay. You aren't ready for this."

"I'm ready. I am." She resumed her task, her face a mask

of concentrated effort, but not one iota of enjoyment was evident in any part of her body.

He wanted to grab her and yank her close and kiss her until her body responded, but he'd promised not to touch her and who knew how far back he'd set her if he frightened her. "Fia!" This time he put enough bite in his words to draw her attention.

"Oh God." She groaned and covered her face with her hands as her shoulders slumped. "This is so unbelievably not sexy. How do you even have an erection?"

He chuckled. "I'm pretty much hard whenever you're within fifty feet of me."

She lowered her hands so her eyes peeked over her fingertips. "You are?"

"Yep. Now scoot forward and sit on my stomach." She bit her lip and shook her head. "Do it."

Fia walked her knees up the sides of his hips until she was positioned low over his abdomen.

"Sit."

She sat, and the heat from her sex seared him like a brand. He clenched his teeth and breathed through his nose, willing his body to remain under his command.

"You're not ready, Fia." She opened her mouth. "Uh uh." He shook his head. "You may think you are, you may have convinced yourself that you are, but your body is telling a very different story. Why are you forcing this tonight?"

She sighed and traced a finger over the hills of his abdominal muscles. They quivered under her touch. His biceps ached with the force he exerted on the damn pillow. This was an exercise in self-control like he'd never experienced.

"Acer, I've always liked sex. I had sex, not enough to make me a slut, but enough that I know what I like and I know how I like it. Then I met you, and you were raw and dominant and so unlike anyone I've ever been with."

The thought of her with other men made him want to scream, but he held his tongue. Wherever she was going with this, she needed to get it out.

"That night with you? It was...powerful. It was like you awoke something wanton inside of me. The things we did, the things you said you wanted to do if we had more time? I thought about each and every one of those things for six months. I craved how you made me feel. You whispered to me about things I'd never tried, never wanted to try, but with you, I wanted it all. That was the real reason I came to the gym, I couldn't stay away from you anymore."

Guilt assailed him at the mention of that night, but he shoved it aside. She didn't need that from him right now.

She reached out and skimmed her finger over the side of the barbell through his nipple. His eyes rolled back and he prayed for the strength to survive this sexual torture.

"My body remembers each and every touch. Every time your mouth was on me, every time you were inside me, and how amazing it felt, how much I wanted to feel it again and again. But my mind? My mind is stuck in this state of constant fear and panic. It's so deep, I'm afraid I'll never break free. So, please, I just need to do this. To try and get past some of the fear and get some part of myself back."

Her eyes filled with tears, but she blinked in rapid succession, managing to keep any wetness from falling. That was his Fia, so strong, so determined.

"Baby, I'm not telling you no. I just want to try something, see if I can make it good for you. Okay?" His voice sounded strangled and tense.

"I don't need to enjoy it, Acer. I just need to do it."

That was a tragedy in and of itself. That she was at the

point where she felt her sexual pleasure didn't matter. It damned well mattered to him. "Well, I need you to enjoy it, so humor me, okay?"

She gifted him a small grin. "Well, okay, if you insist that I actually get pleasure from the sex, I guess that's fine."

"There's my smartass. Okay, close your eyes. I promise my hands will not leave the pillow, I'm just going to talk to you, but I want you to concentrate on my voice."

She assessed him for a second, then dropped her eyelids.

He admired her so much, couldn't imagine the courage it took for her to come to him like this despite her obvious anxiety. The trust she placed in him was baffling. After what she endured, to trust him with her body, with her greatest fear.

It humbled him.

It shamed him. She gave far more than he deserved. More than he gave her.

His caveman reaction to her presence at his fight was the reason she was assaulted in the first place, and he'd walk through the fires of hell to make her whole again.

"I want you to think back to the night in LA. What? Did we do it four times?"

"Five," she said with a smile, her eyes still closed, hands resting on his ribs. "But I came six."

"Five, that's right. You have a favorite?"

She flushed a pretty pink and nodded.

"Tell me."

"In the middle of the night, against the window." Her voice was low, husky.

"Damn, that was my favorite too. I woke up alone in the bed, but it only took me a second to find you standing by that entire wall of windows, staring at the city lights. You were completely naked, your gorgeous ass right in my field of vision. I ever tell you I just watched you for a few minutes?"

"No," she whispered with a shake of her head.

"Well I did, but not for too long, because the need to touch you was consuming. As I walked toward you, I couldn't keep my eyes off your backside. I had this unbelievably hot fantasy about fucking that ass some time. Did I tell you that?"

Her voice was breathy. "You told me. Whispered it in my ear when you were inside me."

"Oh yeah? Was that one of the things you thought about? One of the things you'd never tried?"

She nodded and a drop of fluid beaded on his dick inside the condom he still wore. This plan had better work. He wasn't quite asshole enough to go jerk off if she couldn't go through with this, which meant he'd be stuck in blue-ball hell.

He swallowed, bringing himself back under control. "I came up behind you and plastered myself against your back. Your skin was soft and warm against my chest, incredible. You remember what I did next?"

Her enthusiastic nod made him smile. "I remember every second."

"I picked up your hands, one at a time, and pressed your palms against the cool window, told you to leave them there. That was the only words we spoke. Then, starting just above your ass, I ran my hands up your back, over your shoulders, and down to your breasts. Your nipples were so hard they could have cut right through that glass. You cried out when I pinched them, loud." He paused, remembering the exact moment. "God, I loved hearing that satisfied sound, loved that you weren't shy about making it. Every time I did something you liked, I was rewarded with that sound. After I had you panting, I stroked my hands down your sexy stomach to your hungry pussy, didn't I?"

"Yes," she whispered, her voice beginning to sound just a bit needy. Her nipples were visible against the thin fabric of her top. She was responding to his words.

"You were wet, fuckin' drenched. It coated your thighs. Your pussy was so slick and greedy it sucked my finger right in and clamped tight around it."

He glanced down at where her sex rested against his stomach. With small, tiny, almost imperceptible movements, she rocked her pelvis against his abs, pausing when she tilted forward and her clit met his skin. Christ, she was gorgeous. This encounter had gone from tense to unbelievably erotic and he worried he might not last long enough to make it good for her.

He swallowed hard. "I had you completely at my mercy with your palms on the window and my fingers deep in you. Or so I thought. Then you arched your back and wiggled that curvy ass all over my cock. That ended my game real quick. All I could think about was getting inside you, feeling you gripping me as I drove into you."

Her sex became slippery. Arousal coated his skin, assisting the tilts of her pelvis on his stomach. Acer wanted to shout out the victory. She slid back and forth on him, the movements more pronounced, quicker, and a small whimper escaped her as she ground against him.

Her scent filled the room and Acer's sac drew tight. Christ, there was a very high chance he'd blow without ever feeling her around his shaft. "You remember when you came? Remember how it felt? Remember what you screamed?" he asked, his voice harsh and strained.

"I screamed your name." Her voice shook for different reasons now.

"Goddamn right, you did." He was almost growling; the animalistic need to be back inside her clawed at him. "Say it now. I was the one fucking you then, and I'm the only who's gonna fuck you now. Say it."

"Acer," she choked out. Her eyes flew open, holding his gaze. "Acer," she said again, his name almost a plea on her lips.

His dick twitched so hard it bumped against her ass. Fia jolted, but no fear was evident on her face. Just a dazed look of desire.

She held his stare and lifted her hips, shimmying back until she once again had his rod at her opening. This time, though, she slid down with ease.

Fiery heat surrounded him and overtook all his senses. He gripped the pillow so hard, he expected feathers to fly around the room any second.

~ ~ ~ ~

Fia let out a low moan as she took Acer into her. She had walked in here tonight a ball of nerves, determined to take control of her life and just get it over with. But he'd changed all that. He'd squashed her fears, turned her on, and made it so she actually wanted the sensation of him filling her up.

And it didn't disappoint.

"Ride me, Fia. Please," he ground out through gritted teeth. On either side of his head, he gripped the pillow so hard his biceps bulged and his neck corded with tension.

It was in that moment she understood just how far out of character this man went for her, and how he'd sacrificed himself for her pleasure. He needed to always be in control of every situation, in bed and out, yet he lay under her forcing himself to avoid touching her. He gave her complete command, and the strain showed.

She rewarded him with the slow, steady rise and fall of her hips along his rigid shaft. It felt good, so good, so different from— No. She wouldn't go there. There wasn't any room for those thoughts now.

"Stay with me, baby."

She brought her gaze back to Acer's. Sweat dotted his forehead and his nostrils flared. On a normal day, he'd probably grab her hips and slam into her with everything he had. She needed to put the poor man out of his misery. "I'm with you."

"With who?"

"You, Acer."

"That's right, baby. Keep looking at me."

Fia braced her hands against Acer's stomach and moved with purpose now. A familiar pressure coiled low in her belly, but the prize stayed just out of reach. It was okay, she hadn't expected to come. She couldn't completely turn off her brain and give into the moment.

"Touch yourself, Fia."

"What?"

"Touch yourself. Make yourself come."

"It's okay, Acer, I didn't expect to."

He shook his head, his breath coming in ragged spurts. "I promised you I wouldn't touch you, and I promised myself I wouldn't come without you, so, for God's sake, unless you want me to die from a severe case of blue balls, please get yourself off."

Despite the tenseness of the moment, Fia laughed, the action causing her to squeeze tight around him.

"Fuck." He groaned, a tortured sound.

She removed one hand from his chest, brought it to her clit, and rubbed in tight circles, before stroking directly over it. Pleasure shot through her limbs and she rode Acer with abandon. After just a minute or two, the pleasure crested in a wave and she cried out as her pussy clamped around him.

It wasn't an earth-shattering orgasm, not the biggest or

best she'd ever had, but it was far more than she'd anticipated.

A mere second later, as if he'd been holding out just for her, Acer groaned and he shook below her with his own climax. He finally let go of the pillow and his arms flopped to his sides.

He'd waited for her. And he'd enjoyed himself, if the satisfied smile playing across his lips was any indication. A small thrill of feminine power washed over her.

Now that it was over, she was unsure of herself. She pushed off him, smiling when he flinched, and sat on the bed next to him. "I guess I'll head back to my room."

His gaze stayed on her for a time. He was observant, too observant, saw far too much. "You're more than welcome to sleep the rest of the night here," he said as he stood and strolled into the bathroom. After he'd taken care of the condom, he returned to the bed and lay on his side, facing away from her. "You're safe here, Fia. I won't invade your space."

To anyone else, him turning his back to her might look like he gave her the brush off, but she knew better. He offered her space, options, making her feel safe. She could sleep next to him and he wouldn't touch her, wouldn't crowd her.

Fia shifted on the bed until she was on her side as well, facing opposite Acer. In LA, she'd slept wrapped in his arms all night. Well, during the few hours they weren't going at it, anyway. She'd love nothing more than to be there again but didn't quite have the courage. The idea of being held down, surrounded and under a man's weight still terrified her.

She stared into the dark of the room for a moment before she rolled onto her back and slid her arm across the bed until her fingertips just grazed Acer's arm. He'd probably never know she touched him as he slept, but she still enjoyed the connection. She closed her eyes and concentrated on the sounds of Acer's even breathing.

A moment later, her eyes flew open. Acer shifted so he was on his back as well, the hand closest to her linking with her fingers on the mattress between their bodies. He didn't say a word, just gripped her hand.

Fia closed her eyes again, and for the first time in weeks, fell asleep without fear.

Chapter Twenty-Three

Fia stood in the entryway to Acer's kitchen and smiled at the picture he presented. A frown marred his handsome face as he stood at the counter glaring at his laptop. That computer was never more than a stone's throw away. Something club related had been on his mind the past few days, and while she itched to know what was happening, she kept her questions to herself.

Now that she'd slept with him again, she was a little more confident and just might ask him about it.

He raised his arms over his head, and stretched to the right with a groan. His back had to be sore from hunching over the computer all day. She hadn't seen much of him today. He'd worked on the computer from sun up to sun down and she'd spent the majority of the day adhering Swarovski crystals to the cups of a custom bra for a very ritzy client. The finished product was going to be a showstopper, well worth an aching back and stiff fingers.

Acer lowered his arms and returned his fingers to the keyboard. They flew over the keys with an impressive speed. Fia chuckled under her breath. This man was such a mess of contradictions, and for some reason she found that appealing. He was barefoot and shirtless, two things that always made a man sexy. The yards of ink over taut muscles gave him a bad-ass appeal, but the Calvin Klein sweatpants and perfectly styled hair was high class all the way.

He was a locked vault with regard to his past. Would he open up to her if she asked some of the many questions living with him had made her eager to ask?

Only one way to find out.

She pushed off the wall and cleared her throat as she entered the room. He looked over his shoulder, and his sexy mouth turned up in a genuine smile. "Hey, beautiful."

The compliment warmed her face and her heart.

Acer closed the laptop and met her in the middle of the kitchen. He lifted her hand and pressed his lips to her palm. Tingles originated under his lips and shot straight to her core.

She tilted her head and looked at him. "Any word on Mike?"

A scowl formed on his sexy mouth. "Nothing, not so much as a blip on the radar. I'm sorry, babe. I know you want this over." He squeezed her hand. "Hell, I want it over."

She hoped he didn't mean because he was ready for her to go. "Can I ask you something I've been dying to know the answer to for almost seven months?"

He laughed and rolled his eyes, but she didn't miss the thinning of his lips or the tension in his stance. Answering personal questions wasn't easy for him.

"Okay, shoot. But I reserve the right to plead the fifth."

She smiled. Small victory. "Why do you go to the same one charity event each year?"

His eyes clouded and for a long moment she worried he wasn't going to answer. Then, he pulled her with him to the table, sat in a chair and drew her down to his lap. The second his arm landed across her thighs, the room flip-flopped and she tensed, the sensation of being trapped stealing her breath. Acer either didn't notice, or ignored her brief panic. He rubbed a hand up and down her spine in a hypnotic caress. The very near freak out receded as she realized she wasn't trapped at all. Sure, his hands were on her, but she wasn't restrained, wasn't held down in any way. She wanted out, all she had to do was hop off his lap.

With a deep breath, the tension receded and she relaxed into his warm, comforting touch. Once she settled against him, he began to speak.

"When I was a teenager, I had a friend, Derek. He was from the shit part of town. His family was dirt poor, but despite the difference in our family's finances, we had a lot in common. Both did well in school, both girl crazy." He brushed her hair off her neck and rubbed his thumb across the sensitive skin at the nape. Goosebumps followed his finger like a row of ducklings trailing their mama.

"You were close?" Part of her didn't want to hear the story. She sensed it would end in tragedy and hearing about Acer's suffering would be difficult to endure. But this was the first time he'd opened up to her and she wouldn't stop him for anything.

"Like brothers." He shook his head. "Derek had a sister, Penny, who was just a couple years behind us. She worshiped us, our constant shadow. Neither of us minded. She was such a sweet kid." He sifted his fingers through her hair. "Anyway, Penny was invited to my fancy high school's senior prom by a guy on the football team." He gave her hair a gentle tug.

She shifted in his lap, wanting to see his face as he finished the story.

"Derek flipped his shit, but Penny had him, and me, wrapped around her little pinkie. He eventually caved and let her go."

Pain filled Acer's expressive eyes. She wanted to wrap her arms around him and tell him to forget it, to keep whatever caused that pain buried deep, but he just might need to get it out.

He sighed. "I'll spare you all the details, but he attacked her at an after party. I walked in on him just seconds away from raping her."

Fia swallowed, empathy flowing through her blood. Geez, to go through something like that at such a young age. Devastating. "What did you do?"

"Derek and I beat the shit out of him. Bad. Almost killed him if you want the truth."

Old Fia might have been concerned by his admission of violence, but New Fia understood the horror and almost wished Penny's attacker had ended up dead. Or maybe that was her wishes for Mike bleeding through. What would Acer have done if Mike had been there when he and his brother's busted in. Though he deserved whatever he got, the thought made her shiver, because the murderous expression on Acer's face was telling. "Did you get in trouble?"

Acer nodded. "His family pressed charges against both Derek and me. My old man was buddies with the judge. Conflict of interest, sure, but you're from that world, you know how things work."

She nodded. Money and connections greased the wheels for the wealthy. Rules and laws were ignored, and people were more than willing to look the other way as long as the right amount of green changed hands. It disgusted her, and she'd never used her family's money to her advantage in that manner.

"My dad always detested Derek, said he was just white trash. He screwed Derek over. I got off scot-free, not even a slap on the wrist, not so much as a lecture from the judge. Derek? He got five years. Five fucking years for defending his sister from a fucking rapist piece of shit. He was supposed to join the Marines." He dropped his forehead to hers. "Such a fucking waste."

"What happened to him?" she whispered, dreading the answer.

"After they locked him up, he spiraled downward so fast. I visited him every week, and I watched the depression consume him. They had counseling services at the prison, but so many needed it, he couldn't get an appointment for months. About six months into his sentence, he hung himself from the bars on his cell."

His voice was thick with emotion. She should say something, anything to quell his sadness, but the words died in her throat, inadequate. This explained so much. The animosity with his father, his lack of trust in anyone, his need to have control over every situation. This one betrayal shaped Acer's entire adult life.

"After it became apparent what my father did, I left his house, never went back, and never took another dime from him. My grandmother helped me through college and gave me a place to live on breaks, bought me my first bike." He smiled. "She was quite the rebel when she was young, or so I was told. Anyway, she left everything she had to me, except for her shares in my father's company. I wanted nothing to do with them, so she left them to my father. But a stipulation of the will was that he had to organize one fundraising event each year to benefit state penitentiaries. She set up the prison charity in Derek's honor and I promised her I'd attend the gala each year." He shrugged like it was no big deal when in fact she knew it was the basis for every decision he'd made in his life since then.

"After she died, I met Striker and Jester at a bike rally in Sturgis, South Dakota. They were both prospects at the time. I was on my own, looking for a connection, but I didn't trust for shit. Still don't. The club makes it simple. You're not trust worthy you're out on your ass, at the very least, usually with an array of broken bones, sometimes worse depending on the offense. I never looked back."

"What happened to Penny?"

His face grew even darker. "For a long time, she blamed me for her brother's death. For years, she cut off all contact. Now I get a birthday card from her, but that's about it. She's doing well though. Married, couple of kids. She never knew it, but—" He shrugged and shook his head.

"What?"

"I...uh...I paid for her to go to college. She thinks she won a generic scholarship, but I sponsored it. I had to do something to atone for what happened to Derek, and while that will never touch it, it was something I could do for her."

He had so many layers to him, and the more she uncovered, the more she liked him, even the darker parts. "Was that the anniversary you wanted to forget?"

A look of confusion crossed his face. "What do you mean?"

"The girls. The ones that came to the bar."

"Ahh, yeah. I tend to have a rough time each year on the anniversary of Derek's death." He dropped a kiss to her bare shoulder.

Well, maybe this year she could help him through—oh no, she could not think along those lines. This was temporary. Who knew if she would be anywhere near Arizona on that day. The thought of him turning to another woman incited some violent feelings of her own.

She sensed there was a lot more to the story, a lot more

pain and family upheaval, but she didn't press. He'd opened up to her more than she ever expected. It was a victory she'd revel in. "Thank you for sharing that with me."

He let out a long sigh. "I've never told anyone that entire story."

"Really? Not even anyone in the club?"

He shook his head, his eyes dropping to her mouth. "Not a soul."

"Why did you tell me?"

A quick look of surprise crossed his face, then his eyes shuttered. It was almost as if he just realized he'd poured his heart out to her. "I—well I'm not really sure. We've been through a lot together. It just felt right, like I knew you'd understand."

Acer cupped her face in his hand, stroking a thumb over her cheek. She leaned into his touch, enjoying a light caress from a man without fear. His story had provided enough of a distraction from her own mess of a life that she hadn't even thought to fear his increasing hold on her.

Now he stared at her mouth as though he wanted to devour her. He lowered his head until she could feel his warm breath tickling her lips. "Stop me," he ordered.

Fia shook her head. Never.

He claimed her mouth in a kiss that made the room spin and her heart stutter in her chest. Her first kiss in far too many months. He tasted of coffee and, if she wasn't mistaken, cigars. He liked to sneak them when he knew she wasn't looking, like they were some old married couple.

She slid her tongue into his open mouth, tangling it with his, unable to keep from smiling when she felt him harden against her hip. Breathing heavy, he broke away and rubbed his lips back and forth over hers. "Feeling smug?"

She chuckled. "Just a little." She cocked her head to the

side. "Do you hear that?"

Acer kissed her forehead then leaned against the back of the chair. "Bikes. The guys are swinging by; we're heading out for a while."

"Now? It's almost midnight."

He nodded and patted her hip. She scooted off his lap and he stood, grabbing the computer off the counter. "Yeah, I'll be out for a good few hours, so don't wait up."

Fia frowned. Where was he going? A party? A bar? Ugly jealously twisted her insides. Not a pleasant feeling.

"Hey, what's wrong? You were like warm putty in my arms a few minutes ago and now you're tense again."

She gave him what she hoped was a convincing smile. "Nothing. Have fun tonight."

Acer snorted. "No fun will be had, trust me. Just business."

Oh well. She perked right up. This wasn't good. The more time she spent with Acer, the more she wanted him in her life for the long-term. He'd made her no promises beyond eliminating the threat from Mike.

"Was that—" He crossed his arms over his chest and speared her with an intense stare. "Serafina Caldwell, did you think I was gonna go party and leave you here alone?"

"Oh...uh..." She stared at the floor. Maybe it would just open up and swallow her whole. Anything would be preferable to admitting envy. "Well...no, not really."

His mouth rose into a smug smirk.

She jammed her hands on her hips and rolled her eyes. "Okay fine, yes that's what I thought."

Acer gripped her chin. "I think I like you jealous, babe." He gave her a quick, hard kiss.

"I didn't say I was jealous. I was not jealous." She spoke around his lips.

He winked. "You didn't have to say it." He gave her a

playful swat on the ass as he walked past her and down the hallway to his room. Less than a minute later, he emerged wearing black jeans and a plain black hoodie.

"Um, all you're missing is the ski mask and you could rob a bank. Wait, you're not going to rob a bank, are you?" Hands on her hips, she blocked his way in the hall.

Acer threw back his head and laughed. "No, babe, I'm not going to rob a bank. Give me a little credit, please."

"Right, sorry." Embarrassment heated her skin.

"No worries. Set the alarm behind me. Shit." He rubbed a hand through his hair, mussing the strands for the first time. "I didn't even think to ask if you'll be okay here by yourself."

She waved him away. "Yes, of course. I've been here alone before, and with your elaborate security system, I pretty much know if someone is coming here before they know. You be careful with whatever it is you're doing."

"Always." He pressed his lips to hers again. "Be in my bed when I get back. I want to sleep next to you for a few hours."

There was that warm, squishy feeling again. "Okay," she whispered.

He left and she coded the alarm.

This was all so oddly domestic. Sitting on his lap in the kitchen while they chatted, talking about napping together, sending him off with a kiss.

Fia rolled her eyes. "Don't get used to it, sister. He's not yours to keep."

Chapter Twenty-Four

His buddies' ol' ladies frequently complained about the eerie feeling the quiet, ink-black desert nights evoked, but it was a draw for Acer. The vast night sky and peaceful silence was one of the few benefits to living in a small desert community. If he rode his bike just a few minutes out of town, he could turn three hundred and sixty degrees and see nothing but blackness and the twinkle of stars for endless miles.

Something about the infinite, open terrain soothed his soul. Reminded him the world was so much bigger than his issues. For most bikers, riding on a clear night was a near spiritual experience.

Not the case tonight.

"So, what's the game plan here?" Jester asked as he rolled his bike up alongside Acer.

The two of them, along with Striker, Hook, and Lucky straddled their parked bikes in a row at the end of the road where Acer tailed the faux club brother. Up ahead, about two hundred yards, two yellow beams of light shot out from a large semi, cutting through the shadows.

It hadn't taken long to determine a predictable pattern. Acer had been illegally monitoring satellite images of the area since he learned about it. Each night between midnight and three am, the action happened.

He and his brothers coasted the last mile on their bikes, headlights off, to avoid tipping off anyone on lookout. One thing Harleys weren't, was stealthy. Each man donned all black, and he would never admit it to Fia, but in fact, they each had a black ski mask in case this got up close and personal.

"Plan is to get close enough see what their set-up is, where the weak spots are," Acer said as he scanned his surroundings. I'd also like to get eyes on some of these guys' faces, pics with your phones if possible. I can run them through my computer and try to find out who some of these fuckers are."

Lucky snorted. "So what, we're just supposed to waltz on up there and ask them to strike a pose and say cheese?"

Acer rubbed the back of his neck. "I don't quite have that part figured out yet. That's why I wanted you all here tonight, so we can scope it out and see where the best point of entry is."

Jester snorted. "Some genius you are. Shouldn't you have this all worked out already?"

"Okay, shut it you guys." Striker held up a hand. "Looks like quite the operation they have up there. Maybe our best bet is to try to get someone hired by these assholes. They can feed us info and I don't have to spend too many nights in the fucking cold, away from my bed and my woman."

Acer nodded. "I think that's a good idea. Anyone owe us a favor that's not in the MC?" He pointed toward the activity in front of them. "If any of these workers are local, they'd recognize most of us."

"I can do it," Lucky said. "I'm new enough in town that hardly anyone knows me."

Striker nodded and shoved an unlit cigarette between his lips. "That's not a bad idea. Let me run it by Shiv before I give you the go ahead."

"Lila hasn't beaten that habit out of you yet, VP?" Hook asked.

"I don't know what you're talking about." Striker shot his friend a death glare.

Hook laughed. "I'm talking about that cigarette."

"What cigarette?"

"Yeah, like she can't smell. Your funeral, brother." Hook held his hands up.

"That's right, mine. And it ain't even fuckin' lit, so shut the fuck up about it."

Hook snickered. "First off, you were gonna light it eventually, and secondly...you've been married long enough now to know that she will have your balls for this. Lit or not."

"Fuck." With a scowl for Hook, he tossed the butt to the ground and kicked sand over it.

Lila was always on their assess about smoking, but none more than her husband. He was having a bitch of a time kicking the habit.

"Hey, look." Jester elbowed Acer and pointed toward a pair of headlights moving in their direction.

"Shit. Looks like it's time to roll out, boys." Acer looked over his shoulder. "Or maybe not."

Another two sets of headlights descended upon them, essentially boxing them in on the road. Hiding was impossible in the open desert. They could hop on their bikes, split up, and head off-road in the desert, but as dark as it was, and with as many tiny shrubs as there were, it was a recipe for disaster on a bike.

"Oh, fuck me," said Jester.

"No thanks," Lucky replied. "I like my playthings with a

little less cock."

Jester grabbed his crotch and smirked. "Ahh, so you finally admit my dick's huge."

Striker choked on a laugh. "Will you two shut the fuck up and cover your fugly mugs. Shit's about to get real."

Acer dismounted his bike and pulled the wool mask over his head just as two pickup trucks cruised to a halt about fifty feet up the road. The vehicle behind stopped about the same distance out.

Three men spilled out of each truck in front of them and a quick peek over his shoulder revealed two climbing from the truck to their rear. Adrenaline zinged through Acer's blood as he flexed his fists. He could use a good fight. He hadn't had much opportunity to train since Fia's kidnapping. Any trip to the gym reminded him of what she went through.

It had been weeks since he felt the energy release of his fists making contact with something, even just a heavy bag. Combine that with the frustration of not being able to locate Mike, and he could definitely get behind pounding the shit out of someone.

"You boys lost? You looking for the nearest bank? Ain't no ski slopes around here." A big man with a bushy red beard slapped a wooden baseball bat against his palm. Acer didn't know his name, but he was local. He'd seen the guy around town on various occasions.

Jesus, Fia would laugh her face off when he relayed the asshole's bank robbery insinuation. Wait—what? He wasn't going to tell her any of this.

The ringleader smiled, revealing at least two missing teeth. "Some rich assholes pay us a lot of dough to keep garbage like you out of their business."

"Well, you have the asshole part right," Acer said.

"Wellington is definitely a grade-A asshole."

If Red was surprised Acer and his crew knew the name of his employer, he didn't show it. "Like I said, he and Caldwell pay us well to keep their business private, so you being here is a problem for us."

Wellington *and* Caldwell.

What. The. Fuck. Fia's father was involved in this? Shit. How had Acer not discovered this yet? Could Fia know about this?

No.

Fuck no!

Last time he'd been this confident of someone's loyalty, his best friend ended up in prison. As much as he wanted to believe Fia wouldn't betray him, he just couldn't take the risk.

"Fuck it, this turns into a brawl we ain't gonna be able to see for shit with these on." Striker muttered as he pulled his mask off and stepped forward. He wasn't one to shy away from a physical altercation.

Red snorted and looked to his goons on either side of him. They weren't as tall or bulky, but they each had a homicidal gleam in their eyes, like they couldn't wait to get a piece of Striker. Guess they didn't know how lethal the VP was with his fists. "Oh this is gonna be fun, men. I've been itching to take out some biker trash for years."

Jester scoffed and pulled his ski mask off as well. "You sure you want to start something, dude? You can just drive around us and get back to your little operation without any broken bones."

The ringleader laughed. "Bigger they are, the harder they fall," he said. Jester had about five inches on the guy. "And we outnumber you. Think we'll take our chances."

Acer wasn't worried. Hell, two of their guys were named for their boxing abilities. He himself was better on the ground, but could hold his own when punches flew. Jester was just plain huge, so one thump from his meaty fist was often enough to end a brawl, and Lucky was a trained Marine. No, he wasn't worried at all.

He glanced to his right. Jester and Striker wore similar evil grins. On his left Lucky rubbed his knuckles and Hook bounced on the balls of his feet.

The hairs on the back of Acer's neck rose to full attention and he whirled around, just in time to dodge a fist flying toward his face. Jester wasn't quite as fast and he grunted as a man half his size barreled into his back.

Years of MMA training kicked in and Acer raised his hands, protecting his face. He jabbed at the lanky man who attacked him, catching him under the chin. Apparently, his opponent had no clue how to fight, because he left his soft face wide the fuck open.

Without warning, Red's wooden bat landed right across his sternum, immobilizing his arms and leaving him vulnerable to the lanky man's knuckles. A punch to the gut stole his breath and another to the jaw had him spitting blood on the sand.

Fuck this.

He rammed his head back and smiled when Red cried out. The pressure around his chest dissipated immediately as the bat fell and he charged forward, catching the lanky guy with a punch to the side of his head that had him crashing to the ground. He spun, knuckles up, prepared for more, but no attack came. Seven of the eight meatheads who'd confronted them lay sprawled out on the floor groaning and clutching some part of their anatomy. Acer smiled a broad grin at the scene before him

His brothers also looked a little worse for wear, but nothing some ice and a little TLC from their women wouldn't cure.

Red, in better shape than his cronies, wobbled to his feet spitting bloody phlegm to the ground. His bat lay about fifteen feet away in the sand. "Big fucking mistake," he said, attention on Acer.

Acer raised an eyebrow. "Care to tell me why?"

He swiped at the blood flowing from his nose. "You No Prisoners think you're fuckin' invincible." He grinned a bloody smile. "You have no idea what's coming. Only a matter of time before you're all in the slammer." He shook his head. "What a shame it will be, all those whores, what do you call them? Ol' ladies? All those ol' ladies without their men, lonely and looking for some dick. I'll be sure to pay each one of them a visit." He thrust his hips forward and back.

Acer clenched his jaw. He wouldn't be baited by this shithead.

"You got an ol' lady? She'll be first on my list." He rubbed his crotch.

Acer's blood sizzled in his veins. He took a deep breath to keep the rousing beast asleep.

His brothers only half paid attention, each using some plastic zip cuffs to secure the rest of the thugs. Hook rummaged through each vehicle one by one.

"She'll beg me for it. And if she don't?" The piece of shit shrugged. "Maybe I'll just take it anyway."

"Oh shit." Jester's warning registered somewhere in the back of Acer's mind, but it didn't matter. He snapped, straight in two.

Acer charged, caught his bearded opponent around the waist, and crashed him to the ground, flat on his back. He rose to his knees, straddling the guy, his full weight on his chest. The guy struggled for breath, so focused on getting air, he never saw the first blow coming.

Acer's fist collided with the side of the brute's head. A satisfying pain shot from his knuckles to his shoulder. Damn that felt good. It didn't take much imagination to swap out Mike's face for this loser. He swung again, colliding again with the guy's face. Then again, and again, until his mind was clear of everything except thoughts of keeping Fia safe.

"Acer! Yo, Ace. That's enough. He's had enough, brother." Jester's voice cut through the red haze.

A sturdy hand gripped his bicep, halting the next blow. Acer shook his head to clear the violent intentions and rose to his feet. On the ground, Red lay bloodied and moaning.

He should feel regret, guilt, some kind of repentance for losing his shit all over this guy, but he didn't. Any threat to Fia was a threat he'd gladly eliminate.

"Hands gonna be okay to ride?" Striker asked.

Acer flexed his fingers and hid a wince. Knuckles on both hands were split and bloodied. His ribs hurt like a son of a bitch from where he'd taken a hit to the flank. "I'm fine. We ready to roll?"

Lucky snorted then grimaced, rubbing a hand over his face. The shiner Acer had given him was re-swelling in a grotesque palette of dark purples. "While you had all the fun, the rest of us were on cleanup duty. We can bug out whenever."

Striker nodded. "Nothing useful in their trucks. We did snag their ID's so you can do your thing, Acer." Striker was sporting a split lip and bloody nose. "Damn," he said as he dabbed at his mouth. "Lila's gonna kill me." He pointed to his mouth and winked. "Kinda alters my plans for her for the rest of the night."

Acer laughed and mounted his bike. "I'm sure your woman will survive one night without."

"Either way," Striker said. "I'm ready to get back home to her, so lead the way."

Acer revved his engine and sped off into the night. No point in trying to be quiet when they'd already been discovered.

His hands stung and his head throbbed. He gripped the handlebars with as gentle a grip as he could manage. All he could think about was getting home to Fia.

Christ, here he was thinking along the same lines as Striker, a married man. He might be going home, and Fia might be there, but he wasn't going *home to Fia*. He'd do well to remember that.

Chapter Twenty-Five

Fia woke to a crescendo of motorcycles engines. She rolled on her side and glanced at the glowing clock on the nightstand. Two-fifty-nine in the morning. Geez, Acer had been gone a while.

She slipped out of bed as she heard the alarm deactivate and the door rustle open. She slid her feet into her slippers and padded down the hallway rubbing at her chilled arms. Acer kept the place just a hair on the cold side, though it always felt amazing when she returned from the sweltering outdoors.

"Man, do I need a fucking drink."

Was that Lucky?

"Keep it down, asshole. Fia's sleeping."

She smiled at Acer's grouchy tone. Always looking out for her. She stepped into the kitchen. "I'm awake. Everything go ok—holy crap! What the hell happened to you two?" Bruising mottled both handsome faces and each man's gait was stiff and stilted.

She rushed forward and cupped Acer's swollen cheek. "Do I need to call Lila?" Her stomach rolled. They'd obviously been in a fight. A million questions ran through her mind, but she held them back...for now.

He pulled her hand from his face and pressed a kiss to her palm. "No babe, we're good. Besides, she's got her own battered biker to attend to."

With a gasp, she yanked her hand from his grasp. "Acer! Your knuckles! They look awful. Let me get you some ice. Then we'll clean off your hands and see if you need stitches or anything. After that you can tell me everything that happened tonight." He raised an eyebrow and she gave him the look right back. Damn man wouldn't tell her if it was going to rain because he wouldn't want her to worry about getting wet.

Well, that was going to change. She wasn't some fragile flower who would wilt at the first sign of trouble. A laugh almost bubbled out. Given the past few weeks, Acer had no reason to believe she wouldn't lose her mind over a bit of bad information. She'd just have to show him, and herself, that she could handle life's uglier side just fine. If she was going to resume her life in California without the crutch of Acer's presence, she had to be able to stand on her own two feet, and that meant dealing with shit as it came. She brushed aside the feeling of sadness that swarmed her whenever she thought of leaving. Now was not the time for that.

Acer chuckled. "Yes, ma'am," he said, saluting with bloodied fingers.

She gave him a quick peck on the cheek and moved to retrieve some ice from the freezer.

Lucky rummaged through Acer's cabinets and pulled out a bottle of whiskey. "What the fuck am I? Chopped liver? My face hurts like a bastard. You gonna come kiss up on me too?"

"No." Acer's answer was out of his mouth almost before

Lucky finished the question.

Fia rolled her eyes and chuckled. "I've got a bag of ice for you too, Lucky. I'm sure you'll have no problem finding a warm and willing female to nurse you back to health."

He bobbed his eyebrows then winced when the puffy skin around his eye contracted. "You're right, baby doll, I could totally milk a slutty nurse fantasy out of this." He took a drink straight from the more than half-full bottle. "Damn, that's some smooth shit." He held up the bottle. "This is why I like you, buddy."

Fia pressed a Ziploc bag full of ice into Acer's free hand as he flipped Lucky off. "You owe me about seventy-five dollars for that sip alone." He took the other bag out of her hand and tossed it to a grinning Lucky before pulling her close to his side, his arm around her shoulders as though he didn't want her close to his brother.

She hid her smile. The swell of happiness Acer's subtle possessive and jealous gesture inspired would be her little secret.

Lucky took another swig from the bottle before setting it down on the counter and lifting the baggie of ice to his eye. "Damn that feels good."

Acer grunted his agreement.

"Well, I know it's early, but I won't be able to go back to sleep now and I'm sure between the two of you, there's enough adrenaline and testosterone flowing through your veins to fuel a rocket. Why don't I make some breakfast?" She pointed to the rapidly emptying bottle next to Lucky. "You're gonna need something to absorb all that anyway."

"Only a fool turns down the offer of a home-cooked meal by a gorgeous woman." Lucky winked at her with the one human-looking eye.

She chuckled. "You can't be too injured if you can still flirt like that." She patted Acer on his flat stomach then pulled away, rummaging through the fridge. "Pancakes and bacon good?"

"That's perfect, babe. And you could cut Lucky's tongue out, but he'd still manage to flirt."

"That's true, but it would severely limit me in some other extra-curricular activities that I typically excel at. Fia, any time you like a demonstration, you just say the word." He winked and ran his tongue along his top lip.

She turned away from them, focusing on the task of pancake making. This guy was too much, although she got the impression his outrageous bravado was an overinflated way to hide a deep-seated pain. She barely knew the man and it wasn't her place to ask, but maybe she'd mention it to Acer. She owed Lucky some time in the therapist's chair after he'd helped her out the other day.

"So," she said as she leveled the cup of flour and dumped it into a bowl. "What the hell happened tonight? And don't bother giving me some bullshit excuse about how, for my own good, you won't tell me." Next went the sugar.

Crickets.

She looked over her shoulder and pinned Acer with a hard stare.

Lucky cracked up and took another drink of whiskey. "She's kinda feisty, Ace."

Acer snorted. "You have no fucking idea, brother." He winked at her.

She turned back to the bowl and whisked the ingredients, tears forming in her eyes. She was feisty, at least Old Fia was. That she was reclaiming that part of herself was the most amazing compliment either man could have ever given her.

Behind her, Acer sighed. "My father is fucking with the club."

She dropped the whisk in the bowl and whirled. "Does this have to do with what I overheard? What does he want with your club?"

Acer shook his head. "Nothing, he wants nothing beyond the chance to be a chafe on my ass." He ran the water in the sink and stuck his hand under the stream, hissing when the water cascaded over his split skin. "He's running people across the border to work for next to nothing on his new hotel. His original plan was to have our club do the dirty work, but as you can guess, I passed on the offer."

Lucky nodded "We had a run in with some of their lackeys tonight. Took 'em out, easy-peasy. You'd think Wellington and—"

Acer shot him a look and Lucky stopped talking.

Fia waited for him to finish his sentence, but he brought the bottle to his lips instead. Wellington and whom? What was Lucky about to say, and why didn't Acer want it said? Fia whistled. "That would be a serious federal investigation into your club if his guys were caught."

Lucky grinned. "Sassy and smart. You looking for a husband, darlin'?"

Both she and Acer ignored him, though she didn't miss the flare of annoyance in Acer's eyes. And speaking of flares, his possessiveness had a direct link to her own flare of desire.

"You're absolutely right, Fia, which is why I told him to fuck off." He ran a hand through his already rumpled hair. He looked good like this, minus the bruises, but he looked good a little mussed and disheveled. "Since he's always behaved like a toddler, he's throwing a tantrum and has guys being his coyotes, wearing cuts that look exactly like ours. We went to do some reconnaissance and ended up rumbling with a few of them."

She barely took in anything after the part about the

identical cuts. "Whoa, whoa, wait a minute. You're telling me that your own father is almost certainly setting you up to be investigated by the Feds?"

"That's the gist of it." No reaction registered on his face. No anger, no sadness, frustration, nothing. He might as well have been reporting on the weather. The man knew how to hide his emotions, that was for damned sure. No way was it possible to feel nothing when you found out your father was actively trying to harm you, was there?

"God," she said. "And I thought my parents were assholes." She hoped to wrangle a chuckle out of Acer, but all she got was a ticking in his jaw. Maybe he was still pissed over her parents' lack of care when she went to stay with them.

Lucky cleared his throat and held up his filthy hands. "I'm gonna go take care of these. Don't eat my portion." He ducked out of the kitchen leaving her alone with Acer.

She pulled a handful of paper towels off the roll and stood next to Acer at the sink. Without saying a word, she shut off the water and softly dabbed his wet skin with the absorbent towels. "I'm sorry about all this, Acer. I know it's stupid to say because it doesn't actually help anything." She shrugged. "I want you to know that I can handle things if you need to vent or run ideas by me. Despite what you've seen since I got here, I'm not usually weak. I can actually be pretty tough." She gave him a small smile.

He didn't speak, but cupped her cheek with his clean hand. He bent down until his lips were less than a breath away from hers. "There hasn't been a single second since I've met you that I thought you were weak."

He closed the miniscule distance, capturing her mouth in a hot kiss. Snagging her bottom lip between his teeth, he gave a small tug. She opened to him immediately and welcomed the invasion of his tongue.

She'd almost forgotten how intoxicating his kisses could be. How they could fire her blood and need in an instant. He'd kissed her earlier in this very kitchen, but this time it had a desperation to it. An almost savage quality. Her nipples puckered, reminding her she'd been hanging out with them in nothing but panties and Acer's T-shirt, no bra. Thank God, his shirt hung to her knees.

He tilted his head, deepening the kiss and she moaned into his mouth. Between her legs, moisture pooled. She felt hot, she felt sexy, she felt...normal. Acer kept a few inches between them, not wrapping her in his arms or pulling her flush against him. It was the only indication that she wasn't quite back to normal and while she appreciated the way he always made her feel safe, it was a reminder that she wasn't whole yet.

He abruptly pulled back and stepped away from her. Fia blinked and pressed a hand to her swollen lips. Between the three of them they now had each part of the face covered in terms of swelling.

Lucky stepped in the room. "My pancakes ready yet, woman?"

Ahh. Acer must have heard him approaching. At least someone had enough presence of mind to listen for interruptions. Or was it bad that he wasn't as absorbed in the kiss?

She turned back to the bowl and rolled her eyes at herself. With a smile, she resumed whisking. A mild tingling between her legs kept her mind on the kiss while her arm stirred the batter. Damn, it felt good to be normal for a few minutes.

Her smiled faded as she ladled batter onto the griddle. What information had Acer stopped Lucky from sharing?

Chapter Twenty-Six

"Brother, you got something better to be doing tonight?" Lucky did a shitty job of hiding his amusement.

Acer rolled his eyes. "What the hell are you talking about?"

Lucky shrugged and tossed back the last of his drink before rapping it against the bar. "You need to keep up with me here, Prospect."

The tired looking prospect rushed over and refilled Lucky's drink.

"You keep peeking at your watch like your gonna miss something if you blink too long. What gives?"

Acer resisted the urge to check his watch yet again. "Nothing, man. Fia will be here soon and I don't want her to have to walk in by herself."

Lucky grinned. "I like her, brother." He bobbed his eyebrows up and down.

"Yeah, you like her a little too much. Eyes on your own paper unless you're looking for another shiner." Lucky's offer to sleep with Fia still grated on him, even though he was well aware Fia had no interest in the man.

After Fia patched them up last night, well this morning,

they'd eaten and passed out for a few hours. Lucky crashed on the couch, and his buddy's presence combined with the throb in Acer's hands and ribs, meant he didn't put any moves on Fia.

Plus, he wasn't quite sure where she stood after the other night. She came, but that didn't mean she was over the trauma. Christ, he was pretty much ready to jump on her anywhere anytime, but he wanted to give her the time and space she needed to process what was happening between them and what was happening within her.

She was healing; more of the old Fia emerged every day. It wouldn't be long before she was ready to fly on her own. And he'd let her. The horrors she endured would never completely fade away, but soon she'd be able to look toward the future instead of drowning in the past.

While he hadn't made any overt sexual advances, he had ramped up his campaign to make her more comfortable with being touched. He found countless ways to touch her whenever they spent time together, always making sure to avoid boxing her in or crowding her. He made sure she felt safe and able to remove herself if she became uncomfortable, but he brushed against her in the kitchen, put his hands on her shoulders when he moved past her, tucked her hair behind her ear, and even gave her quick pecks when he left the house.

It was torture on his dick, her skin was soft, warm, and so damned enticing, it took all his strength not to throw her down and pounce on her.

Then there was the whole issue of how he'd left out a huge chunk of his story last night. The part that included her father's involvement with his club's troubles. Guilt ate at his stomach like acid, yet two decades of distrusting everyone he met, kept him from coughing up the entire story.

218

Male laughter brought him back to reality.

"Dude, you've got it bad. I've been talking to you for at least two minutes and you're off in la la land dreaming about your girl. You get her name tattooed on your ass yet?"

"Lucky, you patched over five minutes ago. You sure you want your new brothers to see my boot up your ass so soon?"

Lucky laughed and tossed back another drink. He held up his hands, palms out. "Okay, okay. I'm wasting my time here anyway. She's gonna kick your ass to the curb the second she realizes you straight up lied to her." Lucky narrowed his eyes, all teasing gone.

Acer scowled. "Mind your own fuckin' business, Lucky."

"Just sayin', brother. You're making a big ass mistake. Hell hath no fury and all that." He shrugged.

He was right, but something inside Acer had broken twenty years ago. And that something wouldn't allow him to fully trust her, even if he didn't really think she was guilty. He learned long ago his gut instinct wasn't always accurate.

"Anyway, I'm off to find someone a little more warm and willing to spend my evening with."

Acer snorted. "Knock yourself out brother." He slapped a hand on Lucky's shoulder. "All bullshit aside, it's damned good to have you here."

Lucky's grin grew. "I'm hoping that some pretty little thing will be saying those exact words to me in the next thirty minutes." He returned Acer's manly slap and danced his way to a group of women grinding against each other across the room.

Acer didn't bother to check the time again. Fia should be here any second. This would be her first No Prisoners party. He smiled, thinking of the contrast to the party where they met. Night and day.

Just as he stepped out into the cool night air, Fia's BMW

pulled into the lot, followed by the prospect he'd ordered to tail her from the apartment. He rested his back on the warm wall next to the door while he waited for her to exit the car.

She studied her surroundings before making her way toward the clubhouse, her gait stiff and her gaze darting in multiple directions. The moment her focus landed on him, her entire posture changed. She visibly relaxed, a genuine smile crossed her face, and her eyes sparkled.

Damned if that didn't make a man feel like a fuckin' king.

There was no way she was in on her father's dealings. Was there?

As her heels click-clacked across the lot, she stepped into the direct path of a flood light and Acer almost swallowed his tongue. "Holy shit, Fia."

She stopped dead in her tracks about fifteen feet from him. "What?" She glanced around. "Is something wrong?"

Acer shifted his stance, the fit of his jeans suddenly much tighter than it had been just seconds ago. "Baby, you look…"

Her smile fell and she peered down at her outfit. "Is my outfit no good?"

Acer snorted. "Fia, it's so good I'm gonna need a few minutes before I can walk back inside."

Her smile returned, even more radiant this time. Her outfit was simple, tiny, ass-hugging black shorts with a hot pink skimpy tank top that bared about an inch of her smooth, creamy stomach. Man, he'd love to start at that expanse of skin and lick his way down until she moaned and fisted his hair. Her dainty feet were in sky-high heels and she'd done something with her hair to make it look like she just rolled out of bed after hours of hot sex.

"Turn."

"Acer." Her face flushed red, but she did as he commanded. "Won't that just make your little problem worse?"

He groaned. Those damned shorts were so fuckin' lucky to be molded to her ass like that. His palms itched to slide over the round globes. God, she had a fine ass. "First off, as you well know, there is nothing small about my problem."

She chuckled and her gaze darted to his crotch for just a second before returning to his face.

He winked and her face grew even more crimson.

"And second, it's well worth it for a view of that ass. By the way, you catch anyone else staring at it, let me know. I'll gouge their eyes out."

She rolled her eyes and grabbed his hand, spinning him around and tugging him toward the door. "Come on."

He gave her hand a gentle squeeze. The rare times she initiated any kind of touch was priceless. "You look amazing, Fia. Much better than the bags you've been wearing. Had a feeling they weren't the real you."

She smoothed a hand over her flat stomach. "It's just clothes, but for some reason it feels so much bigger."

He wouldn't be able to keep his hands off her tonight. It just wasn't going to be physically possible. "It is a big deal, baby. It's you getting your life back."

She smiled and blew him a kiss. Hand in hand, they entered the dim and smoky clubhouse.

"Yikes."

Acer laughed. "A bit different from where we met, huh?" Straight ahead of them, a woman stood with a shot glass wedged between her very generous cleavage. Gumby winked at the woman before licking salt off her neck. He then wrapped his lips around the shot glass, tossed it back, and sucked a lime from her mouth into his. Not quite champagne and ball gowns.

"Uh, yeah. That's one way of putting it." Her wide eyes

gave away party-virgin status.

It was always a trip to observe someone's reactions the first time they came to a No Prisoners party, especially if they weren't used to loud music, large bikers, and in your face sexuality.

Fia's posture was stiff, but she stayed tense most of the time, and she didn't look afraid. Instead, she looked... intrigued. She shifted her gaze from the body shot duo to another couple making out on a barstool. "You guys sure know how to have fun, don't you?"

"That we do, babe. Follow me."

He reversed their positions and preceded her to the bar. "Hop up." He patted an empty stool and Fia shimmied her sexy ass onto it. "You want a drink?"

"Just a beer."

With a wave of his hand, he signaled the prospect and asked for two beers. Fia probably wouldn't indulge in much more than that, but he hoped she'd allow herself to lower her guard and let loose a bit. There were no threats to her safety here; he'd make sure of it.

As she sipped her beer and gazed around at the crowd of drunken dancers, Acer stepped around her and molded his front to her back. The urge to wrap his arms around her and hold her tight against him was intense, but he resisted. This way, if she felt nervous at all, she could jump right off the barstool.

He followed her gaze to the center of the room, where Hook and Marcie were dancing it up. Dancing may have been a bit sedate a term. Hook's hands were under his wife's miniskirt, full of her ass and he held her close, unashamedly grinding his cock against her. Their mouths tangled as their bodies moved, somewhat in time with the pounding beat of the music.

Acer glanced down at Fia and bit back a groan. Her nipples were visible, hard points jutting against her figure-hugging top. Inability to experience desire was not this woman's problem. He leaned down and grazed his teeth over her neck, right where the muscles curved to meet her shoulder. She shivered and tilted her head ever so slightly, giving better access.

Acer smiled. Small victories were the name of this game.

He kissed his way up the column of her throat, her breathy sigh all the encouragement he needed. With slow movements, so as not to startle her, he rested a hand on each of her hips. She was still free to escape anytime she felt smothered.

Acer captured her earlobe between his teeth and gave a gentle tug. "You enjoying the show?"

She didn't meet his gaze, but kept her attention on Hook and Marcie's erotic display as their encounter grew even more heated. "Such public displays aren't really my style, but...well it's kinda hot to watch them. Does that make me a perv?"

Acer groaned. "No, babe, it doesn't. If it wasn't common to get off on watching others, the porn industry wouldn't be worth billions."

She chuckled softly. "Good point."

"Speaking of points." Acer ran one hand up her side and brushed it against the underside of her breast before returning it to her hip.

She looked down at her tight nipples and gasped, but didn't move to cover herself. Instead, she turned her head until their gazes met, their mouths a breath apart.

There wasn't anything Acer wanted more in that moment than the feel of her mouth on his, so he took it. She tasted of mint toothpaste, beer and her own unique flavor. It was her essence that was intoxicating.

He kept the kiss light, teasing, until the gentle probing of her tongue against his lips became insistent. He smiled. His girl was getting her spunk back.

Fia took advantage of his parted lips and slipped her tongue into his mouth. He answered by pulling her hips closer and sinking everything into the kiss. With a slow slide, she spun her body on the stool and eased her hands around his back and down into the rear pockets of his jeans. Damn, this was the first time in seven months that he'd felt her embrace. Sure, they'd fucked, but she hadn't had her arms around him, hadn't draped that curvy body all over him. And her hands on his ass? Fuckin' heaven.

His cock surged, straining behind its denim jailer. Fia smiled against his mouth and rocked her hips into his. Hell, this was the hottest physical encounter he had in seven months and he was in his damned clubhouse surrounded by

—

"Well, don't you two look cozy." Lila's voice held a note of laughter.

Fia jolted against him and he gave her a soft, comforting squeeze as he pulled back.

Damn Lila and her shitty timing.

One look at Lila's smug grin revealed her complete lack of remorse for interrupting them.

Fia's face was bright pink, but she laughed and gave Lila a hug.

"You guys drinking beer? I could go for one of those." She turned around. "Want one Emily? Jester?"

Jester shook his head and held up his half-full glass.

Emily shook her head as well. "No thanks. I'm good."

Lila frowned. "Okay, girl, what gives? This is the third time we've been out that you haven't had a drink. What's up with—oh my God!" Lila squealed, the sound so high pitched, Acer flinched.

What the hell?

Lila threw her arms around Emily and screeched again.

Acer glanced down at Fia. She wore a radiant, excited smile.

"You're—"

"Lila, shh," Emily whispered, placing her palm over Lila's mouth. "Please be quiet. I haven't even told Jes—"

"Haven't told me what? What the fuck is going on?" Hands on his hips, Jester scowled from at least a foot above Emily and Lila.

As clueless as Jester, Acer stared between the beaming women, his head whipping back and forth like he was a spectator at a tennis match.

Poor Emily's face was beet red and she chewed her bottom lip. Jester stepped closer to her and ran his thumb along her mouth. She released the abused lip and spoke in a low voice. "This is not how I wanted to tell you. I'm sorry. We hadn't planned for this."

"Hadn't planned for what? Woman, if you don't tell me what the fuck is going on—" Jester's big body coiled with tension and looked about five seconds from exploding.

"I'm pregnant." Emily looked at the floor, wringing her hands at her waist.

Jester's reaction was pure comedy. His mouth opened and closed about three times and his eyes went cartoon-wide. If he wasn't careful, they'd fall right out of his head. "You're… holy shit." He let out a whoop worthy of his size and picked up his woman, spinning her around and laughing. "We're gonna have a baby? Fuck yeah! Emily, I love you so fucking much." He placed her back on her feet.

"You're happy about this?" Emily's voice was almost as

stunned as Jester's.

Jester bent his big body down and whispered something to his girlfriend. This wasn't a moment anyone should have been present for, yet part of Acer was glad to see his brother's unfiltered surprised reaction to Emily's news.

Her face lost its tense distress as Jester spoke in her ear, replaced by a pretty pink blush.

"We'll be back." Jester scooped her up and stalked away without another word for the group.

Acer couldn't help but smile. Those two had been through a hell of their own and emerged stronger and very much in love. Fia had a wistful expression on her face that sobered him. Did she want that? That happily ever after? The family? Of course, she did. She was a woman.

At some point, he would have to let her go, and sooner would be better than later. He wasn't going to be her Prince Charming, wasn't going to give her that happy ever after. He just didn't possess the ability to do that. That pill was easy to swallow when she first moved in, why did he now feel like he'd be making a huge mistake to let her go?

"This is so fantastic. I have to tell Striker." Lila darted off into the crowd leaving him alone with Fia.

"Exciting news," she said.

"Yeah, they—"

"Hey, Acer? Sorry to interrupt, but Shiv wants to see you in the office for a second. I'll sit with your girl." Lucky winked at Fia.

Acer tipped his bottle back and drained the rest of his beer. "Duty calls. You gonna be okay to wait for me here?"

Fia nodded. "I'll be fine."

He pressed a quick kiss to her lips before turning toward Lucky. "Hands off, brother."

Lucky made a big show of sticking his hands in his pockets

as he smirked.

Acer flipped him off and made his way through the crowd. He missed Fia's presence even before he reached Shiv's office. Christ, his head was such a mess. With every fiber of his being, he felt that Fia was ignorant of her father's nefarious dealings. His gut screamed at him to tell her, he could trust her with the information and maybe she'd have some helpful insight.

But he just couldn't do it. He had some sort of mental block that refused to allow him to trust her. And that was why he wasn't good for her. That was why she'd eventually leave. He was far too fucked up to give her what she wanted and needed.

Chapter Twenty-Seven

The minute Acer stepped away, a bit of unease settled low in Fia's belly, as though he was directly linked to her confidence and safety. At some point, she'd have to cut the cord and learn to stand on her own two feet again. Needing something to do with her hands, she lifted the bottle to her lips.

"So, you think about my offer at all?"

Liquid sloshed its way down her trachea, and she coughed.

A large hand pounded her back, nearly tossing her off the barstool. "Woah, sorry, hon. Didn't mean make ya choke." Lucky's smirk said he wasn't really all that sorry.

"I...um." She cleared her throat and blinked, her eyes watery from aspirating the beer. "Um, yeah, I'm gonna have to pass on your offer." She couldn't meet his eye.

"You sure? I—wait a second. I'm too late, aren't I?"

Fia sputtered. Could she feel any more like a kid caught making out by their parents?

Lucky's grin grew into a full-blown smile, the purple skin around his eye crinkling with mirth. "Good for you, hon. Acer's a good guy. Since I'm assuming I was a close second choice, I'm going to give you some advice."

She raised one eyebrow. Somehow, taking relationship

advice from a man named for his penchant for getting laid didn't seem wise.

He chuckled, then grew serious. "Don't go spinning any fairy tales, sweetheart. Use Acer to work through your shit, but don't expect a happy ever after. He's a closed off bastard and doesn't trust for shit."

Pop. There went her newly formed bubble of happiness. His words weren't anything she didn't know, but she was beginning to let herself drift from the knowledge. Lucky's reminder cemented the fact that she had to think of Acer as an amazing friend who helped her through a horrible ordeal, but nothing more. Nothing permanent. "He's your brother. Why are you telling me this?"

He shrugged. "I like you. You've been through enough; you don't need a broken heart to top it all off."

Smart advice.

She wouldn't be here all that much longer. Each day she felt more equipped to handle life. She was able to work from Acer's apartment but it would be more convenient in her own space. If she didn't leave soon, she was bound to start dreaming of those fairy tales Lucky mentioned. "I'll keep it in mind."

"You do that, hon. Since you gave me the brush off—are you fucking kidding me?"

Fia followed Lucky's gaze to two men who looked about ready to rip each other's throats out. One was huge, nearly Jester's size, and the other not much smaller. The bigger guy swung a meaty fist in a wild arc that came close to taking out an innocent bystander. The smaller of the men laughed and curled his upturned hands in a bring-it-on motion.

"Shit, I hate to leave you alone but I need to help break that up before it explodes."

Uh, yeah, he did, before someone was seriously injured.

"Go, go. I'll be fine." She gave him a gentle shove.

Lucky dashed off, grabbing the smaller man around his chest a fraction of a second before the man's fist would have collided with his opponent's face. Thankfully, a few men latched onto the bigger man as well.

She sucked in a breath and rolled her shoulders. Lucky would be back in a second, and Acer shortly after that. She'd be alone for a few moments at most. Nothing to freak out about.

Fia shifted her attention to the oblivious and intoxicated dancers, blissfully unaware of the ensuing fight just steps away. Sitting a stone's throw from men attempting to demolish each other didn't help her nerves. She needed something else to focus on.

She was so absorbed watching a woman who had to be an exotic dancer use a man like a stripper pole, she didn't notice when a large, leather-bound biker approached. He had an MC cut, like Acer's but the patch said *Hermanos de Sangue*. What did that mean? She shoved the cobwebs aside and dug back to high school Spanish. Brothers in blood, or something like that?

"What's a pretty *chica* like you doing over here all by yourself? Want some company?" He spoke loud to be heard over the pulsing music.

Not from you. Old Fia's retort was on the tip of her tongue, but New Fia's fear clogged her throat and rendered her mute.

"Aww, you shy, *princesa*? Don't worry, I'm *real* good at getting women to open up." He leaned close, until his face was level with hers and he rested his hands on the bar on either side of her body.

She was caged in, couldn't escape without touching him. The uninvited tightening in her chest was instantaneous. Her eyes flooded with tears and her muscles trembled. She wanted to scream at him to back away, but it was though a hand squeezed her windpipe, cutting off her air and ability to vocalize.

"Speechless, huh, *princesa?*" He ran a hand up her thigh, the touch enough to kick her into action.

"N-no! Don't t-touch me." She tried to smack his hand away, but the quaking of her muscles made it impossible to put any power into the action. Her breaths became labored and the man's image swam before her eyes.

She had to get out of here. She needed to be alone with her humiliation and fear.

~ ~ ~ ~

Lucky swiped at the blood on his lip and shook his head. Leave it to drunk bikers to fight over a woman who charged by the hour. "Thanks for the assist, Gumby."

Gumby grinned as he ran a hand through his disheveled hair. "No problem, brother. Arizona's turning out to be more exciting than Vegas so far, ain't it?"

Lucky snorted. "My face ain't exactly happy with my decision to move here." He needed to get back to Fia. She was fun to tease, but she'd been through hell and he didn't want her to be afraid sitting by herself. Not to mention the beating Acer would give him if she felt one ounce of discomfort. For a man who had no interest in having an ol' lady, Acer sure acted like a smitten son of a bitch.

"What the fuck's wrong with you? Jesus, lady, you're crazy." An angry male shout of pain rang out over the beat of the music.

Christ, what now? Lucky raised to his tip-toes to see over the crowd and locate the source the shouting.

Fuck.

A biker he didn't know had Fia completely dwarfed by his

size and stance, captive against the bar. Fia was shaking so hard, her stool wobbled. Lucky picked up the pace, shouldering anyone in his way aside to get to her. Just as he was about to yank the biker off Fia and beat the tar out of him, the guy jumped back.

"Fuck. Crazy bitch scratched me." He held a hand over his right forearm. "Someone needs to teach this *puta* a lesson."

"Back the fuck away from her, asshole." Lucky snarled and plowed into the man, using his side to shove him away from a trembling Fia.

He stumbled back and raised his hands in surrender. "No problem, man. She's your problem now." He moved away, muttering under his breath.

Tears flowed down her cheeks and she gasped for breath.

Lucky stepped next to her stool. "Honey, it's Lucky. He's gone. Want to come with me to find Acer?"

Fia shook her head, her body still quivered and her eyes were unfocused. "No, no...Don't bother Acer. Please...I just need to go home."

Shit. She was about two seconds away from a meltdown like she had in the park. He could not let her leave. "Honey, there is no way you can drive, and Acer will castrate me if I put you on the back of my bike. Let's go find him so he can take you home. Okay? Follow me. I'll go first so no one bumps you."

He turned and took three steps away from the bar before he glanced over his shoulder. That was his mistake. In that brief time, Fia slipped from the barstool and was halfway to the exit.

Fuck! How the hell had she moved that fast when her legs were trembling like they were brand new?

Lucky ran after her, but his larger frame wasn't able to zigzag through the drunken bodies nearly as fast as she had. He burst outside just in time to see Fia's taillights speeding out of the parking lot.

He had two choices, follow her, or go back in and get Acer. He needed to follow. He could call Acer on the way. He shoved his hand in his pocket.

Goddamnit! Could one thing go the way it was supposed to?

He'd stashed his keys and phone behind the bar so he wouldn't lose track of them after the party got going.

With another curse, he turned and jogged back into the clubhouse. He could see the headline now, *Ladies man murdered by his brother for not protecting his woman.*

Fuck.

Chapter Twenty-Eight

"Sorry to yank you from the party, Acer, but I wanted to keep tonight's meeting about Lucky patching over and nothing else. Now I need to ask you about this shit down at the border. Where are you with it?"

Acer nodded and sat across the table from Shiv. "No problem, pres."

As usual, the No Prisoners' president had a thick stogie dangling from the corner of his mouth, the rising smoke mixing with the permanent smog of the room.

He hated to mention Fia's father's involvement, but it's not like he could keep details from Shiv. "It looks like my old man and Fia's old man have teamed up to try and fuck us. After our scuffle at the border, I hacked into Wellington's emails." His father's cyber security was good, but he was better. "He had a shit ton of communication with Terrance Caldwell. Details about their trafficking operation. I pissed my father off when I turned down his offer to shuttle illegals across the border, and I pissed Fia's old man off when I chewed his ass out about wanting to go to the media. This must be revenge."

Shiv rubbed a hand over a scar that ran the length of his

left cheek. No one knew for sure where it came from, but rumor had it the wound was inflicted when he was in prison. He served ten years for weapons trafficking back when he was in his twenties. It was also how he got his nickname. He'd survived a stabbing in the prison yard. "You gonna make this chick your ol' lady?"

Acer choked on his saliva. Where the hell had that come from? He cleared his throat. "Uh, no pres, I'm not. She's just rooming with me until she gets back on her own two feet. That's all."

If he said it enough, maybe he'd believe it.

Shiv pulled the cigar out of his mouth. "We'll see. You boys are dropping like flies." He waved the cigar. "Anyway, you got a plan to deal with this shit from the rich fathers?"

"I've got photos of Fia's old man with a woman younger than she is. He's been fucking her and does not want it leaked. It will ruin his reputation, his family, and potentially his business. I'm going to increase the pressure on him, let him know I won't hesitate to release them to the media. Maybe send him some fake headlines. Make him sweat a little. My old man is a different story. He's much more cautious with his dealings. I'm working on getting some dirt on him."

Shiv leaned back in his chair and ran a hand over the new beard growth on his face. He'd been growing it for the past half year and it hung nearly to his chest, the graying color matching his long hair. "Maybe Caldwell will give you something if you squeeze him hard enough. We need them fucking gone. It's just too risky to have anyone with a connection to us working the border. Even if we scare them into getting rid of the fake cuts, what's to say they won't find another way to pin the whole fuckin' thing on us if they get caught?"

It was a risk. His old man's typical style was to throw money around and make problems disappear, but if he was running short on cash, he may look for other ways to keep his ass out of trouble. He needed something big enough to make Reginald abandon the entire project. "Alright, give me a few more days to get a solid plan together. Aside from his sloppy emails to Caldwell, Wellington's been very discrete. I'll find a way to drive them out of Arizona. I'm sorry my family shit fell on the club's doorstep, Pres."

Shiv shrugged. "Don't worry about it. If it wasn't this it would be something else, right?"

"Guess so." His president's easy acceptance didn't alleviate the guilt he felt over his old life's intrusion into his current life. His brothers were now at risk, a pawn in his father's games. Just as Derek had been.

"You need more help from the club, you let me know. This isn't just your problem." Shiv pierced him with a stern look.

"I can handle it."

"I know you can, Acer. Just saying you don't have to do this entire thing on your own. You got brothers." He raised one eyebrow and removed the cigar from between his lips, flicking ash into a ceramic bowl.

Yeah, he did. And they had his back the other night. He could hand off some of this responsibility to a few of his brothers. It was just easier to do it himself, easier to have control over how much people found out about his shitty family. And the only one he fully trusted was himself.

"Have you told your girl about her old man's involvement?" He inhaled from the cigar then blew rings of smoke into the air. The pungent odor followed him wherever he went.

Everyone referred to Fia as his. He supposed she was since she was living with him and now sleeping with him. Or had slept with him once. But she wasn't his to keep. He needed to distance himself a bit, start laying the groundwork that she wasn't a fixture in his life. "No."

Shiv nodded and puffed on his cigar. "Not yet, or just no?"

Acer shifted in his seat, uncomfortable under Shiv's assessing stare. "Uh, just no."

"You think there's any chance she's in on this?"

His gut screamed *no*, but he didn't listen to his gut anymore, at least not when it told him to trust someone. "I just don't think she needs to know. It will only add to her stress." That was more than him looking for an easy out from the guilt of keeping secrets, it was partly true. Her entire world had been rocked just a few short weeks ago. Her family failed to help her when she needed it, finding out now that they were a part in his troubles *would* add to her stress. She just didn't need it.

Shiv snickered. "Playing with fire, my man."

Didn't he know it.

A loud pounding had both men turning toward the door.

"What?" Shiv called.

Lucky poked his head in the room. "Sorry, pres. Acer, we got a problem."

Acer looked at Shiv who nodded. "You're free to go. Let me know if you need anything from me."

"Thanks." If Lucky was at the door, where the hell was Fia?

He closed the chapel door behind him and advanced on Lucky. "Where is she?" He looked around expecting Fia to be steps away.

Lucky held his hand out. "Stay calm, brother. I had to help break up a fight, and while I was gone, some asshole came on to her real strong. Freaked her out big time. Not quite as bad as the other day, but bad enough."

Tension radiated from him, so thick, he could almost see the waves flowing toward Lucky. "I asked you where she was." He kept the panic out of his voice, but couldn't keep the deadly intent hidden.

"She took off. I tried to catch up, but she was too fast. I'm sorry, brother." Lucky's eyes were bleak and there wasn't a hint of the cocky swagger and bravado he usually employed.

Fuck! She was out at night. Alone. Unprotected. Sweat broke out across his forehead and his mind ran in a million directions. Sure, there had been no peep from Mike, but still. He couldn't bear the thought of her alone and afraid. The attack hadn't just affected her, it fucked with his head as well. All he could see was the image of her, battered and terrified, chained to the floor at the mercy of that monster.

"She said she wanted to go home. I'm guessing she went to your apart—"

Acer didn't stick around to hear the rest of Lucky's statement. He shoved his way through the crowed and out into the crisp desert air. His heart pounded in his chest as he ran toward his bike. Not for the first time since he met Fia, he felt completely out of control and helpless.

Fear wasn't something he did. Lack of control wasn't something he did. Was this how Fia felt? Constantly afraid and powerless. If so, she was a fucking hero, because two minutes of it and Acer was ready to claw his own eyes out.

He hopped on his bike, revved the engine, and sped off in search of his woman.

That's right.

His fucking woman.

At least for today.

~ ~ ~ ~

Fia made it to Acer's apartment in record time. Driving alone, in the dark, not far from where she'd been abducted did nothing to calm her. Grateful for Acer's bright security lighting, she clung to the handrail and made her way up the stairs on shaky legs. Once inside, she stumbled into the apartment and straight for the bathroom, shedding clothes as she went. She needed a shower, scalding water to cleanse away the pain and grimy memories.

She reached into Acer's large spa shower and flipped the water on, hot. While she waited for the stream to heat, she stared at herself in the mirror.

The circular scars forming an M over her ribs seared as though fresh wounds. Whenever she was in a panic, the fiery pain of the burns flared. The pink spheres glowed against her tanned complexion like neon lights, mocking her. Reminding her she was weak, helpless, a basket case who couldn't even tell an overgrown frat boy who didn't understand the word no to fuck off.

With a snort of disgust, she stepped into the shower and grabbed her body scrubber. The water was just shy of too hot, and she backed under until it fell in sheets around her head. Fresh tears, as hot as the soaking water ran down her face.

Fia stared down at the marks on her side. She loathed them and everything they stood for. The constant reminder of being completely at the mercy of a malevolent psychopath. How, in the blink of an eye, she transformed from a strong and confident woman to a panicked and timid shadow of that individual.

Acer had no idea her body bore Mike's brand. He hadn't noticed it the night he rescued her and she'd left her camisole on when they had sex. What man would want to stare at a physical reminder that his woman had been violated? And not an ordinary reminder at that, but a mark that screamed, "Mike was here."

Acer already felt unwarranted guilt over what she went through. A nasty scar staring him in the face would be intolerable. But it was more than just that. This reminder would be with her forever. Any man she showed herself to in the future would want an explanation and would have a front row seat to her shame. Shame that she'd look at every day for the rest of her life in the mirror.

She ran her scrubber over the small round blemishes as though she could wash them off. After a few swipes, she increased the pressure, abrading her skin with the rough sponge.

The sobs came then, her entire body heaved with the force of her sorrow.

Who was she kidding, thinking she'd be back to her real life any time soon? She was such a fucking head case. Just as her body bore scars and would never be the same again, neither would her life.

Chapter Twenty-Nine

Acer shoved his door open. It slammed against the wall and bounced back, smacking him in the shoulder as he burst through the entryway. There'd be a mark for sure—both on the wall and his shoulder. He stared at the alarm panel. It hadn't beeped. Fia's car was parked around back, so she had to be here. Had she forgotten to set the alarm, or had something happened?

"Fia? Baby, you here?" He listened for a response, but the rushing of blood in his ears overpowered any reply. He quickly trekked through the apartment, following a trail of clothes toward the guestroom.

She wasn't in there. Where the fuck was she?

Acer stepped into his own bedroom, drawn by the sound of the running shower. Relief almost brought him to his knees. He took a cleansing breath before opening the door. She needed him to have his shit together.

He pushed the bathroom door open and waved the steam away. It was hotter than a sauna. As some of the steam cleared, he noticed Fia through the glass shower door. She stood under the spray, sobbing and rubbing a sponge over her stomach.

Her agony was palpable, and Acer ached as he watched her suffer through the anguish alone. He itched to run out of the room, into the night so he could scream his rage into the quiet desert. But he didn't leave. In that moment, he'd have done anything, given anything to take away some of her pain.

The raw skin beneath the scouring sponge was an angry red, so much so, it was easily visible from his position outside the shower. "Fia!" He spoke loud enough to be heard over the rushing water.

She jumped and stilled, staring at him through ravaged eyes.

"Baby, what are you doing to yourself?" His voice broke and he worked to keep his own eyes from tearing. He'd cried one time in his life, years ago, at the news of Derek's death. Seeing Fia suffer this way was just as horrific.

"I just want it to go away. It won't go away." Tears poured from her bloodshot eyes, and she started scrubbing at her stomach again.

Acer wasted no time stripping out of his clothes and opening the shower door. He stepped into the large stall and slowly reached out to still her movements. "Honey." He kept his touch gentle and soft despite the urge to drag her into his arms and never let her go. "You need to stop. Your skin is bleeding. You're hurting yourself."

Fia dropped the sponge and it landed with a soggy plop. Without lifting her head to look at him, she whispered, "I'm sorry."

She seemed to have no idea that he was naked, a foot and a half away from her in the shower.

He didn't answer, he couldn't. Rage began low in his gut and clawed its way up, wrapping around his windpipe and cutting off his ability to speak. His vision tunneled to a single spot on her dripping body. Through the abraded skin covering her ribs, small pink discs arranged in the shape of an *M* mocked him. It took three breaths before he felt under control enough to speak. "Did he do that to you? Did he fucking brand you?" His voice was a whisper, as rough as her scraped skin.

She finally looked at him and flinched. He could only imagine the fury reflected in his gaze, and tried to tamp it down, for her sake, but it was impossible.

"Y-yes." She swallowed, and folded her arms over her sides. "He burned me with cigarettes. I'm sorry, I didn't want you to ever see it."

If he'd been alone, Acer would have punched the tile wall until chunks of ceramic fell to the ground and his knuckles bled. Maybe then, some of the murderous rage coursing through his veins would abate. Instead, he took one step closer, ignoring the boiling water that beat against him. "Please don't say you're sorry. Don't every say you're sorry. I'm the one who's sorry. Sorry you worried about me seeing this, sorry I didn't find you sooner, sorry for so many fucking things. Christ, baby, you survived something people can't even fathom. Do you have any idea how strong that makes you? How amazing you are?"

She laughed, a humorless sound full of disgust. "You've got to be kidding me. I am not strong, Acer. Do you have any idea what happened tonight? Some jerk got a little fresh and I freaked out. Freaked out! I couldn't tell him to go to hell, I couldn't even breathe. Three months ago, I would have kicked him in the nuts so hard they popped out of his mouth. Tonight, I panicked, ran away, and now I'm in the shower trying to scrub a freaking scar off my body." She pointed to herself with both hands. "This is not strength. This is the complete opposite of strength."

Her words sliced at the cage around his heart. Her chest heaved, her gorgeous breasts rose and fell with her heavy inhalations. While he detested the words of self-hatred, he could handle her anger better than her consuming grief. Anger brought a spark of life to her eyes that was so much closer to the old Fia than she realized. Her beautiful face was flushed and she looked like a warrior ready for battle.

A very sexy female warrior.

"I'm not me." She pushed her wet hair out of her eyes and stepped closer to him. "I'm someone else. I hate this person." Her voice rose. "I hate her! This timid mouse with her fear and her panic attacks, afraid of every dark corner and every man who comes within ten feet."

He reached out and placed one warm hand over the scars on her body. She tensed beneath his palm, but he didn't move, waiting until her body slowly relaxed. "These scars mean nothing. They define nothing about you. They're just pink skin. I don't see them when I look at you. I see a beautiful woman fighting like hell to regain something that was taken from her against her will."

"Acer…" she whispered.

He cupped her face between his hands, ensuring she kept her gaze on him while he spoke. This was far too important for her to miss a single word. She stared at him like he held the key to the universe. "I see a woman who's come so far she can work again, laugh again, she can be a sassy smartass again, she can even fuck again."

She huffed out a tiny chuckle and a ghost of a smile graced her sweet mouth. "Thank you."

"And you're not afraid of me." The sound of the water splattering on the tiled floor was as loud as a herd of elephants as he waited for her response.

"No…I'm not." The words were spoken so low he almost

didn't hear them over the stampede.

As though a light switch flipped in her head and she realized he was nude, her gaze flicked to his cock then back up to meet his. Before his eyes, her nipples tightened and her body tensed, but for a different reason this time.

There wasn't a single thing he could have done in that moment to prevent the rush of blood southward.

They stared at each other across the shower, the air thick with steam and desire.

One, two, three seconds ticked by.

~ ~ ~ ~

Fia couldn't tear her attention away from Acer if her life depended on it. How was it he saw her so differently than she saw herself? Was he right? She did find herself acting more and more like Old Fia each day, laughing, giving him sass, allowing him to touch her. While he seemed angry she had to endure pain from Mike burning her, he didn't seem disgusted or turned off by the scars. In fact, he'd barely looked at them, focusing instead on boosting her confidence and squashing her insecurities. Maybe it was time to focus on the progress she had made and look to the future instead of living in the past.

She held his gaze for long seconds. Then, like someone lit a match in a room full of gas, they exploded toward each other. Acer was bigger and faster, backing her up until she hit the tile wall the same time his hungry mouth came down on hers.

All thoughts fled her mind. There wasn't room for fear or sadness. There wasn't room for anything but the consuming need to feel his hands on her, his mouth on her, and—dear God please—his cock inside her.

Their mouths ate at each other. Gone was the patient man from two nights ago, the man who let her take control. The man who ignored his own needs in favor of hers. In his place was a man who wanted her to remember how amazing the physical connection between a man and a woman could be.

He pressed her to the wall, his slick, muscular torso flush against hers, but it wasn't close enough. Without breaking the kiss, Fia lifted a leg and wrapped it around his hips. The movement nestled his erection between her thighs. Almost where she needed it, but not quite.

She moaned against his mouth. If he didn't get inside her soon, she might combust.

Acer must have sensed her desperation, or maybe his own matched it. He slid one hand down her slippery body and filled it with the soft skin of her ass, holding her leg in place around his waist. His other hand tangled in her hair and with a firm tug, he tilted her head back.

Fia's mind spun with the overwhelming onslaught of sensation. Her beaded nipples pressed into the hard planes of his chest, his mouth sucked at the sensitive spot where her neck met her shoulder and his—

Oh my God.

Acer bent his legs and entered her in one fierce thrust.

She cried out and her knee buckled, the pleasure so intense she'd have fallen straight to the shower floor if he hadn't been holding her up by her ass cheek.

His thrusts were short, fast and choppy. This wasn't going to be a long drawn out lovemaking session where he commanded the pace and when she came. This was going to be a hard and fast race to the finish.

Fia could no longer distinguish between the sensations rioting through her. All she felt was pleasure, swamping every cell in her being. It went far beyond the physical, touching somewhere deep, and mending her fractured soul.

She wrenched her head against his hold on her hair, her

lips seeking his. When his tongue found hers again, she moaned into his mouth. Acer thrust twice more, his pelvis bumping her clit with each slam, and just as suddenly as this began, Fia came.

Weeks of tension and strain fled her body in a rush of sensation so intense, it brought tears to her eyes. She cried out as she jerked in his arms, her pussy squeezing his thick length, demanding every last drop he had to give.

Acer tore his mouth from hers. "Fuck, Fia." He grunted next to her ear as his body convulsed in her arms and propped her against the wall, preventing her from melting to the floor and down the drain in a satisfied puddle. She held him close as he came, loving how she could make him lose his mind as completely as he did her.

Wow. She'd had no idea how much she'd needed that. She'd just had crazy, intense sex with Acer without a hint of fear or panic. She smiled, her face buried against his chest as tears fell, happy tears this time. Tears of relief and hope.

She wasn't completely broken.

She was one hundred percent certain she couldn't have done that with any man beside Acer, but that didn't matter. He was the only one she wanted now, anyway. Maybe the only one she'd ever want.

He released her bottom and she flinched. There'd be a few finger shaped bruises there tomorrow. She couldn't wait to see them, to remember how they'd attacked each other like starving animals.

She enjoyed the feel of his flexing muscles sliding under her palms as he pulled back. Blinking through the tears, she looked up at his face, anticipating the contented look of a sated man. She expected him to be as proud of her as she was. Instead, she encountered horrified eyes full of revulsion.

"Christ, Fia, I'm sorry." He stared at his hands as though

they didn't belong to him.

"What? Acer—"

"I'm sorry." He backed out of the shower and left the bathroom without grabbing a towel. The door slammed behind him and Fia jumped.

What the hell just happened? All the insecurities he'd quelled just minutes before rushed back full force. She shivered, the warm water having disappeared at some point in the last few minutes. With a frown, she turned off the spray and leaned against the shower wall.

Had she read him wrong? Maybe, despite what he said, he really was repulsed by the scars. She wiped a tear...the tears! It had to be the tears. He misunderstood them. Well, who could blame him? She'd been a weepy mess since she'd come back into his life.

Damnit.

Fia blew out a breath and pushed off the wall. She needed to fix this. No way could she allow him to think he'd hurt her. Not when he'd given her exactly what she hadn't known she needed. Not when, for the first time in over three weeks, she felt like she had a fighting chance for a normal life again.

She quickly toweled off. Acer's T-shirt and zippered hoodie lay on the floor so she threw them on over her nakedness along with her discarded panties. She never heard the rumble of his bike, so hopefully he hadn't left. The idea of driving around town in the dark looking for a pissed off biker wasn't appealing, but she'd do it to find him. Even though they had no chance for a future, for a happy ever after, she'd do damned near anything for him.

Chapter Thirty

Acer sat on the cold, concrete steps leading from his apartment to the parking lot, his head in his hands. It was somewhere around midnight, and quiet as a tomb in the desert. His was the only apartment above the coffee shop—which had closed an hour ago—so he had privacy and peace.

Well, privacy anyway.

What he yearned to do was hop on his bike and ride out into the dark night until he left behind what just happened, but leaving Fia alone after he'd fucked up so royally would make him an even bigger bastard.

Christ, he'd really screwed this up. She trusted him, with her body, with her fears. And he'd attacked her like he was no better than Mike.

To top it all off, he hadn't used a condom. Protection hadn't even entered his consciousness. Damn, she'd been hot as hell and wetter than the water that had soaked them.

This was exactly why he didn't trust anyone. This was why Fia never should have trusted him. It was only a matter of time before he broke that trust. Because in the end, it wasn't just that he shouldn't trust others. They shouldn't trust him either. Hadn't he destroyed Derek? Now he'd done the same to Fia.

The door creaked open above him and he tensed. Fia's soft footsteps sounded on the hard stairs. She walked down, around him, until she stood one step below, her smooth stomach pressing against his flexed knees.

"Go back inside, Fia. You don't want to be around me right now." He couldn't look at her. Couldn't bear to view the hatred and blame in her eyes.

"Acer—"

"Don't trust anyone, Fia. Not Lucky, not me, not anyone. No matter how well intentioned, people will fuck you over. Every single time. I think I just proved that."

"Are you done yet?"

His head snapped up at the bite in her voice. Her hands were on her hips, and she frowned at him, but didn't look like she hated him.

She cocked a hip and raised an eyebrow. "Can I speak now?"

He nodded. She could say whatever the hell she wanted. He deserved it.

"Did you lie to me in there?" She pointed toward the apartment.

"What?" He stared up at her, the words not registering.

"Did you lie to me about the scars? Do they turn you off?"

He gasped. "No. No! What the fuck, Fia? I'm not sitting out here because you have a few scars."

"Well, then I only have one thing to say to you." She frowned at him, hands still perched on her hips.

Here it comes.

A radiant smile broke out across her pretty face. "Thank you, Acer."

What? He blinked at her like an owl.

"You forgot, and I forgot, and it was so freakin' fantastic.

That's why I cried. I wasn't upset, I wasn't hurt. I was relieved, and it felt so incredible."

He shook his head, his thoughts racing. "Forgot what?"

She pushed his knees apart and stepped between his legs. The jeans covering his firm thighs were cold and damp since he hadn't bothered to towel off. "Forgot to treat me like I was damaged. Forgot that I *am* damaged."

"Fia, I crushed you against the wall. I didn't give you an out. Christ, I held you so tight you'll probably have bruises tomorrow." He put his hands on her feminine hips. He had no right to touch her, but he couldn't stop himself from needing her softness under his fingertips.

She leaned forward and gave him a gentle kiss. Just like that, he was hard again. What was it about this woman that made his legendary control blow right out the window?

"And I inhaled you like I was starving, and held you against me because I couldn't get you close enough, and I think I may have clawed at your back trying to keep you close. So, you may have a few marks of your own." She smirked, the look so full of self-pride, he couldn't help but smile back. "Acer, you've seen me in freak out mode enough over the past few weeks to know when I'm afraid. I have no doubt in my mind, not a single one, that if I'd wanted you to stop, you would have."

He shook his head and gave her a gentle squeeze. He loved the way her soft flesh molded in his hands, like warm clay. "I told you not to trust me."

She kissed him again, longer this time, hotter. "Well, you're just going to have to find a way to deal with the fact that I do. Sorry."

He chuckled. Her voice was full of sass. Old Fia sass.

"I didn't use a condom."

"I know. It's okay. I have an IUD and I was tested for

everything under the sun right after…you know, and again before I came here. I'm clean. As long as you are, we're good."

"I'm clean. I swear it." He stared at her stomach. Anger, sadness, fear, frustration, tenderness and an unfamiliar warm feeling all swirled through him in one barrage of emotion. For someone unused to shoving all emotion aside, it was overwhelming. He couldn't begin to sort through and process it all right now.

The one feeling he knew exactly how to manage was the anger. He had an intense and morbid need to memorize the scars on her body, to use the image of her marred skin to fuel his fury. Maybe he'd gift Mike a similar treatment before ending the fucker's life. "Can I see it?"

She tensed in his arms, but nodded.

The night was quiet, no one around for miles. They may have been outdoors, but they were isolated, behind the building on his steps. He nudged the too-large T-shirt up her torso until it rested just below her breasts. Damn, that lacy thong was sexy. She was a master at her craft.

The scars on the right side of her ribs rested just about eye level given their position on the steps. Illuminated by the security light adjacent to his front door, the marks were clearly visible. The small circles and the skin around them were an angry red from the abuse she'd inflicted in the shower. He pressed a kiss over the ridged skin before resting his forehead on her stomach. The scent of her arousal, either from this intimacy, or from what they shared in the shower, was intoxicating.

"Acer," she whispered as she slid her hands into his wet hair with a soothing touch.

He'd find Mike, and make the motherfucker pay, if it was his last act on this earth. The noble thing would be to want justice for Fia, and he did, but he wanted to hurt Mike for himself too. He wanted, needed the satisfaction of seeing terror and pain in the man's eyes. Yes, his sense of justice was warped, but he'd come to terms with that part of himself years ago. It's just who he was.

"I'm so sorry he did this to you, but don't say you hate the scars, baby. We all have things that have broken us and left their mark, both physically and mentally. Just shows what a survivor you are." He kissed the burns again and trailed his lips across her stomach. He'd devour her whole if he could. The touch of her delicate and capable artist's hands sifting through his hair was a heavenly combination of comfort and arousal.

"I'm only a survivor because of you, Acer. You got me out of there, you've helped me heal. I was drowning at my parent's house, suffocating in my own fears and misery."

After one more kiss he looked up at her. "Don't put me on a pedestal, baby. I don't belong there."

She rolled her eyes, and, with her hands still in his hair, gave his head a little shake. "I'm not. Don't worry, I know you're full of flaws." The admiration shining from her eyes defied her words.

He didn't want hero worship from her. Nor did he want growing emotions. So what the hell did he want? This conversation was sliding into dangerous territory, so he steered it to safer ground.

"You know, that smart mouth is going to get you into trouble sometime, babe." He nuzzled his nose against her stomach. The combination of the clean, fresh shower smell mixed with her pungent arousal. His shaft twitched in his pants.

She smiled. "I thought my smart mouth was one of the things you liked best about me."

"Oh, it is."

Her smile grew seductive. She stepped backward, down one step as she shrugged out of the borrowed hoodie. When she was free of the material, she laid it along the length of the step between them. "Let's see if we can't find another reason for you to like my mouth," she said with a wink as she dropped to her knees on the sweatshirt.

The chilly night air did nothing to stomp out the fiery heat that suffused every inch of him. Whatever water still remained on his skin from the shower must have evaporated from the heat coming off his body. Though he'd thrown on a pair of jeans but hadn't bothered to zip them and had forgone a shirt as well.

Fia maneuvered the open fly of his jeans so his now aching dick was free for her touch. She wrapped her small hand around him and gave a firm squeeze. He jolted at the harsh shock of pleasure. "Oh fuck! Fia!"

"Hmm?" she hummed as she lowered her head. She licked a circle around the crown of his dick and his eyes rolled back in his head. With a puff of air, she blew on the wet skin she'd just licked.

Acer gripped the edge of the step until the rough concrete abraded his fingertips. He should stop her. He needed to stop her. It wasn't that he was worried someone would catch them out in the open on the steps, it was plenty private, but somehow, he felt like he should be the one pleasuring her, not the one on the receiving end. "Fia, wait."

She rose up on her knees and rested her elbows on his spread thighs. "Acer, don't be selfish."

He snorted. "I'm trying not to be, baby. I'm trying really hard not to be." He ran a thumb across a puckered nipple through the fabric of her shirt and enjoyed the shudder of desire that quivered through her.

"Then let me have my wicked way with you."

He searched her gaze, not finding inflated hero worship, only desire. He nodded.

Fia winked. "Good. Now lean back and enjoy."

"Only if you get yourself off too, babe."

"What?" Her eyes widened.

"Finger yourself. While you suck me. I want to see you come again." With a light pinch, he rolled her nipple between his fingers.

Her hands flew to his thighs as though to anchor herself against the pleasure. She blinked at him, pink tingeing her cheeks, but she nodded. Leaning on his thighs for support, she spread her knees wider. When she was in position, she moved one hand between her legs and gasped at the contact.

Acer shifted his hips so they were closer to the edge of the step, allowing him to lean back somewhat, and brace his elbows on the concrete one step above.

"Good boy." Fia sent him a sassy grin as she lowered her head once again. This time, she opened her mouth wide and drew him deep into the warm, wet heat of her mouth. After she closed her lips around his length, she sucked, hard.

"Christ, Fi."

"Hmm?" She made the same humming noise she had a moment ago, this time around his dick and the vibrations nearly did him in.

"That feels so fucking good." Wars could be fought over a mouth like hers.

She drove him crazy, licking, sucking, occasionally throwing in a small hum until he could barely see, all the while rocking her pelvis on her little hand and hopefully getting as close as he was.

He lifted one arm off the step and sifted her silky hair through his fingers.

She pulled off him, replacing her talented mouth with her clever hand. "Go ahead," she said around a gasp, still fingering herself.

"What?" He almost couldn't process the words.

She nudged his hand with her head. "Go ahead." Her eyes were unfocused, glazed with desire. "God, that feels good," she said, increasing the speed of her fingers in her channel. "I trust you, Acer. Guide my head."

Even though she was a fool to trust him, her words melted something long frozen inside him. He fisted her hair with a firm hold and guided her back down. This time, he controlled the pace, thrusting into her wide mouth. He was careful not to lose control, not to scare or hurt her, but she let him take over and kept up with him while he fucked her mouth, her fingers thrusting in her pussy in time with his cock.

It didn't take along at all before his balls drew tight and the pressure built to near bursting. "I'm not gonna last, Fia. It's now or never if you don't want me to come down your throat."

Little moans escaped her, the vocalizations squeezing the tip of his cock at the back of her throat and she trembled. Christ, she was coming. Her grip on his thigh tightened to near painful and sent him over the edge.

"Fuck, babe, that mouth." He curled forward and shot down her throat, his hands tightening in her hair as he lost the ability to command his muscles. He came hard for the second time that night. He always came hard with Fia.

It was a high he'd never experienced with another woman, and it was more addicting than any drug.

A few moments later, she rested on her heels and winked, her expression sleepy and content. "I think it's safe to say I've still got it."

Acer threw back his head and laughed. Damn that felt good. Another experience he had with Fia more than anyone else. "Come on, smart-mouth, let's go to bed." He stood, drew her up from the step, and threw an arm around her shoulders.

"Don't you think you should call it *amazing mouth* or something? Maybe *gives-best-head-ever mouth*? Or how about ___"

Acer kissed said mouth until he couldn't remember what she'd been teasing him about. "Smart-mouth. By the way, you're sleeping in my bed tonight, and every night."

"Okay," she whispered, pressing a hand to her swollen lips.

Something significant had shifted tonight, both with Fia's recovery and between them. If only her trust in him wouldn't end with Fia walking away more broken than when she arrived. If only he wasn't keeping important information about her family from her. If only his own ability to trust hadn't been snuffed out.

Chapter Thirty-One

"Acer, knock it off. We're in public." Fia pushed Acer's shoulders with a halfhearted effort. Really, she didn't want him to stop; she never wanted him to stop.

But they were in public.

"Acer." It came out as half moan, half whine. His mouth was on her neck, his hands on her breasts, under her shirt. One thumb brushed over a nipple and she groaned. In the four days since Lucky's party, Acer hadn't been able to keep his hands—or mouth—off her. He took advantage of every opportunity to kiss or touch her, and she loved it.

Gone was any tension or fear. With Acer at least. Around other men, she was still wary and a bit skittish, but with him, she felt free and whole again.

"Can't stop, baby. Your tits are far too sexy for me to stop. Besides, we aren't in public. We're in the privacy of Striker and Lila's kitchen while everyone else is outside stuffing their faces."

"But I just came in to get a corkscrew. They're going to know something's up if I'm not back soon."

"I've got a screw for you, baby."

Laughter bubbled out despite her desire. "That just might

be the worst line I've ever h—oh." She gasped as Acer pinched a nipple and bit down on her shoulder at the same time. If she didn't put a stop to this in the next ten seconds, she'd be begging him to fuck her on Lila's granite countertops regardless of that fact that one of the other six people here could walk in at any time.

"Fia? You having trouble finding—whoops!" Lila threw an arm across her eyes, a shit-eating grin on her face. "So, whatcha guys doing?"

They both laughed, and Acer slid his hands from beneath her shirt. She swatted him away as he attempted to right her clothes in a most unproductive way.

"Sorry, Lila, we're decent. You can uncover your eyes." She looked ridiculous, standing in the entrance to her own kitchen with her eyes concealed.

"You sure? Cuz I can wait if you two want to finish up." She barely got the sentence out around her laughter.

"Oh, well in that case—"

"No!" Fia shoved Acer away and hopped off the counter. "We're done." She smiled sheepishly at Lila and started for the doors to the backyard.

"Babe?"

Fia turned.

A silver corkscrew dangled from Acer's pinky, and a smirk played across his tempting mouth.

"Oh, right, thanks."

Lila and Acer laughed as she snatched the corkscrew and dashed back outside.

Luckily, Lila kept her mouth shut, but the knowing grins around the picnic table told her they weren't fooling anyone.

Striker shoved his chair back and stood. "We gotta roll, boys. Church is in forty-five minutes. You girls gonna be able to keep yourselves entertained for a few hours?"

"Oh, we sure are." Marcie's eyes sparkled with mischief.

Hook tugged on her ponytail, tipping her head back for a kiss. "I feel as though something is going on that we should know about, but don't. And that usually implies trouble."

She gave him an innocent smile. "Now, honey, do we ever cause you guys any trouble?"

Jester snorted. "I think you should just leave that one hanging out there." He kissed the pregnant Emily who glowed with happiness, and followed Striker and Hook into the house.

"See you in a few hours, babe." Acer's mouth met hers. He wasn't satisfied with a chaste peck. No, he tangled his tongue with hers and kissed her until a buzzing started in her ears and her panties grew damp.

Okay, damper. The little tryst in the kitchen had been the original culprit.

"Uh, yeah, bye." Whew, the man melted her brain. She was falling, hard and fast, the knowledge of the hard, solid ground below her doing nothing to stop her from diving in head first.

He winked and left her with the other women whose expressions resembled those of hungry vultures.

Marcie was the first to break the silence "Sooo, seems like you two are getting along well."

Heat rushed to Fia's face, but she couldn't keep the grin at bay. "We are."

Lila squeezed her hand under the table. "We love to gossip and tease, but first I just want to say how happy we are for you, Fia. You're a different woman than when you arrived."

Her eyes misted with tears, but she refused to let them fall. She was done crying, for any reason. "Thank you." She looked around the table at each woman.

"You thinking of sticking around?" Emily asked the

question Fia hadn't been allowing herself to think of.

"Oh, um, no. I don't think so. My apartment, my…life is in LA, you know?" The excuse sounded weak to her own ears.

The women exchanged a look, but didn't press then issue. Thank God. She wasn't ready to talk about her growing feelings for Acer. Wasn't ready to admit aloud that if he asked her to stay she'd say yes. Wasn't ready—or able—to admit that the man she just might love didn't possess the ability to trust her. That fact was the last nail in the coffin of their doomed relationship.

"Well," Lila said, rubbing her hands together. "Let's get to the important stuff, shall we?"

"Yes, yes!" Emily bounced in her seat. "I need mine soon or I'll be too fat to fit into it. My boobs have already grown to twice their normal size, which was too big to begin with."

"Oh man," Marcie said around a giggle. "Jester must be in absolute heaven. Be careful, or he's going to keep you knocked up forever."

Emily's face turned bright red, but she didn't deny Marcie's comment.

"Don't worry, Emily, I took that into account when making yours. It should be fine." She lifted the box she'd brought to the table and drew out three bra and panty sets. "Here, you go, ladies." Each woman reached out to receive their lingerie. "Go on in and try them on. If you're comfortable with me getting up close and personal, I'll make some adjustments. Then it will just take me a few days to get them finalized."

"We're comfortable." Marcie grabbed Lila's hand and tugged her into the house. "Come on, you two!"

Fia followed the bouncing women into the house. Each disappeared into a different room, but emerged a few moments later.

"Wow, Fia, no wonder you charge so much. This is amazing. The quality is outstanding and I swear my boobs have never looked so good!" Marcie twirled in her lingerie and struck a pose.

Fia busied herself making small adjustments as the women chattered on about how much their men would love her creations. Each bra and panty set was different, but true to the initial design.

"Hmm, never had a woman kneeling at my feet while I stood around in my naughty things before." Marcie winked down at Fia.

She laughed from her spot on the floor and removed the pin from the pin cushion her teeth often served as. "Sorry! Am I making you uncomfortable? I do this so often I forget that it can be weird for people."

"Nah." She waved a hand in the air then burst out laughing. "Oh, my God, can you imagine the guy's reaction if they walked in right now?"

The other girls laughed along with Marcie. "I think their heads would just explode right here in your living room."

"Which heads?" Fia muttered.

They all cracked up again until Fia had to wipe tears from her eyes. These girls were so much fun to be around. Her problems just faded away when they were together.

"Hey, Fia, do you usually wear your own designs?" Lila asked.

She stood and flexed her knees one at a time. They ached from kneeling for three rounds of fittings. "I do. I have a slight obsession with pretty underwear."

"Ooh, let's see what you have on?" With a laugh, Marcie grabbed for the hem of Fia's shirt.

She stepped out of Marcie's reach, folding her arms over

her midsection, the phantom burn of the scars coming to life.

Marcie frowned and dropped her hands. "Gosh, I'm sorry Fia. I didn't mean to make you uncomfortable."

Lila stepped up and put an arm around her shoulders. "I'm sure it's a hundred times worse in your head than it really is," she said, her voice full of gentle understanding.

She gaped at Lila. How did she—oh, of course Lila knew. She'd been the one to treat the very burns that now felt like a hot poker boring into her side.

The women stared at her and Emily took a breath. They were her friends. New friends, but good, kind, and supportive friends. They'd each been through their own ordeals as well. Acer had told her all about how each of the women met their men. There was no reason to hide who she was from these women.

She blew out a breath and lifted her shirt, revealing the lacy bra that was a recent creation. She loved it so much, she'd sent the design to the factory that made her retail pieces. In a few weeks, she'd have stock to sell.

The room was silent long enough that heat rose to Fia's cheeks. Then Marcie let out a low whistle. "That's some sexy stuff, girl. I think from now on, I'll be coming to you for all my unmentionables."

Lila gave her shoulders a squeeze and pressed a kiss to her temple. "You never have to feel self-conscious with us. About anything."

Emily stepped forward and gave her a hug. "Your strength is admirable, Fia."

"Trust me, girl. No one will ever notice you have scars if you keep wearing undies like that." Leave it to Marcie to shake her out of her negative thoughts.

Fia laughed and lowered her shirt.

It had been almost twenty-four hours since any thoughts of Mike or what she went through disturbed her happiness. Acer and her new friends were responsible for that. It would be hard to leave these women when it was time to go. And soon it would be that time. She was running out of excuses to stay with Acer.

She hoped he'd ask her to stay, not because she needed a place to hide away from the world, but because he wanted her with him. For days, she'd pretended that wasn't what she longed for, but she could only ignore the truth for so long. She wanted him, wanted to stay with him, but she wouldn't ask. It wasn't the deal they made, and he'd been so amazing to her. He didn't deserve her changing the rules so late in the game. And bottom line, she couldn't live her life with a man that would never trust her.

It wasn't her, she knew that. But the fact that he didn't trust anyone fully didn't make the pill any easier to swallow. She longed to be the one to break through his barriers, as he'd done for her, but she didn't see a way to tear down the walls he'd erected around his heart.

So she'd leave, soon. And she'd miss these women.

It was nothing compared to how much she would miss Acer. It was time to stop kidding herself. She was in love with the man. The man who was part biker, part intellectual. The man who was patient, supportive, protective, and loyal.

Fia was healing from her trauma, but part of her feared she'd never recover from the heartbreak that loomed ahead.

~ ~ ~ ~

"What the fuck were those four up to when we left?" Jester's hands were on his hips and he hovered over Acer as he dismounted his bike.

Acer leaned back in an attempt to get Jester out of his personal space. "Will you back up, you giant ape? I have no idea what they are doing. All I know, is Fia has been working on something she won't let me within twenty feet of. Given what she does for a living I'm sure it has something to do with lingerie for the ladies."

Jester backed up a step, a grin spreading across his face. "Oh, well, that I can get behind."

"What did you think they were doing?" Acer hung his helmet off the end of his handle bar.

Jester shrugged. "Didn't even have a guess. It's dangerous to try to figure out what women are thinking."

"Especially when one of them's knocked up." Hook punched Jester in his massive bicep.

Jester snorted. "You ain't kidding. Yesterday Emily cried for twenty minutes because her damned jeans were hard to button. Um, isn't that a given? She's pregnant, she's gonna get bigger."

Striker rolled his eyes. "Brother, it's going to be a long nine months if you don't even realize women hate to gain weight, for any reason."

"Fia seems like she's doing real well." Hook changed the subject.

Acer nodded. "She is. Come a long way." He kept his face impassive in an attempt to keep the guys from knowing he was sleeping with her, but their sly grins showed they were on to him.

"Any word on Mike?" Jester's stare was intense. He'd been the first to see Fia cowering in the corner at Mike's house. He probably wouldn't mind taking a shot at the fucker himself. Too bad. Mike was Acer's.

"Had a hit on his credit card, yesterday actually. At a motel in Iowa."

"Iowa? Fuck. We need to make a trip there?" Jester cracked the knuckles on his right hand.

Acer loved that his brothers were so ready to jump in and kick ass on his behalf. He shook his head. "I talked to a number of people at the hotel. No one by his description was seen. They have a security system as well, it's shitty, but catches the door to each room. I hacked in and viewed the footage. No Mike."

Striker frowned. "You think his card was stolen? Kinda far-fetched, don't ya think?"

Acer climbed off his bike. "No I think he gave the card to someone to throw us, or the cops, off his trail."

Striker grunted. "Fuckin' piece of shit. You think he's still a danger to your girl?"

Acer exhaled and shrugged. That question had been taunting him for the past few weeks. "No fuckin' idea. That's what's so maddening about this. Not only do I want to rip his balls off and shove them down his throat before I slit it, but he still owes us a shit ton of money. He'd be the worst kind of fool to be anywhere around here, but who the hell knows how stupid he actually is."

Jester clapped a meaty paw on Acer's shoulder. "Sorry, brother, I know this shit is making you crazy. We'll get the bastard eventually, and in the meantime, you get to keep your girl close."

Keep his girl close. He and Fia were involved in this monogamous pseudo-relationship, and the most frustrating part of the entire thing was how fuckin' happy she made him. But he was keeping secrets from her. At this point, he wasn't even sure why anymore. He didn't actually think she knew anything about their father's plans. But something made him mute every time he thought of coming clean.

"Hey!" Shiv stood in the doorway to the clubhouse. "You ladies interested in joining us, or you too busy talking about your fuckin' periods?"

"Sorry, pres." Hook elbowed Jester. "Jest was just telling us about how he called his woman fat."

"What! I did not—"

"Christ, Jester. You better sleep with one eye open." Shiv rolled his eyes and moved to the side, allowing the group to enter the clubhouse.

Once everyone was seated in the chapel, Shiv slapped his hand against the metal table. "All right, listen up. You all know we've got shit going on at the border. Guys trafficking illegals through our territory wearing our cuts, or at least a replica of our cuts that's good enough to fuck us with the Feds if they're caught. We've got good reason to believe they're gonna be caught at some point. Acer, I'll let you fill everyone in." He leaned back in his chair and puffed on his thick cigar.

Acer opened his laptop and pulled up a satellite image from the day before. He cleared his throat and ignored the gnawing burn of acid in his stomach. "Robert Wellington, the billionaire hotel mogul and owner of the Wellington Hotel group is trafficking Mexican immigrants across the border and shuttling them to his most recent construction site in the desert outside of Vegas." He pointed to the satellite image where men were hanging out along the border.

"Your old man is a piece of work, ain't he, Ace?" Gumby asked. Murmurs of disbelief floated around the room.

This was why Acer didn't talk about his past; this was why he didn't talk about his family. This fucking pity from his brothers. Yet, he spilled his guts to Fia, and even felt a smidge lighter after unloading his baggage.

"Shut the fuck up and let the man finish." Shiv slapped a hand on the table in rapid succession.

When all the shocked eyes were back on him, Acer

continued. "About eight months ago, Wellington came to me and requested our club be the coyotes for this very project. I told him to fuck off. I have no interest in helping the man in general, plus with the ICE presence down there it would have been far too fuckin' risky. The men in fake NP cuts are his way of fucking with us, with me." A snug band wound its way around Acer's head tightening with each word he spoke. "I anticipate he'll feed info to ICE when he's about ready to wrap up the operation. The Feds will find these assholes wearing the NP cuts and open a huge fuckin' investigation into our club. Won't make a lick of difference that it's not really our club. By the time we are able to convince the Feds of that, we'll already be up a creek."

"That's something we cannot afford." Striker lit a cigarette. He only smoked now when he was stressed. Lila would rip him a new one when she found out, as she always did. "We moved all artillery off premises to the warehouse, but that's not a perfect solution should ATF come knocking. I don't recommend riding around unarmed, but be on alert. We're moving on a plan to shut this shit down, but we don't know what's already been communicated to the Feds. Don't get caught with a piece that will get your ass tossed in county jail."

"So what is the plan?" Lucky spoke up. He sat directly across the table from Striker.

"I've got some dirt on Wellington's partner." He specifically left out the fact that it was Fia's father. She didn't know and he didn't want someone mouthing it off to her. "Dirt that would be devastating to him personally and professionally. Wellington himself has been very good at covering his tracks, but I'm hoping if I turn up the heat on his partner, he'll crack and give me some shit on Wellington. Then, I'll take him apart."

Gumby looked at him. "You okay with throwing this all in your old man's lap? One thing to hate the guy, another to destroy him."

"Yes. I owe him one." It was all he was going to say on the matter, and combined with the cold stare he shot Gumby's way, it must have been enough, because his brother nodded.

"Good enough."

"Acer, you squeeze your old man's partner and keep us posted on everything. Let me know if you need anything from us." Shiv ground his cigar into an ashtray. "Watch your sixes out there, gentlemen."

Chapter Thirty-Two

"All right, Isabella, I have your measurements, and you like all the designs?"

"Love, darling, I love the designs."

Fia smiled and, since she was clearly visible on Skype, managed to resist the urge to do a happy dance. Isabella DeBlasis was one of the biggest snobs with whom she'd ever had the privilege of doing business. Luckily, the younger woman was obsessed with her merchandise and had been a loyal client for almost five years. "I'm glad you're pleased with them. Just to run through the details one final time, I'm creating seven pieces, one for each night of your honeymoon, plus lingerie for your wedding day. It will take me about a month to complete everything. When we get closer, I'll contact you to set up a time and place to meet for a fitting. I'm more than happy to travel to you."

"Sounds wonderful, darling." It wasn't a conversation with Isabella if the word darling wasn't dropped at least fifty times.

"I'll just need half down as a deposit," Fia said to the laptop screen. Conducting meetings on Skype had its perks. Isabella was clueless to the fact Fia wore sweatpants and her feet were bare.

She waved her hand in the air, her permanently upturned nose rising even farther into the air. "Please, darling, you have my American Express on file, no? Charge the whole fee now, it's no bother."

Cha-ching. This was a significant sale. Isabella demanded only the finest materials, including imported silks, gold threads, and crystals. She was a true attention whore and loved nothing more than to show off to her elitist friends as well. Fia always had a surge in clientele after working with the socialite. Her peers were just as affluent and not willing to be out-styled by Isabella.

"Okay, Isabella, I will. It's been lovely to speak with you. I'll contact you in a few weeks."

"Thank you, darling. Have yourself a fabulous day." She disconnected the Skype call.

Fia glanced at the clock on her laptop, her heart rate kicking up in a nervous rhythm. Twenty minutes until Acer would be home.

Back, not home. This wasn't her home. Acer would be back to *his* home in twenty minutes.

She blew out a breath. Tonight was the night. If she had any hope of fully conquering her fears and truly putting the trauma behind her, there was one last hurdle she had to jump. It was a high one, but if she was successful, it would be worth it. Mentally and physically.

A shiver ran through her. It would be so worth it. And then she'd be free. Free to resume the life that had been put on pause weeks ago. She sighed. At this point, she wasn't even sure that's what she wanted anymore.

She hopped off the bed and slid her top dresser drawer open. Two weeks ago, Acer surprised her when he moved the dresser from the guestroom into his bedroom declaring she'd be spending every night with him. Doing little things to make her life easier was his modus operandi.

Since then, the nights, and sometimes mornings—okay, sometimes afternoons too—had been filled with passionate encounters. She fell further under his spell with each passing day, but neither breathed a word of what was to come.

He had feelings for her, strong ones, she was sure of it. He may even love her, but he'd never admit that to himself, let alone to her. For now, it was enough to view it in his smoldering gazes and feel it in his sensual touch.

Or so she told herself.

She pulled out the teeny tiny thong she'd just finished stitching that morning. It was a deep, dark purple, Acer's favorite color on her. The silk in the front barely covered her mound and the G-string style bands rode low across her ass in the back, drawing attention to the curve of her backside.

Acer loved her ass.

She smiled to herself. For years, she'd tried every exercise she could to tighten her behind up, but could never quite get rid of a bit of jiggle. Acer told her almost every day how he loved her softness and how amazing it felt in his hands or against his body.

There was no disagreeing with that. His competent hands and hard body felt just as wonderful on her skin. If only he could express his emotions as easily as he expressed his love of her body.

She shimmied into the panties and snatched the bra out of the drawer next. It was the same silky material as the thong and the same deep purple. The cups gave her good lift and dipped low enough to tease with a tiny peek of nipple.

When she had the lingerie in place, she slid her feet into a pair of sky-high purple heels she bought online a week ago. They did amazing things for her legs and ass.

Acer was going to flip his shit.

Fia shook her hips in an excited dance around the room and stopped in her tracks at the sight of herself in a full-length mirror behind the closed door. The scar on her ribs was as visible as ever. It might as well be a red stop sign with the way her eyes were drawn to it. The good news was, until she saw it just now, she hadn't even considered it when making her plan for tonight.

Progress.

She held up her middle finger to the scars in the mirror. Just distorted skin; it didn't define her. She could go for whole days now without thinking of it.

Acer's doing.

Fuck the scars. The woman shining in the mirror was a sexy, confident woman who knew the effect her body had on her man.

Hell yeah, she did.

"Fia?" The walls shook with the force of the front door slamming shut, jarring Fia out of her daze. She dashed to the dresser to grab the last item she needed for tonight. Her hand stilled over the open drawer.

Deep breath. She could do this. It would be good, beyond good; Acer would make sure of that.

She snatched the silken ropes and moved to the bed. Assuming the pre-planned pose, she leaned against one of the long uprights of the four-poster bed, and cocked her hip to the side.

She should have felt stupid, but the fluttering of excitement and nerves in her belly outweighed any foolishness she might have experienced. "I'm in here!"

Acer's footsteps approaching down the hall was all it took to have her nipples tightening and her clit throbbing. The small strip of fabric between her legs wouldn't contain a raindrop, let alone the amount of moisture already dripping from her. She pressed her legs together and squirmed, the action ineffective at quelling the need.

Only Acer could do that.

~ ~ ~ ~

"You in bed already, babe?" Acer opened his bedroom door and let it swing into the room. He took one step toward his bed and stopped dead, as though someone had pulled an emergency brake on his momentum.

The light was low, but positioned behind Fia so that all attention was drawn to her glowing form. She mentioned something once about how she learned tons of lighting tricks during photo shoots for her website.

She leaned against his bed, her curvy hip tilted at a seductive angle. Two pebbled nipples peeked over the top of a sinful bra. A miniscule scrap of fabric scarcely covered her pussy, drawing his gaze with a force stronger than gravity.

He hardened so fast it was just shy of painful.

The smile on Fia's face said she knew exactly the effect she had on him, and she loved it.

Fuck, this woman was amazing. She'd come so far and that she could be so giving with her sexuality around him after all she'd endured was nothing short of astounding. She stayed plastered to him when around other men and she still tensed when one came too close. But with him, she was everything she'd been the first night they'd met.

A shameful part of him loved that he was the only man she felt comfortable around. The only man who got to see and experience that gorgeous body, the sexy sounds she made as she came, and her growing sense of sexual adventure.

She no longer seemed self-conscious about the scars on her ribs. Anger and the desire to rip Mike's throat out still rose sharp and fast whenever he saw them, but he worked very hard to keep those feelings from showing on his face. It wasn't about him.

"You just gonna gawk at me all night, handsome?" A sexy grin played across her face and she raised one eyebrow.

"No." He stalked toward her. "I'm going to fuck you until you pass out from the pleasure."

Her whiskey eyes dilated and darkened. Yeah, his girl liked it when he talked dirty to her. She liked when he got dirty with her.

When she was close enough to touch, he filled his hands with her lush ass and jerked her against his straining erection. God, she felt so good, so soft and yielding. Her body was made for this, for him.

She tilted her pelvis, rubbing along his length and he swore she purred like a contented cat.

"Wait," she said as he dipped in to take her lips.

He froze. Even though they'd come so far, he was always alert and aware that something might push her too far. He never allowed himself to lose control as he had in the shower. The risk of scaring her and fucking up her progress was too great.

"What's wrong?"

She squeezed her arms around him once before letting go. "Nothing's wrong." She held up a hand. "I want you to do something for me."

Dangling from her fingers were two long, silken strips of fabric. They matched the lingerie she wore. She must have made them.

"I want you to tie me to the bed."

The breath stilled in his lungs. If she had any idea the fantasies he had about this very thing. Not since he'd rescued her, but for months after he slept with her. But after what she'd been through? "No, Fi—"

A soft hand covered his mouth, determination glowing in her eyes. "I want this, Acer. I need it. When we first met, you whispered about how you wanted to tie me up and fuck me."

The word fuck coming from her lips always made him harder.

"I dreamed about that for months. I've never done it and couldn't stop thinking about it. I need to do this to take back the last part of myself. I promise I'm not afraid."

He tilted his head and stared down at her, her gentle fingers still pressed to his lips.

She chuckled. "Okay, I'm a little nervous. But I really do want this. For more reasons than just getting over a fear. And I trust you, completely."

He growled around her fingers and she laughed.

"I told you you're going to have to deal with it. Please, Acer. I can handle this." She winked at him. "I may even like it."

He slipped his tongue between the gap in her fingers. A subtle shiver ran through her and her throat worked as she swallowed. He pressed a kiss to her palm and pulled her hand down, sliding the cool fabric from her hand. "Okay, baby, on one condition. You feel any discomfort, any fear, anything remotely bad I want to know. Got it? Our word will be smart-mouth. You say that and I'll stop, no questions asked."

She pouted. "Acer, I don't need a safe word."

He wouldn't budge on this. "Safe word or nothing."

She rolled her eyes. "Okay, smart-mouth it is."

"Great." Without warning, he crushed his mouth to hers, lifting her with hands under her ass. She jolted in his arms and wrapped her legs tight around his waist, the spikes of her fuck-me heels an erotic bite of pain in his back. They kissed for long minutes, until her growl of frustration had him chuckling. "Patience, baby. There's no rush tonight."

"Easy for you to say."

He ground his cock against her. Christ, the front of his pants were growing soaked with the evidence of her arousal. "It's really not."

He placed her on the large bed and she scooted back, maintaining eye contact and stopping when she was in the center. She laid down and lifted her arms over her head, waiting for him to tie her up.

The woman looked like the sexiest sacrifice imaginable. His cock was so hard and pulsed with so much blood, his head spun from lack of oxygen.

She smiled at him and the steel doors around his heart flew up. She was so beautiful, so brave, and so trusting.

How was it this one woman made him question two decades of thinking?

Chapter Thirty-Three

Fia tugged at the satin fabric, testing the strength. Pretty sturdy. She wasn't going anywhere.

"You good, babe? Want me to keep going?"

She took a deep breath and willed the drumming of her heart to slow down. "Yes. I'm a little nervous, but it's more anticipation than fear. I promise I'll let you know if it gets to be too much. Keep going. Over thinking is what will make me back out."

Acer secured her other wrist then pressed his mouth to her ear. "Give me ten minutes and you won't be able to think at all."

Oh yeah. The man could make her swoon with that silver tongue of his.

He backed up until his feet hit the floor and he stood at the end of the bed. "Spread your legs."

She took her time obeying his command. There wasn't much she could do to him bound to the bed, but she'd find little ways to torture him as well. His smirk said he was on to her game.

"You're wet."

Understatement of the year. Spread out and immobile, she

felt exposed and vulnerable, but not in a frightened way. The anticipation of what he'd do to her was a strong aphrodisiac. Her nipples were aching points of need and her clit throbbed and swelled. "I'm soaked. It coated the fly of your jeans."

"I know. But there's something about seeing that fabric barely covering your pussy all dark and drenched with your arousal. All for me, right? No other man can make you wet like this. It's all mine."

Truer words had never been spoken. She could barely tolerate another man within ten feet of her. With time, she was becoming more comfortable with his friends, but hadn't felt even a smidge of sexual attraction to any man besides Acer.

"Only you, Acer. It's all for you." And when she left? What then? Would it even be possible to experience a fraction of the desire she felt for Acer with another man? She wasn't sure she could ever even try.

His nostrils flared as he nodded. He pulled his T-shirt over his head and went to work on his belt, his eyes never leaving her body. No man should be that sexy. It almost wasn't fair to the rest of them.

As he shed his clothing, the ink on his skin highlighted the play of muscles and the bar though his nipple gleamed in the dim lighting.

If she could just press her legs together, put some pressure on her clit, find some relief—

Acer shook his head and circled an ankle with his large hand, pulling her thighs wide apart. "Uh uh."

Fia sighed and stilled her movements. Tonight would be on his timeline.

He stroked a hand over his length and her mouth watered. Maybe this had been a mistake. Not because she was scared, but it was obvious he planned to draw this out until she was a mess of need. She might not survive the buildup.

Acer crawled up onto the bed, between her legs, and bent near her ear. "I don't want you to be scared, so I'm going to tell you exactly how this is going to go. Okay?" His voice was tight, strained.

She nodded.

"I need you to say it out loud. So I can be certain."

"Okay." So okay.

"First," he said, nipping her earlobe. "I'm going to unwrap these gorgeous tits and play with them for a while. Did you make this for me?" He trailed a finger along the top edge of a bra cup, just glancing over a nipple and she shivered with need.

"Yes."

"I highly approve. When I'm done up here, I'm going to move down and eat you out until you come on my face." He brushed his knuckles across the damp silk covering her mound.

Fia moaned. If she got any wetter, they were going to need to grab a towel. She squirmed, trying to rub her nipples against the fabric of her bra. Anything to relieve the ache.

"And finally, I'm going fuck you, long and hard until you scream my name as you come again. You good with the plan?"

Good? Good was such a pale word for the excitement and need his words evoked.

"Babe?"

"I'm good." Her throat was so dry the words came out as a croak.

He pressed his lips to her neck and moved downward, forging a fiery path to her breasts. Every time his mouth met her skin, her pussy clenched she let out a soft moan.

When he reached her breasts, she held her breath, not

wanting to miss a millisecond of his plan.

He nuzzled a nipple with his nose, just where it peeked out from her bra, and inhaled a deep breath. "You smell amazing." Warm air wafted over her sensitive skin as he spoke. It was as though every pore on her skin was ultra-sensitive, responding to the slightest input.

"It's...um...vanilla?" She could barely think. Her mind was too busy trying to send him telepathic messages about how much she needed his mouth on her.

He chuckled against her skin. "I hope you're not asking me, because I don't have a fucking clue. All I know is it makes me hard."

Huh? What did he say? He flicked the front clasp of the bra open and pushed the cups aside, freeing her breasts. In the next instant, his mouth closed over her and pleasure shot straight from her nipple to her clit. "Yesss," she said on a moan.

He wasn't gentle, and he sucked until she pulled against the restraints and tried in vain to grind her pelvis against his. She groaned when he switched to the other nipple.

"Acer, that feels so good." Instinct had her wanting to dive her fingers into his hair and hold his head against her breast, or push it between her legs, but she was helpless to do anything but lie there and take it as he gave it.

"Tell me," he said. He gently raked his teeth across her nipple. "Tell me what you feel." He lifted his head and watched her. One hand pinched a nipple and the other moved between her legs and lightly stroked a finger over the satin covering her with a maddeningly insufficient touch. He winked. "I'm diverting from the plan just a bit. Tell me."

She swallowed as best she could, the saliva in her mouth having dried up at his first touch. "I want to touch you." She moved her hips, trying to get his finger to enter her. "But I can't. You have all the control, and I think I really like that. All I can do is lie here and feel what you're doing to me. It's kind of freeing."

"That's right, baby." He pressed an open mouth kiss between her breasts, then continued his journey over her quivering belly.

"Did you make this for me too?" he asked as he nuzzled string of her panties, right over her sensitive hipbone.

"Yes." She raised her hips, seeking relief, but he denied her for now.

He slipped a strong finger under the fabric and through her slick folds.

She moaned and pressed her hips into his touch. If he didn't get some part of his anatomy inside her soon, she wouldn't be held responsible for her actions.

"And this?" he asked, rimming her entrance, his laser focus on her face. "Is this drenched pussy for me?"

"Y-yes."

"Only me."

They'd been through this already. Was that insecurity she heard in his voice? How could he even begin to question her desire for him, only him? She could barely stand to be in another man's presence let alone think of allowing one access to her naked body. "Only you. It's been only you since LA."

His eyes darkened and his pupils dilated, a growl of male possession rumbling in his chest. He bent down and grasped the string between his perfect teeth, drawing back and letting it go with a snap against her skin. "Goddamned right it's mine."

Fia jumped and gasped, straining against the bindings. She wanted to grab his head and hold him against her center until he made her come, but she was trapped, unable to end this sensual torture. His claiming words were as hot as his touch.

"Was it a lot of work?"

"What?" Why was he still talking? She couldn't process anything but the need spiraling through her. "Um, no, it wasn't."

"Good." He ripped the G-string from her.

It wouldn't have mattered if she'd spent a year crafting the lingerie. The sound of the material tearing from her body almost made her come.

"Bend your knees."

She obeyed at once.

He didn't move, poised over her pussy, for unknown seconds.

"Acer, please." She groaned and tilted her pelvis closer to his face.

He slid his thumbs up the seam of her pussy, spreading her lips until he reached her clit. A warm stream of air wafted over the throbbing nub.

"Holy shit!"

He chuckled and pressed his thumb to her clit.

Fia jerked at the harsh lash of pleasure. She was so far beyond turned on, her body so sensitized, it was almost too much. Acer buried his mouth in her folds and she fisted the fabric ropes in her hand. She needed something to hold, something to yank on, something to keep her from shooting off into space.

The man was a God. His mouth should be licensed, registered, and come with a warning label. *Do not use unless prepared to be ruined for all other men.*

He ate at her sex, using his tongue, lips, and teeth to drive into a frenzy. She thrashed against the bindings, her biceps bulging with the force of her grip.

He showed her no mercy, and in no time, her limbs tingled and her vision blurred. "Oh God, Acer, I'm gonna come."

He inserted a thick finger deep into her and curled it forward as he flicked her clit with his tongue again and again.

Pleasure crested and she shattered, coming against his face as promised. Her back arched, pushing her against his mouth. He didn't guide her over the edge easily, he flung her into oblivion, fucking her with his finger and his mouth until the intense pressure built a second time.

"Ahh," she cried out as another orgasm swamped her. Lights flashed behind her eyelids and her arms lost the strength to tug on the ropes. Every last ounce of energy leeched out of her as she came down from a high she'd never imagined.

The next thing she knew, Acer was pressing into her, filling her with his heavy cock. She moaned as he seated himself to the hilt. He stayed still, deep inside her, and kissed her. It was a passionate kiss, full of all the emotion he could never voice.

She tasted her essence on his lips, a reminder of the pleasure she'd just experienced. Not that she needed a reminder, her muscles still twitched with aftershocks.

Without breaking the kiss, Acer pulled the knots out of her bindings, liberating her arms. He'd used a quick release knot. One pull of the rope by him, and she was free even though the bindings held strong through her fierce tugging.

She wrapped her arms around him the instant she could, drawing him close, loving the way his muscles bunched and flexed in her embrace. She stroked her hands over every surface she could reach.

"Thank you for trusting me." His tone was so low she almost missed the words whispered into her neck. Had he meant for her to hear them? Probably not, but her heart soared just the same.

He rocked his pelvis into her, small movements that quickly became inadequate. When they both needed something more, he rose on his knees and filled his hands with her ass, lifting her to meet the increasing force of his thrusts.

She dragged her hands from his shoulders, down his chest, pausing to play with his nipple ring. When she gave it a light tug, he grunted and slammed his hips into her even harder.

With each drive of his shaft into her channel, the pleasure built until she was moaning once again.

***

~ ~ ~ ~

The heat of Fia's tight pussy seared him until his eyes crossed. With her, he discovered something he'd never experienced anywhere else. And it wasn't just the physical pleasure, which far surpassed any other, but it was an awe-inspiring sense of rightness. A feeling that he found where he belonged, where he should stay.

He shoved those confounded feelings aside and focused on the physical. Not hard to do. "One more, baby, give me one more."

Fia moaned. "I don't think I can, Acer."

Oh, hell yes she could. He thrust in and out with furious strokes, his control beginning a slippery slide into non-existence. He yanked her hips up farther so he hit deeper inside and her clit bumped against his pelvis with every stroke.

"Oh my God," she cried out, her hands fisting in the comforter on each side of her body. Her core clamped down on him, trying to keep him just where he was. He grinned. There's the spot.

She did it again, squeezing his dick like a fist and he groaned. Fuck it. He surrendered to the madness, control flying out the window. With his hands full of her ass, he pummeled her with his cock. He dominated every aspect of the encounter, using his firm grip to slam his sex into her again and again.

She whimpered every time he bottomed out, her head thrashing back and forth on the pillow. "Acer." Her voice was strangled, full of passion and hunger.

"I know, baby. Play with your tits."

She released the comforter, and pinched and rolled her nipples. Around his cock, her walls began to spasm. She gave one more tug on her nipples at the same time he pushed, hard, into her and she let out a wailing cry. Her body shook and she convulsed around him.

"Fuck," he cried out, her orgasm triggering his. His body stiffened and jolted over her as the pleasure crested. "Goddamn." He collapsed on her and smiled when she let out a weak chuckle.

After a moment, he tried to roll to his side, but Fia held him tight. "Don't move yet," she whispered against his ear.

He used the last of his strength to push himself off her just slightly so as not to crush her. Lying with her like this, in the aftermath of the storm, was almost as good as the sex. He rested his head on her chest. As her heart rate leveled, the steady beat lulled him to near sleep. Fia's breathing evened and she didn't stir or speak. He assumed she was asleep and had just given himself permission to doze as well, when her voice startled him back to alertness.

"Acer?"

"Yeah, baby?" He lifted his head and looked into her

somber eyes.

Her voice was low and a little sad. "I think…I think it's time for me to go home."

An unfamiliar ache settled in the left side of his chest. He'd fallen so far down the rabbit hole with Fia, he wasn't quite sure what he'd do once she left. But he had to let her go. He freed her, and it was time to let her fly. It was what they agreed on when she first arrived.

"I know it is, baby. I know."

Chapter Thirty-Four

Jester cleared his throat. "Fia, I had an idea I wanted to run by you."

She looked up at him, the fork freezing halfway to her mouth. What on earth could he want to discuss with her? She'd be leaving tomorrow. There wasn't any time for her to do him any kind of favor.

Emily choked on her water. "Jester!" She shot daggers at her man with her eyes.

He winked at her and plowed on. "You ever think about getting a tattoo to cover your scars?"

Well, the man didn't beat around the bush.

A loud crack had her and Emily jumping in their chairs. Foam oozed over the top of the beer bottle Acer slammed on the table, his expression an icy mask of fury. He'd been difficult to read since she announced her plans to leave last night. He'd acted upset, broody and distant, but hadn't voiced his feelings one way or the other.

"Oh, my gosh, Fia, I'm so sorry." Emily's cheeks grew red and she looked about two seconds away from crying. The tick in Acer's clenched jaw and his fisted fingers under the table were more concerning than Emily's embarrassment. A physical fight at the dinner table wasn't exactly how Fia imagined her last night in Arizona.

She placed her hand on Acer's under the table, amazed at how the starch left his spine the moment she touched him. "Emily, please don't worry about it. I never asked you to keep it to yourself and I wouldn't expect you to keep anything from Jester. It's not a secret. I'm sure everyone knows exactly what happened to me."

The thought was uncomfortable, but the hot boil of shame she'd once felt dissipated to a low simmer. Thanks to Acer and his amazing group of friends, or really, his family.

She turned to Jester, who smiled, completely unrepentant. "Actually, I think I appreciate you not tip-toeing around it. I have thought about it a little, but not too seriously. It's impossible to spend any time around you guys and not think of getting a tattoo."

He snorted and ran a hand across the stubble on his chin. "It can be tricky, and the options vary depending on the integrity of your skin, but typically something can be done. Even if the scar tissue itself is too thick or would cause the ink to spread, a lot of times you can ink around it, blending it into the design."

Huh. It was definitely something to consider. She loved Acer's ink. It was hot as hell. Would he think it was sexy on her?

Not that it mattered. She was going home in the morning.

The man monopolizing her thoughts turned his hand over until their palms touched, and linked his fingers with hers. Always strong and supportive. Sadness threatened to swamp her and she forced it away. Plenty of time for that over the next few days. No point in wasting the last few hours on sorrow.

"How do you know so much about this, Jester?"

"He's an amazing tattoo artist." Emily smiled, her complexion back to its normal creamy color, and her pale eyes shining with pride in her boyfriend.

"Really? I had no idea."

Jester shrugged and took a sip of his beer. "I can hold my own."

Emily rolled her eyes. "The only time he's modest."

Acer laughed. "Don't worry, I'm sure it won't last."

"Okay, fine. I'm pretty fucking good at it." Jester leaned his massive body back in his chair, a smirk on his face.

"Do you have any tattoos, Emily?" Fia asked.

Emily rolled her eyes at the same time Jester said, "Fuck, no she doesn't."

Beside her, Acer laughed. "I don't get it. What's so funny?"

Emily sighed. "I'd love to get one, but he—" she jerked a thumb in Jester' direction, "—won't let me."

Fia chuckled. "Jester, you have to have hundreds of tattoos. Why don't you want Emily to get one?"

Jester looked at Emily as he spoke. He picked up her hand and pressed a kiss to her palm. "Because I love all this smooth, sexy skin and I don't want her to mark it up in any way."

Emily shook her head, but her eyes shone with love. She winked at Fia. "I guess when he puts it like that, it's something I can live with."

Acer snorted. "You know you could get him to change his mind if you just bat those pretty eyes at him."

Emily grinned. Seems like she didn't really care about getting the tattoo. Who could blame her when Jester was so open with how much he loved her body the way it was. The same thing Acer had said to her so many times.

"If I decide to get a tattoo, could you do it for me?"

Jester tapped his beer bottle on the table twice before

sipping again. "I could lay your ink, but I'm probably not the best one to work on a scar. Just haven't done enough to have mastered it. I know a guy though." He glanced at Acer. "Dude who did Lila's ink. He's fuckin' amazing. Done tons of work with scars. People come from all over to have him ink over burns and shit."

He looked at Acer as he spoke, as though he'd be a part of the decision. As though he and Fia were a package deal and his opinion mattered.

Her stomach rolled, the chocolate mousse settling like a rock. The sad part was, it did matter. Even though he'd be out of her life in less than twenty hours, his opinion held more weight than anyone's.

She bit back a sigh. Lila and Marcie couldn't make it to dinner tonight. She was having breakfast with them on her way out of town tomorrow. Tonight would be her last night with Acer. She probably should have just left today, but she needed time to say good-bye and thank the girls. She also needed one more night with Acer, desperately. One more deposit for her memory bank. It was all she'd have after tomorrow.

A sharp rap on the door had Acer frowning.

"You expecting anyone?" Jester tensed, muscles on alert and ready.

"No." He looked at Fia and she shook her head. No one was expected to stop by this evening.

Acer rose and pulled a pistol from the top of the refrigerator. The man had multiple weapons stashed around the apartment. "Don't move."

Fia rolled her eyes. "Yes, sir."

~ ~ ~ ~

"Fuck me." Acer rested his forehead against the door. There was no way this could possibly end well. He peered at the panel on the wall next to him. Terrance Caldwell still stood in full view of the security camera. Not a figment of his imagination.

He opened the door, but filled the entrance with his body, blocking Terrance's path into his home. "What the fuck are you doing here?"

"I—I, um." He cleared his throat and ran a hand through disheveled gray hair. His expensive suit was rumpled, the shirt untucked, a missed buttonhole throwing the shape off kilter. "I need to speak with you."

Acer ground his teeth together, biting back the words of hatred that threatened to escape. There was no way to keep Fia out of it at this point. He moved aside, and allowed Caldwell to enter the apartment.

"Dad?"

Goddamnit. *Yes, sir* his ass.

"Sorry, bro, she's fast." Jester stood behind Fia in the mouth of the hallway.

"What are you doing here? You look awful. Is something wrong with mom?" Dark circles rimmed both eyes and his skin had a grayish pallor to it, as though he hadn't slept in weeks and wasn't taking proper care of himself.

Not an ounce of sympathy stirred in Acer. Instead, he was glad to see the other man looking like shit. It was the least he deserved.

Caldwell ignored her and spoke to Acer. "She in on this? She know you're trying to destroy me? Ruin everything I've worked my whole life for?"

Acer risked a glance at Fia. Surprise flickered across her face, but she masked it, keeping her expression neutral.

"She has nothing to do with this, Caldwell."

He turned toward his daughter, a sneer on his face. "You're not going to try to do a thing to stop this?" His voice rose and spittle flew from his mouth. "Your gang-banger boyfriend threatened to ruin my entire life, my business, my reputation, my—hell, *your* family—and you're just going to stand by and watch?"

"I don't have a c-clue what's going on right now." Fia's voiced wavered. "We have our issues, but you've never spoken to me like you did just now. And Acer has been amazing. He's helped me so much more than you know." Her confused gaze shifted from her father to Acer, millions of questions in her eyes.

Jesus, she must want to rip his balls off and stuff them down his throat. Acer couldn't begin to imagine the feelings of hatred and betrayal she must be experiencing as she realized he kept information from her, but she didn't turn on him. She didn't scream and demand an explanation, she backed him up without even knowing if Acer was even in the right.

She trusted him.

He admired her so much in that moment, so much it was almost like he—

Fuck.

He loved her.

Fucking loved her.

And a giant bomb of his own making had just blown any chance he had with her straight to hell. He never should have kept any information from her. Caldwell sputtered, drawing Acer's attention off Fia and back to him.

"You. You're no daughter of mine. You're a heartless bit—"

"That's enough." Acer stepped closer to Caldwell, so he stood just two feet away from the man, keeping the attention on himself. "Speak to her like that again and you'll be leaving on a gurney. You're obviously here for something more than whining in my living room. Start talking. You've got three minutes."

There was zero chance Fia would leave the room if he asked her, so why bother? Besides, she deserved to know the truth. He should have told her when he filled her in on his own father's sins.

Caldwell's bluster evaporated like a balloon with the air let out of it. "You can't release those photos. If it's money you want, you can have it. Just don't release the photos." His shoulders slumped and he looked every bit the seventy-year-old man he was. The suave businessman who'd been compared to Richard Gere so many times was gone, in his place remained a defeated man.

~ ~ ~ ~

Photos? What photos? What the hell was going on? Fia sunk her teeth into her bottom lip to keep the hundreds of questions inside her mouth. Something big was happening. Acer wouldn't go after her father for no reason. Sure, he'd been pissed on her behalf at the way her family had reacted after her kidnapping, but she didn't think this was related. This had to be about the trouble his club was having with his own father.

What the hell had her dad done? And why the hell was she just finding out about it now?

"You're gonna have to do better than that, Terry. You know I'm not interested in your money." Hatred dripped from Acer's mocking tone. "As I told you two days ago, the border is fucking huge. Move your apes to another state and burn the copy-cat cuts."

"I don't—I don't have that authority. This isn't my show." His voice actually trembled and he stared at the floor. This wasn't her father. The beaten-down man before her was unrecognizable.

It hurt to see him like this. Sure, they had their problems, but she never hated her family. She should have paid more attention to the escalating troubles between them, first her job, then her disagreement over how to handle her abduction, then their dissatisfaction with her association with Acer. She'd been blind to what was occurring right under her nose. What a fool she'd been. She just couldn't conjure up sympathy for her father. If he was involved in illegal activities with Acer's father, then he made his bed.

"Not my problem." Acer said. "My problem is uninvited guys on my turf."

Acer was cool as a cucumber while her father fidgeted and squirmed more with each passing second. Behind her, Jester growled under his breath. If the situation wasn't so tense, so confusing and messed up, she might have laughed. To those who knew him, Jester was like a giant joking teddy bear, but when you needed an enforcer, his size and stature was the perfect way to put the fear of God in just about anyone.

Sure enough, her father paled. He remained silent for long moments, then his shoulders slumped and his arms hung limp at his sides. "I've got something on your father. Something you can use. It's the one thing that will make him back off. He just can't know it came from me." He stared at the floor as he spoke in a low, almost whispered voice.

Acer tensed. It wouldn't be obvious to just anyone, but for someone who knew every inch of his body, it was. "Two and a half minutes."

"He's bleeding money. Hemorrhaging really. If this new hotel isn't an immediate success he's through." His words were rushed, a slight panic in his tone.

Fia held her breath, not wanting to miss a word of her father's confession. She shifted her gaze to Acer. How would he take the news of his father's financial troubles?

Acer rolled his eyes and shook his head. "Nothing I don't already know, Terry. You're down to two minutes, and so far, you haven't told me anything that a first grader couldn't find with Google."

Her father swayed on his feet and Fia had a momentary urge to stabilize him. Not all of her memories of her father were bad. It was only when she became an adult and made independent decisions that his disapproval and scorn became apparent. Unfortunately, it only grew. He believed women belonged at their husband's sides, a fancy ornament to be looked at and appreciated. Especially rich women who didn't have to work for a living. How Fia could break the mold and start a business—a business loosely associated with sex, no less—he just couldn't wrap his mind around. And since he didn't understand it, he had to put a stop to it. Her mother was too passive to ever stand up to her overbearing husband, so Fia had no support.

He didn't look overbearing now. He looked like a man who had hit rock bottom.

"Jesus Christ." Her father rubbed his hands over his pale face.

"Minute forty-five."

"Stop fucking counting down." He glared at Acer, a spark igniting his eyes. "This information could very well get me killed."

Fia's stomach dipped. What the hell had he gotten himself into?

"Ninety seconds."

A strangled sound flew from deep within her father. For a moment, Fia feared he'd charge Acer, but he held his ground. Acer looked as calm and cool as ever.

"Reginald is in deep with the mob. *Deep.* Millions deep. They invested in three of his hotel designs, hotels that never got off the ground. Reginald pissed away their investment. Women, gambling...I'm not exactly sure where it all went, but it's gone. I—I think—" He stared at the ceiling. "Jesus," he whispered. "I think it may have all been part of some psychotic plan to screw the mob out of money. I think he sabotaged the hotels to keep the money, but I have no proof of that."

Fia kept her gaze on Acer as her father spoke, gauging his reaction. He was so in control of his emotions, not a flicker of response crossed his expressionless face. The man should start playing poker. She dug deep, using him for inspiration as she tried to keep her own face blank while her heart raced and her stomach rolled with nausea.

Paying attention to the conversation was growing difficult with her thoughts spiraling out of control. They all revolved around Acer. Surprisingly she felt almost numb toward her father. Here he was, in serious, potentially lethal trouble, and all she could think about was Acer. What would this mean for him and his club? Was he okay? Why hadn't he told her any of this? She might have been able to help.

It's not like she would have spilled his secrets to her fath—

Oh my God. That was it. The realization was like running full speed into a brick wall. How many times had he warned her not to trust anyone? It was a code he lived by. She'd been stupid enough to believe she was different, that she would gain his trust eventually. Well, she was just like anyone else, and he didn't trust her.

It gutted her, but she didn't let it show. She shoved the despair and anguish down deep. Lashing out right now would only hurt Acer's position with her father. She'd never put him or Jester, or any of the No Prisoners in jeopardy. She owed them far too much.

And she loved Acer. Despite the fact that he didn't trust

her.

Fool was too generous a word.

Damn, her heart ached.

Chapter Thirty-Five

The mob? Really? Christ, Acer wanted no part of that mess. Sure, the No Prisoners had a few contacts with different mob bosses throughout the country, but their reach tended to be great and their wrath deadly.

He glanced at Fia, but couldn't read any of her feelings in her face. Her rigid stance and rapid rise and fall of her chest was the only indication of any distress.

Jester still hovered behind her, his forearms braced on the walls of the hallway. Emily remained out of sight. Nice for him that his ol' lady obeyed and stayed put.

Fia's not your ol' lady.

Christ, she'd probably think of him as an enemy after this.

"Keep talking," Acer said. Caldwell needed to get this story over with. "What does any of this have to do with you?"

"The woman. From the pictures." He shifted his eyes to Fia then back to Acer. "She's the daughter of the mob boss your father did business with. I won't tell you his name."

Acer almost laughed. He'd have the name five minutes after Caldwell left. "What was your young plaything's name? Alicia, right?" He paused as realization set in. "Did my old man set you up?"

He nodded. "Looks that way. I met her when I was with him. It's how he got me to help with the smuggling. Blackmailed me." He pierced Acer with his gaze. "Like you're doing."

This story was getting boring. "So Reggie introduced you to a girl younger than your daughter, and you couldn't keep your dirty hands off her. You then find out that she's the daughter of the mob boss Reggie owes money to. I'm missing something here. What's the big deal? Aside from the fact that you're a cheating scumbag. You afraid her daddy's gonna find out his little girl is fucking a married piece of shit? Probably not her first, Terry."

Caldwell shook his head and peeked at Fia one more time before lowering his gaze to the floor.

Christ, Acer wanted her out of this room. She stood so ramrod straight he worried she might snap. He couldn't for the life of him tell what was going on behind her impassive mask. Maybe if he'd been honest with her she'd be willing to let him handle this on his own. One more check in the asshole column.

"She's pregnant and married too. The baby is mine." The words were whispered so low they were almost inaudible.

Fia's gasp sounded like a thunderclap in the shocked silence of the room. Man, Caldwell made himself quite the mess. It all made sense now. If the mob boss found out Caldwell knocked up his precious, and married, daughter there would be some serious hell to pay. Perfect blackmail material for Reginald.

"Ahh, now we're getting somewhere." He'd give his left nut to know what was going on in Fia's mind. On top of everything else she'd been through in the past few weeks, the news that her family was falling apart had to be devastating.

"My bastard of a father must be thrilled at this turn of events. Hell, he couldn't have planned it better. So, he's blackmailing you. You invest in the hotel, help him at the border and he'll keep your name away from your new kid's grandfather." He smiled. "Now, I'm pushing you to get Reggie to pull back or I'll release photos of you with the little adulteress to the media."

Fia's eyes widened but she remained silent.

"Whatever you do with this information, Reginald can't know it came from me." Caldwell's voice shook like he was on the verge of tears.

Acer laughed. "It won't matter what the fuck I say. You think her daddy won't find out? You're delusional as well as stupid. Get out of here Caldwell. You've successfully saved your own ass for the time being."

Caldwell turned toward Fia. Would he lash out at her again? Maybe beg her for forgiveness? Didn't matter. Fia didn't deserve the first, and Caldwell didn't deserve her good graces. Neither did Acer. "I—"

"You have nothing to say that she wants to hear. Get the hell out." After all that Fia had been through in the past few weeks, he wasn't going to let her father heap his garbage on her.

Fia's eyes narrowed slightly in his direction, but she didn't contradict him. Part of him wanted to laugh. Leave it to Fia to grumble at his protection.

Without another word, Caldwell left the apartment. The door closed behind him and it was as though he took all the air in the room with him.

A heavy blanket of silence and unanswered questions descended.

"Jester," Emily whispered. She pulled Jester's arm, dragging him back into the kitchen.

Acer was alone with Fia.

Alone with a woman whose face was no longer impassive. Profound sadness radiated from her in waves so thick they were almost palpable. He'd let her down. He'd betrayed her. He broke her heart.

Jesus Christ, he'd done what his father had done to him twenty years ago.

~ ~ ~ ~

Where to even begin? What would come out of her mouth if she opened it? Would she scream at him for keeping her in the dark? For not trusting her? For allowing her to be blindsided by her father's treachery? Would tears fall from her eyes as she railed at him for breaking her heart? Would words of forgiveness make their way past her lips?

Each of these feelings swirled inside of her like a brewing hurricane whose strength and path was still in question.

Acer didn't speak, and for the first time since she'd met him, he looked uncertain. Maybe he was wary of the storm as well.

They stared at each other and her heart sank farther with each silent second that ticked by.

He was so handsome. Memories of the hours spent beneath his hard body hit her with the force of an avalanche. They combined with the memories of his gentle care and protection over the past weeks. She was strong because of him. That's what she'd stayed here for. Not to fall in love, but to recover from a trauma. He'd given her that gift. Falling in love with him was on her.

She cleared her throat. "I think it would be best if I left now."

"Fia—"

She held up a hand. "Acer, let's not do this. I'm leaving tomorrow, anyway. I could yell and flip out and you could apologize and tell me why you kept me in the dark, but it won't change anything. I'm still leaving. All it will do is drag us through a bunch of emotional shit neither of us has the energy for."

He didn't move, didn't speak, but his eyes implored her to do just that. To yell at him, to cry and beat on his chest with her fists. Maybe it would make him feel better, but she couldn't do it.

Because she loved him, and because in this moment, the agony of betrayal was too great. If she let it bubble out her eyes and her mouth, she'd end up in a hysterical heap on the floor. She didn't move to him, didn't hug him, didn't kiss him. She wasn't strong enough.

With soft steps, she moved toward the door. "Please apologize to Emily and the other women for me. I'll call and say a proper goodbye to them in a few days. And, if you wouldn't mind, can you have Jester bring my bags down to my car?"

He nodded and she opened the door. With her hand on the door, a surge of anger rose from deep in her soul. He was just going to stand there and let her walk out the door without so much as a word of apology or explanation. Well, fuck that. Old Fia was back, and she didn't take shit from anyone.

She turned and stared at him. He wore a bleak expression that an hour ago, she would have attributed to sadness over her leaving. Now she wasn't sure what to think. "You could have told me about my father's involvement at any time over the past week. But you didn't. In fact, you purposefully left that very important piece of information out of your story the night you and the boys got in a fight, didn't you?" Her chest heaved and she fought to keep herself from screaming at him. Jester and Emily were still in the apartment.

"You've been through so much. You don't deserve more shi—"

"You're goddamned right I've been through a lot," she yelled. So much for keeping her cool. "And you're goddamned right I don't deserve more shit. But that's exactly what you're giving me now. Aren't you the one who keeps telling me how strong I am? How well I handle what life has thrown at me? So try again, Acer. Tell me the real reason you kept my father's involvement a secret."

He took a step toward her. "Fia—"

She held out a hand, warding him off. "How about I tell you my theory." God, how could this have happened? Ten minutes ago, she was imagining the amazing night they were going to spend exploring each other and making each other scream with pleasure. Now she could barely stand to breathe the same air as him. "I think you were worried that I might call him up and warn him. I think you didn't trust me not to betray you and your club. Am I warm?"

Guilt burned bright in his eyes, answering her question without words.

"That's what I thought," she said. She sighed and wiped at an errant tear. "I owe you, and your club, so much more than I can ever repay. Never in a million years would I have betrayed you, or anyone in your club. If you don't know that, then you don't know one single thing about me. Please don't contact me when I leave." Her voice hitched. She was dangerously close to a breakdown.

She turned back to the door. This couldn't be further from the way she wanted to leave things between them. Well, he certainly made it easier to walk out that door.

"Please let me have a prospect follow you. We still don't know where Mike is," he spoke so low she almost missed it. Like he knew there was no way in hell she'd agree to that,

Acer

but needed to get it out in the universe anyway.

She snorted. "He's gone, Acer. There hasn't been a blip from him on anyone's radar. When I get home, I'll hire security until he's found, but I do not want anyone following me out of town. If I so much as see a motorcycle in my rearview mirror, I'll call the police. Goodbye, Acer."

She stepped through the door and started down the steps, her head held high. When she was halfway to the ground, the door closed with a click that might as well have been the sound of a steel door slamming in the path of her future.

She doubled over as a sob ripped from the very depths of her soul.

Chapter Thirty-Six

The sight of Fia turning her back on him and walking out of his life would haunt him for the rest of his days. He hadn't said a word of apology. What was there to say? He was sorry? He hadn't meant to keep the information from her?

He had. Because he didn't trust her.

Of course, he was sorry. So damned sorry he could barely draw in a breath. What difference would the words actually make?

He rubbed a hand over the left side of his chest in an inadequate attempt to ease the squeezing pain. When had he allowed himself to feel? When had his heart re-opened and become vulnerable?

About seven months ago, in his father's hotel in LA. That's when.

Jester stomped down the hallway, a dark scowl on his face, Fia's duffle over his shoulder and suitcase rolling behind him. Emily trailed after him, but didn't follow him out the door. Instead, she turned to Acer. "Go sit on your couch."

"Em—"

"Uh uh." She shook her head and pointed to his couch. "You want me to tell Jester you gave his pregnant girlfriend a hard time?" She raised an eyebrow and planted a hand on her hip.

Acer snorted. "You play dirty."

"When I have to. When someone is being so stupid they can't see two inches past their own bullshit."

Yikes. Emily didn't curse too often.

She sat next to him on the couch and took one of his hands between both of hers. He was surprised by how soft and fragile her fingers felt in his. She was tough; she'd have to be to put up with a big gorilla like Jester. Plus, she'd been to hell and clawed her way back out. He had nothing but respect for Emily. She reminded him of Penny, bringing out a hidden brotherly protectiveness.

"Acer you gave me the benefit of the doubt when I was in some deep trouble. I'm going to pay you back with some advice."

"Look, Emily. I know I fucked up. She—"

"And you will listen to my advice." She shook her teacher finger at him.

Acer chuckled. She'd spoken over him like he hadn't uttered a word. "Yes, ma'am."

She smiled and squeezed his hand. "That's better. I just want you to think about something. Is this really about you not trusting Fia? Is that really why you kept information from her? Because from where I'm standing, it seems like the person you don't trust is you."

Acer rolled his eyes. "Seriously, Emily? This is not that type of couch, and you teach first grade. You're not a therapist."

She narrowed her light eyes. "Well you're acting like my six-year-old students right now, so you get to listen to my lecture."

Ouch.

"Telling Fia about her father's involvement, letting her get closer to you, would have given her the power to hurt you. I don't believe for a second that you thought she'd run to her family with the information. You've just been so emotionally stunted and have hidden behind your self-erected walls for so long that you don't trust yourself to open up to a woman. I hate to break it to you, buddy, but it seems to me like you fell in love with her anyway, despite your best efforts." She patted his hand. "Let that marinate for a while."

Unease settled into his stomach as her words hit too close to home.

"One more thing. Just remember what an unbelievable amount of trust Fia had to put in you to allow your relationship to progress to the level it did. She's no dummy. Perhaps if she trusted you that much, it was well deserved. Maybe you could trust yourself even half as much. Scary thought, but worth it." She leaned forward and brushed a kiss against his cheek.

Jester's rumbled growl of disapproval caused them both to chuckle.

"Sorry, honey, just trying to help out your dumb brother. I'm ready to leave." She stood and moved to her man.

Jester nodded at him before dipping his head and kissing Emily. His hands cupped her ass and he tugged her close. They had a rocky beginning, but were solid now. And expecting a kid of all things. Could he do that? Could he put aside his *bullshit* as Emily called it and reach for something like she and Jester had?

"You two think you could take that nonsense about five feet over and do it on the steps outside instead of in front of my face?" The mention of sex on the steps had him thinking of the night Fia swallowed his cock on those very steps. Not what he needed to be reminded of in this moment.

Emily giggled. "Sorry, Acer. We'll get out of your hair. And we'll try to make it home before we rip each other's clothes off." Her cheeks pinked. Even after more than a year of hanging out with Jester's crew, she still blushed like a schoolgirl.

"No promises, babe," Jester muttered.

She smiled and towed him outside.

"Emily?" Acer called through the open door. "Thanks."

Her grin was genuine. "Really think about what I said, and you're welcome."

Alone in his noiseless apartment, Acer leaned his head back against the couch cushions. Now what? He inhaled a deep breath and the faint smell of vanilla tickled his senses, same as it had for the past few months. She'd left her mark on his apartment like she'd left her mark on his heart.

He'd been alone in the apartment a number of times since Fia moved in. Mostly when she was out with the ol' ladies. This was different. There was a finality to the emptiness. He'd lived alone for almost fifteen years. Two months of rooming with Fia and the return to solitude was suffocating.

Emotions he hadn't allowed himself to experience in eighteen years threatened to drown him. It was like being in a glass tank as it rapidly filled with water. He floated up with the rising water level, soon to hit the ceiling and be engulfed.

Was Emily right? Did he not trust himself? Not have faith that he could handle what came along with giving himself over to Fia?

Suddenly exhausted, he scrubbed his hands over his face and glanced at a clock on the wall. Christ, he'd been in this one spot for over an hour. Fia was probably halfway to California by now.

He dragged himself off the couch and toward his room, stripping off his clothes as he walked. When he reached the bed, he pitched forward, face-first, eager to forget this shitty day.

The idea of leaving the day at the bottom of a bottle of Jack was even more appealing, but tomorrow he'd have to deal with the issue of his father, and the trouble at the border. A nasty hangover would make that unpleasant task even more so.

He closed his eyes and buried his face in a pillow. Emily's words ran through his mind over and over. He fell asleep to visions of Fia walking out of his life.

Acer woke to the early morning light blazing through the window. Christ, it was bright. He must have forgotten to close the blinds. Vanilla wafted from his pillow and shot straight to his cock. He smiled. Fia loved it when he woke her at dawn, eager to start their day lost in each other.

He rolled over, anxious to sink into heated clasp of her body only to encounter cold, flat sheets where her body should be. The events of the previous evening smacked him hard, like he ran full on into an impenetrable brick wall.

He wanted her. He needed her. He had to go find her.

His phone blared from somewhere in the apartment. With a groan, he jogged toward the sound, finding the offensive noisemaker jangling against the counter. He peeked at the screen.

Lucky.

Why the hell was he calling at six on a Saturday? Better not be any fucking trouble at the border.

"What's up, Luck?" As he spoke, he filled the coffee carafe with water.

"Hey man, what the fuck is your girl doing out at the Starlight motel? You know the one about forty-five minutes out of town on the way to California. She's loading a suitcase into her trunk. You fuck that up?"

Acer's heart rate kicked up. "You could say that. Listen bro, I'm leaving now, but can you follow her until I catch up?" She hadn't left Arizona yet. If he pushed it, he could be there in half hour. What he'd say when he got there was a different problem entirely.

"Man, you owe me."

"Thanks, see you soon. Wait!"

"Yeah?" Lucky asked around a yawn.

"What the fuck are you doing out there? Everything okay?"

"Yeah, man, just taking care of some personal shit. It's all good."

"Let me know if I can help."

Lucky snorted. "Seems like you got enough to worry about. Move your ass." He disconnected the call.

Coffee forgotten, he dashed back to his room, and threw on the first pair of jeans he encountered. Lucky's problems would have to wait, but he made a mental note to press his brother later.

Exactly two minutes later, Acer roared off into the early morning light in search of his woman.

Chapter Thirty-Seven

Fia grunted as she hefted the heavy bag into the car. It seemed to have gained fifty pounds in the time she'd been in Arizona. She slammed the trunk and yawned wide, the crack of her jaw reverberating through the peaceful morning. She'd been far too upset and nervous to make the journey at night by herself, so she drove out of town and found a motel. A well-lit motel an entire town away from where she'd been abducted.

Sleep hadn't been much of a reality last night. Anxiety at not only being alone, but alone in a motel once again, kept her awake and jittery until just a few hours ago. Still, she hadn't had a full-blown panic attack and a little tiredness was a small price to pay for that victory.

She missed Acer until she felt the loss like a hole in her wounded heart. A huge part of her wanted to drive back to Crystal Rock, bang on his door, and beg to stay. But she didn't. Living with a man who could never trust her, never love her would eventually eat away at her soul. She'd lived on her own for years—she could do it again.

Alone in the car, she cranked up a country station until the music was so loud it drowned out the thoughts in her head.

"Good bye, Acer," she whispered as she maneuvered her car out of the lot and onto the two-lane highway that would take her to California.

After thirty minutes of driving past nothing but sand and small rock formations, her head began to pound and she killed the music. She longed to close her eyes and rest her head back against the seat, but a devastating crash was the last thing she needed. With a sigh, she rolled her shoulders. It would have to do for now.

Any chance at relaxation flew out the window when the roar of an engine rose up behind her, way too loud to be a safe distance away. Her gaze flew to the rear-view mirror.

Jesus! A rusted-out, faded blue pickup barreled down the highway toward her at an alarming speed. She returned her attention to the barren road ahead, thankful to see no one was traveling toward her in the opposition lane. Mario Andretti could just go around her.

Another check of the mirror revealed he was edging perilously close to her rear bumper, still at a speed that far exceeded the highway's limit. A niggle of unease worked its way up Fia's spine until the hair on the back of her neck stood at attention.

"Chill out, girl," she whispered. She flicked the signal switch, turning on her right blinker. She'd just pull onto the shoulder and allow him to pass. It was a narrow portion of the highway, with rock formations on either side of the road, but the thin shoulder lane was wide enough for her car.

She removed her foot from the gas and veered onto the shoulder, coasting to a slower speed to allow the pickup to pass.

She looked in the mirror and screamed as the grating screech of metal on metal assaulted her ears. With a violent lurch, her body was thrown against the seat belt. A giant boom, comparable to an explosion shook the BMW and she was slammed back into the leather seat. Sharp stinging pains lashed at her arms as the sound of shattering glass registered. Confused, she tried to blink the cobwebs out of her head.

Airbag. The noise and punch back had been the airbag deploying. She took a shuddering breath, wincing when her chest ached as though she'd been kicked by a horse. Damn, that seatbelt may have saved her life, but she was going to have one hell of a bruise.

She lifted her hands to her face and gingerly prodded around her nose and eyes. No blood, no apparent broken bones. So far, so good. With a groan of discomfort, she slapped the airbag down. Sharp slivers of broken glass scattered to the seat and floorboards. Careful not to slice her fingers, she unbuckled the seatbelt and yanked on the door handle. It stuck at first, but with a painful shove from her shoulder, it creaked open.

That pickup driver had been crazy...the pickup driver! Her head snapped up and her ribs smarted in protest. Was the driver okay? With slow, cautious movements, she stood from the car. Shards of glass flew in every direction and her entire body screamed in protest. Man, her chest hurt. Is this what a broken rib felt like?

What she needed to do was call the police and possibly an ambulance. Where the hell was her phone?

The phone could wait until she checked on the pickup driver. She took two wobbly steps toward the truck and frowned. The driver's seat was empty and the windshield remained intact. He or she wasn't thrown from the car. Where were they?

"You fucking bitch."

Fia screamed and jumped, gasping as pain shot through her chest. She whirled and screamed again. Mike loomed ten feet away, a gun pointed at her.

His hair stood on end and his eyes were sunken and red-rimmed. A stream of blood ran from his nose, dripping to the rocky ground.

Fia's vision wavered and pins and needles began to tingle in the tips of her fingers. The pain in her sternum morphed into a tightness that made breathing difficult.

Christ, she could not have a panic attack right now. It would leave her completely vulnerable to whatever Mike had planned. If she'd only stayed at Acer's. She should have forced him to have it out with her, then made up. She could still be there now, wrapped in the warmth of his protective embrace.

The only time she felt completely safe was in his arms.

She inhaled, fresh oxygen filling her lungs and clearing her vision. Yes! *Keep thinking about Acer.* As though breathing in power, each breath cleared her head and infused her with the strength to survive. "How did you find me?"

He snickered. "I've been here all along, eyes on you, just waiting." His face morphed into a mask of fury. "There are fucking bikers looking for me everywhere! They don't even want their money back. There's a fucking bounty on my head." As he spoke, he moved closer until he stood just two feet away.

She stared at the gun, but thought of Acer's smile, his care, his ink, the way he always kept an arm around her when there were too many men in the room. His invisible support buffered her and gave her the courage to stand up to Mike. "Just go. Leave the state. They won't follow you. I'll make sure of it."

He laughed, the sound high pitched and crazy. Then his laughter died and his eyes darted around. "Shut the fuck up." He kept the barrel of the gun trained on her. "I think someone's coming."

She heard it too. A rumble. Was it a motorcycle? She crossed her fingers and prayed for a savior. Even if the rider blew past them, she wouldn't become a victim again. She would kill him if she could only get hold of that gun. There wasn't a chance in hell he was getting his hands on her again.

~ ~ ~ ~

Acer owed him big time. After the night he had, all Lucky wanted was a hot shower and a vat of coffee. Instead, he was cruising through the desert at six thirty on a Saturday morning, on babysitting detail.

All right, he didn't really mind helping his brother out with Fia. Christ, after witnessing her panic attack a little over a week ago, he felt almost as protective of her as Acer did. He was just exhausted.

It had been one shitty night.

"Oh, come on, asshole." Lucky growled as a rust bucket made a right turn and rattled its way onto the highway about two hundred yards out, obscuring his view of Fia.

He drifted over the yellow line to get a better line of sight. Fia traveled along at the same speed, a bit ahead of the truck.

Lucky frowned. The truck closed the distance to Fia's little BMW at an alarming pace. He increased his speed as Fia pulled off to the right shoulder. He blew out a breath. Smart girl, letting the fucker pass.

He eased off the throttle and—holy shit!

The truck slammed in to Fia's sporty car, with a screech Lucky felt in his bones. He raced toward them, only to decrease his speed at a rate that would have sent a less skilled biker skidding across the road. A man stumbled out of the pickup, pistol in hand, and jogged toward Fia's car.

Lucky pulled to the shoulder, about a hundred and fifty

yards out from the collision. The only weapons on him were a knife and a disassembled rifle in his pack. It would have to do. He grabbed the pack and scrambled over the cover of the rocks, on his way to rescue Fia.

~ ~ ~ ~

Acer squinted. Nothing but road and desert lie ahead. Where the hell were they? He'd been on the road almost an hour soaring at more than twenty-five miles over the limit. He should reach them any second.

He narrowed his eyes again as the sun glinted off something metallic up ahead. Lucky's fender. Relief and nerves coursed through him in equal measures. If he didn't get his shit under control, he'd be stuttering like some high school kid meeting his crush for the first time.

As he neared Lucky's bike a dark prickle of unease that had nothing to do with the fear of Fia's rejection worked its way up his spine. Why the hell was Lucky's bike parked on the side of the road? He glanced farther up the road. A beat up old pickup had crashed into a—

As though in a vacuum, the air was sucked out of Acer's lungs and his heart seized in his chest.

Fia's car. She could be injured. His stomach rolled and almost lost the contents, but he forced himself to move forward. If Fia was hurt, or worse, and he hadn't had the chance to make things right—

He couldn't finish the thought. She had to be okay, there simply wasn't another option.

He zoomed past Lucky's bike and skidded to a stop. He jumped off the bike as he laid it down, still traveling forward, in a move that would have impressed a professional stuntman. His feet hit the ground running and he threw his helmet somewhere in the road as he ran flat out toward the wreck. He didn't bother trying to be quiet or stealthy. He barreled forward with no thoughts beside reaching Fia as fast as possible.

The morning sun was climbing in the sky, heating the day to an uncomfortable level already. Sweat poured off his face, and his heart pounded as though he'd run ten miles instead of fifty feet.

He drew up next to the crash and the second shock of the day slammed into him. Mike stood directly in front of a wide-eyed, trembling Fia. The fucker aimed a pistol at the woman who owned his soul.

White-hot rage heated his blood and tensed his muscles. Forget killing the man; death would be too easy for him. Acer would tear him apart piece by fucking piece until nothing existed, until he no longer had nightmares of finding Fia beaten and violated. "You just signed your death warrant, motherfucker."

"Acer!" Fia's exclamation was full of terror.

Mike grabbed her by the arm, whirling her around and locking her against his bony chest. He jammed the gun against her temple with such force, in a few seconds a trickle of blood ran down the side of her chalky face.

Acer stared at the dark red river, channeling all his murderous fury, controlling his actions. He was stronger, smarter, and far deadlier than Mike. The dead man walking just didn't know it yet.

"You got a gun? Toss it down," Mike ordered.

Acer hesitated a moment too long and Mike ground the gun against Fia's temple. She whimpered then bit her lip, holding in any other sounds.

"Back the fuck off, asshole," Acer said as he pulled his forty-five out of the shoulder holster beneath his cut and tossed it to the ground between him and Fia.

"I'm sorry." Fia whispered on a choked sob. "I shouldn't

have left like that."

Acer risked taking his attention off Mike for a beat to gaze into Fia's frightened eyes. The combination of stark terror, and trust radiating from her gutted him like he'd been flayed with a knife. He forced himself to temper his reaction and winked at her. "You're not the one who has to apologize, baby. Just tell me you're coming home with me after we get rid of this shithead."

Tears spilled down her face and she actually chuckled, the sound wrapping around his overworked heart. "I wouldn't go anywhere else."

"Shut the fuck up, bitch." Mike pressed the muzzle of the gun harder against Fia's soft skin and she whimpered. Gasping sounds flew from her throat with each breath, and she shivered like it was twenty degrees instead of a hundred.

"Just keep looking at me, baby. Focus on me."

Where the fuck was Lucky?

Chapter Thirty-Eight

Fia focused on Acer's face, contorted into a mask of anger she'd yet to see from him. The anger was well controlled, but no doubt would be lethal when unleashed. No fear or uncertainty was evident in his stance. Only pure, poisonous confidence.

Mike would die today. Of that, she became certain.

Maybe later, when the waters calmed, she'd feel guilt and shame for her thoughts, but for now, she wanted his death. She wanted to know she could live her life, maybe with Acer, without jumping at shadows and peeking over her shoulder every ten seconds. And part of her wanted Mike to know what true fear was.

Acer's confidence bolstered her and her breathing leveled once again, or as best it could with a firm arm banded across her already tender chest. She kept her concentration on Acer as he'd ordered.

Anything she could do to help him, she'd do. She would not be a liability in this situation.

Acer rolled his shoulders and relaxed his stance, but she wasn't fooled, the man was poised and ready to strike when necessary. "So what's your plan here, Mike? You gonna shoot me, shove Fia in your shitty truck and ride off?"

Mike tensed. The gun scraped along her temple, taking a layer of skin with it. She tried not to react. Who knew what would set Mike off?

His high-pitched laugh vibrated against her back. The cackle reminded her of the Joker from Batman, not completely sane. "I like that plan. What the hell are you gonna do about it?"

Acer shrugged, his gaze flicking back and forth. What was he looking for?

"Guess there's not much I can do about it." A deadly expression crossed his face. "But my brothers?" He laughed. "Yeah, they'll do something about it."

"They want to kill me anyway. Might as well put some lead in your ass, get something out of this. Something besides pussy." He loosened his hold on her enough to run his hand down her chest and squeeze her breast, hard. Bile rose in her throat as horrific memories replayed in her mind.

Acer's eyes darkened and his fists curled. Fia stared at him. If she kept him in the forefront of her mind, she could almost ignore Mike's hand on her breast. Acer sent a small nod her way, as though he understood her intense focus.

The wind gusted and a small dust devil spun up behind Acer. It blew across the road so fast, there wasn't time to react. Fia held her breath and closed her eyes as millions of tiny sand grains accosted her skin.

"Fuck!" The gun fell away from her temple and the pressure against her chest disappeared as Mike coughed and sputtered behind her. Fia's fight-or-flight response kicked in with a powerful surge. She lunged forward.

Pop, pop.

What the hell?

Strong arms wrapped around her back and in the next

instant, she found herself pressed roughly against another chest. This chest was solid and comforting. This chest she knew.

"Acer? Wh-what's happening?" Her entire body shook with relief and bewilderment.

"Shh, baby, are you hurt?" His large hand cupped the back of her head, keeping her face buried in his pecs.

"I don't think so." She spoke into his shirt. The sound of a man screaming in pain registered and despite the hot sun beating down on the open road, Fia shivered. With her face still mashed against Acer's firm chest, she couldn't see, but the agonizing screams seemed to be coming from Mike.

Acer turned, still holding her. "Take her for a minute."

What, who was he talking to?

Acer pressed his mouth against her ear, his warm breath tickled her skin. "Stay with Lucky while I end this."

Fia's head spun and she could barely process Acer's words. Lucky? Where had he come from?

Acer released his hold on her and gently handed her off to another pair of strong arms. She immediately missed the feeling of safety, comfort, and arousal only Acer could provide.

She glanced up at Lucky, still clueless as to where he'd materialized from, then looked at Acer. If she hadn't known he was harmless to her, the lethal look of impending violence on his face would have sent her running for the hills. "Be careful," she whispered.

"Always." He stepped away.

"I need to see." She pushed against Lucky's chest, but his arms remained steel bands around her back.

"No way, Fia. You don't want this image in your head."

"Please, Lucky. I need to know it's over." She struggled against his sturdy hold.

He hesitated, but after a few seconds, loosened his hold. She rotated in his arms, watching as Acer stalked the short distance to Mike.

Her attacker lay ten feet away, a puddle of crimson blood expanding beneath him. "What did you do to him?" she asked around Mike's cries of pain.

Lucky paused a second before answering her. "Put a bullet in the hand that held a gun. And a bullet in his leg. Didn't want him running away."

Fia swallowed and kept her focus on Acer. He dropped to one knee at Mike's side and leaned forward, pressing a closed fist into Mike's thigh, inches from the bullet would. The howl ripped from Mike was that of a mortally-wounded animal and Fia couldn't hide her flinch.

Then Acer bent down, so his face hovered above Mike's. He held the muzzle of his gun to the center of Mike's forehead and the man's screams dwindled to whimpers. Fia held her breath. Acer wouldn't let the other man live.

Would guilt set in at some point? Guilt that she wanted this? Wanted another human's death. Guilt that she let Acer do this? Maybe, but it wasn't there now. Now all she felt was the anticipation of freedom from fear.

~ ~ ~ ~

"I've been dreaming of this moment for weeks. Having you at my mercy. Killing you. Gotta say, I was hoping we'd have a little more privacy and a little more time." Acer kept his voice low. Fia didn't need to hear this shit. She didn't need to know how the need make this man suffer pulsed through Acer's body with each pound of his heart.

He'd longed for this moment every second of every day since he discovered Fia in that hot as hell fucking house, her body violated, her mind terrified. He took a deep breath, savoring the moment, the certain knowledge that his woman would be free of this piece of shit.

"P-pl-please do-don't kill m-me." Mike's eyes were saucer-wide and color leeched from his face with every passing second. Sand mixed with the blood and tears running down his face forming a muddy paste. He cradled his injured hand against his chest, the action not nearly sufficient to stem the flow of blood soaking his clothing.

The cowering and sniveling did nothing to soften Acer toward the injured man. In fact, they only made Mike more loathsome. Fucking coward. Couldn't even die like a man. "Ohh, that's good." Acer's mouth rose into an evil grin. "Beg me a little more. Maybe, just maybe I'll have mercy on you." He kept his pistol centered between Mike's glassy brown eyes. "Go on."

"P-please." His voice grew weak. "I'll g-get your m-money. I'll l-leave town."

"Hmm." Acer leaned forward just a hair, letting his body weight rest on the fist on Mike's thigh. The man let out another ear-splitting scream. "You know, I'm just not sure that's good enough, Mike. See, you hurt someone very important to me. You hurt my woman."

"I-I didn't know." Snot dripped from Mike's nose as he started to blubber. "P-please m-man. Please."

Acer chuckled. "You think I care that you didn't know she was mine? You know now and yet, here we are." It was time to end this. While he'd been dreaming of a long drawn out death for Mike, Fia waited behind him, and taking her back home was more important. Mike would be dead, and that's what counted. "I have no fucking intention of letting you live."

He pulled the trigger, the loud pop echoing through the vast desert. Mike went limp beneath him and Acer was filled with a sense of satisfaction. His woman was safe. "Rot in hell, asshole," he muttered, before he rose and turned to Fia.

She'd broken out of Lucky's hold and flew across the distance to Acer. The soft, warm weight of her body slammed into him, soothing him a million times better than any verbal or visual confirmation of her safety. He held her close, careful not to squeeze too hard in case she sustained any injuries in the crash. "It's over, baby."

She trembled in his arms. Moisture seeped through his shirt. Christ, he hated to see her cry.

Lucky turned his attention to Fia; his rifle slung over one shoulder. "You okay, sweetie?"

Fia sniffed and lifted her head from Acer's chest. "I think so. Where did you come from? And how did you—"

"Former Marine sniper." Acer spoke above her. "And he saw you leave the motel. I asked him to follow you until I could catch up." Acer stroked his hand up and down her back in a rhythmic, soothing motion. He wasn't sure if it was her or himself he set out to soothe, but it seemed to have a calming effect on both of them. If he had his way, she wouldn't leave his arms for the next week, but that wasn't possible. They needed to get the hell out of here.

"You guys take off. I called for garbage detail. Should be here soon. Thank fuck this Podunk road doesn't get much traffic." He looked over his shoulder into the barren desert.

This road was sparsely traveled, but that didn't mean they could stand here all day with a dead body in the road and not draw unwanted attention. "You sure, Luck?" Acer asked.

Lucky turned back and met his gaze. "I'm sure. Take your girl home. Give her something to smile about." He winked at Fia and she chuckled.

"Thank you, brother." For so much more than letting them bug out, but Lucky didn't need the extra words.

He nodded. "Anything."

Acer pressed a kiss to Fia's head. Part of him wanted to stand here with her in his arms all day, just feeling the life flow through her, but they needed to leave. He couldn't chance her being here if someone drove by. Plus, he needed to get her alone so he could inspect every inch of her body and assure himself she was unharmed.

But first. "Fia, do you need to go to the hospital? Or need me to call Lila?" He stepped back and ran his hands over her face, her arms, her hips. He couldn't get enough of touching her.

"No, I'm sore, but fine. I just want to get out of here."

"Will you be able to ride on the bike?"

She nodded. "Yes, anything to get out of here. Please take me home."

Home.

Damn, that sounded good.

Chapter Thirty-Nine

The instant the door closed, Fia found herself backed gently against it with Acer's face buried in her neck. He ran his teeth over the corded muscles and licked along her collarbone. "Acer," she said on a moan. She let her head fall back against the wood with a thunk, allowing him easier access to her skin.

This was exactly where she belonged. Pressed between Acer's muscular body and whatever surface happened to be closest. This was her happy place.

He worked her shirt up and yanked it over her head, taking her bra along with it in a slightly awkward push and pull. When she was free of the material, he tossed it over his shoulder. "Fia! That's it, you're going to the hospital."

She glanced down at her chest where a long diagonal bruise was already multiple shades of purple. She'd never admit it to him, but the ride home hurt like hell. It was worth it though, to be wrapped tight around Acer's sculpted back as he drove them farther and farther away from her past. Now, desire outweighed the majority of the discomfort. She cupped Acer's distressed face between her palms. "I'm fine. It will probably hurt later, but it's not bad right now. And if you stop what you were doing, you'll end up with a bruise that makes this look like nothing."

He opened his mouth, then closed it as though considering her words. Assessing whether she was telling the truth. She gifted him a seductive smile that must have done the trick because he returned his mouth to her, trailing biting kisses up her neck. Kisses that would leave a mark, kisses that claimed.

His actions were full of an unfamiliar desperation. He seemed to temper it as he kissed a gentler path down her sore chest, but desperation was still evident in his strong grip on her hips. It was as though he held on by a thin thread, seconds from unraveling. Part of her wanted to ask if he was okay, but then his mouth closed around a puckered nipple and she cried out instead.

He wasn't gentle, almost in a frenzy, but it was exactly what she needed. He released the nipple and moved to the other, swirling his tongue around it and sucking it into his mouth with a strong pull. Fiery pleasure shot from the tight bud straight to her core.

After just a second or two, he dropped to his knees and yanked her shorts down over her hips. His fast motions and minimal time spent on each part of her body had her head spinning to keep up.

"God, you smell fucking amazing." With a hand on each inner thigh, he shoved her legs wide apart and inhaled deeply.

She was exposed to him in the most intimate way possible. Standing over him with her legs spread, dripping pussy poised above his mouth as he drank in the sight and scent of her. Mesmerized, she stared down at him, the anticipation of when his lips would land on her an erotic torture.

He breathed her in a few more times, then swiped his tongue through her drenched folds.

"Ah, Acer." Her hands flew to his head, fisting the soft strands and holding him against her.

"Taste even better, baby. I'm gonna eat every drop of this cream."

She groaned and rocked her pelvis into his face. He gripped her ass in his hands, keeping her locked against his hungry mouth. Not that it was necessary. She wouldn't move for all the money in the world.

With a hum of approval, he swirled his tongue around her clit. Fia's legs trembled as lightning shot up her spine. Thank God for the wide stance, or she might have toppled over.

There was so much unspoken between them. Just because they wanted to lose themselves in the life-affirming passion of sex, didn't mean he'd want her for good. The sad thought only lasted for the blink of an eye because he opened his mouth wider and fitted it against her pussy, thrusting his tongue deep inside her.

"Yes, Acer, oh my God, that's so good." Between his grip on her bottom and her hold on his hair, his face was pressed so tightly to her center she was surprised he could still breathe. Tension coiled low in her belly as the pleasure reached an almost unbearable intensity.

Acer ate at her like she was a life-giving source.

"Please, don't stop. Don't stop." She was so close, the pressure so great her head might shoot right off her body.

He grunted against her sex and she detonated like a match in a room full of propane. Her head slammed back against the door and her muscles quivered with electric pleasure. If not for his firm hold on her ass, she'd have melted into a puddle of satisfaction on the floor.

Acer remained where he was, running his tongue along her over sensitized folds with gentle strokes as her body calmed. He laid a soft kiss on her clit and only then did she realize her hands were still clenched in his hair like she was holding the mane of a bronco.

Her fingers ached as she uncurled them. Yikes, her grip had been strong. Poor guy probably had a bald patch now. "Sorry." She patted the top of his head, not enough energy for anything else.

He chuckled. "Nothing a little Rogaine won't fix."

She laughed with him. Acer rose to a tall kneel and wrapped his arms around her waist. After one kiss to her scarred skin, he laid his cheek against her flat stomach. "I'm so fucking sorry, Fia. Please stay here with me. I can't—" He swallowed and turned his face into her abdomen. "I can't be without you."

Unsure of what to do with her hands, Fia left them hanging in midair. This strong man, whose biggest fear was appearing emotionally vulnerable, laid his soul bare on his knees before her. "Stand up," she whispered.

He rose, his muscles sliding against her, igniting the fire once again, until he stood above her, looking down into her eyes.

"Acer, you don't need to go to your knees for me, for anyone. You are everything to me. You saved me, you protect me, but that's not why I want you. I—"

He cut off her words with a kiss. "I'm so fucking sorry I kept important information from you. So sorry that I didn't trust you." Acer kissed a trail from her mouth to her ear. "Emily made me realize it wasn't you I didn't trust…it was myself. I didn't trust myself enough to be the man needed, to keep you safe, to not let you down. Fia, I trust you, more than anyone, and I will prove that to you every day if you stay with me."

His words were like a balm to her soul. It wasn't a proclamation of love, but that was okay. For now. They both had emotional baggage, and him admitting to his trust issues and putting his trust in her went a long way toward building a solid foundation. She smiled and turned her face until her mouth met his. "That Emily is pretty smart." She captured his lips in a quick kiss. "And I'm not going anywhere."

His breath of relief was almost comical. "Thank fuck."

Running her hands over the rise and fall of the muscles in his back, she grinned. "Guess that just leaves one thing."

He pulled back and frowned down at her. "What's that?"

With a sassy grin, she wrapped her hand around his cock and stroked the smooth skin. "Please, fuck me."

He growled and spun her until her front pressed against the door. "Yes, ma'am."

~ ~ ~ ~

Why he'd been gifted with this strong, sexy, independent, and forgiving woman, he'd never know, but he was done questioning it. She was here and she wanted to stay. He planned to grab onto her with both hands and never let her go.

Acer nestled his throbbing erection against the soft curve of Fia's ass. He molded his chest to her back and linked his fingers with hers where they rested against the door near her head. With a small tilt of his pelvis, he ground himself against her.

"Have I told you how hard this ass makes me?"

She laughed. "Once or twice."

"Well then, let me make it an uneven three." He nipped at her earlobe, enjoying the slight shiver that racked her. "This okay?" Mike may be dead, and Fia may be miles away from the skittish girl she was when she first arrived, be he'd be damned if he did anything to spook her and he wasn't arrogant enough to think there wouldn't be some hard times ahead.

"No, it's not okay."

He started to take a step back, but five sharp nails bit into his ass as she reached behind her and anchored him to her.

"It will be okay once you're inside me."

Jesus. She'd scared the crap out of him. He growled against her hair. "You'll pay for that little stunt."

He could almost feel the grin spread across her face. "I sure hope so, but so far it's just more talking."

He took a step back and slipped one hand around her waist, yanking her hips away from the wall. The other hand pushed against her lower back until she arched, her ass on display for his pleasure. He stroked over the rounded globes, squeezing occasionally. "Keep your hands there on the wall, next to your head. Don't move them. No touching your tits, no touching your clit. We clear?"

She didn't answer right away and he slapped a palm against her ass.

She gasped, then moaned.

"I asked if we were clear?"

"Crystal. Though if you wanted to punish me, maybe you shouldn't have done something to make me even wetter."

Smart-mouth. Damn he loved his woman.

Acer shoved his boxer-briefs over his hips and kicked them away. With a stable grip, he fisted his cock in his hand and ran it up the seam of Fia's ass. She moaned and did a little shimmy with her bottom. "Spread your legs."

She complied immediately. There wasn't much he loved more than when she submitted to him in the bedroom. She may tease him and in the day-to-day sass him, but in here, she obeyed his every command.

Fuckin sexy.

"This reminds me of LA. Against the window." He slipped the head of his cock between her folds, coating it with her wetness and rubbing along her slit.

"Yes." She gasped and shifted, trying to impale herself on his cock. He allowed the tip to rest right at her opening, but not enter her. "Acer," she moaned. "You're killing me. Please, fuck me already."

He chuckled, the motion pushing his cock more snuggly against her heat. Okay, enough teasing. With a steady stroke, he pushed into her to the hilt. "Nothing better than this, baby. You're so fucking hot and tight around me, I can barely hold back every time I get inside of you. Nothing better."

"Better when you move." Her voice was breathy, full of desire and need.

He laughed. "Smart-mouth. You move, fuck yourself on my cock."

With the angle of her arched back and her hands splayed against the wall, her movements were limited. But she did as he asked, and pumped her hips on his shaft.

After a minute, she let out a feminine growl. "Acer." Her voice was nearly a whine.

"You need something, baby?" God, he loved her like this, wanton and needy, begging for him.

"It's not enough!"

He smiled. When was the last time he had this lightness in his chest? This sense of peace? More than twenty years ago.

He clasped her hips, stilling her frenzied movements. At an agonizingly slow pace, he drew out until he nearly lost the blazing clasp of her body. Their mixed moans filled the room. He paused for a second, letting the anticipation build. Fia's back rose and fell with her heaving breaths.

He slammed back into her and pulled immediately back out in a fast and furious rhythm.

"Yes," Fia cried. "Just like that." Her head dropped down between her shoulders and she panted for breath. Against the dark door, her knuckles and fingertips were stark white.

He fucked her until his breathing was ragged and harsh. His balls slapping her ass with every deep thrust. As he raced toward completion, his dick swelled and his balls drew tight to his body. "Shit. I'm not gonna last. You close, baby?"

"Yes, yes, yes."

He reached beneath their bodies and found her clit, pinching it lightly between his thumb and forefinger. She clenched around him, and with one last thrust, he emptied into her welcoming body, holding her tight against him.

Thank God she'd been right there with him because he couldn't have held back for anything. With his fingers, still on her clit, Fia's head fell back, her mouth dropped open, and a wail pierced his ears.

After her body calmed, he kissed the middle of her spine and smiled at her contented sigh. Damn, he may have shot his soul into her.

He slipped one arm under her knees and the other around her shoulders and scooped her into his arms. She was soft and pliant and curled against his sweat-slicked chest.

"Oh good, you're carrying me. Not sure I could have walked if I wanted to."

He looked down into her eyes, at the love shining from her sleepy face. "I'll always carry you, babe."

I love you. The three words were on the tip of his tongue, but there was one thing that needed to be settled before he could put his own past behind him and move forward with a life with Fia.

Chapter Forty

As the doors slid open, Acer stepped out of the elevator and into Reginald Wellington's world. The opulent design, complete with heavy drapes, carved wooden pillars, and dark colors, that adorned Reggie's Vegas office fit in well with his hotel décor.

He hated to leave Fia so soon after the incident with Mike yesterday, but this had to be done. Fia was fully supportive, and to his satisfied surprise, insisted he go alone. He didn't want her anywhere near his prick of an old man. Two and a half hours each way to Vegas, two if he pushed it. He'd be back by mid-afternoon, and she was working on some secret project anyway.

Acer sidled up to a large mahogany reception desk and crossed his arms over his chest. A young lady—probably no older than twenty-one and probably fucking his father on that very desk every night—stared up at him with wide, wary eyes.

He'd worn his No Prisoners cut on purpose. The MC was known, respected, and feared—if the receptionist's expression was any indication—in the Vegas area. He pressed his lips together to hold back a grin. The girl's only sin was working for an asshole, but he had to admit it was fun messing with her. "I'm here to see Reginald Wellington." He kept his tone unfriendly, no-nonsense.

She cleared her throat and played with the end of a long red braid draped over one shoulder. "Um…Mr. Wellington keeps a very tight schedule. Do you have an appointment?" She pushed her glasses up her freckled nose then went back to fidgeting with her hair.

"Nope. Don't need one. He'll see me. I guarantee it." He widened his stance and glowered at her.

"Let me call him." She fumbled with the phone and Acer almost laughed. This was too much fun.

"Mr. Wellington?" Her voice took on a different quality as she spoke into the phone, softer, almost seductive. Yeah, she was definitely fucking the bastard. "There's a man here to see you. Um, no he did not give a name and doesn't have an appointment." She looked at Acer. "Your name, sir?"

"Acer," he said loud enough for Reggie to have heard through the phone.

His father yelled something he couldn't make out, but the receptionist's face paled and she hung up the phone. "You can head down the hallway. His office is the double doors at the end," she nearly whispered.

"Thank you. Word of advice, things are about to get pretty shitty for Reggie. You may want to find yourself a new sugar daddy." He tapped his hand on the desk then turned and strode in the direction she'd indicated.

The mahogany double doors were open by the time he reached the end of the poorly lit hallway. Money must be tight if Reggie couldn't afford better light bulbs. Acer slipped through the doors and met his father's cold stare across the room.

Reginald rose from his leather chair and placed both

palms on the meticulous desktop. "What the fuck have you done?"

"Not happy to see me, old man?" Acer asked. He took a seat in an antique chair across from Reginald's desk.

"Do you have any idea what you've done to me?" Reggie asked.

Acer leaned back in the uncomfortable chair and propped his right foot on his left thigh. "I have no idea what you mean." He smirked at his father.

Reginald slapped a palm against the desk, his face turning a deep shade of red, almost purple. If he kept ramping up, smoke would billow from his ears. "You did something. I got a call from Tony Chicarelli this morning."

Acer was well aware the mob boss had called his father. "Hmm, not sure I can place the name. Who is he?"

"Really?" Reggie's lip turned up in a snarl.

Damn, this was the most fun he'd had in a while. Maybe he should have brought Fia with him. She deserved a little fun.

"He certainly claims to know you. In fact, he says you're such good buddies, he won't tolerate my company's presence in Arizona." Reggie twisted the lavish ring on the finger of his right hand.

Acer almost laughed. Calling his illegal human smuggling ring *his company's presence* was truly hilarious. "Huh, would you look at that. Maybe the name does ring a bell."

"What. The. Hell. Did. You. Do?" Spittle flew from Reginald's mouth. The man looked on the verge of a heart attack.

"Simmer down there, old man. I didn't do much. Just a quick favor for a friend who you happen to owe five million dollars to."

Reginald turned stark white and he dropped into his chair.

"Ahh, didn't know I was aware of that tidbit, did you? I also know that you don't have even a tenth of that to pay back, and your deadline is soon. This new hotel needs to be erected, fast and cheap, and it needs to be a huge success. Hence you scrambling for inexpensive labor." Acer tsked. "Tony was not pleased to hear the news."

In reality, Acer offered Tony something he desperately wanted in exchange for the mob boss demanding Wellington scrap the activity in Arizona.

"He threatened to ruin me. Christ, he threatened to kill me!"

Acer shrugged. "That is what happens when you piss off the mob." He dropped his foot back to the floor and leaned forward. "Be careful who you fuck with, old man. I think I've proved I'm no longer a child you can fuck over. I trust the border will be clear by the time I arrive home."

He stood and walked toward the door, leaving a defeated Reginald staring at the wall. Before he exited, he turned back around. "I warned you my connections were more impressive than yours. I'll fulfill my promise to your mother, my grandmother, and honor my friendship to Derek by attending the prison fund raising event each year. But I expect you to find a reason not to be there from now on. In fact, I expect this will be our last conversation. Ever."

He stepped into the hallway and blew out breath as the door clicked shut behind him. He was done. Rid of Mike. Rid of his father. He'd gotten so used to the substantial weight pressing down on his shoulders over the last twenty years, he almost felt like he'd levitate off the ground as the heaviness disappeared. He raised his gaze to the ceiling. "That was for you, Derek," he whispered.

Time to return to Arizona, to Fia. He had something very important to tell her.

Chapter Forty-One

Fia threw the door open as Acer's heavy boots sounded on the steps. She jumped up and he caught her mid-flight, his hand cupping her ass to hold her against him. "Hi," she whispered. He'd been gone just a little over five hours, and it felt like a lifetime. After everything that happened with Mike yesterday, Fia was a little needier than usual and wanted him in her arms.

Of course, she fully understood his need to put his issues with his father to bed, so she'd encouraged his trip to Vegas. She spent the day working and checking the clock. The wait was finally over.

"Fuck, I missed you," he said as he walked them into the apartment and straight to the couch. He fused their mouths and lowered her to the cushions, his big body dwarfing her. This was exactly what she needed. She kissed him back, letting all her love flow into the act. They hadn't spoken words of love yet, but she loved him with every cell in her body and was pretty sure he felt the same.

"Need you now, baby," he said, wrestling with the zipper on his jeans.

Yes. Now. She could barely wait the time it would take

them to undress. As she reached for the waistband of her white denim shorts, a shrill melody sounded through the house and she froze.

"Ignore it," Acer said of the ringing phone.

"It's my father's ring tone."

Acer sat up straight and ran a hand through his mussed hair. "Fuck. You better get it. Put it on speaker."

She nodded as she scrambled to a sitting position. She reached for her phone, resting on Acer's coffee table. "Okay," she whispered, then pushed talk and speaker. "H-Hello?" She tried to sound unaffected, but her mind whirled and her heart raced.

"Fia?" He sounded so small, beaten down.

"Yes." She worked to keep a tremor out of her voice. Despite everything that had gone down between them, he was her father, her blood, and she couldn't remain unaffected by his distress.

Acer rubbed a hand up and down her back, always there, always supporting her.

Her father cleared this throat. "I, um, I just wanted to say thank you. Whatever Acer said to get Wellington to stop blackmailing me, it worked."

She remained quiet. As part of his deal with the mob boss, Acer demanded his father stop blackmailing hers. How was she supposed to respond? He hadn't done it for her father's own good, but for hers. To keep any additional drama and heartache from touching her.

"You still have a lot of trouble on your plate," she said instead of acknowledging his thanks.

"I know. I'm going to take care of it." He paused, the silence made him seem a million miles away. "And I want you to know, I will not interfere with your business anymore."

Her jaw dropped and she turned to Acer. He pressed a

soundless kiss to her cheek. Her dad sounded sincere, sounded remorseful. She wanted to believe him, wanted to think they could have some sort of father-daughter relationship moving forward, but it was just too soon. After dealing with so much trauma and stress, she just couldn't add to it at this time.

"You've said, and done some pretty serious things, dad." Had he even told her mother about the affair? A dull ache throbbed behind her eyes. This was all just too much so soon after everything with Mike. She just didn't have the energy to deal with the problems he created.

His heavy sigh was clear through the phone. "I have a lot of amends to make."

She rolled her eyes. He had a lot more to do than just making amends. "I think...I think maybe we shouldn't talk for a while. Not forever, but for now. I need time. Time for me."

"I understand. Take as much time as you need. Goodbye, Fia."

"Bye, Dad." Fia ended the call and dropped her face into her hands. "I'm not sure I handled that right."

Acer brushed her hair to the side and pressed a kiss to the back of her neck. Then another. She smiled into her hands. God, she loved this man. It was time to tell him. Even if he couldn't say it back.

"Acer," she said, and she lifted her head and made eye contact with him.

He clasped her face between both hands and stared deep into her eyes. For a second, the serious look on his face worried her. Was something wrong?

"I love you, Fia." He kissed her. "I couldn't say it until I was free of all this, it didn't seem fair, but I love you so fucking much."

Tears filled her eyes and spilled out as a giant smile grew on her face. Those three words coming off his lips were the sweetest sound. After all that she'd been through in the past month, to have it all end with Acer's love was unbelievable. "I love you too. So much, Acer. You have no idea."

Tension fled his body until he almost sagged into her. It was like he'd been afraid she wouldn't return his feelings.

Not possible.

He wrapped his arms around her and crushed her too him, so tight it was as though he wanted to absorb her into his body. "God I don't deserve you, baby, but I'm so fucking thankful for you."

Tears flowed freely down her cheeks now and she laughed. "You just haven't seen my mean side yet."

He chuckled and rested his forehead against hers. "I hate to say this when all I want to do is take you to bed and stay there for the next week, but I have church in half an hour."

Fia groaned. "I forgot." She sighed. "All right, let's get it over with. I'll tag along. I have something for the girls."

"What is it?"

She winked. "Nothing for you to worry about." She pulled him off the couch with a light heart and feeling like her life had taking an amazing turn.

~ ~ ~ ~

"So, how'd you run 'em off? I was looking forward to kicking some ass. This was too easy." Hook rubbed a hand over his fisted knuckles.

Acer smiled at his brothers. He felt great, like he'd woken up from hibernation. Fia was officially his, and he planned to keep it that way for the rest of their lives.

Striker laughed. "You're still rocking that shiner from the last time we ran into them. You that anxious for its twin?"

Hook scoffed. "Screw that." He touched the faint purple

bruise ringing his right eye. "This ain't nothing'. You saw what I did to the dude, right?"

The men laughed until Shiv cleared his throat. "Think you jerk-offs can focus for five minutes?"

"Sorry, pres." Hook's grin was unrepentant.

Acer rolled his eyes. "Anyway, looks like Reggie was so far buried under the shit he would have needed a whole crew of excavators to dig out. A little discrete digging revealed he owed more than five million to the mob."

Jester snorted. "Discrete digging, huh? What's that mean? You hacking bank accounts now?"

Acer flipped Jester off. "You want to hear the rest or not?"

"Go on, go on."

"The bill is due soon and Reggie doesn't have nearly what he needs to pay up. Looks like he was hoping to build this new hotel on the cheap so he could pay off his debts, but even then, it didn't look promising. Anyway, that's why he was trying to get migrants across the border to build his latest monstrosity for next to nothing."

"So how'd you get him to back off?" Lucky spoke this time.

Acer was glad Lucky's transition to Arizona seemed to be smooth. He hadn't had a chance to talk to his buddy about what he was doing at the motel out of town last weekend, but he'd get to it soon. If Lucky needed help, Acer would do anything for him. There was a good chance he'd saved both his and Fia's lives that morning.

"I had some information the mob boss could use, so I passed it along. He then let Reggie know we were tight and he wouldn't tolerate them fucking around in our turf. He backed off in a heartbeat."

"What did you give to the mob boss?" Jester asked.

Acer hesitated. "The FBI has been up their asses and they

have a pending trial that goes to court in a month." He cleared his throat. Everyone knew he could make a computer get up and dance, but they didn't all know the full extent of his skills. "I tracked down some files that would give them a leg up."

The room grew quiet as more than fifteen pairs of eyes blinked at him.

Finally, Jester snorted. "Christ, remind me not to piss you off. You can do some scary shit."

"Seriously," Gumby agreed. "I'd like my skeletons to stay locked in my closet."

The room cracked up, ribbing and backslaps making the rounds.

"A'ight, meeting adjourned." Shiv stood and nodded to Acer. "Thanks for taking care of all that shit. Glad it didn't end up with anyone behind bars or bloodied."

Except his father. There was a good chance he'd end up six feet under if he couldn't pay his debt.

"Damn straight." Jester rubbed his hands together. "Ain't got time for any of that shit. I got a woman to keep satisfied."

"Speaking of, any of you guys ever figure out what those ladies are up to? I swear they've got something planning and I'm starting to sweat," Striker said.

"Aww, you afraid of your ol' lady, VP?" Jester asked.

Striker snorted. "You mean, you ain't? Yours is knocked up, brother, you're the one who should be shaking in your clown boots."

Acer trailed the group out of the chapel and over to the bar, where the four women giggled. Each lady had a sly smile for their man. Striker was right, something was up their non-existent sleeves.

"And what is that?" Hook asked, pointing to Marcie's

hand.

Each woman held a small bag overflowing with different colored tissue paper.

Marcie hopped off her barstool and swung the bag in front of Hook's eyes. "Wouldn't you like to know?"

He made a quick grab for the bag and Marcie yelped. She stashed it behind her and backed up. "Now, Hook. It will be better as a surprise."

He advanced on his grinning wife. She yelped again when her back hit the bar, then turned and bolted toward the door. Hook laughed and jogged after her. "You better hope I don't catch you," he called out as he chased her.

The women said their goodbyes and Acer nodded at each of his brothers before turning his attention to Fia. He bent down and kissed her until she moaned softly. "Thanks for waiting for me."

She bobbed her eyebrows. "It was no problem. The girls and I had our own meeting."

"So, where's your little bag?"

"At home."

He wasn't buying her sweet and innocent act for a dollar. He recognized the logo for her company on the bags. Something naughty was in each of those little packages. "Well then, maybe that's where we should be."

She hopped off the stool and strolled past him, her fingertips grazing low across his abdomen as she passed. He groaned as his dick came to life.

"You coming?"

"Right after we get home."

She blew him a kiss. "Love you," she mouthed.

"Fuckin' love you too, Fia. You know this makes you my ol' lady, right?"

She walked toward the exit, a little extra sway in her hips.

When she reached the door, she looked over her shoulder and winked.

Damn, he was one lucky bastard.

Epilogue

"How you holding up, honey?" The tall tattoo artist with the bushy beard and four facial piercings didn't shift focus from his work, but he somehow seemed aware of every reaction she had.

Acer let out a harsh breath from the chair next to her and Fia couldn't hold back the laugh.

"Uh uh, don't move." The gruff voice held a no-nonsense tone.

"Sorry, Crank." Every time the tattoo artist called her honey—which was pretty much every time he addressed her —and every time he moved the needle too close to her breast, Acer let out a little growl. After hours of listening to it, she couldn't keep the laughter at bay any longer.

The buzzing quieted and Crank rose to his full height, which rivaled Jester's six-foot-five. "Seriously, Acer? I've got a needle in her skin, and my rep on the line. I ain't about to hop on this table and show her where my real talent lies." He winked at Fia. "At least not until I'm done with this masterpiece."

Acer practically snarled and this time it wasn't a chuckle that bubbled out, but full-blown hilarity. Jealous Acer was a sight to behold.

"Fuck you," Acer turned his middle finger up to Crank.

Crank stowed his tattoo gun and held out a hand to Fia. She grasped it, allowing him to assist her to a full sitting position, ignoring Acer's frown of disapproval. The man was a professional, for crying out loud. Not to mention she found his tattooed scalp and perpetual scowl more than intimidating.

"Check it out in the mirror, then I'll grease you up and review the aftercare one more time."

A flutter of excitement coursed through her as she essentially skipped to the mirror.

She closed her eyes, took a deep breath, and gazed at what would be permanently showcased on her body. A gorgeous sunrise rose over the ribs on the right side of her body. Vivid swirls of pinks, oranges, and yellows morphed into a stunning palette.

"Oh my God." Tears filled her eye and her hand flew to her mouth.

Crank was a genius. An absolute genius.

He'd been reluctant to tattoo directly over a few of the scars since they were rounded and raised. The ink had a high chance of bleeding. Instead, he'd planned to weave the pink scars into the image with a promise that the marks would disappear into the design.

She couldn't deny her skepticism. In her mind, she envisioned a sunrise tattoo with seven pink circles making it look like a child's connect-the-dots game.

She couldn't have been more wrong.

Crank coordinated the colors so perfectly, even she couldn't discern the pink scars from the pink in morning sky, and she knew the exact shape and placement of each burn. The finished product was so much more than she'd allowed herself to hope for.

This tattoo was the final rung on the tall ladder of recovery. It was a long, hard, and slippery climb, but she'd triumphed. The physical reminder on her skin had been replaced with an image of strength and splendor. Now she viewed her life like the rising sun, a cheerful dawn of new beginnings full of beautiful possibilities and wonder.

She owed it all to Acer.

~ ~ ~ ~

Acer stood about three feet behind the woman he loved, letting her have a private moment to absorb the impact of Crank's spectacular work. She was bound to have an emotional reaction after months of worry over those marks. Despite how much progress Fia made, those scars still bothered her.

He shifted his focus to the tattoo artist and sent the man a nod of thanks. Crank winked and resumed his task of cleaning the station. He'd been at this long enough to appreciate the significance of this tattoo for both Fia and Acer.

When he returned his gaze to the mirror, he locked eyes with Fia. A luminous smile and glossy sheen of tears met his stare. With two extended steps, he closed the gap and wrapped his arms around her from behind, careful not to disturb the fresh ink.

"What do you think?" Her voice was low and choked up with emotion.

"I think it's stunning. But then I think everything about you is stunning."

She smiled and crossed her arms over his where they lay against her chest and lower stomach.

Acer pressed a kiss to her temple. "The sunrise is incredible, but the quote is my favorite part." Written in a scrolling script under the glorious sunrise were the words, *Through darkness comes light, through fear comes love, and through pain comes triumph.*

It was the perfect axiom for what Fia had been through. She'd taken an experience so full of darkness and despair, and emerged victorious and even stronger than she'd been.

Fia spun in his arms, and while he wanted nothing more than to crush her against his body, he controlled himself for the sake of the brand-new ink.

"Thank you," she said as a tear slipped down her cheek.

He shook his head and swiped a thumb across her cheek, catching the tear. He'd held her through more than one crying jag or anxiety attack, but it had been weeks since she shed tears or felt any true panic. Each tear was a knife to his heart. "Don't, baby. You never have to thank me for anything. You've given me as much, or more than I've given you."

She smiled up at him. "Not possible, but I love you for saying that."

"Love you too, babe. How about you let Crank bandage that up so I can take you home and show you just how sexy that ink is."

Her pupils dilated her breathing hitched. Damn, there was nothing that made a man feel higher than a woman who responded like Fia did to him.

His dick stiffened and Fia smirked. "Hey, Crank? Let's get this show on the road. Acer's developing a little problem."

"Ain't nothing little about my problem," he rumbled against her ear as he pressed his *problem* into her soft stomach.

She chuckled and kissed him hard on the lips before spinning around and walking back to Crank's station. She looked over her shoulder and winked. "Hold that thought."

Acer stood back and watched his woman as Crank applied

salve to her tattoo and bandaged the fresh ink. After a moment, she was back in his arms and Crank disappeared into his office.

She looked up at him with watery eyes. "I don't know if I've ever said thank you." She squeezed tight around his waist. "But I want you to know—" Her voice cracked "—that I'm not just better because of time."

For twenty years, Acer kept his heart hard as a cinder block. Now, since Fia, he felt a strong, burning love that powered him through each day. Her words were unnecessary, but he loved her all the more for her ability to make him feel ten feet tall.

"I haven't moved on because Mike is gone, or because my scars are covered. There is only one reason that I'm happy and healed. And that reason is you. All you. You supported me, held me while I cried, were patient with me, gave me strength and confidence. You made me feel desirable, and made me want again." She sniffed as a tear leaked from her eyes. "I just love you. So much, it's almost scary."

He sealed his mouth over hers in a tender kiss. "You don't need to thank me for anything, baby," he said when he pulled away. "I love you just as fuckin' fierce. Now let's go home so I can show you properly. Otherwise, Crank is likely to get a show he'll never forget."

She laughed, the sound music to his ears. He'd never forget what she went through, but the memories faded into the distance with each passing day. Now, they both looked to the future and let the past lie where it lay.

Thank you so much for spending some time in the No Prisoners' world. If you enjoyed the book please feel free to leave a review on Amazon or Goodreads.

Join Lilly's mailing list for a free 9000 word novella A No Prisoners Wedding.

www.lillyatlas.com

**Look for Hook and Marcie's story
in a No Prisoners Novella
April 11, 2017**

About the Author

Lilly Atlas is a contemporary romance author. She's a proud Navy wife and mother of two spunky girls. Every time Lilly downloads a new eBook she expects her Kindle App to tell her it's exhausted and overworked, and to beg for some rest. Thankfully that hasn't happened yet so she can often be found absorbed in a good book.